THE

QUICK

AND

THE

DEAD

BOOKS BY RANDY LEE EICKHOFF

NOVELS

The Fourth Horseman

Bowie (with Leonard C. Lewis)

A Hand to Execute

The Gombeen Man

Fallon's Wake

Return to Ithaca

Then Came Christmas

And Not to Yield

The Quick and the Dead

THE ULSTER CYCLE

The Raid

The Feast

The Sorrows

The Destruction of the Inn

He Stands Alone

The Red Branch Tales

The Odyssey: A Modern Translation of Homer's Classic Tale

NONFICTION

Exiled

THE QUICK AND THE DEAD

Randy Lee Eickhoff

A Tom Doherty Associates Book
New York

FORGE®

This is a work of fiction. All the characters and events portrayed in this novel are either fictitious or are used fictitiously.

THE QUICK AND THE DEAD

This book is printed on acid-free paper.

A Forge Book
Published by Tom Doherty Associates, LLC
175 Fifth Avenue
New York, NY 10010

www.tor.com

Forge® is a registered trademark of Tom Doherty Associates, LLC.

Library of Congress Cataloging-in-Publication Data

Eickhoff, Randy Lee.
    The quick and the dead / Randy Lee Eickhoff.—1st ed.
        p.   cm.
    "A Tom Doherty Associates book."
    ISBN 0-765-30776-6
    EAN 978-0-765-30776-7
    1. Vietnamese Conflict, 1961-1975—Fiction.   2. Americans—Vietnam—
Fiction.   3. Women spies—Fiction.   I. Title.

PS3555.I23Q53 2005
813'.54—dc22

                                                                2004066428

First Edition: July 2005

0   9   8   7   6   5   4   3   2

For my mother, Eldina

And a special thanks to

Robert Gleason

for his continued belief in this project

On the third day, He rose into heaven
where He sitteth at the right hand of God, the Father Almighty.
From thence He shall come to judge
the quick and the dead.

THE
QUICK
AND
THE
DEAD

1 We walked well into the afternoon through the thick forest of ferns and banyan trees, making our way through the An Lou Valley. The thick canopy overhead trapped the sweltering heat on the forest floor, and gnats buzzed around us, trying to feed on the salt from our sweat as we made our way cautiously to the end of the valley. We would have to make a dry camp there until night, when we would move out of the valley and into what should be a vast region of rolling hills near the Laos border. At least, we would have some rest there before we made our assault on the prisoner of war camp where some Americans were being held captive by the Vietcong.

I wasn't interested in all of the captives, just in one: John Fell, one of the soldiers who had gone through special training with me when the army had decided to train twenty-seven of us to man small Special Operations Groups scattered around both North and South Vietnam. The experiment had been a disaster and only a few of us remained alive. My team was still intact, but Fell's team had stepped into an ambush and Fell had been captured and moved from camp to camp over the past few weeks while Special Operations tried to get a fix on where he was being kept long enough for us to go in and pull him out. Or eliminate him. The information that he had was vital, and although I knew Fell well and knew that he would resist interrogation as long as possible, I also knew that every man has a breaking point and the longer we waited, the more time the Vietcong had to work on him. They were masters at that and could keep a man alive long after he began to pray to whatever god he prayed to, to allow him to die. In the end, just before the captive went insane, he would begin to babble in desperation, and if that happened to Fell, then we would have to collapse what was left of the groups and begin again.

Nor, I reflected, would that be a waste. So far, we had been lucky, my team and I. Most of us had come through the past eight months relatively unharmed. There were a couple of other teams that had been as lucky, but Lady Luck can only be pushed so far before she gets tired of granting you grace and leaves. You had to learn and learn quickly in Vietnam just how far you could push luck before it disappeared. That, and remember patience.

Since I had come to the hills and mountains, however, all the past on the reservation had suddenly disappeared. The old pains and misfortunes of being an Indian had slipped away, and those fears and troubles that I had known, but I had not learned happiness. Sometimes, I wondered if I had ever known happiness or ever would, because the emotion of what I had felt growing up on the reservation still stayed with me. Yet, for the first time, I felt that I was like a spider weaving my own web of destiny.

I wrenched my thoughts away from my musings and looked around at the five others that formed my Special Operations Group team. All had been carefully chosen. The best warriors had to do the dirtiest part of the war:

Solomon Johnson: "Solly," our gun-carrying medic; a large black man from Chicago with a knife scar snaking down from his left eye to his chin;

"Sparks" Gonzalez: our radio operator; what he could do with a Prick-Ten was pure magic; but everyone knew enough not to turn their backs to him when he got to drinking; he sometimes forgot where he was and who he was and who we were;

Earl Cameron: "Duke," who everyone thought came from a rich family, as he was always reading books on many esoteric subjects, as if there wasn't enough knowledge in the world for him to gather; once, he was reading a book on Pluto and got into a fight with Sparks after laughing at him when Sparks wondered why anyone would write a book about Mickey Mouse's dog;

Theodore "Heaven" Templar: our scout, a bit dreamy, but if a religion was part of his dreams, I shudder to think what religion it might be; sadistic, to the point of being nearly out of control—which made him perfect for the up-country—once he checked out a garrote he had made by flipping it over the head of a chicken and decapitating the bird with one sharp twist of his wrist, then announced himself satisfied;

Herman "Cornpone" Henderson: a nickname he hated but had grudgingly given over to accepting from the others, but no one outside the team dared to mention his nickname to his face—which most did upon hearing his Tennessee accent—he was our "shooter";

And myself. Benjamin Wingfoot, although everyone called me "Wingo"—a nickname I hated but had become resigned to—lately from the Rosebud Indian Reservation in South Dakota and the University of South Dakota, where I had earned a degree in teaching with the idea of going back to the reservation to teach at the Saint Francis Indian Mission. That was before the U.S. Army came calling and, after a battery of tests, I found myself going through Military Intelligence School and later Ranger and Airborne training at Fort Benning.

Now, here I was, leading a mission given to us to correct a situation that the army had found potentially dangerous to the war effort, far from Barthelemy Pass, our home base, where we were teamed with a group of Montagnards to lead raids on the Ho Chi Minh Trail and do whatever other dirty work came down to us from Nha Trang or Saigon.

Heaven suddenly motioned and dropped into a squat as he studied the thick trees in front of us. I immediately crouched down along with the others and duckwalked my way up close to him.

"What is it?" I whispered. My eyes flickered around the thick cover in front of us, looking for something that didn't belong. The trick is not to stare hard at something but to hope to catch it in the quick glance.

He shook his head. "I don't know. Something ain't right. When was the last time you heard the birds?"

I held my breath, straining to listen. Silence gathered like cotton balls around my ears. I shook my head.

"It's late afternoon. They're probably lying up in the heat."

He nodded and shifted a wad of chewing tobacco from one cheek to the other before whispering, "Yeah, well, pigs might fly, too, but there's something. Don't know what it is. I feel it, though."

That was good enough for me. If Heaven felt something, then something was usually there, and even if it wasn't, we had survived long enough to learn to play hunches when they came along.

"I'll send Duke around on the right flank. You take the left. And keep it quiet, you understand? I would rather detour around than open a can of worms with gunfire. We don't know how far that will carry. The Tay Son Pass isn't that far away."

He nodded and slipped away to his left as I turned to motion Duke up to us.

He slid in next to me. "What's up?"

"Heaven has a hunch," I said. "He's on the left. You take the right. Check things out. And watch yourself," I added as he began to move away. "Keep it quiet and watch for spider holes."

He frowned irritably at me and nodded. The warning was not needed, but I always gave it anyway. It made me feel better even though I knew that all of us had been in the field long enough to watch for small holes that would drop down into tunnels that led to underground rest areas, barracks, and even hospitals. The whole damn country was covered with tunnels that had been dug when the French had tried to keep control of Indochina before the Dien Bien Phu fiasco, where the French forces had been soundly defeated. Sometimes I wondered if those damn tunnels went all the way up to Peking or even Paris.

I waited patiently, watching and trying to will the birds into singing again, but they didn't. I had a feeling that Heaven was right; there was something up there that was keeping the jungle silent. I didn't even hear mice scuttling through the underbrush. That usually meant more than a small patrol. I frowned and tried to think. When Colonel Black had sent us up here, he had said that air recon had indicated two large troop movements, but that didn't mean anything. The Vietcong and the NVA regulars were used to moving rapidly and could have made their way into the valley from the other end. If that was the case, then we would have to either hide up somewhere or make a long detour up and over the side of the valley.

Heaven was back first. He slid next to me and whispered. "About a couple of clicks ahead. There's a supply group resting. They're heavily loaded. Ammunition, food, medical supplies. I could see the Red Cross on some of the boxes. I think they're coming this way. We have one, maybe two hours at the most."

Duke came in at the end of Heaven's words and nodded. "I found the same. No flankers on my side, though."

"Any point men?" I asked.

Both shook their heads.

"All right, so we have a couple of minutes. Meanwhile, let's move to the north side of the valley. Don't cut a trail. I'll tell Cornpone to drag our track clean so they won't stumble across it."

"They will eventually," Heaven said, nodding toward the rear of the party. "They'll eventually stumble upon our trail and then they'll know that we are somewhere in the area. They'll send out searchers."

"They have enough men with them that they can afford to do that?"

Duke nodded. "Yes, they could spring a couple of scouts loose. But if we move fast, we should be able to make it up and over. They won't follow us that far."

"But they'll have radios," I said. "We might find ourselves walking into an ambush before we get to the camp. We're only thirty or so clicks from there. Remember, we're on a tight schedule. We don't want the dust-offs coming into a hot zone. Those helicopter pilots have a tendency to roll away from hot zones."

"What do you want to do, Wingo?" Heaven asked.

"Let's go to the north," I said. "I think the walls there are better to climb up than the south walls. And that puts us closer to the camp. I'd like to make it by nightfall and hit them before the moon comes up."

The men nodded and rose, Heaven moving off to the right, Duke falling back to tell the others our plans. I knew Cornpone would be pissed at having to handle drag again, but he was meticulous about such things and I knew that for a couple hundred meters he would cover our passing well enough that no one would know that we had even been there. After that, it wouldn't matter. Charlie seldom sent flankers out farther than that unless it was a big detachment. We might even get lucky. After all, An Lou was known as the Valley of Ghosts. I grinned. Maybe Charlie would think that ghosts had been coming up the trail toward them and move off to the south as we were going north.

I rose and slipped through the thick brush after Heaven, trying not to snap any twigs or kick up the dead leaves that lay like a thick blanket over the forest floor. I didn't hear the others moving behind me, but I hadn't expected them to make any noise and knew that most of them were slipping through the shadows that lay darker in the dim light formed by the canopy of branches and leaves above us. Sunlight streamed through like light bars in places with dust motes moving slowly in the bars, but they were spread far enough apart that we could slip around them and stay in the shadows.

I felt a strong urge to urinate but knew that was common to men who were suddenly on the verge of a possible firefight. I thought briefly about that, wondering why a man didn't react differently, such as breaking out in a rash and getting the sudden urge to scratch himself all over. Perhaps it was the subconscious desire to make his body clean before the possibility of dying, or was it the male concern about being wounded there?

I could feel the slope of the floor beginning to rise toward the valley wall and walked faster, leaning forward slightly against the pull of my pack on my shoulders although we were packed lightly. I moved on the balls of my feet, keeping Heaven just in sight as he made his way through the thick vegetation, stepping over trailing vines.

I tried to empty my mind of thought, concentrating on the silence surrounding us. Composure plus balance and awareness were the keys to security, but you had to be careful not to be lulled into the mind state that became a sedative of sensation. The senses had to be all alert. It sounded simple, but it was something you could only learn through long practice, and few had the time to practice long in this area of the world. You had to be able to will the rush of adrenaline through your veins, and that rush made you feel invulnerable and that was needed in times like this.

War is not always dirty if it brought man to this type of awareness, I thought. What was it Fell had once said when we had met at the Racquet Club back in Saigon before he was sent up to the Tay Son Pass? The world would always revolve to progress, and progress was always hurried along by war, because war changed things faster than natural evolution. The seed of tomorrow. Yes, that's it: the soldier is the seed of tomorrow, planting himself in the soil for the world to grow and progress.

Heaven stopped and waited as the rest of us came up to him. Above us, the walls of the valley loomed like a ladder laid short against a house. But a goat trail snaked up the side of the wall, narrow but climbable. There would be about a hundred meters where we would be exposed, but I counted on the thick canopy of the forest to hide us.

"Dangerous," Heaven murmured, reading my thoughts. "If we're caught halfway up, we'll have no cover."

I nodded. I looked up and saw where the sun left part of the face of the wall near the top in glaring sunlight. The trail wasn't much, but waiting for night to cover it would be more dangerous and the moon would be up before we reached the top. I squatted and took the map out of its map case and spread it on the ground, studying it. Even after we climbed to the top, we had to cross a plateau before we came to the hills where the camp was nestled in a ravine near a stream that flowed south, winding its way down to the Mekong River. Risky, but we were running out of time.

"Let's do it," I decided. I folded the map and placed it back in the map case.

Heaven sighed and removed his black beret, scratching the close-cropped hair on his head vigorously with the knuckles of his hand. "Well," he said, "no sense waiting for a better moment."

He moved gingerly onto the trail and began to follow it up the face of the wall, leaning forward far enough to almost touch the trail itself. I glanced at my watch, then hitched the pack higher on my shoulders and followed, feeling immediately the strain on my calves from the steep trail barely wide enough to push one leg ahead of the other, concentrating on each step. Halfway up, I glanced back and saw the others following gingerly. Sparks had swung the radio to the front of his chest, keeping it as close to the wall as possible. If he fell, he would be able to slip the radio free and hope that it landed on the trail. Without the radio, we would be in deep trouble. I made a mental note to compliment him on his thinking.

It took us two hours to make it up the wall, and the sun was low on the horizon and turning red. The men started to drop down to rest, but I motioned them back up.

"Come on," I said. I took a canteen from my web belt and took a long drink. I lowered the canteen and replaced it. "We have a long way to go before nightfall."

The men glanced over the plateau to the vast region of rolling hills in the distance. Brambles and camphor trees would give us some cover while we made our way across the plateau and found the camp in the hills. The wind from Laos blew across the plateau, drying the sweat on our bodies. At least up here we would not be draining the sweat as much from our bodies. All of us carried three canteens and knew enough to ration the water as closely as possible without becoming dehydrated.

"Check your weapons," I ordered needlessly. Cornpone already had the bolt of his Springfield out and was running a rag through the barrel. The others followed suit: Duke with his grease gun, Sparks and Heaven with their M16s, and Solly with his carbine. I slipped the Thompson off my shoulder and pulled the magazine, ejecting the round in the chamber.

Within minutes, we were up and moving at a near trot across the plateau, making our way through elephant grass and small stands of bamboo. Briefly I wondered what bamboo was doing growing this high, then dismissed the thought as I concentrated on following Heaven as he made his way through the brush.

The sun was a red crescent on the horizon by the time we made it across the plateau and took refuge in a small stand of camphor trees. We dropped wearily to the ground and slipped out of our packs. I took a can of ham and lima beans from my pack and opened it with a P-38, a small folding can opener. The others were following my lead. Cornpone pinched a couple of inches off the square of C-4 explosive that he carried and divided it among the rest of us. C-4 was the soldier's delight. You could do anything with it and it was harmless as long as a detonator wasn't planted in it. It made a hot and smokeless fire that warmed anything up within a minute.

I took the piece that Cornpone passed to me, rolled it into a tiny ball, and placed it between three stones. I used a match to start it. Immediately I balanced the ham and lima beans on the stones and watched as it began to bubble almost instantly.

I took a scarf from around my neck, wrapped it around my hand, and gingerly picked up the can and began to eat. It was almost too hot to eat, but I forced it down anyway. Solly took a small bottle of Tabasco sauce from his pack and liberally doused the can of pureed ham and eggs that he had chosen for his dinner. Most soldiers carried a bottle of Tabasco sauce to kill the taste of the C rations—especially ham and eggs, which came out of the can gray-yellow, like vomit.

I took the map out and used my compass to find an azimuth and waited as Cornpone took his entrenching tool and dug a small hole to bury our cans. Then I rose and motioned for Heaven.

"I think the camp is to the west of us about ten kilometers," I said. "At least, it should be. The border is somewhere around here and the camp is on the border. Be careful; there's bound to be guards close to it."

He nodded and again we set off, moving rapidly through the trees. Shadows lengthened as the sun slipped below the horizon, and then Heaven stopped and waved me forward. He pointed to where lights gleamed faintly through the trees in a small cutback in the hills. He pointed again, and I saw the guard stationed on a small platform built from bamboo in the fork of a tree. The guard was resting with his back against the trunk of the tree, the barrel of his rifle protruding over the edge of the bamboo where he had laid it down by his side. He was smoking a cigarette and making no attempt to hide the coal in the cup of his hand. That was still dangerous, as smoke carried in the night air. Careless, but we were far enough north above the parallel that separated North from South Vietnam that lethargy had set in with the knowledge that they were safe.

"Any others?" I whispered.

Heaven shook his head. "None that I've noticed."

I felt movement behind me, and Duke and Cornpone slipped up on either side of us.

I studied the camp, noticing the three low buildings at the far end built on short stilts against the rainy season, when water would stream off the roof and flood the camp. A small generator was on the porch of the center building, and I knew that would be the commandant's. The generator was only enough for that building, but the others were lighted by lanterns, and light flickered through the open windows. In the center of the camp stood twelve small bamboo cages that allowed prisoners to neither stand nor sit down. Bad enough, but not the worst torture the prisoners would have been put through. Only three of the cages were occupied. At the end of the camp a series of mounds showed where prisoners had died and been buried. Nothing marked the graves except the mounds of dirt, and I knew that would settle as the rain soaked the ground and the bodies became dust.

Tinny music came from the camp, and faint laughter, and I knew the guards were being entertained by some women from a nearby village. I took a small set of binoculars from my belt and studied the camp. The prisoners were naked so the night cold would make them shiver and bring even more pain into their thighs. A bucket of water with a dipper stood just an arm's length from each cage, and the sight of that during the heat of the day would drive them mad with thirst.

I took the binoculars away and placed them in the small pouch on my belt.

"All right," I whispered. "Cornpone, you think you can take out the watch and take his place? You should have a fine field of fire from that platform. And," I added, "if we don't make it, take out Fell before you cut and run with Sparks. If you can't get Fell, Cornpone, you'll have to end it. You think you can get a good enough sight from up there?"

Cornpone nodded and took a Colt .45 from its holster. He reached in a small pouch attached to his pack and removed a silencer. He screwed it on the end of the .45, slipped the Springfield over his shoulder, and started to crawl away.

"All right," I continued. "Heaven and Duke, you each take one of the outbuildings. Solly, you and I'll take the one with the generator. We'll have to move fast."

"Should we use C-4?" Heaven asked.

I shook my head, then realized that the night had fallen enough that they might not be able to see me.

"No. There's no sense in killing those we don't want to kill. Sparks, I want you to stay with Cornpone. As soon as we get clear, you call in for the dust-off. You have the coordinates?"

"Yes," he whispered.

"If we don't make it, then you call in an air strike on the village."

He nodded and crawled off after Cornpone.

"Everybody know what to do?"

"Who gets the prisoners?" Heaven asked.

I nodded at Solly. "Solly and me. You keep the others off us until we clear the camp. Then come after us."

"It's gonna be touchy," Solly said solemnly. "We take out the building, then have to cross that clear patch of ground to get to the cages. That's a lot of ground without cover."

"Yes, but workable as long as Heaven and Duke keep the others pinned down away from the doors and windows."

Solly sighed and moved his massive arms, easing the nerves in his bunched shoulders. He grinned, his teeth suddenly white in his black face.

"Well, I guess we'd better start," Heaven said, glancing at the sky. "I make it about an hour, maybe less, from moonrise."

A faint pop came from the guard's tree. He jerked, then slumped to his side, hanging head down over the platform. I could just barely make out Cornpone making his way up the side of the tree to the platform. He bent over the guard, then kicked him off the platform and waved to us.

"Let's go," I said. "Remember: quick and low."

We rose and ran lightly on the balls of our feet, crouched and ready to fall flat if we were discovered.

Within minutes, Solly and I flattened ourselves against the commandant's building. Heaven and Duke each scurried to the corner of one of the other buildings. I took a deep breath and slipped up quietly onto the porch, hoping the rattle of the generator would cover my steps. I moved to a window and glanced quickly in. The room was bare except for two tables and a desk. On one of the tables stood a field telephone with long wires attached to it and rolled neatly next to it. I knew what that was for: the wires would be wrapped around a prisoner's genitals while the handset was cranked, the nerve ends screaming from the jolt of electricity. The pain would be excruciating. A neat pile of thin-cut, small splinters was next to it. I shivered, imagining them being forced in a prisoner's fingernails and toenails, then set on fire. A thin fishing knife rested next to the pile of splinters. That would be used to peel the flesh from the more stubborn prisoners. At the end of the room was a small partition where the commandant would have his private quarters. A small lamp glowed from behind it, and I knew the commandant was in bed. I hoped alone.

I nodded at Solly. He came up beside me and took a position at the window to cover me as I went to the front door. I took a deep breath and opened the door, sliding inside quickly, moving to the partition.

The commandant rose from his bed, his eyes drawn to the Thompson leveled at him.

"*Cái này là cái gì?*" he said in a high-pitched voice. "What's this?"

"A reckoning," I answered, and killed him with a short burst. Blood splattered over the back wall like a Pollock painting.

I turned and ran from the building as Heaven and Duke began firing at the windows and doors. Solly ran after me as we crossed to the cages. I took my pistol and shot off the locks on the chains holding the doors shut.

Fell looked up, his face haggard and taut with pain. A week's growth of beard stubbled his cheeks. I reached in and grabbed him. He gasped from pain. I pulled him roughly out of the cage. Solly grabbed him and threw him over his shoulder like a sack of grain and ran for the trees.

The other prisoners looked hollow-eyed at me, uncomprehending.

"Come on," I shouted. "Let's go."

They tried to stand and fell down. I swore and pulled them out of their cages. They sprawled in the dirt. I hauled them to their feet and shoved them toward the trees. They began to run in a stumbling gait.

"Heaven! Duke! Go! Go! Go!" I roared.

They fired a last blast at the windows and doors, then sprinted across the compound. I ran after the prisoners. Bullets started flying around us. One of the prisoners straightened and screamed, then fell forward on his face. His legs twitched twice; then he lay still. I sprinted past him, hearing Duke and Heaven pause to fire another burst behind them as they came.

I reached trees and heard Cornpone's rifle as he sniped at the doors and windows; screams sounded from behind me and I knew that we had left some wounded Vietcong behind us. That would lessen the pursuit some, as many would have to stay behind to care for them.

I caught up with Solly. He was swearing gently. Fell had spattered him with diarrhea and vomit. I paused as Duke and Heaven joined me.

"Everyone all right?"

They nodded as Cornpone called down from his perch, "They're coming."

"Use your grenades and C-4 now," I ordered.

Explosions followed hard on my words as Heaven and Duke began throwing grenades high and far into the camp. Cornpone dropped down from his perch and handed his rifle to Sparks.

"Get," he said curtly. "I'll catch up."

He took the square of C-4 from his pack and broke it into chunks, sliding a detonator into each. He crimped a fuse into the detonators, then glanced up at me.

"Better git," he drawled. "I'm cuttin' these here fuses short."

I nodded and glanced at Sparks, standing nearby, holding Cornpone's Springfield.

"I've already called in the dust-off," he said. "We got three hours. You want an air strike as well?"

I glanced back at the camp. The Vietcong were moving warily from their buildings. I shook my head.

"No, the C-4 will keep them guessing for a while." I turned to Cornpone. "Can you space them? Give us a little more time?"

He grinned. "No problem."

He lit the first block and threw it toward the camp. The blast was deafening. The Vietcong scattered, diving under the buildings. Methodically, he began lighting the other fuses and lobbing them into the camp.

"Catch up soon," I said. "Sparks, leave his rifle and come with me. We'll need the radio."

He propped the Springfield against the tree trunk and set off in a mile-eating jog after the others.

I gripped Cornpone's shoulder. "Don't be too long. We don't know who else might be around."

"Don't y'all worry," he said, lobbing another block into the camp. "I have no intention of staying around a moment longer'n necessary. You ain't careful, you may find my size elevens pounding up your ass."

I laughed and took after Sparks.

We ran through the trees, making for the pickup point. Behind us explosions sounded like the rhythmic beat of bass drums. We broke through the trees on top of the plateau as the moon came up, full and bright. I could see Solly ahead, still running easily as Fell flapped over his shoulder. Heaven and Duke stayed on Solly's heels. I caught up with Sparks. He glanced over at me.

"They coming?" he asked.

"Don't think so. Cornpone's keeping them pretty occupied."

Sparks turned and concentrated on the run practiced long enough that we all could maintain it for miles, a ground-gaining lope that ate up the miles. I glanced behind and saw Cornpone break onto the flat and stretch out his long legs to catch up with us.

We ran for two hours before I called for a halt. Solly immediately placed Fell on the ground and started tending to him, pulling morphine Syrettes from his medical bag and stabbing Fell in the thighs with them. He wept from relief and pain. I glanced at his hands where the nails had been burnt black. His clothing hung in rags and had been fouled repeatedly with his bodily wastes. Solly used a knife to rip open a pant leg and exposed a wound that looked green in the moonlight. He swore.

"Sumbitches left him untended," Solly said. He glanced up at me. "Be best if I open it now and dump in some sulfa. That might help some before he gets back to the hospital in Saigon. Might save his leg."

"Do it," I said. My chest heaved slightly, and the night wind began to cool the sweat on my body. "We have a minute or two."

He nodded and drew a small scalpel from his bag. "This is gonna hurt a bit," he warned. He sliced into the raw flesh. Fell screamed. His eyes rolled up and he passed out as Solly pressed his huge hands hard against the wound, forcing pus to squirt out in a small fountain. Rapidly he took two sulfa packets from his kit, packed the wound, and bound it with gauze. He glanced down at his jungle blouse and pants and swore.

"Gonna need new ones. Ain't nothing gonna clean these up. Didn't think a man this thin would have that much shit in him. He's lost a lot of weight." He looked up at me. "He's in a bad way, Wingo. They did him bad back there. Real bad."

I didn't say anything. Anyone who fell into Charlie's hands and made it to a prison camp could expect treatment like that. I looked around. "Where's the other prisoner?"

"He went off on his own way," Duke said. He shook his head, breathing deeply. "I don't think he'll get far before they catch him. I wouldn't want to be him when they do."

"You want us to go back?" Heaven asked.

"No," I said curtly. "He made his choice. Besides, some of them will go after him. That'll lessen the odds some if they come up on us before the helicopters get here."

They nodded, accepting the decision. Practicality took precedence over gallantry out here. All of us knew it. I took a deep breath, smelling the thick slaughterhouse smell of wet blood mingling with sweat and cordite. I looked down at Solly.

"You need a break?"

He shook his head and stood. He lifted Fell and slid him easily over his shoulder. "I been shit on enough that a little more won't matter none. 'Sides, he ain't heavy."

"Yeah," Heaven drawled, "but he ain't your brother."

Solly grinned. "Close enough out here. We all equal out here."

"Let's go," I said, and motioned for Heaven to take the lead.

We set off toward the rendezvous, moving through the night like wraiths, making no attempt to cover our trail. We had Fell; that was enough. I knew what it would be like if Charlie caught the other prisoner. There were many tiny camps hidden in the mountains and the forest and the jungle where law and rules were invented daily at the whim of the man in charge. There he would be dead as far as the world was concerned, along with others like him, concerned only with the spark that pulsed through their veins and with each beat of their hearts, clinging fearfully to that and living between the beats and wondering if each beat would bring another.

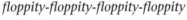

floppity-floppity-floppity-floppity

Helicopters.

Every time I remember back to Vietnam and up-country, I hear the sound of helicopters beating, beating, beating like an overworked sound track in a *ciné noir*. We can never get away from helicopters. Each time we hear their approach, talk stops and everyone stares to the south, waiting. The dull *thud-thud-thud* of their approach merges with the beats of our hearts, thumping in our temples as the squat bugs come quickly toward us, high at first in the gray sky (always the gray sky), then dropping swiftly to whatever landing they can manage. Or hover above us while someone pitches a weighted pouch out to us, using green smoke from grenades we have thrown out to mark a "safe patch."

At times, I'd be in that twilight that we call sleep in the up-country and I'd hear the helicopters approaching and snap awake, feeling my heart beat hard in my throat. For a moment, the walls seemed to close in a little tighter, and I'd wish I was back home on the Rosebud Indian Reservation, but then I'd remember that there was nothing for me to go back to and that this place was as good as any. Growing up on the "rez" made me quite familiar with poverty, despair, and hopelessness. I didn't catch the scent of ten dollars until I was enrolled at the University of South Dakota in Vermillion. During football season I'd get a weekly mysterious envelope with one hundred dollars in cash stuck in my locker. I made the mistake of taking the first one to one of the coaches. He looked at me strangely, then muttered something about looking into the whole affair and stuck the envelope in his back pocket. I never saw that envelope again, but the next week a second one appeared in my locker, and by then I had learned enough to keep my mouth shut and quietly placed the envelope in my gym bag before I left the field house.

I never thought about the rez anymore except briefly upon awakening from a nightmare, remembering the bellow of a steer my uncle stole from a nearby rancher when its throat was cut. The women caught the blood to make sausage, working around the men who butchered the animal as quickly as they could before one of the reservation police caught them. We didn't butcher animals here in the up-country, but the smell of blood was there anyway. It seemed to soak in the ground and roll back out during the steamy days before the monsoon rains hit. The whole country seemed to be steeped in blood. The rains washed the smell away momentarily, but when the sun burnt down upon the earth, the rank blood smell would roll back up.

Whatever money came our way, trickling down from the tribal council to those of us who lived away from Mission, was quickly spent by the men. On the tenth of every month, the men would take the women down to Valentine, across the border in Nebraska. There they would buy what food they thought they would need for the rest of the month, but we always ran out a week before the next allotment came to us and the women would dress themselves silently in their town clothes, painting their faces the best they could, using a thin paste they made out of flour and water to cover their faces so the deep pits and wrinkles wouldn't show as much, rouge their cheeks, and spread lipstick clumsily upon their lips and the men would drive them to the various small towns around the rez. The men would park their cars behind the taverns and sit inside, nursing beers, while the women used the backseats of the cars as mattresses to earn a few dollars to help buy more food for the rest of the month.

When the tenth of the month came again, the cycle would begin again—supermarkets, then to the various hardware stores where the men would make small payments on presents for Christmas or birthdays, then the liquor stores, and back to the hardware stores, where they would buy tins of Sterno. But they never wasted the Sterno on heating or cooking. When the whiskey ran out, they would strain the Sterno through cheesecloth or a few slices of old bread and drink the liquid to get drunk again so they would be able to forget the dignity that once belonged to their grandfathers.

And now, I was here in Vietnam, in the up-country, having traded one hellhole for another. But that didn't matter; one reservation was like any other reservation: it was all the same to me. Strangely, I came to regard the up-country as home, but I never told anyone about my feeling. The army would have considered me a mental problem and sent me home. Sometimes, I would think about the strangeness of that situation: to survive in the war, one needed to be insane, but if he let others know he was insane, he would be sent home and placed in an institution until the army finally decided it had enough from him, and then only after several treatments that included frying the brain with electric jolts or carefully monitored overdoses of insulin. I heard once about a hospital somewhere that was using psycho-expanding drugs for treatment, sending men into their own nightmares to confront them in a controlled atmosphere. But that didn't work because the men were insane because they couldn't handle their nightmares and confronting them anywhere was a trip back to the interior of Vietnam.

Insanity. The sin of man. At least out here, alone with my team, we could make our own rules.

floppity-floppity-floppity

Any other day and the rains would have kept the helicopter away, for we were in the rainy season, when it seemed to rain every hour like clockwork. Some rare days the sun would shine, but mostly it rained. We didn't mind the rain, although if we weren't careful a soft gray fungus would begin to crawl over everything. We would rather put up with the fungus, though, than sunny days. The rains brought the war to a brief halt. Not even Charlie liked to move through the red mud that clung stubbornly to your feet as thick and heavy as cement. The rains made the war a soldier's war despite the myth of Dien Bien Phu, when the French army lost to Ho Chi Minh's determined soldiers who dragged cannons up impossible terrain during the rains to surround the overconfident French. But Dien Bien Phu had been an accident caused by the French, who refused to see the Vietnamese as determined soldiers instead of docile workers on the French rubber plantations, and soldiers knew the accident and greeted the rains with weary relief, even though they knew that the rains would also bring malaria and typhus and other sickness.

So far, we had been lucky, but I knew that luck in war was an illusion. Anyone who tried to make it through the country on luck went home in a body bag. Although home was an illusion for me, I knew the other five members of my team had homes, and I had an obligation to them. This wasn't their war; it was mine, and I was in no hurry for it to end. But I also knew that the odds were against them. When a man has something to lose, he becomes vulnerable. The longer he remains waiting and looking forward to the end, the more vulnerable he becomes. We were very vulnerable, now, for the members of my team had entered that twilight known as the "short-timer's list," when the days could be marked off with a certainty that soon there was going to be an end and a hopefulness that the end wouldn't be the anonymity of an aluminum casket stacked with others like cordwood in the belly of a transport plane. Entering the short-timer's list made a man very vulnerable, and we were very vulnerable. So when the rains came, sheeting down like Noah's deluge, I breathed a sigh of relief that we were back in the Montagnard camp and broke out a bottle of scotch to celebrate the end of yet another season. We had been lucky—for the most part—but the last two missions had been a little too close, a little too rough. The last one had been the worst. We had been up around Barthelemy Pass—far north of the Demilitarized Zone—in an attempt to stop arms shipments from coming through the mountains and into Laos. We traveled by night and held up in the highlands during the day in an attempt to slip past the border guards. But when we tried to make our way up and around the pass, we stumbled across a large North Vietnamese division and were lucky to escape. We had spent the better part of three days fleeing south, trying to lose the patrols after us in the mountains. We made it back to our base camp and now wanted nothing more than a few days to unwind from the constant strain of trying to stay one step ahead of our pursuers. We thought we were going to get those days when the rains began to fall hesitantly off and on, building up to the torrential downpour that would begin the monsoon season and let us have a little breather—eat some steaks, maybe; drink some booze, certainly.

floppity-floppity-floppity

"Wingo?"

A brief wave of annoyance came over me. That nickname followed me wherever I went. It seemed to have slipped ahead of me when I left the Rosebud Indian Reservation in South Dakota as if someone was sending it ahead with drumbeats or smoke signals. It didn't matter how many fights I had; my name was always Wingo.

When I went away to the university, I made a point of always intro-
ducing myself with my full name, Benjamin Wingfoot, but everyone soon came to call me "Wingo."

I looked up as Sparks slipped in through the tent. Rain thundered
on the canvas over our heads and dripped from his shoulders. Behind him, I watched puddles form in the red mud. Then, as if someone had turned off the faucet, the rain stopped and the sun came
out, bright and lending a false sense of cleanliness and warmth and
happiness.

"I don't want it," I said, raising the bottle of scotch and wagging
it at the flimsy he held in his hand.

"Wonder what the hell we're getting into now," Duke muttered. I
glanced at him. He sat beside me, bare-chested, arms folded, one
hand clutching Nietzsche's book on Zarathustra, a thick forefinger
marking his spot.

Sparks spat and shook his head sadly. "Well, I tell you. It's some
lieutenant from Saigon coming up to pay a little visit. I'd guess he
wants a few hours up here so he can claim his CIB."

Solly grunted, shaking his massive head. "So. We get another
wannabe hero who needs the Combat Infantryman Badge for his
two-oh-one file. Grand."

We were all familiar with that. When we were back in our base
camp—wherever that might be, sometimes in Laos, or Burma, or
Thailand, or Cambodia—one of the green officers tucked safely in
Nha Trang or Saigon would decide to pay us a short visit so he could
claim the Combat Infantryman Badge for having spent some time
in the "zone."

"Remember? Remember when we got that message that a chopper was coming up with some major new in-country and we had
that case of Black Jack Solly liberated from Hung Yang Duc or whatever the fuck his name was? We got that call asking for green smoke
and Sparks hit the button and fired off his .45 and yelled that we
were in a hot zone? Man. I never saw a chopper turn as fast as that
one and head back. Like a honeybee going to his hive after nosediv-
ing a rose."

We all laughed at the memory. It wasn't really funny, but you
took the humor where you could get it. Sometimes, the humor was
a little raw. Like the time when we got a captain up from Lincoln

Library—what we called the building where the Central Intelligence Agency had its Saigon headquarters on the Tan Son Nhut airfield—who came up for a brief visit. The captain arrived in full glory: four ammo pouches crammed full of clips for his M16, a bowie knife as large as a machete tied to one leg, two canteens filled with *purified* water (he was quick to let us know), a small tent, a sleeping bag (for he had heard it got cold in the highlands), and jungle fatigues starched and pressed to knife-edge creases that would have slit the throat of Charlie as easily as a razor.

Right from the beginning, the captain made our lives miserable, assuming command of our team and demanding that we set out claymore mines around our position in case we were attacked in the night. Then he put Solly to setting up his tent while he took a brief hike around the "perimeter" of our post and was appalled to discover that we hadn't cut the brush back to clear a field of fire. I tried to explain to the captain that we weren't going to be there long enough to have a need for cutting the brush, but he wouldn't listen. So, we brought up some of the Montagnards to help us sweep back a field of fire. Mystified, they used their heavy parangs—like a machete only with a wider blade and thicker ridge on the back that made it more like a wide-head hatchet—to cut back the brush.

That night, the captain retired to his tent and immediately began screaming about a snake that had promptly bitten him when he slipped into his sleeping bag. The captain came bolting out of his tent, wild-eyed, clutching his M16 in his hand. He turned and emptied the clip back into the tent, slammed a new clip home, and emptied that as well into the tent. Then, he collapsed, eyes rolling back into his head, moaning about being snake-bit and dying. Heaven cut back the captain's pant leg and discovered ants running all over him. Solly had pitched his tent over a fire-ant hill. I slammed a shot of Benadryl into him to bring down the swelling and we stripped him and stood him under our "shower"—a homemade affair with a washed-out fifty-five-gallon gas drum filled with rainwater up on stilts; you pulled out the plug to sluice down with water, soaped, then pulled out the plug to wash the soap off, primitive but better than nothing—and rinsed off the ants.

I tried to explain to the captain what had happened, but he would have nothing to do with my explanation, demanding that we radio for an evac chopper to take him to Nha Trang. When Sparks told him that the radio was down for the night, the captain lay back against the ground, his hands fluttering weakly beside him like white moths, and moaned, *"Guhdam, guhdam, guhdam,"* and passed out.

We got a chopper in at first light, and Heaven rode back with him to Nha Trang, told the doctors at the hospital what had happened. The captain got his nickname Guhdam from that and the doctors at the hospital had a good laugh as well. Heaven spent the night in the whorehouses in Nha Trang, beat the hell out of a couple of marines, stole a case of scotch from a master sergeant's hooch supply, and came back, happy with his brief vacation. He shared the scotch with us, so we were happy for him as well.

I suppose that isn't really funny, but it sure was to us—true dark humor. I never found out what happened to that captain, but I think his days were numbered from that point on. The army has a problem with fools making themselves known as fools. The wise man is the fool who lets others talk and nods his head with great wisdom when the others make wise statements and shakes his head when mistakes are given voice. After a while, he blends in with the rest of the command force, finding refuge in anonymity and promotion with a hundred-dollar bill wrapped around a bottle of Johnnie Walker or Black Jack Daniel discreetly left for certain clerks.

This is true wisdom. The Simplex Method for Linear Programming—a pompous algorithm but valuable when used practically.

Yet here we were, stuck on a hilltop in a country where we didn't want to be, and where most of the people back home didn't want us to be, and where most of the people in the country didn't want us to be. It didn't matter which way we turned; we were outcasts from ourselves, our country, and the country we were trying to save from itself. We became the natural enemy for all.

Once, my plan had been to return to the rez and become a teacher and work at bringing the truth out about the many murders that went unsolved or, in most cases, undetected, by the F.B.I. The Indians who *live* on the rez know the truth, but they also know another truth, and that is if they talk to someone outside the rez, the F.B.I. will find another dead. *If* they are found. The Rosebud covers a lot of miles—empty miles—and much of it near and on the Badlands, where people disappear forever with more frequency than the

Park Service will admit. Tourism must be protected at all costs. The heart of Crazy Horse is buried in the Badlands, but damn few know where. It's just as well. Crazy Horse is the Indian's King Arthur— many still believe that he will return when the Indian needs him the most. I guess White Buffalo Woman has failed to keep his spirit informed, because the Indian could not need him more than he needs Crazy Horse now. Still, the myth gives the Indians slim hope, and they wait, patiently, just as the fervently religious wait for the Second Coming with a hope that they will at long last see the sacred heavens.

I graduated *summa cum laude* from the university. That was a big mistake, but I knew also that a lesser degree wouldn't do me any good, as an Indian with only an honors degree doesn't have as much hiring power as the white man who graduates at the bottom of the class, despite the Equal Opportunity people who swear up and down that they are making a difference. If they are, we can't tell it. In fact, things were better for the Indian *before* the Equal Opportunity laws went into effect. Then, we at least knew where we stood, for anyone who hired us *before* those white man laws went into effect hired us because he believed in us. Now, it's federal law and we are hired by all, even those who are forced to hire us and spend most of their time trying to find a way to legally get rid of us.

As I said, I made a big mistake graduating *summa,* for Uncle Sam took a big interest in graduates like me—especially those of us with minority backgrounds, minority *Indian* backgrounds, that is. Although I'm a good head taller than most of the Vietnamese, I still have brown skin, black eyes, and black hair and can easily blend into a crowd of others with brown skin, black eyes, and black hair. My nose gives me away, or would if it hadn't obviously been broken many times in the past and so has become its own explanation, and if someone is paying close attention, my eyes do not quite tilt in the same way as the eyes of the Vietnamese. But the interesting part of blending in is that you are really not blending in with the real people but only as far as your employers *think* you are blending in. The Vietnamese knew at a glance that I wasn't one of them, but the U.S. Army Military Intelligence Corps believed that I did: the Vietnamese were brown-skinned, black-haired, and black-eyed; I was brown-skinned, black-haired, and black-eyed; *ergo,* we were the same. A faulty syllogism that the intelligence group had convinced themselves was true. I suppose this belief came about when someone remembered an old and worthless anthropological theory about the American Indian having made his way across the Bering Strait when it was actually a land bridge connecting Alaska with Siberia—although they weren't called Alaska and Siberia at the time. Whatever name they had, if they had any name—that is, if man had evolved enough to learn how to give names to things instead of identifying them with a grunt—had died with the dinosaurs, and the anthropologists' theory was just another myth to explain why the American Indian was like all the other brown-skinned, black-haired, and black-eyed races in the world: we all had a common ancestor.

I had a gift for languages. The army quickly discovered that, and so I was drafted, inducted, basic-trained, security-vetted, and military-intelligenced before the ink had dried on my diploma. Once, a specialist who taught Vietnamese at Presidio, then the premier language school for the armed forces, asked how I could pick up languages so quickly. I tried to explain my theory that all languages conformed to six or eight rules of grammar and once those were understood and which rules were applied to a language, then all that remained was to memorize the words. He didn't believe me, because learning another language had to be more complicated than that. I didn't bother to correct him; he hadn't been forced to live on a reservation where the United States government had jammed all Indians regardless of individual tribes under the belief that an Indian was an Indian and all of us shared everything in common—a belief as ludicrous as if I suggested that all white men spoke the same language and came from a universal place called White Country.

Yes, once I was an idealist and told all who would listen about my grand plans, but deep within my secret self I knew it was self-delusion, and after a while I came to understand the strange looks others gave me when I told them about my plans. I had gotten out of the rez and to go back to it was insanity. By then, I had grown away from the rez and there would be no going back. But another problem surfaced: I had become directionless. I drifted mentally for a while, trying to decide what to do, where to go, and while I was trying to resolve my future, the government stepped in and put it all on hold. I accepted the moment for what it was worth—a further delaying of any decision I had to make about the future—and went into the U.S. Army for the pocket change and three square meals a day. I thought I would have the leisure time to ponder possibilities, but through a strange twist of fate I found my future being decided for me. The Law of Diminishing Returns—delay too long and the Second Sister will weave a new pattern in the fabric of your life.

So here I was, the leader of a five-man Special Operations Group team that was perched on a red soil hill somewhere up north where we weren't supposed to be, helping the Montagnards to understand that it was in their best interest to kill the Vietnamese from the North because the Vietnamese from the South were really the Vietnamese who cared for them. This was also an absurdity, for the Montagnards were quite aware that the last Vietnamese emperor as late as the mid-fifties was fond of organizing hunting parties to hunt the Montagnards like his royal peers in England organized grouse or fox hunts. So reality became a question of who could offer the best bribe for some of the Montagnard tribes, while others, such as the Rhandes, were quite willing to kill any Vietnamese for any excuse. The excuses that we brought to them they knew were probably lies but would do until a better excuse came along. It was the principle of the whole affair; one needed to have *reason* to justify killing another—even the Montagnards, who were only a step away from the stone age but rapidly learning how to walk in the modern age of war.

floppity-floppity-floppity

And now I wondered what new wisdom was being brought to us in the helicopter rapidly approaching from out of the sun, swooping down to a makeshift landing pad. We flinched away as the helicopter hovered a bit above the ground, the blades beating the dust up into a fine grit that stung the eyes, then gently lowered, bumping softly on the pad. A second lieutenant dressed in starched jungle fatigues stepped down from the helicopter, paused, then hurried over to us, ducking needlessly as he stepped under the flapping blades.

"Mr. Wingfoot?" he shouted, looking at Sparks. Sparks jerked his thumb toward me. The lieutenant hesitated, and you could see in his eyes that he wanted to say something but thought better of it. He stepped over to me, started to salute, then grabbed hold of his baseball cap as it threatened to blow off his head. Behind him, the pilot shut down the beating blades.

"Yes, I'm Wingfoot," I replied. I glanced down, expecting to see a briefcase, but he held only a manilla envelope.

"I'm from COMSAC," he shouted, then lowered his voice as the roar of the helicopter diminished. "Colonel Black sends his compliments."

He handed the envelope to me. Behind me, Duke muttered an obscenity. I ignored him and took the envelope. I turned away and opened it and removed a single sheet of paper with a short message ordering me to accompany the lieutenant back to Saigon. I read it twice, then slipped the sheet back inside the envelope and secured the metal tabs to close the flap.

"What's this about, Lieutenant?" I asked. I knew the words were perfunctory, however. If the lieutenant had been told, there would have been no need for the message—although the message didn't reveal anything, either. That was the army way: a simple radio call would have been enough.

"I don't know," the lieutenant said. I glanced at the black name tag above his right pocket: Koestler. "I was told to fly up here and bring you back immediately."

He glanced around the camp, then turned and looked down the mountain and across the valley. In the distance, a ground fog was beginning to gather at the far end of the valley and the hills looked lush and green and inviting—until you stepped into the greenery and smelled the decay of spent time and felt the back of your throat dry with anticipation.

"Pretty," he said, a touch of enthusiasm in his voice.

"Pretty," Solly imitated, rolling his eyes at the rest of us. Heaven laughed. The lieutenant flushed.

"That's enough," I said automatically. It takes time before new lieutenants lose the new polish of self-importance, and in that time many mistakes are made and sometimes people are hurt when the lieutenant is quick to take offense.

I looked at Cornpone. "Why don't you and Solly get a fire going, and we'll cook up some of that meat Heaven brought in yesterday. We don't want it to spoil."

Heaven had taken the breather to move down into the valley and shoot a small pig at a watering hole. The carcass had been hanging in the shade of a stunted oak next to the canvas Lister bag we kept filled with water. In the high heat of the day, it didn't take long to turn.

Cornpone shrugged and glared at Solly. "You shoot your mouth off and I get the punishment. Figures."

"You can cook," I said easily. "I give it to Solly to do and we'll eat charcoal tonight."

Grumbling, but mollified with the compliment, Cornpone turned, saying over his shoulder, "Come on, Solly. At least you can start the fire and help butcher. It don't take no great skill to cut meat. Even you can probably manage that."

"Fuck you," Solly said cheerfully. He nodded at the lieutenant and ambled away, following Cornpone back toward the command post.

I turned back to the lieutenant. "You'll have to excuse the men, Lieutenant," I said. "They were expecting a couple of days' break."

He shook his head. "I understand. It must be rough, living on the edge out here."

"Up-country's not for the fainthearted," Duke said. "But if you want to try it, I'll trade places with you for a few days." He looked half-hopefully at me. "What do you say, Wingo? Want me to go back to Saigon in your place?"

"You'd never last. The lotus honeys would eat you up back there," I said.

"Yeah," he answered wistfully. "But what a way to go."

Saigon 1966 was just like Saigon 1965, and I knew 1967 would be like 1964. A time warp into eternity, everything collapsing in onto itself. No present, no future, only the past over and over again. In a way, there is a comfort in that, a strange melancholy, *une génération perdue?*—perhaps, although that is a bit too romantic. The air was so gray that it appeared grainy. You breathed differently here in the city than you did in the mountains. Saigon had a toxic, insidious smell about her like a great evil whore: painted, primitive, hypnotic, and when you walked through her at night, she panted wantonly and you felt like eyes were always upon you, like the cold eyes of a vulture waiting hook-necked upon the dead limb of a tamarind tree for you to fall.

The Paris of the East that had become the asshole of the world in one quick year after Lyndon Baines Johnson decided to honor an old and worthless treaty and commit American soldiers to Vietnam. Within one year, the Americans had corrupted a country and its capital with their arrogance that made the Vietnamese believe that their culture—that had been old when Leif Eriksson first shat upon the beach of what became America five hundred years later—was inferior to the one brought into the country by apple-cheeked boys who still shaved beginning beards. The Saigon tearooms and cafés, where once gentle and polite conversations had been conducted, quickly became cheap copies of the San Francisco clubs where Carol Doda had invented a new pastime with a G-string and silicone implants. The new South Vietnam government cut down the chestnut trees that lined Rue Catinat to allow American tanks to proceed easier and renamed the avenue Tu-Do Street.

The American soldiers were rock-and-rollers with one foot in the grave, and they knew it. They spent money wildly and lavishly, and the Vietnamese families who had a daughter reasonably attractive placed her dancing and whoring in the clubs lining Tu-Do Street such as the Casino Club and Papillon Bar, where the bar girls were referred to as "butterflies," or down at the brothel called The Flowers, which wasn't far from the Rose Bar. The families' fortunes increased quickly if the daughter was a fast learner and had no reluctance to satisfy whatever jaded interests the Americans brought with them when they arrived at Tan Son Nhut Airport eager to experience the mysticism of the Orient.

Fortunately, however, there were a few places that held grimly to honor and dignity and not the American dollar that inflated an already deflated currency: the Hotel Continental Palace, the symbol of the literary world (where Graham Greene had allegedly stayed while writing *The Quiet American* in another generation; perhaps he did, although the Majestic Hotel down by the Saigon River still had his signature on a couple of bar tabs; frankly, I hold with the Continental; the Majestic is too close to the river, which smells like an unbridled sewer, especially at night), the Racquet Club off Old Plantation Road, the Club Eve on Tu-Do Street (which the owner still called Rue Catinat), and many places in Cholon where Chinese and older Vietnamese held to their traditions while flooding the willing market across the Saigon River with willing country girls bought from their fathers.

I preferred staying at the Continental, although most soldiers coming in from the country preferred the Hotel Caravelle across Lam Son Square, a sleek and American-chic hotel where you could watch the nightly Tan Son Nhut fire from the rooftop bar. Sometimes, if you were lucky, you'd see a parachute flare descend slowly over the country until it became lost below the black skyline. The Caravelle staff didn't know an aperitif from an apricot, but whoever stayed there was expected to get drunk and spend lots of money. It was a gathering place for the soldiers and the civilian hard hats who worked for Morrison & Knudson or other contractors who had latched onto lucrative bids, and the staff turned a discreet eye away from soldiers bringing in their nightly romp. The Continental had high-vaulted ceilings with large, slowly rotating mahogany blade fans pushing the humid air around to give an illusion of coolness, and if you were willing to pay a little more (and I was), your room could have fresh flowers from the marketplace on Le Loi Boulevard placed in it daily. At the Continental, you could forget that Saigon had become a garrison town with huge coils of razor wire snaking around the American Embassy and that the city resembled Paris only in the most illusory manner. The principal buildings, except the *fin de siècle* arrangements such as the Gia Long Palace, which tended toward art deco curves of opaque glass resembling illustrations on the old *Normandie*'s breakfast menus, were battered and pockmarked from bullets, paint flecking from the thick walls, yet you could still get a good meal at the Guillaume Tell in Khanh Hoi near the Ben Nghe Canal. Only a few years before, you could get a good meal anywhere; that was before secularism became communism and *modernism* only a euphemism for "godlessness."

We landed at Tan Son Nhut in late afternoon, when the scarred city still appeared golden in the setting sun, before the neon glitter took command of the streets, and it was still easy to get a small cab before the off-duty soldiers flocked to the cabstand off base, impatient to get to their watering holes, traveling in pairs always against the groups of long-haired juvenile delinquents who lurked just inside dark alleys to catch drunks weaving their way down the inner districts. The driver's eyebrows rose slightly when I ordered him to take me to the Continental, but he stayed silent after quoting his base price in piasters for the ride. I knew the ride would be cheaper if I offered to pay him in U.S. dollars, but that was illegal and this close to Tan Son Nhut one had to be careful to trade dollars with the Vietnamese, as some of the drivers were agents for Nguyen Ngoc Loan's Saigon police or the Military Police and could earn a month's wages for turning in an unsuspecting soldier. The day when the American was a small god not to be tampered with was rapidly disappearing, and it was best not to take chances based on one's own feeling of being under the aegis of the American eagle. To the Vietnamese, the eagle was a bird of prey, not royalty.

Saigon had changed, but not so I could not recognize it. More peddlers haunted street corners, and short skirts and sling-backed high heels—whores' shoes, we called them—were being worn by many more young women near the same bars and walking the same streets. Before the murders of her husband and brother-in-law, Madame Nhu had tried to establish a series of morality laws, casting herself as the reincarnation of the legendary Trung sisters, who had led Vietnam's revolt against China in the first century. Madame Nhu had had a statue erected in their honor, although it was obvious to the observer that she had modeled for the sisters herself. All had to laugh at her attempt to raise the morality of the people, as Madame Nhu wore sexually suggestive décolleté gowns and had a series of lovers, with one always standing in the wings in case the current one should prove unsatisfactory.

Now, with the Diem regime long past—although memories are long and frequently reincarnated in different ways in Vietnam—rumors abound about the similarities between Madame Nhu and Ky's wife today, although "Madame" Ky wisely kept herself politically neutral and conducted her affairs, if any, with utmost discretion.

Still, one could still see the influence of Madame Nhu and her V-necked *ao dais* upon the prostitutes on the streets of Saigon.

Traffic from Tan Son Nhut to the heart of Saigon crept along at its own pace in a choking blanket of exhaust leading to a narrow bridge jammed with bicycles, pedicabs, and Lambrettas. Two enormous piles of garbage mark the entrance to a distinct quarter of the city. Near a place called Whore's Street or Bring Cash Alley, or whatever it is someone wants, girls teeter on spindly heels as they make their way over piles of rotting fruit to the concrete on the other side, where rind peels clog the spidery cracks in the pavement. Behind those garbage piles, the alley is carpeted alternately with garbage and human refuse or a fine silt of mud that winds back into a warren of houses, some made from sheets of tin still bearing the marks of Schlitz, Budweiser, Hamm's, or other beer cans carelessly tossed into dumps by soldiers, some thatched huts with tin roofs. This is Bui Phat, the oldest of refugee quarters, which lies just across the dung-colored river from the spacious French villas and streets lined with old trees.

In Bui Phat, boys in white shirts push their Vespas past groups of black-clad women and men who carry water and goods on coolie poles. Children scamper underfoot, playing games they invent upon the moment. Crime is rampant here and life can be bought for a few dollars as the police are afraid to enter the quarter because of the gang of teenagers led by a young army deserter who learned the principles of organization from the Binh Xuyen, the Vietnamese mafia. At one time the Binh Xuyen *were* the police, that right having been sold to them by the last emperor for a tidy sum that allowed him to maintain an extravagant lifestyle in Paris, but later they were forced to go underground after a battle with the army.

But Bui Phat reminded me of the backwaters of the Rosebud where my aunt lived in a gutted 1958 Chevrolet, a hole cut in the roof for a stovepipe that canted from a cut-down fifty-five-gallon barrel of motor oil, the front hacksawed down to make an entrance for chunks of wood, dried cow dung, or even old tires as the fall came ambling in and the winter roaring down from Canada. My uncle lived in a cave he dug out of an old buffalo wallow, and another uncle froze to death when he got drunk from drinking squeezed Sterno and went out in a blizzard in '56 to find the outhouse. We found him frozen not more than ten yards from the front door of our shack that had been hammered together from driftwood and old railroad ties, the roof shingled with entwined willow branches laid like mats on top of each other, with gramma grass between each layer for insulation.

My taxi pulled to the corner of the Continental and swiftly unloaded my bag and myself. The square in front of the Continental was notorious as a terrorist hunting ground, and the wise man was not the one who tarried but the one who conducted business as swiftly as possible and left. Dutifully the staff of the Continental gathered luggage and guests and swept them inside the building, where the thick walls provided safety.

"Mr. Wingfoot," the concierge said, smiling politely. "It is good to see you back again. The usual?"

The "usual" indicated my preference for a room above the second floor. It would take a good arm to lob a grenade that high, although the windows of any room were vulnerable to a rocket. But one took safety measures in numbers and adhered to the Decree of Lessening Opportunities as much as possible. After a while, it became instinctive and one moved around Saigon with an animal's subconscious awareness that preempted the cautions issued by the Saigon command: avoid outdoor cafés, frequent only those bars with grenade-proof windows, stay out of taxis, and avoid *cyclos* at all costs. Once one became used to the situation, safety lay in the freedom to move quickly out of harm's way, in not being confined within small areas for the convenience of the terrorist. And as for taxis, the driver was as vulnerable as his passenger. There were, of course, the zealots, the fanatics, the suicide bombers, but those were not as common as the press or command would like one to believe. And after a while they, too, became grist for the survival instinct. Tiny gestures, a shifting of the eyes, even the *smell,* were keys for the wise man. But more important was the willingness to listen to one's own feelings about a situation. If something didn't *feel* right, it wasn't. Vacate.

"Yes, please," I said, returning the concierge's smile.

And as quickly as that, my bag was taken up to my room, and by the time I had made my way up to the third floor a bath had been drawn, bottles of scotch whisky and gin and mixes readied, and my bag unpacked. I kept a small trunk in the storeroom at the Continental, and that, too, was unpacked, my suits being taken down to the hotel's valet service for pressing.

I sighed.

The Continental was a long way from the Rosebud Indian Reservation.

As I sat on the terrace of the Continental Hotel, the day looked golden. Light filtered through a couple of the chestnut trees still left from the time before the Diem government had cut them down to allow tanks to roll through the streets at the start of the war, back when I was only a thought. Yet I could still see the markings of war across the square where broken glass from bottles thrown the night before against the Caravelle's walls still littered the street. The violence made me remember the bicycle bombs that had torn through the crowd across Lam Son Square at high noon in an attempt to catch unwary Americans leaving for Mass at the Saigon cathedral. But the timers on the bombs had not been set correctly and instead of tripping at eleven o'clock went off at one, sending nails and iron fragments ripping through the market crowd, leaving torn bodies of women and children lying around on the concrete in the midst of bright splashes of blood that soaked deep into the pores of the concrete. Even now, I could see the faint shadows on the concrete as remembrances of that moment. But that was not unusual, because everywhere I looked I could see reminders of war and rebellion. It was almost as if the city had a huge keltoid scar lying over it as a reminder of despair.

I glanced at my watch: only eight—0800 for the military. I looked around the square; already the torn and the lame veterans of past battles were finding their places on the concrete where they would spread their pallets from which they would beg for a few piasters from passersby. Was there anything good about the city? I wondered. Perhaps behind the high concrete walls whose tops were set with broken glass and strung with razor wire to keep people out. Perhaps there behind those walls from which one could sometimes get a glimpse of a bougainvillea vine crawling or the tops of a decorative tree. Perhaps there where people still had ornamental ponds from which fountains sprayed small columns of water and one could walk under the coolness in the shade cast by palm fronds that formed a canopy over crushed stone and shell paths. Yes, perhaps there the war had not yet found people, unless the people themselves brought the war behind those walls on Cam Don Street. Some of those palatial homes had been taken by the government and were now homes to politicians who were driven to work behind smoked glass in highly polished black Mercedes. Some of the homes housed members of Westmoreland's staff and some houses were homes to the political neutrals who had found great wealth in the black market, where they sold manufactured battlefield souvenirs to U.S. soldiers who had never been out of Saigon and never would be out of Saigon. Many of the souvenirs were illegal, such as North Vietnamese flags, which were mass-produced in a sweatshop owned by someone named Trang—everyone involved with the black market seemed to be named Trang—and were a popular item and brought food to the tables of women who risked torture and possible imprisonment for making the flags. In a few years there would be more North Vietnamese flags hanging on walnut-paneled den walls in the United States than would ever fly over North Vietnam—or united Vietnam, if the war continued the way it was.

Vuong brought a cup of *café au lait* to my table. He looked cool and crisp in his white shirt and jacket, and his slacks had knife-edged creases in them. I doubted his name was Vuong, but in Saigon everyone had a name they weren't born with or one that suggested the aura they were trying to project. It made no difference to me. I sighed, contented. The Continental still stubbornly maintained the distinction of the past, when it was the symbol of French *esprit* before Dien Bien Phu made all things French *passé*.

"Will you be going to the Library today, Mr. Wingfoot?" he asked tactfully.

"Lincoln Library" was the nickname for the building where the C.I.A. pretended anonymity while surrounded with tanks and jeeps mounted with M60 machine guns and trucks with large .50-caliber guns mounted, which Westmoreland kept to impress visiting dignitaries from the United States. Had Westmoreland ever released those tanks and guns, the combined ARVN forces would have rolled down the streets of Hanoi months before. At the least, the Kontum–Pleiku highway would have been kept permanently open. As it was, the marines went through one day, and the next day the Vietcong closed it down until the marines went through again.

The marines were the country bad boys, but not as bad as they would like to believe their reputations made them. More than once the 173rd Airborne Brigade (Separate) had to go in and pull them out of the difficulties into which their arrogance had led them. One thing about those paratroopers: they didn't have to live up to their reputation; they carried it with them and made it with their actions over and over again. For my money, they were the best. Compared to them, the marines were bar fluff. The last time the Kontum–Pleiku highway closed down, the marines got bogged down and then surrounded. After two weeks of trying to fight their way out, the paratroopers went in, pulled the marines out, then opened the highway, all in less than a week.

"Yes, later," I said. I lifted the cup and sipped. The coffee was rich and rightly laced with warm milk. At least, to my palate it was correct. I suppose someone with more *élan* would have been able to criticize the bean for having been taken two rows too far down the hillside, but the Continental produced the finest cup of coffee that I had ever tasted. In fact, the Continental produced the finest of everything that I had ever encountered. I could understand why Graham Greene had spent so much time as a guest here while writing his novel, even during those times when he would stay at the Majestic until the stench of the river drove him out. There might be more fun at the Caravelle for those soldiers who lived frantically from one day to the next, knowing that tomorrow they might die, but I had learned patience long ago in another world on the Rosebud. All Indians did. They had to. And patience meant that I didn't like the fast track; I preferred the gentility of the quiet moment, the book on the terrace with a cup of coffee or, in the afternoon, a gin-and-tonic or Pernod, or a whisky-and-soda in the evening.

"Shall I arrange a car?" Vuong asked. He folded his hands and waited quietly.

I hesitated, then nodded, and he slipped away to discreetly arrange for a Renault and driver who could be trusted. I sat and sipped my coffee and stared out over the square, watching people move quietly through the building heat, wondering as I always did which ones were Vietcong. Perhaps the street sweeper who had quietly spent the last fifteen minutes sweeping the same small area over and over again, the flower woman whose flowers appeared more wilted than they should have been, but, I reflected, any could be and it was certain that a few were. That was the difficulty, telling the good guys from the bad guys, as they all looked the same.

The Library hadn't changed much since I'd last been in it, although more desks and cubicles had been added, so you had to weave your way around like a mouse working through a maze toward a piece of overripe cheese he could smell but couldn't see. The point in this was something that never failed to amaze me. Why the cubicles when all one had to do was stand up and casually glance over the top of the thin plasterboard to see what the next person was working on?

Secrecy was in the idea of secrecy, I thought, as I wound my way toward the back of the building. A young lieutenant sat at a field desk outside the door to Colonel Black's office. I didn't remember him. The lieutenant, that is; no one ever forgot Colonel Black once they met him. Short, stocky, balding, the gray fringe closely cropped, a constant chewer of Dutch cigars that made his lips look brown and rubbery.

"Yes?" the lieutenant asked. He frowned. I could understand why; I had chosen to wear a pair of khakis and a white shirt open at the throat.

"Tell Colonel Black that I'm here," I said.

"Who should I say?"

"Me," I said.

"I mean, a name, please?"

I stared at him for a long moment, watching the flush begin to creep up his face. The problem with young lieutenants is that they are important enough to demand a certain respect in the chain of command and ignorant enough that they don't realize they really aren't important at all. I wondered if this one had realized yet that the war hadn't been created for him, that it was simply the natural process all countries go through on their way to building a cultural identity.

"He's waiting," I said patiently.

The lieutenant chewed nervously at his lip. I knew his consternation, but it was something that all second lieutenants had to learn: when to be discreet by sacrificing officiousness. I was interested to see how long it would take this one to figure that out. If he did. The ditches along the road to hell are filled with the corpses of young second lieutenants who never figured that out in their fanatic drive to get their tickets punched to further their career. Actually, "ticket punching" was the minimum amount of time that an officer needed to spend with troops so that he would have a healthy-looking résumé. It was part of the corruption of the army: the more positions an officer held, the more likely he was to be promoted. This created, I imagined, a tidal wave of paper flowing constantly to Command Headquarters. Most officers spent just long enough in a position to royally screw everything up. The great war machine had nearly ground to a halt.

"I'll see if he's free," the lieutenant said, rising. He frowned disagreeably, but at least he was showing himself to be tactful enough to hold his opinions to himself until he knew fully what he was facing.

He knocked softly on the door, waited a moment, then entered, closing the door behind him. I turned and looked over the top of the cubicle next to me. A young private first class sat at a typewriter, slowly working his way through a cold decoding.

"Hi," I said.

Startled, he spun in his seat and stared openmouthed at me. I grinned and waggled my fingers at him. He looked rapidly from the flimsy on the desk beside him to the paper in his typewriter. His eyes flickered back and forth, panic rising. I heard the door open behind me, waggled my fingers at him again, and said, "See you."

I turned and saw the lieutenant standing beside the door. Beyond him, I could see Colonel Black staring across his desk at me. I felt like grinning again and waggling my fingers at him, but Colonel Black was not known for his sense of humor. I think he had lost it somewhere around the Choson Reservoir in Korea. But it could have been long before that. Maybe at Anzio or Berlin. There were plenty of Colonel Black stories to choose from.

"Well?" he growled. "Get in here."

I nodded at the lieutenant and stepped through the doorway into Colonel Black's office. The door closed firmly behind me. I took a quick glance around the room: the walls were covered with regional maps with colored pins stuck in a random pattern known only to the one who stuck them there. I noticed a red pin near Phou Sam Sao and raised an eyebrow. I had thought my team was the northernmost one, but someone or something had become important enough for a pin to be inserted there. I had a rough idea of the area, but only a rough idea. In fact, all our concepts about the country that we drew from our maps had to be taken cautiously. We were still using maps drawn by French cartographers who had sent Vietnamese surveyors in to get information about the land instead of going themselves. The Vietnamese took advantage of this and deliberately lied about plains and valleys and mountains and passes. I remembered one time around Pha Lap when my team went in expecting gentle hills only to find nearly impassable mountains.

"I expected you yesterday," Colonel Black said, drawing my attention away from his maps.

"Sorry," I answered. "I thought I was supposed to look like I was in Saigon for a bit of R & R. Or aren't we using that cover anymore, sir?"

He frowned at me suspiciously, considering whether I was being disrespectful or not. I kept my expression bland, waiting on him. He was right, of course; I was two days late reporting in, but this war was far beyond Ben Franklin's need for a nail and Poor Richard had yet to have a kingdom to trade for the damn horse anyway.

"Uh-huh," he said. Then, he motioned at the chair across from him. "Sit down."

I obeyed, resisting the temptation to cross my legs and relax. I didn't like Colonel Black and doubted if he liked me—if he even gave a thought to liking anyone.

"We have a problem," he began, and stopped. He pressed his lips together and frowned down at his desktop. Then, he surprised me by sighing and scrubbing his hands furiously across his face. He leaned back in his chair and stared at me. Deep pouches had gathered under his eyes, and his lids drooped tiredly. He regarded me steadily for a moment, then picked up a file from his desk, opening it.

"You have a good record, Mr. Wingfoot," he said.

"Thank you, sir," I answered.

He threw me a quick, annoyed glance. "I just said that. There's no reason to state platitudes, Mr. Wingfoot."

I remained silent, staring silently at him. This wasn't an ordinary mission; that had already become painfully obvious; I had never seen him, normally a bit surly with this sense of awkwardness about him, as if he was truly reluctant to give me new "traveling orders" for my team. Abruptly he slapped the folder closed and opened the bottom right-hand drawer of his desk and tossed the folder inside, slamming the drawer shut.

He leaned forward on his desk, folding his hands together, glaring at me. He nodded slightly as if making up his mind, then said, "All right, Mr. Wingfoot, here it is. We have identified a young woman working for the North here in Saigon."

I sat straighter, feeling my face tighten. I had a fair idea where this was going. "You've arrested her? Questioned her?"

He shook his head, his eyes shifting away to the left, then back again, fixing steadily upon mine. "No. There are some . . . 'complications' about doing that."

"I don't understand," I said, breaking in. "If you have an informer"—a crazy thought ranged through my brain at that moment: when had the euphemism for *spy* changed?—"why haven't you dealt with it?"

"We have our reasons," he said.

In other words, not mine.

"But what does this have to do with me?" I asked.

"We want her 'eliminated,'" he said.

Well. There it was. Out in the open and succinctly said. Eliminate. As casual as ordering a burger and fries in the malt shop back in the Land of the Big Milk Shake.

I shook my head slowly, watching to see the effect I had on him.

"You must have plenty of people back here in Saigon who could do that for you. Why bring me all the way down from up-country?"

He spread his hands and raised his eyebrows. "That's it, precisely.

We have plenty of people and those people know each other. This must be kept as quiet as possible."

"Oh. An accident."

"No," he said, shaking his head. "We want it to look like murder. An accident would be too obvious to our northern counterparts. *And* we don't want it to look like an assassination." He hesitated. "This must look like nothing more than a simple murder. Politics or the war cannot be brought into it."

I shook my head. "I don't like this."

His eyes snapped. "I don't personally care if you like it or not, Mr. Wingfoot."

"I don't like it one damn bit," I snapped back.

He straightened in his chair, a dull red moving across his face, making it look like old liver. We stared hard at each other, but for once, I didn't give a damn. Sherman was right that war is hell, but there are degrees of hell. Dante had a huge shopping list that he had made in the fourteenth century. A lot had been added in the five hundred years since.

"It seems," I said quietly, "that you are charging a woman with *maleficiam*. Is that it? I would also like to point out that there is nothing simple about murder. Not even here where it's as common as uniforms at the Army–Navy football game. Murder is murder. I don't care what you try and disguise it as; it's still murder."

"It won't be that difficult," he said equally as quiet. "She's a prostitute down at The Flowers on lower Tu-Do Street."

"A *prostitute*?" I blurted. "What the hell? How could she possibly gather enough information that she would be such a problem?"

He shook his head. "A good cover. But that doesn't concern you, Mr. Wingfoot. We have enough reason to want her, *need* her," he corrected, "dead. This won't be the first time that you have killed someone. Probably not even a woman. How many times have you fired blindly into the bush? Down a trail? In a hamlet?"

"They were shooting back," I said automatically.

"A bullet will only kill one person," he said. "Words can kill thousands. And have. The problem is not that a woman doesn't always say the thing she means but that she means too much with what she says. *And* she says it too often. You were brought back here because few in Saigon know what you do. Now, you have your assignment,

Mr. Wingfoot. Complete it. I don't care how you do it; just that it does not appear to be politics."

"How long—"

"One week," he said firmly. "You are officially back here for a week's R & R."

"My men—"

"Your men will be taken to Long Binh for a little R & R of their own," he said. "We'll put in a Special Forces 'A' team for the week that you and your boys will be out."

I shook my head. "They're going to know that something's coming if you pull the whole team out."

He took a cigar from a box on his desk. He lit it deliberately. "Then they'll be expecting the worst, won't they?" he asked.

He lifted another folder from his desk and handed it across to me. "Here's the file on her. She goes by the name Lisa Lee, but that isn't her real name. She works out of the Casino Club part of the time, the rest of the time out of The Flowers."

I knew what he meant: the girls who worked the bars were usually adolescents acting out the roles they thought the soldiers wanted to see, pretending to be adults in a world where they were too young to belong. Yet here they were, depressives past the initial period, a few old enough to have learned to enjoy what they did, others hating what they had to do and hating those who made it possible for them to do what they did. Many were on phenopsychotic drugs, some eating tranquilizers like candy—perhaps it was, a pleasantry gained in a life of pain, self-administrated occupational therapy.

But the Americans had become used to the Vietnamese women as whores or, better, courtesans, and even the wives of the politicians were seen in that light, for the men knew that even those women, if given the chance, would be whores or courtesans if the opportunity presented itself. It was part of the nature of the beast that had been created as people sought frantic lives in whatever moments they could seize.

And that made the women dangerous, I thought, staring at the plain brown folder in my hands. Because when people live frantic lives in frantic moments, they lose reason and words begin to flow like rivers.

I opened the file and took a look at the pictures of her. She was young and light brown and heavy-breasted. She reminded me of a young Sophia Loren, or what Sophia Loren would have looked like anorexic. Her skin stretched tightly over her bones and face, creating sharp almond-shaped angles. Her legs were long and shapely, the calves set off nicely by the sling-back high heels she wore. I could tell from the picture that she was probably naked under the lime green dress she wore. A delicate lotus blossom design had been woven into her dress with a darker green, meant to be subtle, but on her, it radiated sex. There was a brief and formal description of her, but other than that, the file was relatively slim. I glanced down at the bottom of the narrative; it quit in midsentence, and I knew it had been severely edited.

"Where's the rest of it?" I asked, knowing the answer but knowing as well that he expected the question.

"I suggest that you start at the Casino Club and see if you can find her there. You can manage your own introduction; women like that don't need the formality."

I nodded. I started to take one of the pictures, but he shook his head. "No, leave it. Memorize it. If you can't find her, ask one of the bartenders at the Casino Club for her. You'll want the one who is wearing a small silver and onyx ring on his left ring finger. He's ours."

"What if some of the others are wearing that kind of ring?" I asked.

He smiled like winter. "There won't be after seven P.M. That should be the time to try for her. It's early enough that you shouldn't have much competition, late enough that there shouldn't be any suspicion."

I closed the file and flicked the edge of it with my thumbnail. "You know that this could make me a liability."

"In Saigon?" He laughed and rolled the cigar around in his lips. "Here, everyone is faceless. It's the Year of the Goat. A dangerous time for all."

I stood outside the gate, debating what to do. The day was long, yet, too long to start hitting the clubs. That wouldn't be prosperous until the light turned to neon blasts of blue and yellow and red and green. I thought about Fell and wondered how he was faring. I glanced at my watch. Noon. Perhaps the Racquet Club out on Old Plantation Road.

I hailed a taxi and directed him to the club, then leaned back against the torn seat and watched the traffic as the driver wove his way in and out of lines of cars, making his own lane as most Saigon taxi drivers did, yelling at the rickshaws and pedicabs that refused to get out of his way.

I thought about all that Fell and I had been through. We had already been in the army for nearly a year before we learned why we were going through obscure and, what seemed to us, unrelated training. We finally ended up at Fort Holobird, which, at the time, was where the army sent people for special investigative training skills after they had been put through the Ranger and Airborne courses at Fort Benning. I never knew why Fell had been chosen for this training. The nearest I could figure out was because he had made a mistake in electing to take a Doctor of Philosophy degree from the Jesuits at Georgetown rather than stay in college for the sake of avoiding the war. I put that down to the romanticism of youth and war at the moment.

After that, all of us were sent to Vietnam. This was right at the beginning of the war when Lyndon Baines Johnson was quietly announcing to the public—quietly for political reasons, to avoid drawing broadsides from the doves, as it was the beginning of electioneering—that he was committing troops to Vietnam for an indefinite period. That was a harsh word, as we soon discovered, for the twenty-seven of us who had survived the security checks and training were given teams and sent to particular spots all over the country. We were insurgents, modeled after the old Deer Teams of World War II that had been sent into Southeast Asia to harass the Japanese.

It wasn't a very good idea, however; by October, six months later, there were only four teams still occupational: Fell's, mine, another led by the "Dutchman" Pieter Van Neiderhof, who, I privately believed, was certifiably insane, and the one led by Copperhead Jack— who *was* insane. Being crazy and being able to control that craziness despite the cold brutality needed to do so was instrumental to survival in a country where man is nothing but a wager God places in a crapshoot with Lucifer.

The four teams left created a bit of a problem for the army, as they really didn't know what to do with us. Fell was no problem now, his team destroyed, but mine and Neiderhof's were still operational and Copperhead Jack had proven to be too much even for Saigon. Neiderhof punched out a psychiatrist once in Saigon who tried to probe a little too deep into his psyche, and the last I heard, Neiderhof was up in Burma somewhere, trying to raise a guerrilla army in the Kachin Hills.

But Copperhead Jack was the worst of us. A big, blond man, he had the coldest blue eyes I had ever seen; they seemed to probe like icicles to the back of your mind and read all of your thoughts that you had hidden there. Jack just plain liked to kill. There is no other way to explain him. Once he tested a new garrote he had made by snapping the head off a puppy that had come wandering into the tent in search of food. His face bore no more feeling for that than if he had been slicing a piece of meat upon his plate. He was the only man I knew who carried a small hatchet with him, the head specially weighted by having a strip of brass welded upon the back of it, the edge ground to such a sharpness that it made it useless for cutting wood. I never heard of him using it to cut wood, but you could trace Copperhead Jack's trail through the jungle and mountains by the heads that were left on sticks, facing back from the way that he had come. The army made the mistake of giving him R & R once in Bien Hoa. An airman made an unwise comment while Copperhead Jack was drinking in the Gunslinger's Club on the air base there and spent two months in the hospital being wired back together. The club was wrecked and four other airmen went into the hospital as well. Jack walked out of the club with very few marks upon him and returned to his hotel beside the Dong Xi river in Bien Hoa. When the MPs came to arrest him, he threw one from the second-story balcony of his room, broke the jaw of the second, and when the third made the mistake of drawing his .45 Jack took it from him and shot him in the ass with it. The bullet passed through both cheeks, which, according to the story, made bowel movement so painful that the MP damned near died of constipation.

After that, Copperhead Jack was left alone up around A Sap, which was next to the A Shau Valley. The Ho Chi Minh Trail used to run through A Sap, but once Jack started operating in the area, the trail was moved down to the A Shau Valley. A Sap came to be known as Jack's Valley, and the Vietcong and the NVA left him pretty much alone. The Montagnards loved him and followed him like a god. To them, I guess he was; he never bothered with prisoners, and he never bothered with following any of the rules that we were supposed to follow. To Jack, Geneva was simply a dull place to visit and if there was a convention there, it wasn't for Jack.

It took a while for me to understand how Jack had so much success; then I realized exactly how he made things work. He had made horror his best friend and in the process had made himself something like a priest-king for the Montagnards he led. He had learned how to use horror to take fear away from his men through the use of the heads. In the hill country, some of the Montagnards believed that the head was the seat of the soul and for knowledge to be retained by the tribe, the head of the leader must be severed at the precise moment of death to keep the soul of knowledge from escaping into the darkness of the night. At an appointed time, the successor to the chief would enter the ailing chief's hut and sever the dying man's head and drink from the lips to suck forth the essence of the man. Legend said that Jack united some of the hill tribes by performing the ceremony and mounting the heads of the chieftains on poles facing his hut. But I knew that it was more than legend; there had been seven heads on poles outside Copperhead Jack's hut the last time I had occasion to go through Jack's Valley.

I think that Copperhead Jack had made a pact with God; Jack would stay out of God's business if God stayed out of his valley, and God, being omnipotent, wisely left well enough alone.

At one time, long before we arrived in "the Paris of the East," when we were still innocent and Vietnam had just changed its name from French Indochina, the country was run by armed Hoa Hao and Cao Dai sect members with their own private armies and the Binh Xuyen gangsters who had their main offices in police headquarters and their own army as well. As if that wasn't enough, General Nguyen Van Hinh was issuing a *coup* threat to the "official" government—whatever that was—while the official government of Ngo Dinh Diem attemped to keep some sort of order.

Diem managed to crush the others through a combination of military and political moves (thanks to the support of the United

States), but the damage had pretty well been done. South Vietnam was, at the time, in severe economic depression—its main export, rice, had for the third straight year fallen three million tons short—and the Agency for International Development was created to direct and administer the U.S. economic aid program to South Vietnam in the 1950s and 1960s, with disastrous results. Part of the problem was the "spoils system" that Diem instituted once he had control. He placed family members in key positions with the government whether they were capable of handling the job—and most weren't—or not. It wasn't as if the U.S. hadn't been repeatedly warned about these problems; they had. Dr. Tom Dooley gave them plenty of warnings with his books and reports until his death from cancer in 1961. I suspect that he wasn't listened to, as one of the government's "secret services" had begun a clandestine investigation that questioned Dooley's moral fiber.

The worst case of Diem's appointments was when he named his brother Ngo Dinh Nhu as the Supreme Counselor to the President. Nhu was a ruthless and rigid follower of Machiavelli who created intrigues that didn't need to be created in order to give himself an aura of importance. His office was magnificent: decorated with heads of tiger, buffalo, and deer that Nhu had collected on mini-safaris made to resemble Hemingway's romantic *Green Hills of Africa*. Nhu's favorite hunting grounds were around Dalat. Yet it was the life-sized portrait hanging across from his desk that drew a visitor's eye when he was granted admittance behind the veil into the holy of holies: a beautiful Vietnamese woman dressed in a sheathlike *ao dai,* the traditional dress, that dramatically highlighted full breasts and exuded sensuality with imperious flashing eyes that smoldered with sexuality.

Nhu played the games, but it was Madame Nhu who defined the rules of the games, building everything upon some nefarious communist plot that no one had ever heard before.

There were other members of the president's family who made his government teeter back and forth on the brink of disaster. Ngo Dinh Thuc, his older brother, transformed the archbishopric of Hue into a source of personal revenue, using his governmental position to force sales of apartment buildings, rubber tree estates, and timber. He had soldiers cutting wood for him, and if he took a liking to a certain tract of land, it mysteriously went up for sale with no other bidders showing an interest.

The second-youngest brother, Ngo Dinh Can, made a fortune smuggling rice to North Vietnam and opium to Hue, while another brother, Luyen, made a fortune manipulating currency.

Soon protests about the Diem government began to surface, and it was after the Buddhist monk Thich Quand-Duc set himself afire in Saigon in 1963 that the Diem government began to crumble. Of course, it didn't help matters that Diem was a fervent Catholic and had a tendency to view Buddhists as "naughty boys" who hadn't found the way yet. It wasn't long before the two brothers were assassinated in the back of an armored personnel carrier, and then the government was up for grabs again, this time without Nhu and his wife plotting and planning. The reins of the government slipped through many fingers before finally coming into the grip of Nguyen Cao Ky through a *coup d'état* along with Nguyen Van Thieu that was really little more than a farce to demonstrate that the military could not be controlled by the then government.

And into this mess came we, the soldiers made into something that we didn't want to be but, by the grace of Lucifer, had become in the grand manner of the moment.

We were given "hidden rank," which meant that we could pretty well do any damned thing we wished when we were in the bush. When we came out of the bush, however, it was a different story, and that caused a lot of problems that left quite a few frustrated officers wondering if we were worth the trouble or not. I don't think we were; we were simply an experiment that had gone wrong.

We had become jaundiced by the war, which came from finding soldiers with their peckers cut off and jammed into the back of their throats so they choked to death, bodies carefully flayed so they couldn't be identified except with dental records, others burnt with soldering irons and branding irons, with fingernails and toenails pulled out with forceps, others gutted and hung between two trees just high enough that they could watch the jackals eat their entrails, and those were the lucky ones who had been caught by the Vietcong.

Most of us kept rooms in Saigon against the time when we would be called back for briefings. Fell's was in the Majestic Hotel, which looked across the river to Cholon. The waters of the river moved

slowly and dirtily down toward the South China Sea. Below, on occasion, tanks and jeeps would rumble by and grind dust from the
concrete street. The dust would rise and powder the leaves of the
trees. The trunks of the trees would also have a thin film of dust
upon them that would last until the rains came, and if the rains
came too late; then the leaves would fall from some of the trees and
Vietnamese workers would move slowly through the heat of the day,
sweeping the leaves into piles with long brooms made from swamp
rushes. Late at night, the street would become bare and white because of the curfew, except for the leaves, which rustled with a dry
brittleness like fingernails scraping faintly over blackboards.

The taxi pulled into the drive leading up to the Racquet Club. I
paid the driver and got out to walk up the crushed shell drive beneath the canopy of tamarind trees. The club had been built by the
French, who had owned the country as a colony, and the buildings
were whitewashed, with thick walls, and cool inside, with old fans
with long mahogany blades clicking overhead to pull the heat up
toward the high ceilings. The tennis courts were still well maintained and now were used by the rich Vietnamese who had come
into the club after the French had been defeated.

At first, the French had tried to maintain control of Vietnam by
supporting the emperor, Bao Dai, and educating him as a boy in
France. But all Bao Dai developed in France was an appetite for fine
wine and women and gambling. It was the gambling that had begun the downfall of the French in the midfifties, as Bao Dai gave the
Binh Xuyen, the Vietnamese mafia, control of the police, which
opened the doors of Saigon to corruption that still existed, although
the Binh Xuyen had allegedly been stamped out in the late fifties.
But one has never been able to legislate morality, and once pleasure
is made illegal, it simply goes underground and becomes even more
tantalizing. The Binh Xuyen were still around, but under different
names. That was even reflected in the meaning of the name
Saigon—"gift to the foreigner." The French thought of themselves
as the recipients of that gift and had transformed the city into a
copy of what they had left behind: wide, straight boulevards,
gracious squares, solidly built buildings with rococo designs. That
all changed after Dien Bien Phu, when the French lost control of
their colony.

Now, they lived in their homes in tight security yet still maintained the dignity of coat and tie for dinner, discreetly keeping pistols on laps or by the legs of their chairs while eating their meals from old china and silver, engraved with forgotten coats of arms, maintaining tradition and customs that had been established by their great-grandfathers and -uncles two hundred years before, during the days when Vietnam was a colony.

The tension of the war was seen more upon their wives and women, but their nerves bred a constant gnawing discontent that made them lose weight and look very chic in the new styles. They took to carrying beaded purses lined with leather to keep their pistols from snagging if they had to be removed in a hurry. The most popular were the hammerless .32 calibers or the small .25 Berettas that fit well within a grown man's palm. Some of the women wore long hat pins in the wide-brimmed hats they still affected to keep the tropical sun from bringing out unsightly freckles on their creamy-white skin. Those hat pins were deadly in their hands; long, thin, steel-shafted, and sharp, a hat pin could be inserted between a man's lower ribs before he felt the sting of the point. The women didn't bother going for the eyes with their hat pins; a quick feint at the jugular, then angled in from the left of the sternum. The younger women were the most dangerous, as they had not developed the qualms regarding the sanctity of the human being. They did not hesitate but attacked quickly when they were attacked, never bothering to yell or scream for help.

Some old French families still used the club, those families who refused to move away and had adjusted themselves to the new economics established by a succession of presidents, each making radical changes that were designed to redistribute the wealth of the country but did not allow the wealth to trickle down to those who needed it most, as those who were in charge of collecting the wealth in taxes were reluctant to let it slip away from them. But the club was still the best place to go to relax, for the war seemed to never touch the Racquet Club, thanks in part to its deep wine cellar, although all who were there were always conscious of the war, for the war could never entirely disappear, despite the frantic and frenetic lifestyle that had emerged since people discovered their vulnerabilities.

It was always cool at the Racquet Club, or, I suppose I should say, the fruit trees and chestnut trees and the thick webs of grapevines that were encouraged to grow there lent an atmosphere of coolness even when the temperature soared into the tropical nineties and humidity settled around a hundred and five, forming a condition known as *verga,* when tiny droplets of water seemed to hang in the air and walking through them seemed like walking through a damp and clinging curtain of spiderwebs.

But when it rained, then the club became gloomy, usually in the fall when the branches of the chestnut trees would become bare and the trunks of the trees black with rain and the vineyards became thin and bare-branched and the country seemed to become bare and brown and black and dead all over. Gray mists floated over the river, and when the sun shone from high through the mist the world became a yellow-sulfuric nightmare in which dim shapes like the spirits of the damned floated eerily through space, hovering just off the ground. The air, then, smelled dank like death, and all knew that the winter season would bring even more rain and with the rain would come typhoid fever and, in some outlying villages, cholera, which would bring death to many. But that didn't seem to be of much concern, for the whole country was death simply looking for a place to happen.

Saigon, however, was another world.

If God wanted to give the world an enema, he would stick it in Saigon. Yet there was a deadly fascination to Saigon that drew people to it much in the same way that people flock to watch the deadly snake exhibits in zoos. Except in Saigon, you were part of the exhibit, part of the night that was always within the city. Saigon may have been the city of the living, but for all purposes, it was the city of the dead. Everyone who came to Saigon was anxious to leave it, but when they left, they took with them a strange nostalgia for it and a yearning to return. Once one was in Saigon, Saigon became a part of one.

I found Fell sitting at a table beneath an umbrella, enjoying a Pimm's Cup while reading the *Paris-Match.* He looked up, annoyed, when I pulled the chair out across from him; then he recognized me and his face lifted a little in a smile. He wasn't drunk but trying to work his way toward it. His eyes were bright and focused, but there was a tightness around his lips and cheeks that suggested he had entered that stage where he would drink more and still get no drunker than he was at the moment and remain lucid. Men who have been exposed to combat for a long time develop a self-preservation instinct that allows them to retain an alertness despite enormous intakes of alcohol; when a threat presented itself, they became instantly alert.

"Hello, Fell," I said. "How have you been?"

"Well," he said, folding his paper and laying it beside his drink. "It's been quite a while since I've seen you, Wingo. As you can see"—he nodded toward the cane he had leaned against the edge of the table—"the army is still reluctant to send me home."

"They'll find something for you to do," I said. "They have too much invested in you to turn you loose until they get full interest in return. Have you heard anything about the others?"

He glanced around; we were far enough from others that our conversation would not be overheard. I smiled at his precaution.

"A bit. There's not many left. You, me, Copperhead Jack, perhaps a couple of others. But they're late reporting in. They might still be alive."

I shook my head. "They're alive. Just smart enough to stop reporting in. The radio is our worst enemy, did you realize that? The smart man is the one who ignores it as much as possible. Only bad news comes by radio. Nothing good. What does one have to do to get a drink around here?"

He motioned to a waiter, and when he approached, Fell ordered a gin-and-tonic. He raised his eyebrows at me, but I shook my head.

"Whisky. A double."

He waited until the waiter disappeared, then said, "Bad news, I take it? An assignment that you wished you didn't have?"

"All assignments are ones I wish I didn't have," I said. "They're becoming tighter and tighter. We damn near didn't come back from the last one. You hear about Yen Mong?"

He nodded. Yen Mong was a tiny village or hamlet about sixty kilometers or so west of Hanoi. A *very* hairy area. Rumor had come down the Pike—one of the many nicknames we had for the Ho Chi Minh Trail—that Vo Giap, Ho Chi Minh's leading general, and some of his staff would be in the village for one reason or another. My team had been sent in to eliminate—a popular euphemism for "murder"—Vo

Giap with "extreme prejudice." We damned near didn't make it away from that one. Someone had dropped the intelligence ball somewhere.

The waiter brought a tray with our drinks to the table and a soda siphon for my whisky. He placed the tray upon the table and discreetly left. Fell lifted his gin-and-tonic from the tray.

"Cheers," he said.

I splashed a bit of soda into the whisky and took a swallow.

"Are you getting over your difficulty from Tay Son Pass?" I asked.

A tic developed beneath his left eye. He covered it with his hand and shrugged. "It had to happen sooner or later. A man visits the tiger too often, the tiger gets a piece of him. We knew the odds when we got into this business."

"I don't recall volunteering for this, and if I remember right, you didn't, either."

"There's that," he conceded, taking a larger sip.

Suddenly it began to seem like a good idea to get drunk—or at least as drunk as we could get, given our peculiar situation.

"How long are you back?" he asked, lowering his glass.

"About a week," I answered. "The rest of the team is being sent to Long Binh for a bit of R & R."

"Uh-oh. That sounds ominous," he said. "Sorry."

We all knew what would follow the week's respite; the gods make man happy just before throwing him in harm's way. Or, as was the popular saying, God makes one happy before laying a huge dump on him. The adage works either way.

This time I shrugged. "God must be dicing with Lucifer again and they can't find Job. So, what are they going to do with you?"

"Administrative work for now. I hear the Langley boys are developing a new program. I have a hunch I'll be in on that. Intelligence and Pacification. You know: rebuild what we have already destroyed in a gesture of goodwill."

He tried to sound casual, but I noticed a cold sweat that suddenly broke out on his forehead, and his hands began to tremble. I had a hunch that Fell was near his end. Being captured by the Vietcong takes a lot out of a man.

"Well, look at it this way," I said soothingly. "It might be a good opportunity for coming in the back door with intelligence."

He nodded and finished his drink. He stared brooding into the empty glass.

"Another?" I asked.

He shook his head and continued to stare into the glass. I looked around the grounds of the Racquet Club. My eyes focused on a young girl lying on the close-clipped grass, her arms outstretched as if she had been crucified upon the ground. She wore a short tennis skirt and I could see fully up the golden columns of her legs to where a few pubic hairs escaped her undergarments, and imagined her beneath the mosquito netting over my bed in the hot afternoon and the sweat in tiny beads on her hot skin. But she was too young for me, although only a couple of years probably separated our ages. I had enough mileage on me that made me at least a hundred and ten. At times, I felt my odometer had gone around twice.

"Want to go to Maxim's for lunch?" I asked.

"It's the middle of the afternoon," Fell said. "Closer to dinner."

I shrugged. "Want to go to Maxim's for dinner?"

He sat still, considering. I knew he wanted company and that sometime during the night we would have one of those serious talks that we aren't supposed to have, with the "need to know" mania that establishes a type of aristocracy within the army. But we knew that we *needed* moments like that in order to try to figure out the sense of logic behind the seeming insanity of the orders. Often we could not, and that was all right, too, as once we realized that there was no logic to the order, then everything became its own logic.

"Why not?" he said, shrugging. "I haven't been to Maxim's for quite some time, and a good evening would be a change. Maybe we could visit Le Monde after."

I felt a smile quivering on the corners of my lips. Le Monde was across the river in Cholon, the Chinese section that had been France's "Crown of Thorns." A man could find anything in Cholon, but it was not a place for everybody. It was a place for madmen only, who were caught up in a primitive and retiring way of life or secure in their own invulnerability to visit there after dark or to simply not care one way or the other. But Le Monde was where one could find the practiced courtesan, one who had been trained in her art and not one who lingered at the street corners or in the new bars that had suddenly come into being on lower Tu-Do Street. At Le Monde gentility was still in force and absinthe could be obtained without the raised eyebrows that one might encounter elsewhere, or a discreet visit could be arranged to an opium fumerie. The place reminded me of the old paintings by Toulouse-Lautrec of the Moulin Rouge, a holdover from the old days when a sense of civilized manners prevailed and people still dressed for cocktails and dinner.

But it was a place to go when you had become tired of the soul-destroying days of inward vacancy and despair, knowing that the days would march endlessly on without respite, and a wild longing for strong emotions and sensations began to seethe within you, causing you to rage against the toneless, flat, sterile life that you had no choice but to accept when circumstances were no longer within your control and *free will* had become only a phrase. When days like that came, a strange sadness seemed to sweep over me, and I wanted desperately to smash something, anything, commit some atrocity that would cause others to look aghast at me and know that I really did not fit into their world of carefully preserved optimism filled with fat and prosperous mediocrity.

I looked at Fell. "You still feel it, don't you?"

He hesitated, knowing what I meant, then nodded. "Yes, I do. It's like a narcotic that once into a man's system can never be purged." His hands began to tremble again, and the tic came back. This time, he didn't bother trying to hide it. His eyes moved rapidly back and forth, looking at those who sat at the other tables.

I nodded. "Yes, I feel that way, too. Someday, this war will be over. Then what?"

"You could always go into ascetic solitude and contemplate the trinity: Possibility, Pretense, and Conquest."

I laughed. "I prefer the Four Horsemen of the Apocalypse. Once one has come to understand horror, serenity is no longer desirable. Tell me, which would you rather attend: a good jazz club or an opera with a lot of bad singers? You must make a choice."

"Tonight, the jazz club," he said firmly. "I've had enough of the proprieties for the moment."

I laughed and gave a short, mocking bow with my head. "A gentleman of the arts has spoken. Then, after dinner we shall explore lower Tu-Do Street. I've heard about a place called The Flowers. Do you know it?"

He shuddered. "I know *of* it. Anarchy in its most blessed state. You can make arrangements for anything there."

"Sounds like a plan," I said, rising.

I waited while he drank the water from the melted ice cubes in his drink and climbed painfully to his feet and collected his cane. His hands had ceased shaking and I wondered if I had been making too much out of Fell's earlier appearance.

But it was at The Flowers that I noticed a strange intensity come over Fell's face. At first, I thought it was the result of the three bottles of cold Sancerre that we had drunk with our meal at Maxim's, and the brandy after, but I could see that here was something else that had seized him and held him. Lisa Lee fit the part well. Up close, she seemed too big in the breasts and her hands were long and pale like ivory piano keys and her feet in the sling-back high-heeled shoes were long and narrow and highly arched. Her nails were short and square cut, not the nails of one who sat the day in a beauty parlor but one who had not learned the delicacy of nature that demanded the patronizing care of one's nails if one was to be a courtesan. Yet her wrists were narrow and delicate, almost birdlike, and thin copper and brass bracelets tinkled gently upon her wrists when she lifted her drink to her lips and sipped daintily, her lower lip looking swollen and moist and vulnerable when she took the glass away. Her cheekbones were high and accented the slight hollows of her cheeks and the almond shape of her eyes that drew a man deep into their inky blackness. Men studied her covertly, each locked into his private thoughts about her, although most would have ended their thoughts with visions of her naked body stretched out over their bed, a soft gold against white sheets.

Several young soldiers approached her hopefully, and she laughed and teased them, pulling one on his ear, chucking another under his chin, rubbing her cheek against another and pretending that his young beard had been like sandpaper against her smooth flesh. They all bought her drinks—small shot glasses of bourbon-colored tea served at whiskey prices—but none could convince her to leave with them.

Her eyes kept darting to the door each time someone walked

through, brief lights of hopefulness shining only to be replaced with the flatness and false gaiety of the working girl whose paycheck depended upon the number of soldiers she could tease into buying drinks at the bar.

I watched as several of her friends slipped in and out repeatedly with young soldiers in civilian slacks and sport shirts in tow, reappearing a half hour later, a bit mussed, tired circles under their eyes, as they made their way back to the bar, forcing their painted lips into empty smiles of welcome. Yet the young woman never left.

At last, Fell turned and studied me, raising his voice to be heard over the throbbing beat of Nancy Sinatra's "These Boots Are Made for Walking."

"What is it?"

I shrugged and shook my head. Tiny muscles began to jump at the corners of his jaws. I looked over at the woman again; there was something intriguing about her, something that drew the male attention to her first, then grudgingly to the others. I knew why she was there: she was the flame that attracted the men to her like fluttering moths while the others were the ones who went into the "bam-bam" rooms with the men.

I looked closer at the other women at the bar: one of them had streaks of gray in her hennaed hair, and when she went by I caught the scent of cheap jasmine-scented perfume. Another smiled at a young man and I saw the badly decayed front tooth, her face pockmarked with tiny black grains of dirt dug deep into the pores. Two soldiers came through the beaded curtain at the back of the bar with two little Vietnamese girls. The girls weren't long at the bar before they went back through the beaded curtain, this time with two different soldiers.

I took a deep breath, smelling the stale spilled beer, the sweaty smell of powder-caked whores, the heavy spices of aftershaves.

The lights grew dimmer, and a new bunch of women came in to take their places against the bar. The dim lights would make them look younger, but I knew these were the hard-core whores for whom no degradation mattered anymore, as they had learned to take pleasure in all the debaucheries that came their way. I shook my head and nodded at Fell.

"Time to go," I said. "The dogs of war have arrived."

He nodded and tilted his glass back, finishing his drink as he looked around the room at the changing clientele. There was a hardness to the men who came into the bar at this time of night, their faces looking as if the skin had been enameled onto the skull, the eyes unflinching but not challenging. But once you looked into them, you knew enough to leave these men alone. That, however, also created a problem. Although they came out late at night, occasionally one would wander through the streets during the twilight hours and, sometimes, approach the wrong woman and find himself beneath the savage batons of the police, relishing that pain, as that would make him know that he was, for that brief moment, still alive. That was understandable, as there are times when man needs to be reminded that he is still alive when a deadness has filled his spirit.

We left the bar and stood for a moment among the forced gaiety of the street, the flashing neon lights of pinks and yellows and greens and blues causing a weird change to the night. This would have been the introduction to Dante's hell if he had begun his journey in the twentieth century instead of the fourteenth. There was a strange sensation to the night and the garish colors spotlighting the faces that looked boldly into your own. The night smelled of cheap perfume and rice powder, but beneath all that was a deadlier smell, harsh and acrid, as if you had walked into a room where twenty people had struck a match simultaneously, the sulfur making you slightly nauseous and reckless. Then someone follows you into the room and you know the fear working at him in the back of his throat as he swallows against the sulfur smell.

"Bad thoughts?"

I blinked, bringing myself back to the street and the neon zapping the buildings and shadows with laser colors. "A moment. That's all."

We turned and made our way down toward the Continental, where I stayed. From there, he would take a cab down to his place at the Majestic.

"You want to talk about it?" he asked. "There is something troubling you."

I jammed my hands deep into my pockets. I nodded.

"Let's walk up on up to Notre Dame," he suggested.

I looked at him. "You know what you'll find up there at this time of night, don't you?"

He laughed. "Penitents and sinners waiting to sin some more. Whores waiting to draw the newly cleansed into another night of sin."

"Joke, if you want, but it is not a good place to go at this time of night," I said, warning.

"Then," he said recklessly, "that's precisely the place we should go."

I shrugged again and turned to walk the three blocks down to where the cathedral spires waited deceptively for us. Peace and contentment were an illusion in Saigon and not found in any of the churches. But that didn't stop some from desperately seeking solace when shipwrecked upon the rocks of their own personal seas of troubles by appealing to the Carpenter to build a more seaworthy vessel for them.

We turned into a small park next to the church. Lightning rippled through the thunderheads as we walked under the tamarind and chestnut trees at the edge of the park, following an old stone path deeper into the dark between the trees. My senses prickled and a sense of *déjà vu* slipped over me. There was no resemblance to another time, another place, in the park, but nevertheless the trees and the dark and moldy smell reminded me of too many other places at other times that blurred into a similitude.

Beneath a bush, we saw an old Vietnamese man, mouth open, flies gathering upon his face and in the corners of unseeing eyes. He was emaciated, ribs showing through the tattered shirt he wore, his bare feet thick with old yellow callus. We paused, staring, and I knew that Fell was thinking the same thoughts as I. It was a camaraderie of the spirit, not the soul, for that had been long burnt away with the first napalm attack each of us had gone through, remembering the smell of gasoline in the air long after the last plane had left and how it sucked your soul from you. Napalm flares as hot as the fires of hell, squeezing the air out of your lungs, shoving your blood down to your boots, and burning the light from your eyes. No, this was the reflection of time wasted in a mirror: the faces of the dead always have a story. You can see it in the slack jaw, the mouth stretched tautly in a last-minute cry of outrage or for help or pity, as if the dead person in that last frozen moment of lucidity had discovered the hypocrisy of the world. The eyes stared blankly at the last flicker of light: perhaps a shaft of sunlight through the branches of a banyan tree, or if we had found the body in time, a tear might be frozen in that last singular moment before the sun burnt it away.

I always wanted to believe that there were angels in the world among men when I found a dead body like that, and if it was an American soldier, I hoped that the angels had come fast enough to spirit the life away before the knives of the Vietcong worked upon the body, flaying the flesh, cutting the testicles and penis off and stuffing them into the mouth, eviscerating the man and hanging his entrails around his neck like an obscene scarf.

We moved deeper into the park, watching the shadows automatically. We walked to a small bench that stood in the middle of the park, out from under trees, away from bushes.

"It's not a good idea," Fell said, wincing. "But I must sit down for a moment. I'm getting some of the angries."

"Sorry. Guess I was preoccupied," I said. "Would you rather walk back to the Continental?"

I really didn't want to sit in the moonlight in the middle of the park, a stationary target. But I didn't feel any threat around, the air thick and humid, but not with that *hum* that makes the flesh tingle as if the fine hairs on your arms began to wiggle all at once. If you're lucky, very lucky, you developed this when you went into the field.

"Yes," he said, "but I'm going to have to rest for a minute."

I wiped away the beads of moisture from the bench with the flat of my hand and sat gingerly on the wooden slats. There was no breeze and the palm fronds and banana trees were black-green and motionless in the heat. He sighed and eased his aching leg in front of him.

"You want to talk about it?" he asked again. He gestured around at the darkness. "I think this would be a pretty safe place."

I nodded. "Yes. Probably. You know that girl back in the bar?"

"Which one? There were lots."

"The pretty one. The one who stayed at the bar."

"Oh, the come-on? The bait? What about her?"

"She's the one."

"The one?"

I remained silent, staring out in front of us into the dark across the green. The scent of jasmine and other night-blooming flowers was in the air so thick that it seemed to gather at the back of my throat and wash across my skin.

"She's the reason I was brought back."

He frowned. "Her? They want her eliminated? What in the world for?"

"They claim she's a spy for the North."

He nodded thoughtfully. "Possible. But you can't go around killing everyone on supposition. Hell, half the maids in Saigon that the field officers use are spies. You know that; everyone knows that. As long as it isn't brought to your attention, you pretend that it isn't so."

"Yeah, well, apparently it's been brought to someone's attention."

"But that still doesn't make any sense. There must be a hundred people around here who could do the job. Why bring someone in from out-country? That automatically involves more people. Whatever happened to the doctrine of need to know?"

"That's what worries me. That and the vagueness of everything. Black gave me the assignment, but I could tell there was something there that he didn't like. Something that bothered him greatly. The whole thing has a feel about it that is rubbing me the wrong way."

We all had learned to pay attention to those little feelings. Even when they were false alarms, there would usually be something, some little thing, that would have spelled disaster if we hadn't paid attention to it.

"So, she's the target. And we don't know why except someone has claimed that she is a spy. But what could she possibly pick up in that bar? You saw who uses it. What could they possibly know that would make a difference to whether a squirrel crosses the street or not? That bar's not exactly the place for staff officers, you notice. No, there's something else coming down here."

"I know," I said, and sighed, scrubbing the palms of my hands across the stiff bristle of my short-cut hair.

"What are you going to do?"

I shrugged.

"How long?"

"I have a week. My men are enjoying a bit of R & R."

"A week." He shook his head. "Well, that should be enough time. But are you going to do it?"

"I'm tempted to tell them to 'fuck off' and head back north."

"Bad mistake," he said solemnly. "You can't afford hubris. That's a character defect better left to writers like Sophocles, who make a living out of tragedy."

I grinned at him. "You can't tell me that you haven't done that a time or two."

"Yeah," he said, tapping his leg with his cane, "and look where it got me."

"But did it make you feel better after you did it? Would you do it again?"

He knew what I was referring to. He had been ordered to lead his team down upon a small village in the highlands, as the whole village had been named "unfriendly." After you cut through the officialese language you knew that you were being ordered to wipe the village off the map. He had refused to do so and sent in one of his men to warn the villagers that they would be coming in the next day. When they arrived, even the cooking fires were cold and the only living thing was a scrawny chicken scratching at the hard-packed ground, hoping for a nibble of something.

"Yes," he said irritably. "Damn you, yes, I would do it again."

I shrugged and spread my hands. "There you go."

"Which leaves you?"

"I know. I know. Any ideas?"

"Well," he said cautiously, "I know a man at the university we could talk to. He's pretty good at these sorts of things."

"A man?"

"Dwarf, actually. But he's a professor. One of those Ph.D. folks. He's the only neutral that I know. Completely. His world is literature and he seldom strays into the twentieth century."

"Locked in time, hm? What's he going to do for us?"

He shook his head. "I don't know. But he has friends."

I groaned. "This is beginning to get out of hand already. I don't know. Instinct tells me to keep it short and simple. Do the job and slide back up north."

"The job," he asked. "Is it a wet one?"

I nodded.

"But there's something else, isn't there? What?"

I nibbled my lower lip for a moment, thinking. "I don't know. The vagueness of the whole affair, I suppose. When was the last time that you weren't given all the information? Including that which you probably wouldn't need but was safe to have?"

"Never," he said. "At least," he amended, "not that I know about. Most of the time the problem is ciphering through what is valuable and what is gloss. I take it you have a sketch and that's it?"

"That's it." I sighed and scrubbed my hands over my face, suddenly tired. "Maybe I'm making too much of it, but there is something not quite right about all of this."

"Do you want to see my friend?"

I threw up my hands. "Sure, why not?"

"I'll get in touch with him. Tomorrow afternoon?"

"At his office?"

"Hardly," he said, smiling faintly. "He'll pick a place. Americans aren't popular with all of the students at the university. There's a faction that could make trouble if we visit."

"All right." I looked around. "Shall we go back for a nightcap? I think we've been here long enough."

"Too long at that," he said, pushing himself to his feet.

We hobbled back to the Continental and had a brandy or two before calling it a night. His hands had started to tremble again, and I had a vague uneasiness that Fell had become a war-wearied man who could find delight only in death longing and yet was afraid to die, afraid to be sent back into the jungle.

4 I remember the morning. I have—*had*—always liked Saigon mornings when the sun broke through the smog hanging over the city, the ice wagons peddling snow cones rattling down the street on bicycle wheels, the light soft and buttery and not smelling of hot tar and asphalt—those were good mornings. When it rained the night before, the sunlight seemed to filter through palm fronds, and bamboo and bougainvillea vines and wisteria and azaleas dripped with moisture as heavy as agates and the early morning seemed to have a blue softness about it that suggested the city was a wonderful place with a safe refuge waiting for it in heaven.

Then the day would begin and with it would come the slow rot and decay as the people began to make their way along the streets. The Continental, however, kept the day at bay just a little longer with its quiet breakfasts upon the terrace, and the soft tap of fork and knife upon the plates, the gentle clink of water or juice pitcher to glass, the silver coffee or tea carafe, all prolonged the inevitable but helped to ready the mind for what lay ahead in the course of the day.

After breakfast, I went for a long walk, wandering back off the square and into the side streets where the young women were beginning to make their way from their homes, walking to work or school, strolling through the shade of the chestnut trees, their hard bodies inside white *ao dais,* through a golden tunnel of mist and sunlight that had been created for the young. But I could feel nothing for them except an appreciation of their beauty. I was one of the walking wounded who had been in Vietnam so long and done so much that my soul was ready to commit incremental suicide, as I had done enough for a lifetime's worth of penance and was already storing up for the next incarnation. My head felt like a bad neighborhood that I didn't want to go into alone.

The bright day seemed to disappear, although I knew it was all around me, as my depression deepened. Why were we in Vietnam? A question I had often asked myself during these moments, and I had never really arrived at a satisfactory answer. Now, I realized that the land was our original sin and no baptismal rite would wash it from our lives. We tried and still tried with baptism after baptism of blood as if we were ancient Aztecs seeking to bring down the word of God by offering him human hearts, but the ground only became soaked with it and the ravens and kites and other carrion birds ate of it. We knew the pull of the earth upon our ankles and the claim that the land lay upon us, upon both the quick and the dead.

I glanced at my watch; still a couple of hours before I could expect a message from Fell. I shoved my hands into my pockets, automatically slipping the French Opinel knife with its wooden handle into place, my fingers toying with the blade, opening and shutting it; working the hinge to keep it smooth.

I found myself in a street that still showed the early French influence. High walls with broken glass embedded in the top to discourage thieves from crawling over, intricate iron gates welded into floral designs, most with the initial of the family living in the columned house at the end of the crushed shell drive. Most of the French families who occupied these homes still lived in them, although they had probably given up their mountain homes where they would once have escaped from the summer heat into the cool highlands. Now that would be too dangerous, although I'm certain that many of them still managed to keep most of their property through a complex deal they made with both sides of the war.

I stood in front of one with a coat of arms welded into the center of the gate. I didn't recognize the coat of arms, but I recognized what it and others like it once stood for. These were the people who had pulled the strings on the puppet emperor Bao Dai, making him dance the dance they wanted—a *danse macabre* with intricate movements that involved the Binh Xuyen gangsters, the Cao Dais, the Hoa Haos, and other groups, playing each against the other and against the middle as the fortunes of each swung back and forth on the pendulum of corruption and control. Whoever was the stronger at the moment would draw the largest rake-off, yet that changed as the power structure changed. Yet each had one thing in common: the Montagnards were considered little more than game to be hunted at leisure, usually excursion parties that were formed at Bao Dai's villas south of Nha Trang.

That had caused some problems when I first made contact with them. I could see the suspicion in their eyes and knew the hatred they felt toward outsiders. When the soldiers had galloped down upon the villages of my ancestors, shooting at every man, woman, and child, the French had been slipping into the Montagnard villages and shooting everyone there. When the soldiers cut the breasts off the Indian women to use as tobacco pouches, the French skinned the Montagnards and had the skin tanned and made into wallets. The conceit of the soldiers and French alike was passed down through the generations like malignant heirlooms, genetically coded so the hatred and elitism would be carried through the veins of their offspring like syphilis.

My mother's voice seemed to whisper down through the years to me as I stood in the street, staring through the iron bars of the gate into a world I would never know. Mother's voice seemed faint, disembodied, and for a moment, I thought it was a stranger's voice full of cracks and fissures coming to me.

Yes, I understood the hatred and knew that it really didn't matter if the Montagnards hunted the North Vietnamese or the South Vietnamese. They hunted the northerners only because we had gotten to them first and convinced them that they might have a better deal if the South won the war than if the North won. All Vietnamese were hated by the Montagnards, some more than others, and those who came from Hanoi were the ones despised enough to bring the Montagnards, especially the Rhandes, over to our side. That plus we had made some promises that we had no intention of keeping: providing a place for the Montagnards in the government and allowing them elected representatives. It was complicated, but it worked.

Once in the Valley of Dead Children we were caught in a storm. The wind howled through the valley, sounding like the moans of the dead punctuated by the sobs of those left behind. We took refuge in a bamboo stand, and the wind coming through the bamboo made a macabre symphony of sound that worked deep into our minds, making the tiny hairs on the backs of our necks, wrists, and forearms stand up and quiver as our flesh pebbled. We huddled together, wishing we could sink deep into the night, body and soul. Several times I heard the others whispering and thought I heard a few *Our Fathers* and *Hail Marys* joining the wind. I pulled my poncho liner up over my head, trying to cut out the sound of the wind, but when I did that, the wind seemed to gather strength and howled even louder through the valley.

In the morning, we moved up the valley, not even pausing for breakfast, anxious to get out of the valley. It was then that we discovered the naked bodies of several women, heaped together in the bushes along the side of the trail. The bodies were fresh and mutilated, their genitals hacked out crudely, their breasts sliced off and placed like cups over their eyes. Maggots already were at work in the wounds, fat white larvae that crawled over the bodies in a bacchanalian revelry. Overhead, kites and ravens and vultures wheeled and screamed and cawed, trying to drive us away from their feast.

"Let's bury them," Heaven said.

I shook my head. "If we do, then the NVA will know that we have come this way."

"Do you think the NVA did this?" Heaven said. He spat disgustedly to one side. "These women are from the North. They were probably on the way to join their husbands or boyfriends."

And because I wanted to believe Heaven, we paused to bury them. The earth was hard and shallow, and we carried rocks a long way to bury them. Solly found some flowers somewhere and brought them back and did his best to plant some on each of the graves. Duke and Cornpone tied some rude crosses together. Later, we discovered from the Montagnards that an NVA platoon had watched us discover the women and remained hidden as we were burying them. Heaven read from the Bible he always carried. Our gesture probably saved our lives, although the Montagnards had quietly formed around the NVA platoon from the rear and were ready to fire upon them if they made the slightest hostile gesture toward us.

I turned away from the house and made my way back to Tu-Do Street and the bookstore near the Continental. The bookstore kept a hodgepodge of offerings, English, Vietnamese, Chinese, French, and minor selections in many other languages, including Swedish—although I doubted that many tourists came from Sweden during these times. I went to the Vietnamese section first, curious about the professor I was about to meet. I discovered a shelf of his writings, and a discreet card that listed those that had been translated into

other languages as well. Our professor was apparently highly regarded as an authority on the ancient literature.

I went to the English section and discovered three books by
Nguyen Diem: *The Tale of Kieu, The Influence of Kieu upon Politics,*
and an anthology translated into English of Tang verse. I bought all
three and walked down the street to a small café and ordered *café au
lait* and croissants and settled in the shade under a red-and-white
striped umbrella and opened *The Tale of Kieu* and began reading.

Quickly I found myself swept back to the beginning of the eigh-
teenth century, when Vietnam was larger than the United States
when George Washington stood on a barge and gave his Farewell
Address. While the United States was struggling to find out if it was
a country or not—let alone develop a culture—the Vietnamese people had for centuries realized that they were the devoted heirs to
those traditions of government, philosophy, literature, and moral
and social theory that began with Confucius and Mencius. Buddhism was there, but it was the Mahayana Buddhism that drew the
Vietnamese loyalties, and their sutras were carefully written in the
classical Chinese language.

Yet the Vietnamese literature was not a shallow copy of the Chinese. All things are borrowed and adopted to need. The Vietnamese carefully controlled what culture they borrowed from China
and made it their own. But the Vietnamese like to think of themselves as having always been poets since the ancient days. Nguyen
Diem traced the folk tradition in poetry back to the Dong Son civilization in the fifth century B.C.E. when the Vietnamese worshiped
the sun. But this was all theory, as no literature could be traced directly to that period. The first record of Vietnamese poetry came
during the Han Dynasty invasion in 111 B.C.E., and as time pro-
gressed, the Chinese came to call Vietnam *Van Hien Chi Bang*—
"The Cultured State."

Nguyen Diem identified the first poem as "Two Wild Geese,"
which was written when Li Chueh, a Chinese ambassador of the
Sung court, visited Vietnam to establish diplomatic relations. The
Vietnamese scoured the country for intellectuals who could com-
pete with Li Chueh and his party and found two Buddhist priests.
One, Do Phap Thuan, disguised himself as a ferryman and took the

ambassador across a river. Li Chueh saw two geese swimming in the river and to impress the ferryman with the intellectual ability of China immediately composed a couplet:

> There: wild geese, swimming side-by-side,
> Staring up at the sky!

To which Do Phap Thuan added two lines to complete the quatrain:

> White feathers against a deep blue,
> Red feet burning in green waves.

Suddenly I became aware of the time and closed my book. Rising, I left a hundred-piaster note under the saucer and hurried back to the Continental. Fell's message waited for me: At the Club Eve. Tu-Do Street. Five P.M.

The club interior was dark and cool. Black and white tiles laid like diamonds covered the floor. The tables were small and circular, with upholstered chairs clustered around them. Potted palms stood strategically placed around the room to give a suggestion of privacy. Fell spotted me as soon as I entered, and stood.

"Wingo," he said, smiling. "Fancy meeting you here. Won't you join us?" He indicated a dwarf sitting across from him. I fought to keep my expression neutral as the dwarf reached across to shake my hand. He wore thick, round glasses and his hair was silver and neatly combed.

"Pleased to meet you," he said softly. His accent was French. "I'm Nguyen Diem."

"Ben Wingfoot. This is an honor," I said. "I was just reading your book."

His left eyebrow twitched and a tiny smile forced dimples into each cheek. "Oh? You surprise me, Mr. Wingfoot. May I ask which one?"

"*The Tale of Kieu,*" I answered. "Your translation is very good."

The smile deepened on his face. "And are you aware of the original?"

"A bit," I said, smiling back. "Was Nguyen Du a relative?"

He laughed. "No. 'Nguyen' is as familiar here as 'Smith' is in your country. We all have our pretensions, though, and I imagine my forebears had theirs as well. Adults are only large children. When you were a child, didn't you take on the names of your movie heroes when you played?"

"No," I answered. "Everyone wanted me to be Tonto and not the Lone Ranger."

He frowned politely, but I could see that he couldn't make the connection. The cultural chasm was still too deep at that time for timely reflection. Fell saw it, too, and hurried to cover the awkward moment.

"Are you working on anything at the present, my friend?" he asked Nguyen Diem.

The dwarf shook his head. "No, not at the moment. I have just finished a study in which I compared some of the Western myths with our Eastern ones. Amazingly, there is a lot of similarity, which makes me wonder if all myths don't spring from a single source." He laughed, the sound low and musical in the dark room. "Tell me, Mr. Wingfoot, why do you Westerners refer so much to Prometheus instead of Polonius?"

I frowned, shaking my head. "I think you misunderstand: Polonius is the patron saint of our politicians who send the rest of us on Promethean journeys."

"Or," he asked, his eyes holding a twinkle in their black depths, "an odyssey?"

I shrugged. "If there is a heaven, it must surround the hell holding politicians."

"And not soldiers?"

"They are only the messengers."

"Powerful people used to kill the messengers who brought bad news."

"My point," I said.

He laughed and tapped his fingers gently upon the table between us. He glanced at Fell. "I like your friend. He is most refreshing."

"Wait until you get to know him better," Fell said sourly.

Nguyen Diem laughed and motioned for a waiter. When the man came to our table, Nguyen Diem ordered a bottle of wine for us. A French merlot from an estate whose name I had never heard.

"The San-Martins. You know about them?" he asked when the waiter left.

I shook my head and looked at Fell, who shrugged.

"A bit," Fell said. "They had a vineyard up on the Red River, I believe."

"Yes," Nguyen Diem said. "Yes, and it is still a wonderful place, although the wine has fallen off in years since the last San-Martin left. He was with the Sûreté, a vain and arrogant man who always had a bottle of merlot on his desk when he questioned his prisoners. *This* merlot," he said pointedly as the waiter neared our table, bearing a tray that held a bottle and four glasses that sparkled in the dim light of the room. He placed the tray on the table, produced a corkscrew, and deftly pulled the cork. He handed it to Nguyen Diem, who sniffed it and nodded, then tasted the splash the waiter poured in his glass and nodded again. The waiter filled our glasses and left.

Nguyen Diem held his glass and took a small sip. "It was perhaps the cruelest moment of a prisoner's questioning," he said. "It was meant to remind the one sitting in a chair across from San-Martin that the French had complete power. A subtle suggestion, you see. The wine the blood taken from our Motherland by the French who were draining us at will, at whim. Of course, the allusion didn't work that way for all—some of the prisoners were not educated men, but they could still appreciate the poetry of the gesture. Vietnam is a land of poets, Mr. Wingfoot, as I am certain you are aware if you have been reading my books. The prisoner would have gone through, ah, a certain 'ritual' of questioning in the basement of the police headquarters before he would be taken to San-Martin's office. He would have been beaten and probably resisted that."

He shrugged. "Physical pain is a simple reality to the Vietnamese people, you see. We have been forced to develop stoicism as a significant part of our culture over the centuries. But then, you are in the military and realize that the mind is a far more delicate instrument than the flesh."

"Yes," I said. "I am quite aware of that. But no man is sufficiently strong to resist pain forever."

"True, but can you trust what you get from such a man? Or will he simply tell you what he thinks you want to hear in order to stop it?" He smiled. "And ask yourself: What would you rather go through? Physical or mental torture? Which could you withstand the longest?"

"Why do you drink the wine from the estate of such a man?" I asked.

His lips curved down in a dour smile. "Because I need to be reminded of what *was* in order not to let it happen again."

"The French are gone," I said.

"True, but the Americans and the Australians are not," he answered calmly. His eyes searched mine, probing to see how I would handle the fragility of the moment.

"I am an American Indian," I said quietly. His eyebrow twitched. "One of my relatives was at Black Kettle's village on the Washita River when the American soldiers slaughtered them. The soldiers made tobacco pouches out of the Indian women's breasts and cut out their ovaries and slung them over the backs of their horses as trophies. We have been on reservations for a hundred years. Not as long as your people have been subjects of another country, but at least you still have yours. We are guests only in our own, now. Mental torture is the worst. I know; we have had to live with it every day."

"Frankly," Fell said dryly, lifting his wineglass, "I would prefer to avoid both."

We laughed at that, finding mirth in the darkest of jokes to protect delicate pride. There was little to laugh at in those days, but we always searched for something, if only to assure ourselves one time that there were still moments of sanity in the world and we could keep the simian beast from which we had descended, and which still lived, in a secret place within us locked away from the light of day.

"I understand you have a problem?" Nguyen Diem said.

"Yes," I said, and fell silent for a moment staring at him. He smiled faintly at my hesitance.

"You are reluctant. I understand that. How can you trust a Vietnamese when you cannot tell the difference between those from Hanoi and those from Saigon? The answer is simple: you cannot," Nguyen Diem said. "Either one will tell you what he thinks you wish to hear. But politics are politics and people are people. I believe in people before I believe in politics. You are familiar with your

Bible? Then you may remember that the beast to begin the destruction of man will rise from the eternal sea. The eternal sea is not the ocean but the sea of politics. Do you know why man created politics? That is where he can play at being the god he cannot become. There he can control life and death, and that is the closest he can come to immortality."

"Then what do you serve?" I asked.

"Truth," he said. "I serve truth. At least, that which I see as truth, which is different from man to man. Truth is in the eye of the beholder. To a man who is color-blind, red appears gray, while to the man who is not color-blind, it is red. So, tell me: what is the true color?"

I nodded and took a deep swallow of wine and glanced at Fell. He gave an almost imperceptible nod.

"There is a woman," I began, and told Nguyen Diem the story, beginning with bringing me down from the North and the assignment I was given. Then, I told him my doubts.

"It's not logical," I said. "There are many people in Vietnam—American or Vietnamese—who could do what I have been assigned. *And* why not simply turn your suspicions over to the Vietnamese and let them deal with it? Loan—the police chief—could discover the truth about her."

"It is the secrecy that bothers you," Nguyen Diem said.

"Yes. There is a need for secrecy, but there is logic in that as well. This is not logical."

"What will you do if you discover that she is working with the North Vietnamese?"

I didn't answer. There comes a time when one must take responsibility and not simply assume that his ass is covered because he is obeying orders. Instinct told me that this was wrong, and I had lived a long time up-country to not learn to listen to instinct. She could be the enemy; she might simply be the victim of someone's anger or misinformation. Saigon was a deep well filled with informers, each willing to sell another for a few piasters. There were those who spied upon those who spied upon them, and often it was simply a matter of who got to the master he was serving first that survived and was rewarded with his thirty pieces of silver that made the difference between who lived and who died.

"And what is it you wish me to do?"

"Who is she?" I asked. "I need to know who she is."

"You know that if I did serve the North, she would be warned and would flee?"

I nodded.

"And where would that leave you?"

I shrugged. "If she disappears, then who can say that the job has not been done?"

"And if I do not serve the North and I discover that she is North and tell you, then what will you do?"

I looked at Fell. He stared back, his eyes flat and lifeless, and I knew mine were a mirror of his.

"There is a third possibility," Nguyen Diem said quietly. "What if she is working for the North and I tell you that she is not? What then will you do?"

I shook my head. "The answer will still be the same. If not me, then someone else. Maybe Fell here."

He glanced over at Fell and sat back in his chair, toying with his wineglass. He could barely reach it, his stubby fingers gently rolling the stem back and forth between them. He was troubled by what I had said, and I knew that he could also refuse to help—a fourth possibility that held the same answer as all of them: the young woman would die. So, why should he help? The truth would not be served either way. All that would be helped would be my conscience, knowing that I was doing right or wrong. That was logical; either way, the woman was dead.

But I didn't know what I was going to do. I felt that I was on the edge of a cliff and that if I took the next step, I would fall into another world where I would be something that I did not want to be. It is one thing to be a soldier and kill; it is quite another to be an assassin. Some may think that is splitting hairs, that a soldier is nothing but an assassin, but there is a difference. A tiny difference that makes an individual able to hold firmly to the dignity of his soul. It is that which allows us to continue being men.

Nguyen Diem finished his wine and slid off his chair. The edge of the table came to his chest and I realized he was not so much a dwarf as he was a very short person.

"I must go," he said. He extended his hand to both of us. I was surprised to discover his palm was thick with callus. "Why don't the two of you come out to my home for drinks tomorrow evening? I will have an answer for you."

He turned and left. I glanced over at Fell.

"He'll find out something," Fell said quietly. "I don't know if he will tell you what he has found out or not."

"What would you have done if the assignment had been given to you?" I asked.

He shrugged. "I would have killed her and been done with it."

"Even if she is innocent?"

"In a war, no one is innocent. In *this* war, at any rate," he amended. "Truth doesn't matter. If the soldier hesitates to play with ideas, then he will be dead. There is no good death—Jesus took that away from us."

We went to the casino over in Cholon that night. The casino was a blessing for some Vietnamese who worked frozen-faced around the gaming tables inside the sunless room where cigarette smoke hung like cellophane in the air. But a black mood had descended upon me, and after I placed a few bets upon the roulette wheel and won when red came up four times in a row, I took a scotch-and-soda and watched Fell as he played recklessly with wild abandon, playing the long odds, the single number.

I remembered when I last went on a short R & R down to Vung Tau—that the French called Cap St-Jacques. I sat in a beach chair, staring out at the gray-green waters off the shore. Whitecapped waves came together like alpine peaks as the offshore wind picked up, snapping the stripped canvas awnings stretched in front of the small stores lining the sand behind me. I glanced up and down the beach; no one was going into the water, but they were staring morosely out at the gray eel-like bodies that rolled playfully along the tops of the waves. The sea snakes were migrating, and although they were supposed to be very shy around humans, no one wanted to take a chance on meeting up with a garrulous snake who hadn't had his breakfast. The sea snake bite was the most venomous known, and territoriality was not an issue; they could have the water.

Fell's play was the play of a soldier who refused to admit a tacit honesty about life. He was one of those who had spent enough time in the field to feel the piano wire twist hard around his head. I knew when he closed his eyes he would see the huge clouds of orange flame leaping up out of the rain forest when napalm fell in front of him while he stayed locked on his knees in a muddy, shimmering rice field and shards of claymore mines ripped through the air like hot rain from hell, the souls of children drifting upward like smoke from the village where they lay, and the smell of gasoline hung heavy in the air. When he dreamed, he would see the trunks of blackened trees and birds and monkeys exploding into fireballs, and because he could still dream, he would know that he was, for that brief moment, immortal.

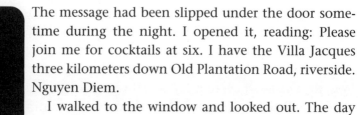

The message had been slipped under the door some-time during the night. I opened it, reading: Please join me for cocktails at six. I have the Villa Jacques three kilometers down Old Plantation Road, riverside. Nguyen Diem.

I walked to the window and looked out. The day was gray, with heat lightning flashing over the city like yellow sheets. There would be rain again, I noted automatically, and, for some strange reason, wondered how my men were enjoying their little break and wished I was with them instead of in Saigon at this precise moment. I glanced again at the note; the words remained the same, the time as well.

I crossed to the bureau and opened the top drawer to slip the message inside. I shut the drawer, then opened it again, staring inside, puzzled. I always used the top drawer for personal items: my billfold at night, money clip, pocket change, my Baby Browning. Something was missing. Then I saw that my dog tags had become singular. That wasn't a problem, as, like most soldiers who had been in the jungle for a while, I tied one to the laces of a boot and tucked the other inside the breast pocket of my jungle blouse. Only a fool wore them on a chain around his neck. Charlie didn't need any help with a garrote; he had his own.

I went to the closet and looked at the laces of the boots that I had worn. They had been cleaned and polished and fresh laces supplied. The staff at the Continental was thorough. I shrugged; probably a slip by the bootblack, nothing more.

I dressed slowly, choosing a pair of double-pleated brown silk trousers and a white cotton shirt tailored to be worn outside the pants. That kept away the need for a shoulder holster and allowed me to carry the small Baby Browning .25 caliber in a special holster inside the waistband of my trousers.

I took a small leather shoulder bag, placed a notebook, pen, and one of Nguyen Diem's books inside, and left. I walked down to the quay where used bookstalls stood and wandered with pleasure among them. Most of the books were old, their bindings water-spotted and the pages showing a slight foxing and smelling of must. But I didn't mind this and selected a copy of Sabatini's *Scaramouche* for myself and a couple of Ian Fleming's James Bond series, remembering how John Kennedy had admitted they were his favorite reading, before Lee Harvey Oswald put a bullet behind his ear. The bookseller promised to have *Scaramouche* delivered to the Continental for me. I took Fleming's books with me.

I moved on through the day, waiting for the first hot drops of rain to hit, enjoying the walk along the river despite the smell of rotting fish and human waste that drifted downstream from Lyonesse, the quay where the boat people lived. You could never get away from the smells in Saigon except along Old Plantation Road and up in the districts where the old families lived in private park-like splendor behind high brick and concrete walls in their own private worlds. For some reason, I preferred it here and in Whore's Alley or Bring Cash Alley, where you could buy anything you wanted, as the police turned a discreet eye away from the black market unless trouble brought them into the area. The people had learned, however, how to handle their own problems, and only two laws applied in either place: live or die and end up by being found floating down the Saigon River after the crabs and fish had nibbled on your body. Even Loan, the police chief who had executed a suspected North Vietnamese spy with a pearl-handled hammerless .38 revolver by placing one bullet in his head in the public square as an object lesson, stayed out of Whore's Alley or Bring Cash Alley. Some of the people who live there are so bad that they go willingly down deep into the abyss where even lizards and snakes don't have eyes because they feel completely at home.

I made my way up to the hospital where I had taken Fell after he collapsed on Tu-Do Street the night before, shivering and shaking, mumbling about snakes and scorpions. I knew the signs of malaria as well as any soldier who had six months in-country, although I had never had malaria myself and crossed my fingers that I would not get it. For some reason, I seemed immune from the parasites and diseases that ran like wildfire over the countryside. I even ate at stalls, secure in the knowledge that I was a "passer" as far as the Vietnamese were concerned. My color and black hair and eyes left them uncertain enough not to work drugs or poison into my drinks or meals. Besides, that is where one could get dried and salted octopus and native beer, two items for which I had developed a taste.

"Mr. Fell?" I asked the nurse at the desk.

She consulted a chart, then asked to see my identification. Sometimes looking like a Vietnamese doesn't have a benefit, but I was used to that: being rousted at will by the rednecked peckerwoods hired as deputy sheriffs in South Dakota leaves you pretty much prepared for anything.

She lifted an eyebrow at my identification card, then gave me a smile and turned away to use the telephone. I walked back to a chair and sat and waited while she made a discreet call to someone. Soon, an orderly who looked like a Green Bay Packer linebacker came and led me down the hall to Fell's room.

"You have fifteen minutes," the orderly said as he opened the door.

"What if I need more?" I asked.

He smiled faintly and silently closed the door.

I turned and looked at Fell, sweating, his eyes bright blue pinpoints but lucid. A saline drip had been tapped into the vein of his left arm. A fan had been placed on a small table and oscillated slowly, moving the sluggish, sterile air around the room. His window had been opened as far as it could. He gestured weakly to the chair beside his bed.

"So. We have a couple of drinks and you slap me in here," he said.

"Seemed the thing to do. You were getting maudlin anyway," I said. I handed him a couple of the Ian Fleming paperbacks I had taken with me from my stroll down the quay.

"Ah," he said, looking at the titles. His hands trembled, but I could see that he was beginning to come out of the relapse. He was lucky; sometimes those relapses went on for a week or longer. "*Goldfinger* and *From Russia, with Love*. Very appropriate."

"Best I could do," I said, leaning back. "How are you?"

He placed the books on the table next to his bed and laughed shakily.

"I feel like my head is the host hotel for a mosquito convention," he said. "But the doctors say I can probably leave tomorrow or the day after." He studied me carefully. "Thank you. You know, I don't know if I thanked you properly for dragging me out of that camp up north when I was captured." His hands began to shake and his eyes took on an unhealthy sheen. "They would have killed me there. Damn near did."

"We don't leave our own behind. You know that. Besides, someone had to do it. My team just happened to be handy."

His eyes slipped away from mine, the eyelashes fluttering, and I knew the nightmares he had of that would always be with him, rolling in upon him like floodwaters when he momentarily let down his guard. He would remember that and the stench of the camp, the "honey pit"—soupy shit—where they dipped him daily and he could feel the tiny bugs eating away at his flesh. I remembered the burn streaks across his chest and belly and lower, although I didn't look because I knew they would be there, from when they had wired him up to a field telephone and cranked away. I had seen the tiny holes flared with red where they had jammed bamboo splinters in and set fire to them. And I had seen the madness in his eyes, the same madness I would have expected to see from someone suddenly jerked back from the ninth circle of hell.

I shrugged. "Don't make more of it than it was. I wasn't about to leave you on the street or in a cab."

"Some would have," he said.

"I'm not some," I answered. "You would have done the same for me."

"Would I?" he murmured. "I wonder. Did you have any trouble with admissions?"

"No," I said. "They thought I was a Vietnamese doing a good deed. They did keep me for a while when they discovered your wallet was empty, but they got over their suspicions in time."

He smiled ruefully. "It was the wine and the scotch. I should have stayed with gin-tonic. The quinine would have helped keep it away."

"Maybe."

He glanced at the door, then turned close to me. "Have you heard from our friend?"

"I had a note in my box today. I'm having cocktails with him at his villa at six. Anything I should know?"

He closed his eyes and shook his head. "I don't know what to tell you. Go armed. It might be a long night. And convey my apologies if he asks where I am. I presume I would have been invited as well."

"Probably."

"He does have a sense of protocol. *And* he works quickly."

"I can tell that. We only explained my problem about eighteen hours ago. He must be tied in with the right people."

He cocked an eyebrow at me. "Meaning?"

"He's your friend, not mine. Could he be tied in with the wrong people as well?"

"Probably." He gave me a crooked smile. "But that's what makes life interesting."

"Pardon me for wishing for boredom now and then," I said.

We made the jokes that were weary by now but still valued because there was a semblance of truth behind them that eased a soldier's worry. I felt a vague uneasiness about Fell, however, as he seemed taut, his nerves strung like piano wires, thrumming to the slightest breeze that came from the fan or through the open window.

I left the hospital around five, promising to return the next day, and made my way back to Lam Son Square, where I hired a taxi to take me down Old Plantation Road to the Villa Jacques after haggling over the price. I didn't care one way or the other, but the Vietnamese lose respect for you if you do not haggle about the price of things. It's a cultural reminder of the time with the French, when the Vietnamese had to haggle to survive. Sometimes, one has to be reminded of the bad times to keep them from coming back.

The taxi had no air-conditioning and the wind blowing in through the open windows felt oily and gritty. I kept my hand on the door handle, ready to leap out. It would take only a moment for someone to lob a grenade into the taxi, and although I knew I could probably pass for a Vietnamese, it was better to remain self-disciplined.

Nguyen Diem lived just off Old Plantation Road. The villa was more a bungalow than the villas of his neighbors, but he had a large garden filled with trailing cassava vines and azaleas and roses growing beneath the shade of banana trees and longan trees. Down at the far corner was an anxiety tree with ash-colored flowers. I wondered if he got any of the fruit from it that tasted like sugar water and then made you feel drunk, your heart beating like Gene Krupa on the drums, before you fell into a deep dream.

He must have seen me coming, for he opened the door before I could knock and, smiling, bade me to enter. Inside, the rooms were cool, the sunlight latticed out with half-open jalousies. Bookshelves lined the walls, some of them double-stacked. In one corner of the room stood a large and cluttered desk with a Smith-Corona typewriter nestled snugly on a small table to the left. A small bamboo bar took up another corner. Light glinted from the various bottles clustered around an ice bucket. Four comfortable chairs had been placed around a circular coffee table. The floor was tiled in black and white diamonds. Overhead, a large fan clicked as its mahogany blades rotated slowly. The room was clean and comfortable, and I felt the satisfaction of a contented man in his surroundings.

"Nice," I murmured. "Mr. Fell sends his regrets. Unfortunately, he became ill last night and is in the hospital."

A concerned look came over Nguyen Diem's face. "I trust he will be all right."

"A malaria relapse," I answered. "But he should be all right."

I glanced at the titles on a couple shelves but did not recognize any.

Nguyen Diem smiled. "The English titles are at the other end along with the French. You will find several there which may interest you."

Obediently, I moved to the other end, noticing quickly the set of Balzac and Hugo.

"I was educated in France. At the Sorbonne," Nguyen Diem said quietly. "Those were the days when wealthy Vietnamese sent their children away, preferably to France, to learn about those who governed us. Our universities and colleges were not considered proper despite being cultural warehouses. Amusing, don't you think? Generations of Vietnamese children were sent away to learn how to become French citizens only to have the French defeated shortly after at Dien Bien Phu. You know about that, Mr. Wingfoot?"

I nodded. The French had been soundly defeated at Dien Bien Phu, a saucer-shaped valley surrounded by what were thought to be impassable mountains. Especially during the rainy season. But Ho Chi Minh and his general Vo Giap had huge guns hauled up the treacherous and slippery slopes anyway and laid a heavy barrage down onto the French encampment while other soldiers tunneled their way in. It took weeks, but the stubbornness of the Vietnamese paid off and the French tricolor was hauled down.

"A big mistake on the part of the French," I said. "You never camp in the low ground. I was surprised when I read that."

"Not a surprise if you consider the arrogance of the French officer," he said. "Did you ever read the biography of de Gaulle and how he insisted that he and his men be the first into Paris after the American soldiers had driven to the outskirts? It took several hours before de Gaulle could make it to Paris. In the meantime, your Hemingway managed to liberate the Ritz Hotel. I understand that de Gaulle was furious when he discovered that Hemingway was already comfortable in one of the suites at the Ritz. That arrogance was their undoing.

"I have been reading about you American Indians lately," he continued, crossing to one of the easy chairs. He picked up a book—*An Ethnographic Study of the Sioux Indian*—and held it out to me. "From what I can understand, your people have developed a certain passivity concerning their relationship with the white man in your own country. Passive resistance worked with Gandhi and his followers, but it will not work with your people. You have not learned how to use the arrogance of your oppressors against them." He clicked his tongue in disappointment. "I do not mean to insult you, Mr. Wingfoot. I am only stating facts as I see them."

"You think the Americans are arrogant?" I asked, handing the book back to him.

"Oh, yes. Yes, they are. Especially your officers. Do you know why?" It was a rhetorical question. "It is because you Americans have always wanted an aristocratic system and within the structure of your army you have one."

I thought briefly about the lieutenant outside Black's office and shrugged. Nguyen Diem was right, of course. We did have an aristocracy within the army that we called the chain of command, but those who managed to make it to the top link of the chain all came from certain families that had clout or a history of service.

"You're probably right," I said. "Although there is hope."

"Ah, yes. Hope. That is a possibility, but a slim one. It depends upon the existence of faith and charity as well. A modest cliché, I admit, but applicable in this instance. You have good officers and bad officers. Unfortunately, the good officers will most often be lost in the shuffle if bad officers are above them. You see how it works? It is the corruptive ability of power. An interesting conundrum, don't you think? Forgive me; I am forgetting my manners." He gestured toward the bamboo bar. "What would you like to drink?"

"You wouldn't happen to have a bottle of that wine we had the other day, would you?" I asked.

A smile wreathed his face. He rubbed his hands together and made his way to the bar and reached under it, sliding a bottle out of the rack. He held the label for me to see, then produced a corkscrew.

"You are a most understanding man, Mr. Wingfoot. But tell me: Do you drink this wine as a favor to me? Or to remind me of the Vietnamese oppression?"

"I drink the wine because I like it," I answered. "Nothing more. Politics and religion have no place in the presence of a good wine."

"Not even in a communion state?" he said, laughing. The cork slid out with a loud *pop!* and he splashed some wine in a glass and handed it to me.

"A good wine rises above the body of each," I replied, tasting and nodding.

"A delightful pun," he said, clapping his hands. He gestured at the coffee table and chairs and we sat. He sipped again, then sighed, and placed the glass on the table between us. He sat back in his chairs and placed his hands upon his knees. His feet barely touched the floor.

"Tell me, Mr. Wingfoot, what will you do if the young girl, Lisa Lee, turns out to be one who works for the North? Will you kill her?"

"What is it? Let me see." I began to tick the points off on my fingers. "She is too poor to do anything else. She has relatives up north who are being held hostage. Her father sold her to someone because he could not afford to feed his family. Her father placed her in prostitution to enhance the family's fortunes. She is truly politically motivated and will do anything for Uncle Ho. She hates the Americans because they remind her of the French who stole her family's farm. She hates the Americans because they accidentally destroyed the family farm. She hates the South *and* the Americans because her idealistic brother joined the North forces and was killed in battle and this is her way of getting even. Her sister was raped by South Vietnamese soldiers or American soldiers. *She* was raped by South Vietnamese soldiers or American soldiers. Or her mother. Or both. Or all three. Have I touched upon the circumstance or should I continue?"

He shook his head. "You are a very cynical young man," he said.

"It comes from being born an Indian," I said. "But the more I see of the world, the more I realize that cynicism is a natural force of life. Like breathing. People have choices and they must make them."

"Cannot the choice be forced upon you?"

"Ah," I said, steepling my fingers beneath my chin. "Now we are talking about principles and honor. That is still a choice, is it not?"

"You are a hard man, Mr. Wingfoot," he said. "Some day, I wonder how you will be when choice is forced upon you."

"It already has been," I answered. "Is she with the North?"

"You know, I could tell you, then warn her. She could disappear. What would you do then?"

"She is, isn't she?"

Resigned, he nodded. "Yes, she is."

"And did you warn her?"

He nodded, watching me carefully.

"Of course," I said, "that makes my job a bit more difficult, doesn't it?"

"A life is a precious thing, Mr. Wingfoot, and we have destroyed enough of it over the past years. Please understand that."

"Oh, I understand, Nguyen Diem; I understand perfectly. But I'm not certain that you do. Your country has been at war so long that it has become an integrated part of your society. If we took war away, the Vietnamese could not survive. They would become socially dysfunctional."

"I would like that chance," he said. "Wars can always be found. Peace and contentment are a rarity, but I think that all men deserve that chance at least once in their lives."

"Whenever someone becomes content with life, another comes along and tries to take that contentment for himself. The gods make men happy, then destroy them. Fact. Fate."

"I think that you are going to be a very unhappy man, Mr. Wingfoot," he said softly. "What are you going to do now?"

I shrugged. "I don't know. That will depend upon my superiors. I don't know if they will give me the time, or if they will turn the case over to the police."

"But you will tell them."

I leaned forward and picked up my wineglass, sipping. The wine tasted vinegary, now, but I knew that was because I was caught in a situation that I didn't like.

"Yes," I said. "I will tell them. But not today, and not tomorrow."
He raised an eyebrow.

"Tell me," I said, settling back against the chair. "Why is *The Tale of Kieu* so important as a cultural icon to the Vietnamese?"

He sat silent for a long moment, his eyes, black and liquid, studying me. Then he offered a small smile and settled back in his chair. His face became animated as he explained how Kieu sold herself as a concubine to save her family, only to be betrayed into becoming a prostitute. Yet she still kept her own sense of honor and was rewarded after several misadventures by being reunited with her family. The tale reflected the life of its author, Nguyen Du, who was forced to betray his own sense of political correctness in order to keep his family safe by serving a government that he did not believe in.

We talked long into the night, listening to the bugs slap against the lights, the crickets sing, smelling the heavy scent of jasmine that floated in through the open windows on the night breeze, and pushing the war away for a few brief hours by immersing ourselves in argument that took us far, far away from the war-torn country. For a few hours, we stepped into a world of books and music and left the uncertainty of a world gone mad for the morrow.

6 The next day the sky was the color of torn purple plums as I made my way back to the hospital to visit Fell. He looked much better, but his skin still had a waxy, yellow look to it under a fine sheen of sweat, and his hand trembled slightly as he lifted it to greet me.

"It's a grim day," he said.

I nodded. "Yes. How do you feel?"

"Better," he answered, and grinned. "The doctors think I can be discharged tomorrow. Maybe noon. You want to come by, maybe we can have something to eat instead of this hospital pap."

I laughed. "That's the same menu the world over in hospitals. There must be a school somewhere that teaches people how to cook bland."

He smiled sourly. "Tapioca. Everything's tapioca. You know what tapioca is? Goddamn rice." He flopped back on the pillow in pretended agony. "Rice."

"The Irish have their potatoes; the Vietnamese have their rice."

He made a face. "I'm English. Bring on the beef."

"How about a Châteaubriand tomorrow? That is, if your stomach can handle it. I understand sometimes soup's better."

"We'll see," he said. Then, glanced at the door and lowered his voice. "Well? What did Nguyen Diem find out?"

"She's dirty," I said. "And he's warned her."

"What are you going to do now?" he asked.

I shook my head. "Nothing. Wait a few days, then tell them she got spooked and left."

He sighed and closed his eyes, passing his hand wearily over them. "Christ, Wingo, you're committing career suicide here. You've got to find her."

"I can't see where the death of one woman is going to make a difference. And why make it a rough death? What's the purpose in that? If she is working for the North, why not turn her over to Nguyen Ngoc Loan and let him and his police work what she knows out of her? Alive, we could get some information from her. Dead, she's nothing but a corpse and everything she knows dies with her. There's something wrong here, John. There's something we're not being told."

"There are some things that we aren't supposed to know," he said.

"Stop it," I said roughly. "You're not Paul or one of the Nuremberg generals. I'm telling you that this is a dirty business. Anyone can pop a cap on her. Wait until she comes out at night, follow her home— you know it's down one of the dipshit alleys somewhere—put the bullet behind her ear, and let her be found the next day. That's the way to do it, not this way."

"Is it the woman's death that bothers you? Or the way it's to be done?"

I remained silent for a long moment, then shook my head. "We have to draw the line somewhere. I'm not meant to be a butcher."

"Object lessons—," he began, but I cut him off.

"Are nonsense," I said. "Charlie's made object lessons routine over the years. How many Americans got their balls cut off and peckers shoved down their throats? Remember Black Virgin Mountain? The small hamlet there that the Special Forces tried to neutralize by sending in medics to inoculate the children against smallpox? The Vietcong came back that night and hacked off the arm of each child that had been touched by a medic's needle. They made a pile of those little arms right in the center of the village. And those were some of their own people."

I began to pace back and forth at the foot of his bed. "That was brilliant, but after a while, object lessons mean nothing. Absolutely nothing. The horror simply becomes mundane. Horror works only when it offends what others take for acceptable behavior. When horror becomes anticipated or touches on normalcy, then it is useless."

"I don't think anyone gets used to having his friend's dick cut off and stuck in his mouth," Fell said, his voice heavy with sarcasm.

"No, not entirely. But it ceases to affect him the same way. The dread of horror is gone. You and I know what will happen if we get caught out in the boonies by the wrong people, right? But that doesn't keep us from going back out there. We have learned to accept the possibility of what might happen to us, and that puts an end to the fear that we would have otherwise."

Fell shook his head and started to speak, then fell silent. His lips pressed tightly together and his eyes met mine, then slid off rapidly to the left, studying the foot of his bed. I walked over to the far corner of his room and picked up his cane, swinging it idly back and forth. His eyes followed the movement of the cane as if mesmerized.

"So, how about dinner tomorrow? Do you want me to come by around noon and collect you?"

"No," he said. "I'll have to go back to the office for a little bit." He made a face. "I may be out to pasture, but there are still some things that the old bull has to do. I'm certain there are several papers I have to sign or initial. Maybe the day after? I'll give you a call."

"The clerk in this man's army is the only one who is truly indispensable," I said, returning the cane to the corner. I touched my forehead in a mock salute. "Until later. We who are about to die salute you, O mighty Caesar!"

"Out with you!" he growled, and reached threateningly for the glass on the table beside his bed.

I laughed and pushed my way through the door. Fell was coming around faster than I would have expected, but I could see that he was still a bit weak. Malaria does that to people, though, and no one knows when it will crop up again. It's like living with ten thousand mosquito eggs somewhere in your body, waiting to hatch at the right moment. A sound metaphor for the war as well. Whenever you feel that you might be able to relax and take things easy for a minute, something is always around to take you down.

Actually, it was three days later before Fell and I could get together again. I had slipped back to The Flowers and the Casino Club each night on the off-chance that Lisa Lee might be there. But she wasn't. I don't know what I would have done had she been, but I seemed to find myself drawn to those dens of iniquity each night, half-hoping that I would find her there; certain that I wouldn't. Nguyen Diem had been thorough, and despite my wanting to see the will-o'-the-wisp, I still felt relief that she had managed to get away. I hoped she made her way back to the North or at least somewhere out of the Big Scene, even if it meant that she would probably work by humping her way along the Trail. At least, there was a fifty-fifty chance of survival there—unless she went through Copperhead Jack's valley, which was suicidal at best.

I think the intensity of my interest in her was because I had only seen her from across a room. I had never spoken to her, never felt her fingers touch my cheek the way that they touched hundreds of cheeks each day, a simple gesture meaningless to her but a memory to the one whose cheek they touched. I felt a momentary jealousy that someone had a memory that I wanted but could not have.

I knew that Fell was disappointed in me, although I knew that he also had misgivings about the way the mission had been handed to me. I could tell as well that he, too, had been touched with her beauty, or perhaps the strange ambiguity surrounding the whole affair. You see a couple whispering across a room and although it isn't any of your business, you are curious about what has caused such an intense need for secrecy. Man has always had this need to know; otherwise, he wouldn't have followed Eve into munching on that apple.

The night that Fell and I went out to eat, he was somewhat quiet and reserved. I didn't think much about that, as we had decided to go to *Elle* for dinner. Afterward, over cognac in a discreet restaurant that had lost none of its French ambiance in a little backstreet that had the cool, dank smell of old brick, we spoke quietly about the nature of war.

"How far do you think a man should go to save his soul?" Fell asked over our third or fourth cognac.

I had drunk enough to treat each question with deliberation before answering.

"That would depend upon the value that a man places upon his soul," I said.

"How much do you value your soul?" he asked.

"I don't. A warrior cannot afford to have a soul."

"Is that why you let the woman go? You don't have a soul? That seems a contradiction to me."

"Guilty as charged," I said. I frowned into the golden light of the cognac in my glass before me as if studying a reflection in a scrying mirror. "I don't think that was a question of my soul insomuch as it was that I felt someone was using me for something beyond my ken. It's a hell of a thing for someone to use the freedom of war as a screen for hiding something."

"*Do* you think someone is hiding something?" he asked quickly, his eyes suddenly intent upon mine.

In the distance I heard the low roll of thunder like the echo of cannon fire, and heat lightning flashed against the window like flash-bulbs lighting the inky blackness.

"I don't know," I said. I lifted the cognac and sipped. "All I know is that I dislike it when an officer becomes a strumpet authoritarian for someone else." I laughed. "Hell, that has to be the answer, doesn't it? Why keep me in the dark? Need to know? Hell, given what we've done over the past few years, people like us should have *carte blanche* clearance to the uppermost or innermost secrets of the government. Right? I mean, look at what we do and bury. We do it, but we always know *why* we have to do it. When someone holds something back and you feel your flesh crawl like centipedes slipping just under your skin, you know that you are being made a Judas goat for someone's sins or something that needs to be hush-hushed. A soldier can't afford principles, but he sure as hell had better hang on to his pride. Besides, what are they going to do to me? Send me to Vietnam? I've got news: I'm already there."

"I hope you're right," he said with misgiving. Suddenly he reached across and grasped my hand. His palm felt dank and cold, like a corpse's hand pulled fresh out of the morgue refrigerator. His lips tightened, his eyes pinprick bits of brilliance. "I owe you."

I frowned and uneasily pulled my hand from under his and used it to lift my glass and finish the cognac. A vague uneasiness came over me like when you see a trail on a dried creek bed too clean and although you don't know why you know, you feel that it has been swept clean and if you go another step farther you'll end up singing soprano in front of the pearly gates when a Bouncing Betty leaps up and blows your balls out your ass.

I glanced at my watch.

"Hey, we'd better get back. Tomorrow's when I go into the Lincoln Library and see Black and tell him I 'fued' the assignment properly. I need to have a little sleep. You don't beard a lion in his den when you're suffering from a hangover."

He smiled. "Or piss into the wind."

"Or fuck with the Lone Ranger. Come on. You can walk me back to the Continental."

We stepped outside. Heat lightning flashed in the distance, followed by the low rumble, but purple clouds still drifted by overhead.

I stared at the full white moon faintly tinted orange and felt a hint of Cassandra's tragic gift that writhed in despair like snakes in my subconscious.

By the time we got back to the Continental, the moon had gone, taking with it the truth of whatever prophecy had lurked at the beginnings of my mind. I knew what Cassandra must have felt.

Heat lightning was already flickering over the tops of the chestnut trees when I stepped out of the Continental into the taxi that had been brought for me. By the time we got to Tan Son Nhut, rain was slamming down on the roof of the taxi like tack hammers, and before I could slip under the roof of the gatehouse I was soaked and already mad at the world. I wasn't looking forward to telling Black that I had blown the assignment, but I felt good about it anyway. It was a small gesture, the life of one young woman for thousands taken, but it was enough of a gesture, the kind a teenager will make to a policeman just before the light turns green and he can drive away before the cop hauls him out of the car for disrespect.

After a while, I decided that the rain wasn't going to let up and talked an MP into taking me to Lincoln Library. By this time, lightning was crackling and large, dark thunderheads were rolling up over the city, turning the day into night. Water sluiced down the concrete, and small waterfalls fell from the roofs. It wouldn't have taken much more to convince me that God had unleashed the forty-days flood again and the whole world was drowning.

I stepped into the main room with its warren of cubicles and made my way back to Black's office. An uneasiness came over me as I felt eyes watching me guardedly. When I got back to the lieutenant's desk, he had already stepped from behind it and was holding the door open. I nodded at him, but his eyes slid away from mine like they'd slipped in grease.

"Shut the door," Black ordered.

I turned, but the lieutenant had already closed it. I took a deep breath and turned back to face Black, gritting my teeth.

His face was set in a sober mask, the wrinkles around his eyes and cheeks deeper than I remembered. He nodded and picked up a folder from his desk and opened it. His lips compressed into a thin line.

"I would like to say 'congratulations,' Mr. Wingfoot, for completing your job. Frankly, I had my doubts when you left."

"Completing—" I frowned and caught the words before they slipped out.

"Yes. But I had no idea that you would go to this extent."

He laid the folder open on the desk, turning it to face me. I looked at the picture of what had once been a human being. The woman was naked and mutilated horribly. Her intestines had been half-pulled from her body cavity and strung across her chest to lie over her right shoulder. Her breasts had been sliced away and placed like cups over her eyes, but her eyes had been removed and lay neatly on what I took to be a pillow above her head. From what I could tell, her throat had been cut before, but the mouth was stretched wide in a rictus of horror, so I could have been mistaken.

I closed the folder and slid it back across the desk to Black.

"You got your wish," I said flatly. "You wanted it messy. Remember?"

He sighed and picked up the folder, holding it by the tips of his fingers as if he was holding something vile and infectious. I had seen worse mutilations in the field, but it had been a long time since Black had been in the field. You could see that in the soft folds of flesh under his chin and, when he stood, the small paunch that threatened to spill over his belt.

He opened a drawer in his desk and placed the folder inside, pushing the drawer closed firmly. He studied me for a long moment, then nodded.

"Yes, you're right; I did tell you that," he said.

"But it's one thing to see it, right?" I asked, feeling the heat build up in my cheeks. "You need to get out more into the real world, Colonel. Ignorance leads men to do careless things."

His face flushed and I knew he wanted to say something, but he held his tongue and rose, moving around his desk to the large map on the wall beside the door. He pointed a large, thick finger at a northern point and said, "Here's something that just came in and needs to be checked. Aerial photos suggest that there is a POW camp up here, or it could be a mass buildup of NVA. The Three-oh-double-eight Regiment has been missing for quite some time. They may be gathering up here for a push south."

"You can't tell the difference from aerial?" I asked.

He shook his head. "Heavily forested and mountainous. This valley"—he traced it with his finger—"is surrounded by steep mountains and seems to be socked in with rain right now. Fog. Mist. We have managed only three snaps in six sorties over the area. So, we're sending your team in to verify what it is. If it isn't a POW camp, then we'll send in an Arc Light strike and level it."

"You're pretty close to the border for that," I pointed out. "A bomb go over into the other side and we might have a problem."

He shook his head. "It would be a hell of a long shot. That place is so rugged that only a few Montagnards live up there. I think some Shans have come down out of Burma, but that's only speculation. Besides, they would have to prove if it was one of ours or one of the North's."

I understood what he was saying. An Arc Light strike was an awesome sight, for you never even heard the planes. Only felt the explosions from the big B-52s that flew so high that no antiaircraft gun could reach them. A heat-seeking missile might bring one down, but first you had to know the planes were there.

"All right," I said. "What about my men?"

"They'll be waiting for you back at your camp. We're pulling the Special Forces 'A' team out. The area's yours. One more thing." He turned back to the map. "We haven't heard from Mr. Langdon, lately." He stabbed a finger at the valley where Copperhead Jack operated. "Swing through on your way back and see if things are all right up there. You know how he is."

"Yes, a loose cannon," I said. "He'll answer in his own good time. No news is good news."

"Maybe," Black grunted. He grimaced and pressed his fingers against his stomach as if a sudden pain had struck him. "But it still makes me nervous. *He* makes me nervous. We'll send you in close with a Strata Team helicopter and arrange a pickup point on your map coordinates. There's a MACVSOG team operating up there somewhere, but SACSA is keeping their lips tight about that." He grinned faintly. "So, it's up to us to affirm."

"This man's war," I said, shaking my head. "You already have a

SOG team up there but can't use them. Seems to me that we're getting ourselves snarled in red tape."

"Yeah, well, everyone has his priorities," Black said. "I'm sending a resupply chopper up in a couple of hours. That give you enough time?"

I shrugged. "It'll do."

The rain had let up to a light mist when I stepped out of the Library, but the day still looked like a sheet of lead had been hung in the sky over the city. I swung by the office to see Fell and tell him the bad news about our dinner, but he had already checked out.

Back at the Continental, I left a message for Fell if he should call, saying simply that "duty calls," and made arrangements for my trunk to be placed back in storage for me. I gathered my gear and returned to Tan Son Nhut and the waiting helicopter to fly back north.

The air felt cool and I leaned into the slipstream of the open door.

"Best you don't do that," the young door gunner said. "You're blocking me."

I grinned at him and slid back, feeling the throbbing beat of the helicopter under my buttocks and the backs of my legs.

"How can you see anything?" I asked, pointing down. Gray clouds scudded past us, giving only a brief glimpse of the ground below.

"Don't need much," he shouted. He patted his machine gun. "Baby can talk through that shit." But he touched the Saint Michael medal hanging outside his flak jacket like some would knock wood to keep the evil spirits away after issuing a challenge to them. Almost everyone carried something for luck, a tattered Bible, a strange-colored pebble found while crossing a stream, small ivory statues of Buddha, whatever had meaning for them. Solly carried a rabbit's foot, the fur rubbed away until only the dried sinews and tiny claws showed. He smacked Duke once when Duke asked him how Solly could imagine the foot to be lucky when it hadn't done the rabbit much good. It's not good to mock the gods. Heaven carried a silver dollar. I carried the Baby Browning. If I was going to hump a good-luck charm, I figured it might as well have a use.

The team was waiting for me when the chopper touched down. The door gunner threw the provisions out as fast as he could and the helicopter lifted off, swinging and running low and fast away, rising as quickly as it could.

"Man," Cornpone drawled. "You think that man's gotta hot one waiting for him back in the snatch?"

I noticed his black eye. "What happened? Walk into a door?"

"Nope, she crossed her legs," Sparks said, laughing. He ducked as Cornpone threw a backhand toward him.

"No way I'm gonna tongue my way through a dink's fur," Cornpone said. "You ain't got no idea what someone left behind."

Sparks sniggered. "Yeah. Might even have a razor in there."

"Or a hand grenade on a trip wire."

"Or punji sticks."

"Gather the stuff and let's get back to the rest of the boys," I said. "I really don't need to know about your preferences. You guys have no taste at all."

"Did you, Wingo?" Solly asked.

"Did I what?"

"Get a taste back in Saigon?"

"A gentleman doesn't talk about things like that," I said with dignity.

They laughed and gathered the provisions, stacking the C-ration boxes into Solly's arms.

"What you think?" he complained. "I'm everybody's nigger?"

"Nope. Just ours," Heaven said. He tucked a box under each arm and turned toward the camp.

Solly's mouth turned up into a grin, the large knife scar crinkling like a dimple down his cheek. "You think that when I put these rats up your ass a can at a time."

"You better mark a spot, then, 'cause he's all ass," Cornpone drawled.

They had come back from the week down south what we called "three-rd": rested, refreshed, ready. Somehow, though, I felt drained, like you do after a three-day drunk and you're trying to make it through the fourth sober while spiders crawled around in your stomach and your head felt like someone had clamped it into a vise and was trying to open the cranium with a hacksaw. But I wasn't suffering from a drunk, and I knew the brass taste in my mouth was only nerves beginning to stretch like piano wires as I thought about where we were going to go the next day when the Strata helicopter swung down out of the clouds to pick us up and zing us north deep into Indian country.

They had lunch waiting on a table they had fashioned out of wooden crates. Like most soldiers who go back on R & R, they hadn't completely wasted the time in bars and whorehouses. They had hit the PX and brought back canned hams and tins of sardines in mustard sauce and small cans of beanie-wienees, the soldier's treat. I noticed several bottles of Tabasco sauce had been brought back as well. Tabasco sauce made even the C rations taste like something other than soggy cardboard.

"What? No rib eyes?" I complained.

They laughed. The last time they had gone to Nha Trang, Solly and Heaven had slipped into the general's private larder and made off with a case of steaks. The marine standing guard had been stoned on marijuana cigarettes soaked in opium and summary court-martialed for negligence. The general had been furious. Those steaks had been meant for a couple of congressmen making a Hail Mary visit during an election year to impress their constituents. Fortunately, Solly and Heaven had waited until the last moment before stealing the steaks, as the general called for a search of all hooches and buildings to find the ones responsible. By the time the theft was discovered, we were winging our way back to our camp.

"Ain't from the lack of trying, Wingo," Cornpone said. "But they just wouldn't leave us alone long enough to make a run. You think they're getting wise to us?"

"What is this, the tenth or eleventh time? Yeah, they've probably got an idea by now," I said. "Military Intelligence, you know."

They all laughed and danced around Solly, exchanging the dap, a complicated handshake that involved hand slapping and fist butting.

"So, what'd they want you for?" Heaven asked as we settled down around the makeshift table. "It must not be good if they bust us free for a little tango. When the REMFs get to being nice to you, that's just before they shove it up your ass without Vaseline."

They all looked at me expectantly, knowing that we were going once again into the breech. I sighed and took a huge bite of ham, shoving it into my cheek as I talked.

"We're going back up north. The long trail again."

They groaned and shook their heads.

"The 'yards going, too?" Heaven asked.

"No, just us. A quick up and down," I answered.

"Man, my feet are just now beginning to recover," Solly complained.

"We're going up by helicopter, then swing down and visit Copperhead Jack before pickup," I said. "We won't be walking the zone all the time."

"Copperhead Jack?" Sparks said. "I don't like that motherfucker. He gives me the willies. You ever look into his eyes? Like looking into your own grave. Why we going back through there? He sure as shit don't need our help. He ain't never needed nobody 'cept hisself."

"Orders. Like everything else," I replied.

"Man," Cornpone said mournfully. "I'm getting a bad feeling about this, Wingo. A really bad feeling."

I said nothing. I had had that same feeling for a long time.

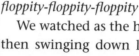

floppity-floppity-floppity

We watched as the helicopter came in, high at first, then swinging down like a darting barn swallow to avoid any small-arms fire around the perimeter. There wouldn't have been anyway because we had set the Montagnards out as perimeter guards until we had lifted off from the makeshift pad. I glanced quickly at my people, double-checking their gear.

Solly carried his medical supplies in addition to a Swedish K that he had become fond of and swore by. He had a .38-caliber Smith & Wesson in a shoulder holster as his "equalizer," and four fragmentation grenades hung like goiters from his belt.

Sparks had the radio but also carried a block of C-4 that he used more for cooking than blowing things up—although that was a possibility if we needed a fast extraction and had to knock down some trees in a hurry. He still carried his M16 but had added a wicked-looking skinning knife and a Colt .45 automatic as well.

Duke had a rocket LAW strapped to the side of his ruck and a machete on the other side for balance. He favored a Fairbairn (as did I) and had a Walther fitted with a silencer that he had collected from a drunken Langley boy back in Saigon. It was a beauty.

Heaven carried a Chi-Com and a Colt .45 he had adapted to fit a Carswell silencer, a rather tricky operation, as he had to go back to the machine shop at Nha Trang to complete it. There were nine millimeters around that were already adapted for the silencer, but Heaven wanted the .45. I think it was probably the only one in-country that had been remodeled according to a soldier's expectations and wants. He had a garrote made out of piano wire he had stolen from a piano in the Officers' Club looped tightly and hung on a strap of his ruck, a Finnish filet knife, and a couple of CS grenades that looked like black baseballs.

Cornpone had his rifle and two scopes, one for the day on tip-off mounts and the starlight scope for night work. His rifle had also been modified with a silencer. He had a .38-caliber revolver in a shoulder holster. Most men, if given a choice, went for the .38, as it had fewer working parts that could get jammed. They carried special pouches with "speed-loads" that allowed them to slip six into the cylinder faster than a man could drop a clip out of a .45 and slam home a new one.

Personally, I preferred the .45. I liked the feel of it and the round that would hit a branch, cut through it, and keep on chugging forward. I carried a Thompson—a little heavier than I liked, but I wasn't fumbling around for rounds. I had a grease gun but seldom used it unless we were going on short night-ops and speed was going to be important. Then, it didn't matter. I had the Baby Browning in its belly holster and a couple blocks of C-4.

All of us carried two-quart canteens and purifying tablets in case we had to make do with forest water, a couple cans of C rations, Swiss Army knives, bug juice (more for getting rid of leeches than using for mosquitoes, which seemed to feast upon it), and emergency field dressings. We carried night vitamins loaded with carotene; detonators; and time fuses. The trick was to pack what you would need but stay light enough to run if you had to. We loaded the rucks last so we could flip them off and still keep our ammo if we had to, in defiance of Basic Training, which taught the soldier to load the ruck first. If you had to be suddenly light-footed, you needed to get rid of all the weight you would probably never need again.

We slid into the helicopter before the skids hit earth and rose immediately as if shot from a cannon, the pilot turning south first, then swinging west in a wide loop, to confuse any spotters as to our direction. I glanced at Solly. He grinned and clapped his big hands together.

"Just like a roller coaster, huh, Wingo?" he asked.

Heaven looked a little green around the gills; he didn't care much for evasive tactics. When I asked him why he went through Airborne training he drawled, "Shit, that just means I can get outta the damn plane faster. It ain't the takeoff that bothers me, Wingo; it's the landing. Most accidents happen then." He also preferred to sit in the back of an airplane, as he had never heard of an airplane backing into a mountain.

Sparks did a quick check of his radio and nodded. He only had one battery. That was all we carried, as the only time we would use the radio was when we needed to call out. In-calls would not be accepted at any time, so most of the time the radio was kept off. When we did use it, we used it for only thirty seconds at a time before shutting down and moving again. I didn't think any sophisticated triangulation equipment would be anywhere we would be, but the Trail wasn't far from us and you could never be certain.

The gunner motioned to earphones on a hook over my head. I slipped them down and heard the captain explaining that we were going to do a run-trail approach. I made a face. A run-trail approach meant that rappelling lines would be trailed behind the helicopter as it made a run over a clearing (if we were lucky) and we would have to slide down quickly to keep from being slammed into trees.

I made a climbing motion with my fists to the team. Solly rolled his eyes and mouthed "motherfucker" and took a towel from around his neck, wrapping it carefully around his hands. Going down ropes fast would burn your hands if you weren't careful. The trick was to capture the rope with your ankles and lean back away from it so your balls wouldn't be broiled by the friction of the rope in descent.

"What the fuck," Duke shouted. "Why not just drop us?"

"Fast insertion," I said.

"It gonna be hot, Wingo?" Cornpone asked.

I shrugged. "Maybe. Fan out when you drop. Get into the trees as fast as you can."

"Motherfuckers will probably drop us in the trees anyway," Sparks added.

My heart flew up into my throat as the helicopter made a sudden drop. The ropes were kicked out and within seconds the gunner made a pumping motion with his fist. I took a deep breath, anchored the nylon rope between my ankles, and slid out into the slipstream.

I could see immediately that we had a problem, as the pilot had not dropped low enough and we would have a pretty fair fall when we reached the end of the rope. But you worried about the fall only after you hit. There wasn't enough time for it otherwise and to think about it only increased your chances of getting hurt. You had to hit relaxed and roll instead of taking the punishment on your legs and hips. Christ, I hated "green" flyboys who avoided chances. Those Air America boys were nuts enough to put you within ten feet of the ground. We liked them. Those who flew by the book were a royal pain in the ass.

Then, I saw the elephant grass and swore even more. Falling into elephant grass was like falling into a field of razor blades. You had to cover your face and hope for the best. The only thing worse was falling through bamboo, as you never knew when you were going to be skewered like Sunday's turkey by a broken shoot.

I felt the end of the line whip through my hands and tucked my elbows close into my sides, covering my face with my palms. I kept my legs pressed together, forcing them to relax, and then the grass sliced through the backs of my hands and I landed with a breath-jarring *whump!* And rolled, spinning on my hips to absorb the impact.

I rose, crouching, ready to fall to the side if I saw lights flickering. You had to be quick for that, as that would be your only key that you were being fired on. You'd see the light before you heard the pop of the rounds zipping past your ear or felt the thud of the bullet hitting you. The tiny red lights, like angry fireflies, were your keys, and if you saw them you had to hit and roll to the side and crawl forward at the same time in case the shooter decided to "walk" the rounds after you.

Quiet.

I saw the black line of brush at the end of the clearing and ran sideways like a crab, balancing on the toes of my feet. I slipped into the brush and fell to the spongy ground, freezing, listening. I slipped a small children's toy cricket from my pocket and clicked it. An answering click came twice in response; then Solly slipped in beside me. I clicked again and was answered by another two clicks, a pause, then a single one. Cornpone came over moments later. Each man had his own answering click. That was protection, for if the enemy had captured him and was quick enough to figure out what we were doing, he wouldn't know the individual response.

Soon the team was assembled around me. I passed my palm over my chest, asking if anyone was hurt. All five shook their heads. I made a motion toward the north and spread my fingers. We would walk parallel through the forest for the first five kilometers before regrouping.

Heaven nodded and slipped forward to take the point. You had to watch carefully, as he could slip through a bramble patch and you would never hear a single scratch of a thorn against him. Solly went to the left along with Cornpone. I went to the right with Sparks. We moved as quickly as possible, but we had to be careful. We were far north and more than likely in Laos, and although the possibility of a booby trap was faint, again, you didn't want to take chances. We were in Montagnard country, and those people were fond of setting out punji pits, bamboo stakes planted in a hole in the ground and covered with feces. We avoided stepping on any palm fronds or piles of leaves. There were other problems as well; snakes were night hunters and we had the krait and cobra and bamboo snakes to contend with in addition to about fifteen other types, each poisonous. The red-headed krait was the biggest problem; like the mamba, it would attack automatically instead of trying to slip away. The rule of thumb was: snake, kill it.

We had to avoid patches of creeper vines, too, for snakes would live in them, waiting for birds or other animals to come. Charlie liked them as well for his toe poppers and Bouncing Bettys, and the vines made good triggering devices for punji drops and bamboo bows and arrows set on trip lines.

The full moon came out, hanging over the forest like a silver dollar, sending streams of light through the forest overhead. I hated that; normally, we avoid deep treks into Indian country when the full moon was out and missions were usually planned around the moon cycles. Suddenly an uneasiness came over me; why was this mission so important that it couldn't have waited for the cycle to end? A few more days wouldn't have mattered one way or the other.

I frowned in the darkness. Too many wrong incidents were beginning to accumulate. I clutched my Thompson harder; sweat leaked out from under my palms and ran down the inside of my thighs. There was no breeze, and for once rain clouds didn't cover the sky. The forest smelled rotten and moldy, and I felt my simian ancestor begin to come alive in my chest.

We rounded a point and looked down into the Valley of the Lowering Mist. Pockets of thick greenery stood out from the thick dirty gray fog that seemed to roil and bubble like a witch's cauldron. I squatted and studied the valley intently. I imagined it as the lepers' valley in *Ben-Hur* or the valley of death's shadow. No birds hovered anywhere. A bad sign.

"We going down there, Wingo?" Solly asked.

"Man, that is depressing," Duke said. "Abandon hope, all you who enter here."

"What's that?" Solly asked.

"Hell," Duke answered.

Solly cast a soulful eye back down into the valley. "Uh-huh."

I rose and slid the bolt of my Thompson partially back, relieved to see the glint of brass in the chamber. I turned to the others.

"Check your loads. We don't need a cap popping off and leaving a round in the chamber."

Sometimes in the jungle the rapid change of temperature and humidity would cause cartridges to swell in the chamber. When the cartridge was fired, the extractor bolt would pop the cap off, leaving the shell casing jammed in the chamber.

I heard the faint slide of metal on metal as the others followed my example. I took a deep breath.

"All right," I said quietly. "The sooner we do it, the sooner we get back. Heaven, you have point."

"Wish I would've paid closer attention in Sunday school," Heaven muttered as he slid quietly down the cliff face, working his way along a faint game trail.

We moved behind him. Soon the clammy tendrils of fog slipped over our faces like cold cobwebs. We moved deeper into the valley and the tendrils became the hands of all the ghosts of our nightmares, sliding over us, caressing us, pulling us deeper down into the bowels of the valley. The very air smelled like copper tastes when you place a penny against your tongue, the taste and smell of old blood that seemed to rise from the ground on noxious, incestuous waves as if the land and the air were both wrapping us in arms of birth and rebirth. I heard the jungle breathing, deep and ragged, a sexual pant as a man and woman will make in rutting when neither loves the other, but they come together for the pure pleasure of rutting, without any strings or attachments other than the act itself. I *felt* it deep within me, a guttural grunting like my ancestors made when they mated, like they still do when they mate without the aloof perspectives of priests and ministers about what constitutes mating: raw, primeval, antediluvian.

I heard my heart pounding and the sound of my blood swishing through my veins and arteries like monsoon rains rushing through thick vines and leaves to spatter the earth in an attempt to leap life from inertness. And then I heard the deep, cognate panting at the same time that I saw Solly raise a clenched fist and gesture left and right, moving us off the faint trail into the brush.

I crawled forward, willing myself to hear beyond my self, beyond the capabilities of my self, projecting an image forward of what I expected or could expect to find. I came upon him, tapping him gently upon the sole of his boot to let him know that it was me.

"What is it?" I whispered so silently a moth's wings could flutter unharmed through the notes of my words.

"Check your map," he whispered back. "Are we on coordinates?"

I looked over his shoulder into the ruins of a large Montagnard village, perhaps a Shan village or Laotian village—after a while lying in ruins, they all begin to merge into the simplicity of the moment. Huts sagged on rotting staves and beams, thatched roofs falling in, creepers sinuously winding themselves through the rills and runs of a village proper. A dog's skeleton lay in the middle by the dead ashes of a dead campfire, bamboo shoots growing through the rib bones. I motioned the team forward, feeling them arrive more than looking for them.

"Fan out," I whispered. "Watch for trips in the doorways. This isn't kosher."

And it wasn't. Even the momentary photos from passing air reconnaissances should have shown that this village had been abandoned for at least six months.

"There's a nigger in the woodpile and it ain't my grandpa," Solly whispered as he rose and moved into the village, gliding on the balls of his feet.

"Couldn't have said it better," Duke murmured, rising and slipping to Solly's right to protect him as they moved rapidly through the village.

The others gave them a ten-second lead to allow for an ambush to show itself, then moved forward behind them, rechecking the places they had checked. I lay back silently on a matted vine bed beneath a bramble bush, trying to solve the enigma before us. Black *had* to have known that this village was deserted. The infrared sensors that photo reconnaissance planes carried would have confirmed it to be uninhabited. It lay if not at the end of the world, at least next door to it. So why were we here? *Why?*

There comes a time when one has to pay close attention to one's instincts. I didn't know what was bothering me, but something was. I whistled a lark's call and saw the others freeze, then move rapidly back from the village, spreading wide as they gathered around me. I motioned for them to fall back and led the way to a small clearing. I crouched and motioned for them to gather around me.

"Something ain't right, Wingo," Solly said. His eyes roamed worriedly, ceaselessly, around the clearing. "There ain't nothing there. Ashes cold, huts empty. Some of the huts even got weeds growing up through the floor. There ain't been no one here for a long time. So why we here?"

Duke coughed and glanced at the map I pulled from my pouch. "We at the right place, Wingo? I mean, could we have misread the coordinates?"

I was happy that he said "we" instead of blaming the possibility upon me. But there was still a cold feeling in my stomach that was warning me not to tarry, to cut our losses and make our way out to a pickup point and to hell with making our way back down to Copperhead Jack's valley.

"I don't know," I confessed. I took a quick azimuth reading, then told Sparks to crank up the PRC.

"Man," Cornpone whispered. "I think we'd better de-de outta here and do that later. We know where we are and it's where we supposed to be. Come on, Wingo; you know damn well you didn't make no mistake. Someone did, but it ain't you and it ain't us. Let's haul ass."

Suddenly I became aware of the silence around us. There is always silence, but tiny noises always creep between the notes of silences so you know that there is a time for thinking and a time for moving. I glanced down at the map again.

"Fuck it," I said to Sparks. "We didn't make the mistake; they did. Let's boogie."

"Wingo," Heaven said. "We *could* be wrong. You know that. It ain't impossible. And if we are and leave without checking and an

Arc Light strike is called where we should have been, there might be a lot of POWs killed. You know that just as certain as hickory nuts."

That moment's hesitation cost us. I caught movement out of the corner of my eye and looked, ducking instinctively. The grenade arched slowly toward us as if coming through thick soup. We scattered, dropped down and hugging the ground. The explosion deafened us for a second, and I felt bits of grenade slapping against me like icy snowballs.

I glanced around and saw the others shaking their heads. Solly crouched, pulling out a grenade and throwing it in reprisal. Heaven was firing as rapidly as he could into the forest in front of him, moving the barrel rapidly back and forth. Duke crawled over to me.

"You okay?" he shouted.

I shrugged. "Doesn't matter. We gotta leave anyway."

"Yeah, but which way?"

Bullets began zipping around us, slapping the ground, the trees, stripping the leaves from the bushes. Cornpone motioned frantically. I nodded in his direction.

"That way," I said.

"Good as any," Duke said, and rose to a crouch, running like a crab, pausing to slap Heaven as he passed. Solly was already moving backward. I heard his grenade explode, a momentary silence, the bullets buzzing and slapping around us like hornets.

"This way!" Cornpone shouted, and moved forward, firing as he went. A shadow stumbled from behind a tree and fell, tried to rise, then jerked as Cornpone's bullets slammed into him.

We zigzagged our way through the trees, trying to keep abreast of one another. Solly glanced over at me and I motioned upward. He shook his head and gestured to stay in the valley. It wasn't a time to argue.

"Heaven!" I shouted. "Take the front!"

Heaven sprinted past Solly, moving rapidly down the valley. His head swiveled rapidly left-right-up-down and I prayed that White Buffalo Woman would help him avoid booby traps. Then, a voice came whispering to me from my ancestral past. I whistled. Heaven froze, then glanced back. I gestured and they all came rapidly around me, crouching, staring away and around at the trees and bushes.

"Damn, man, this ain't no time for a conference," Cornpone said.

"It's a trap," I answered. "They deliberately left this way open. We gotta go up the side."

Heaven glanced at the cliff and shook his head. "We be wide open up there," he whispered. "How you know this a trap?"

I didn't waste time to explain the stories about how Crazy Horse had drawn Fetterman's troops out of the fort to massacre them. The Sioux kept those stories alive, a bardic tradition that was passed down to the children as not only history but a study of tactics as well.

"I just know," I snapped. "But we'll go north. They'll figure we went south. Cross the valley and go up."

Solly shrugged. "You heard the man," he said, and rose, slipping through the trees as rapidly as he could.

Duke sighed, then pressed his lips together and went after Solly.

"Heaven, you take the rear. Cornpone, follow me."

We ran through the trees, winding our way like a python sliding toward a tethered goat. We moved as quietly as possible, yet rapidly, sacrificing complete silence for speed. Dimly I heard the crackle of gunfire behind me, and then it faded into silence, and I knew that Charlie was working his way through the trees toward where we had been like silent shadows, watching for splashes of blood, broken branches, ripped vines, overturned stones, and I knew, although I did not know how I knew, that those who had been set in an ambush were making their way up the valley toward those coming down.

I whistled again and we gathered. Solly slipped his bag and opened it, nodding at me. I glanced down and saw my shirt had been ripped and blood was beginning to leak out.

"Open up, Wingo. We gotta do some quick repair."

Obediently I slipped my ruck and ammo and pulled my jungle blouse off, wincing as it rubbed against the raw sores where tiny grenade fragments had ripped into me like ticks burrowing through the flesh.

"Ain't too bad," Solly said. He worked rapidly, slapping ointment on the wounds, covering what he could. "But you gonna have to go to the hospital when we get back."

"Bad duty," Cornpone said.

"Another Purple Heart," Heaven said. "You gonna need a wheelbarrow to carry all them medals around you ever get back to the Land of the Big Milk Shake."

"Listen," I said. I nodded at Heaven. "Heaven's right. If we try to go up the side, we'll be sitting ducks. We may have lost them for a while, but those boys have been in this area a long time. They'll find our trail in a bit and be after us like shit slipping through a goose."

"So, what now?" Heaven asked.

I pointed upvalley. "We'll take a wide detour and go back through the village. They won't be expecting that. They'll check south first because they'll think that we're in a hurry to get back home."

"Ain't we?" Duke asked.

I ignored him. "Instead, we'll take the long road back."

They fell silent, staring at me.

Heaven shook his head. "Man, you want us to go down the Trail? We don't know what's down there or coming down. That way is murder for certain and I'm too young to commit suicide yet."

I winced as Solly's fingers caught a sensitive spot. "No," I said. "We'll stay on it just long enough to lose our tracks in it. We'll drop off one at a time so they won't find where we all left. Five, six klicks. That's all it'll take. Then, we move over the border and swing down twenty klicks or so and then come in and call for a dust-off."

"Might work," Solly grunted, slapping my shoulder. I reached for my blouse, gingerly shrugging into it. "But it'll take us a couple of days."

"That's why you had R & R," Heaven said. "Get you in shape for a couple days humping the North."

"Wingo," Duke said. "They were waiting for us. They knew we were coming. Someone set us up."

They all looked at me knowingly, their eyes hard like full-metal-jacketed bullets. I felt the heat pouring off them, the hurt, the anger, and the primordial throbbing beat of primitive man in a primitive land. I could smell the rank decay of the universe before a god brought order to it, a foul and feral odor that washed over us more powerful than the waters of the river Jordan.

"Yes," I answered. "I know. But right now, we have more important matters to consider."

"Like hauling ass for the Laotian border?" Duke said.

"You got it," I answered. "Heaven, take the lead."

"We going through Copperhead Jack's valley?" Heaven asked.

"Fuck Copperhead Jack," I answered coldly. "We get clear enough to call for a dust-off and we're outta here."

Heaven gave a quick nod and rose, moving rapidly back the way we came, slipping silently through the trees. Like malignant shadows, we followed him.

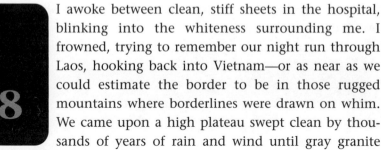

I awoke between clean, stiff sheets in the hospital, blinking into the whiteness surrounding me. I frowned, trying to remember our night run through Laos, hooking back into Vietnam—or as near as we could estimate the border to be in those rugged mountains where borderlines were drawn on whim. We came upon a high plateau swept clean by thousands of years of rain and wind until gray granite lifted its face to the passing of time. Sparks set up and called a dust-off and Solly came back and slammed another morphine Syrette into my leg. The previous one had begun to wear off and the raw edges of the wounds had begun to gnaw at the nerve ends like hungry rats. I may have been delirious—I don't know—but my face felt greasy and my body cold and clammy while sweat soaked through my jungle blouse.

At that moment, Cornpone yelled a warning that Charlie was coming up rapidly on our rear, and again we were up and running. This time, however, we stumbled upon the first battalion, the 503rd from the 173rd Airborne Brigade (Separate), who were on a search-and-destroy mission. A firefight evolved, hot and furious, and we quickly realized that it was not simply a small patrol that had come down the trail after us but a large company from a North Vietnamese regiment, regular soldiers. I was hit twice more before the paratroopers managed to drive the regiment back far enough to call in medevac helicopters. The last time, a hand grenade exploded near me, knocking the wind out of me, tiny pieces of serrated steel wire splattering against me, burning through screaming nerve ends.

I awoke, swinging back and forth in a poncho, hearing the labored breathing of four men racing to carry me back far enough away from the fighting, the tree branches and vines slapping against their helmets, their expressionless faces swinging from side to side in case Charlie had wised up enough to send a couple of patrols wide around our flanks. Solly held one corner of the poncho in one huge hand while his other held a serum albumin bottle high enough to let the fluid drip down through a tube into my arm.

You learn to live with premonitions, despite what the chaplain and others try to tell you is only superstitious nonsense. For thousands of years the Montagnards had held to theirs and still lived. Those who stopped living with their premonitions were dead. I saw a helicopter flap its way toward me out of a bloodred sun and hover over the elephant grass before dropping gingerly down to take the wounded men into its belly. Small-arms fire popped from the tree line and the door gunner racked his M60 machine gun back and forth, his face taut, mouth stretched wide in a soundless scream.

"Duke," I called, and soon his long, lantern-jawed face came over mine. "You're in charge. Take the boys back to Long Binh. If you get any trouble from some of those REMFs, stick a .45 in their mouths and remind them what happens when you pull the trigger."

"What about the 'yards?" he asked. "Shouldn't we go back up there?"

I shook my head, feeling the warm blanket of the morphine begin to unfold over my mind. "No. They'll know where to find you guys there."

"They'll know where we are in Long Binh," Duke pointed out.

"Uh-huh. But there, they'll have too many goddamned witnesses."

"You want one of us to come with you?"

"No," I said. "But whatever you do, keep low. Stay away from the soldier bars and away from the R & R beds. After a week, slip down to Vung Tau and stay at The Blue Orchid—you'll find it back off the beach on the north end, tucked under the hills."

"We'll be AWOL," Duke reminded. But I could tell that wasn't really a concern for them. Most of them had extended to stay in Vietnam after having gone back to what they thought would be the world of roses they had left only to discover that they no longer knew the world they had left. They were all outcasts, flotsam on the stream of time that looped through the oxbows and mountains and fields and forests and jungles of Southeast Asia. Someday the war would end, and what they would do then was anybody's guess. Perhaps the Congo. Mad Mike was always interested in mercenaries there.

That was the case for many who had tried to return to life with the finely tuned survival instincts they had picked up in-country, a fine blend of adrenaline and honed awareness that slipped into the bloodstream at a second's suspicion. We did not climb up; we dropped down.

I laughed. "If you do a good job mixing at Long Binh, they'll just lose sight of you and assume you're around. Don't tell anyone you'll be at The Blue Orchid. I'll find you there as soon as possible. How you fixed for money?"

"What's to spend it on up here?" he groused.

"Live carefully. I don't know when I'll be able to come down from Saigon or Nha Trang—wherever they're taking me."

"Saigon," Duke said. "I'll make certain you get to Saigon."

My tongue felt thick and furry and I tried to mumble a couple last words of warning, but then the black blanket was pulled over me. Dimly I felt hands lifting me and sliding me into the helicopter and heard the pitch of the blades change as the helicopter popped up from the elephant grass like a cork from a shaken bottle of champagne, turned upon its tail, and fled back into the bloodred sun from whence it came. I glanced over at the man next to me on the floor of the helicopter. I didn't know his name. I didn't want to know his name, as a peculiar light began to shine like darts from his eyes. A tiny bubble of blood appeared on his lips and I looked away, afraid for one irrational moment that his soul would fly from his eyes into mine, and there was only room enough within my broken body for one.

The morphine was beginning to wear off and I could feel the spiders and centipedes beginning to crawl under the bandages and wondered how long it would take before I would be taken off the helicopter and carried into an antiseptic white room, my filthy clothes cut away, and another needle jabbed into my thigh. Not long, I hoped. The myth of the soldier taking the pain was for the storytellers. I was caught in the middle of the relativity of the moment and knew it wouldn't be long before each second would seem like an hour.

And I awoke between clean sheets.

I glanced out the window, surprised to see that I had a good view of the garden in which the wounded walked slowly with attendants following closely, watchfully, with them. The palm trees drooped windless-disturbed fronds over the graveled paths the patients followed, shading the paths from the benzine rinsings of the sun. I knew that they were in the process of proceeding to nothingness, to the basic salvation that came not from refusing to take part or running away or drifting on dope-driven dreams but rather from complete surrender. They had lost the means of creating within themselves a boundless and frightful capacity for pain. I knew that if I met one of those in the garden his eyes would always be centered on what was directly in front of him, seeing, but not seeing, knowing, but not knowing.

But I was not ready for repentance.

The door swung open. I swiveled my head and saw Fell standing there, briefcase in hand. His face looked tight and strained, and when he smiled his lips moved up, but the smile never touched his eyes. His hands trembled slightly.

"I should have known you'd find a way to get back here," he said, forcing a note of gaiety to his words. "You can't keep a good field man out of Saigon."

"I could think of better ways of returning," I said ruefully, motioning at the IV drips hooked to needles in my forearms. "These aren't exactly the watermelon days of our youth."

"When did you have watermelon days?" he asked, placing the briefcase beside a chair and sitting.

"You never live in a constant state of misery," I said. "You always find something, no matter how momentary."

He chuckled and lifted a quivering hand in benediction. "Here lies the one truly optimistic man in all Vietnam."

"Welcome to the paranoia," I said.

"Yes," he answered, his face falling suddenly into tight lines. "But sometimes in the midst of paranoia, we discover—things."

I frowned and levered myself up on my elbows to lean against the iron headboard of my bed. A black mist swam across my eyes momentarily; then my sight cleared.

"What's wrong?" I asked.

A fine sheen of perspiration appeared, making his thin face look as if it were melting. "I'm being sent to Bien Hoa. The One-seventy-third. The boys are going ahead with the INTELPAC plan. Remember? We're sending pacification teams out to rebuild what we destroyed and make things better?"

I nodded. "And gather intelligence in that matter from agents. Right?"

"Yes. I'm going to be a field man again."

I glanced at his leg. He still favored a cane. I frowned. "Since when did the doctors clear you for field duty? I thought your profile excluded that."

"It does. Did. But suddenly it became corrected." He laughed. "I guess I've healed faster than they thought I would."

"This isn't right."

"I know."

"Did you tell Black?"

"The orders came down through him."

"From whom?"

"Nha Trang. Wingo, did you tell anyone that I was trying to help you with that wet assignment?"

I shook my head. "You know better than that."

"It's just that I can't figure out any reason why they would want to put me back up on the line. Look at me?" He held his hands up. They trembled. "I'm finished. I knew that when you brought me back six months ago. *They* knew that, too. I'm no good out there anymore. Did you know that the others have bought it? Copperhead Jack, you, and me are the only ones left from Team Twenty-seven."

"When did that happen?" I asked, frowning. "Two weeks ago, the others were alive and well."

He shrugged. "I don't know. I just know that they won't be coming back."

"Cambodia?"

He nodded. "That would be my guess. The Khmer Rouge are acting up over there. I think they went to the well once too often. Slipping back and forth across the borders is tightrope walking. Even up in the mountains. You just never know when you'll stumble across something."

"But you think there's something else," I said pointedly.

He blinked rapidly, then gave a short, quick nod. "My reticent hypocrisy will only go so far. I know there's something wrong. What happened up north?"

I shook my head. "Wrong intelligence. That village had been deserted long enough for the forest to start its reclaiming project. I know there was a problem with getting aerial reconnaissance up there, but it would have to be one dumb sonofabitch not to be able to figure that out even from partial photos."

"There's more," he said. He reached down and opened the briefcase, removing a plain file folder. "A Special Forces 'A' team is operating out of Burma." He handed the folder to me. "They ran a recon patrol through there four months ago on a routine check. That's hard copy, as you can see."

I opened the folder and glanced at the field report, my eyes skimming down the page to the Valley of the Mists. I read carefully, feeling the anger grow within me. The Special Forces captain had declared the valley clean and listed the village as deserted. Of course, four months is a long time and there might be a reason for someone to think that the Vietnamese had gone back into the valley and rebuilt it during that time. But that was doubtful. I looked up at Fell.

"Do we have a date on those recon photos that were used?"

He nodded. "The same time as that report. They were sent up after receiving the report for verification in case Special Forces missed something."

So it was old information that was used to send my team up. Nothing remained static for long in this war. Information over two weeks old was usually deemed worthless and only used for comparative analysis. Never for operation initiation.

"But they didn't."

He shook his head and leaned back in his chair, rubbing his hands over his face. He looked tired and drained, and I could smell the fear coming from him, sour and acrid. Much had been taken from him while he was a prisoner, and now, when he should have been sliding through the rest of his tour, he was being sent back. On the surface, it appeared that he was on "easy street," but any field intelligence operation carried with it a soul-despairing wretchedness with wicked headaches forming behind the eyeballs from anticipating nightmares from the jungle. If one is lucky enough to keep a sense of adventure about him during these moments, then the danger becomes emetic. But once dread slips into the dark crevices of mind and memory, then each day becomes a day of regret with hours dragging past in a blur of dirt and dust.

"So the question is, why send us up there?"

"I've been trying to figure that out ever since I learned about the mission," he said miserably. "But for the life of me, I can't. The files are closed. No one is talking. I mean *no one* is talking," he emphasized.

I tapped my fingers on the file folder, thinking over his words. Regardless of what the Lincoln Library librarians would like everyone to believe and understand, no operation ever went without a whisper being registered here or there. A casual word, a reference, a question— *something* would slip and eventually become common knowledge within the intelligence community. Nothing was ever completely secret away from Langley and, I reflected, perhaps not even there. The interesting thing about secrecy is that it seems to *demand* to be told, as if it had a life of its own.

"So there is a lid on it. But the mission wasn't important enough to warrant that. It was nothing but an exploration. Hell, hundreds of missions like that go out every day. Maybe not that deep into the North, but this was really nothing more than a long-range reconnaissance patrol. Why deep-six information about that?"

"There are other things I don't understand," Fell said. "Why send you back through Copperhead Jack's valley? That's a long detour for nothing when we could do a quick flyby and get the same information. Bringing your team down the Road that far is dangerous. Stupid, in fact. It's almost as if someone . . ." He hesitated, shaking his head back and forth. He chewed a fingernail and spat the shaving onto the floor.

"As if?" I prodded.

"As if someone wanted to keep you in harm's way long enough for an accident to happen. *Or* to make an accident happen. But that doesn't make any sense, does it?"

I shook my head. "Nope." Then a thought occurred to me. "You said word came down from Nha Trang?" He nodded. "From where exactly?"

"COMSACINTEL. Where else?"

"Did you see the original flimsy?" He shook his head. "Then how do we know the origin? Why send the assignment south only to take it back north? The M'nongs are working up there pretty effectively. Hell, they have connections all the way up to Nu Mung Ba. They could have gotten that information faster and with far less risk than running a hot ops assignment through the Saigon office. Right?"

Fell nodded. His face seemed tighter than possible, as if one more turn with a tuning wrench would snap the piano wires holding his face together, and I knew that he was beginning to feel those moments when it seems ticks are burrowing deeply through your flesh, nipping at each nerve as they go until you feel the raw edges burning through your body like a jolt of electricity from a Hot-Shot.

"There's something else," he said softly. His eyes slipped like rolling marbles away from me, staring at the water pitcher on the table beside my bed, my knees bent beneath the sheets, the IV lines trailing down into my arm, the stitches and bandages wrapped around my chest. Everywhere but into my own eyes, as if he was afraid that I would be able to read whatever thoughts he had buried in the deep morass of his mind.

"Lisa Lee."

I frowned. "What about her?"

He glanced toward the door, then leaned forward. His breath smelled like juniper berries and I knew he'd had more than one gin to start the day. His eyes were red-veined like road maps. I had seen that look before on the face of a sergeant in the 101st just before we went back into the A Shau Valley before it became known as the Valley of the Shadow of Death. We *knew* what was in that goddamned valley and we knew that we would never make it through the valley without losing half of those with us. I wondered who would be our Tennyson or if we would even have one who would sing of our bravery.

"They didn't bury the file," he said.

For a moment I didn't understand what he was saying; then it dawned on me: someone was keeping the death of a prostitute in a live investigation in a country where trying to solve murders was like giving out speeding tickets at the Daytona 500. Nobody knew how many prostitutes there were in Saigon. Back in the days of Madame Nhu, a prediction might have been made. But as the war escalated, refugees fled down from the North into Saigon like floodwaters, living hand-to-mouth whichever way they could. Prostitution not only became a fact, it also became a way of life, and in a city where malnutrition and violence and death had become daily statistics generally ignored, to single out one prostitute for followup was ridiculous when the chief of police made an issue of executing a suspected Vietcong spy in Lam Son Square at high noon.

What was even more unusual was that the U.S. Army hadn't discreetly tried to bury the file or even had maintained a file in the first place. The termination of someone suspected of being an agent usually resulted in the file being destroyed to keep "accidents" from happening. The intelligence agencies had learned the lesson of not keeping such files from what had been revealed at the Nuremberg Trials following World War II when the Nazis' own files were turned against them. Of course, there was always a fanatical paper pusher somewhere who insisted on triplicate files in order to keep his sorry ass out of the field by establishing the idea that he was indispensable.

Still, the file should have been buried by now. And the Vietnamese police should have closed the investigation under the pile of paperwork coming in each day—enough to provide toilet paper each day for each soldier in Vietnam for a month. So, why hadn't the case of Lisa Lee been buried?

"Maybe it's because of the way you left the body," Fell said, wiping his lips. "I saw the pictures. What the hell happened?"

I shook my head. "I don't know. I didn't sanction her."

He frowned. "What?"

"It was someone else."

"You telling me that someone took it out of your hands? That someone else cut her like that?"

"I saw the pictures, too," I said quietly. "Do you really think I would have butchered her like that?"

"Black said to make it ugly," he said.

"Black says a lot of things," I answered. "That was different from anything I've ever seen before. It was like—a ritual, almost."

"Ritual?" His eyebrows pinched tightly together, his eyes becoming as flat and lifeless as dolls' eyes. "What kind of ritual?"

I shook my head. "I don't know. A sacrifice of some sort, I'd say."

"Or derangement?"

"Maybe."

"You know," he said carefully, "some psychologists subscribe to an inherited social acceptance of ancient rituals and practices."

"Your point being?"

"Well"—he rubbed his nose with the palm of his hand—"there are the stories of what your ancestors did."

"That's bullshit!" I snapped. "The figment of a bad writer's imagination passed down to other bad writers. You really think a culture could accept something like that?"

"This one has," he said soberly. "You know what can happen out there."

I fell silent for a moment, then said, "And that means that anyone in the Vietnamese culture could have murdered her. More than likely one of them did. Maybe an angry family member, a jilted lover. I don't know." I sighed and shook my head. "All I know is that I didn't do it."

"It doesn't matter what I believe," Fell said. "It's what the others are willing to believe."

I shrugged. "It doesn't mean anything. What are they going to do? Send me to Vietnam?"

"There are worse places," Fell said.

"Like where?"

He shrugged and rose, taking his briefcase with him. "You've been in the North, Burma, Cambodia, Laos. You've seen things that others couldn't even imagine in their worst nightmares. But remember this, Wingo: not everyone has the same nightmares. One man's hell can be another man's heaven because his hell is worse than the one you imagine. I'll see what else I can find."

We shook hands and he slipped out the door. I wiped my hand on the sheet covering me and turned so I could stare out the window into the garden. The garden was empty. As empty as I felt.

9 They came for me the next day at noon right after the doctor had removed the IV lines and changed the dressings on my wounds, flesh wounds mainly, although I would carry a couple of fragments for the rest of my life, as they couldn't be surgically removed without doing greater damage.

The door to my room swung open and a Vietnamese policeman came in followed by two MPs. One took a station at the door and stared hostilely at the Vietnamese, short, chubby, his round face glistening like an oil slick. He wore carefully pressed jungle fatigues, an affectation of several policemen in imitation of American soldiers, and a silk scarf tied under his chin, the ends tucked beneath the blouse. I glanced at the MP who had followed the Vietnamese to the bedside.

"Mr. Wingfoot, this is Le Hung. He's with the Saigon police, investigating the murder of Lisa Lee, a bar girl."

I regarded Hung impassively; he gave a tiny smile—at least, I presume it was a smile, as his lips moved his heavy cheeks up a little, but the smile never touched his black eyes. I looked at the MP.

"And what does that have to do with me?" I asked.

"Do you know Miss Lee?" Hung asked. His English was badly accented, but I refused to speak in his language, as I wanted the MP to hear what was being said.

"No, I don't know her," I answered. "I have never met her."

He sighed and shook his head. I wanted to smile; he had watched too many old detective movies. His mannerisms reminded me of Sidney Greenstreet. "That is not what we have heard," he said.

"And what have you heard?" I asked. "More important, from whom have you heard it?"

"That is privileged information," he said.

"No, not if you are accusing me," I said. "Are you accusing me?"

He considered me silently for a moment, then said, "Should we be accusing you?"

"I've already told you that I've never met her."

"She used to work in The Flowers. Did you ever visit her there?"

"No."

A tiny smile of triumph came over his lips. "We have witnesses who say they have seen you in the bar."

"I never said I wasn't in The Flowers. I just never visited her there."

"What were you doing in The Flowers?"

I shrugged. "Having a nightcap with a couple of friends. What do you do in a bar?" I looked back at the MP. "I think I want a member of JAG here before this goes any further."

He looked uncomfortable and I felt my stomach open up and sink and knew at that moment that we were actors in a farce. At that moment, I could have predicted his words.

"This is a matter for the Saigon police," he said. "Miss Lee was a Saigon civilian and her death comes under their jurisdiction."

"But this is a U.S. military hospital," I said pointedly.

"But it is on South Vietnamese soil," he said. "This matter comes under their jurisdiction. We are here by tolerance."

"And need," I said flatly, turning my attention back to Hung. "If we weren't here, where would you be?"

He curled his lips back from his mossy green teeth in what passed for a predator's smile, and I knew then the lost feeling of predestination as if I was young again and sitting on a ridge in the Black Hills, waiting for my manhood vision, knowing that it would come to me and show me the path I was to try to walk through life. All metaphor and allusion, to be sure, but truth is more often found there than in any attempt by man to discover it on his own.

I listened as Hung talked. His questions were oblique and drifted in and out of sequence in an attempt to confuse me and cause me to contradict myself. But he was not as skilled as he should have been, given the amount of practice he probably had had over the years. Then again, I thought, perhaps most of his interrogations didn't get down to these niceties; it would be much easier and time-saving to simply beat the answers out of the suspect with bamboo canes. As it was, his tangents led nowhere and even confused himself at times. Then he'd flush and his lips would draw down into a thin line and I knew he wanted to shout at me, but he felt a danger in that: I was an American, and although he had jurisdiction for the moment, there was no assurance that he would keep jurisdiction, and then where would he be if he had committed a faux pas of one sort or the other? Political correctness was a delicate tightrope that had to be walked with the utmost care, for there was no telling how much political clout an American might have behind him. I could have saved him the concern; he wouldn't have even been in my room if I had the necessary clout.

At last, he had enough. His eyes had shrunk to tiny black dots, and a small bubble of spittle hung in the corner of his mouth.

"So you continue to deny you killed this girl? This Vietnamese girl?" he asked. It was rhetorical, but I answered it anyway.

"Over and over again," I said. "I've told you all that I can."

"Then!" he exclaimed with a gleam of triumph in his eye. "Then, how do you explain this?"

He opened his hand in front of me. I glanced down. It was my missing dog tag. My heart stopped beating.

"That was taken from my room at the Continental before the girl was killed," I said.

"Did you report it?"

"No."

"Why did you not report it?"

"I still had one."

"Why did you not report it?"

"I told you: I still had one."

"Then how did it get beneath the girl's body?"

"I don't know." I glanced at the MP standing beside my bed. "Do you think I would be that stupid?"

His eyes slid to the left away from mine. "I have no way of knowing your record, Mr. Wingfoot," he said. Tiny beads of perspiration dotted his upper lip. He shook his head. "It's out of my hands, sir."

I looked back at Hung. He smiled a Cheshire cat's smile.

"It means nothing," I said. "That could have been found anywhere."

"It means everything," he answered with satisfaction. "You may be here to help us win this war, Mr. Wingfoot, but you have no right to murder our people."

"Then what is war?" I asked.

But he refused to answer and stood up. He addressed the MP beside my bed. "It is done, then," he said. "Mr. Wingfoot is under arrest by the People's Republic of South Vietnam for murder. We will

station a guard outside his door until the doctor says he may be released. We will then take him to police headquarters for detainment
until his trial."

He looked back at me. "A *Vietnamese* trial, Mr. Wingfoot," he emphasized.

He left and I looked at the MP.

"What the hell is going on?" I demanded. "Why did you bring
him here without a JAG representative?"

"I had my orders, sir," he said.

"From where? Who gave them to you?"

He shook his head. "I can't tell you. Need to know."

"What?!" I exclaimed. "You mean that you don't think this is a
need to know? It's my ass hanging out in the slipstream right now
and you don't think that's important enough to tell me?"

"I have my orders," he repeated stoutly, and, turning, he nodded
and left.

"Tell me!" I shouted.

My words echoed back emptily at me.

The cells were tiny, six by four feet, all right for a Vietnamese, but
too short for an American. Most of the inmates lay on bare steel-
slatted cots without blankets or sheets. The toilet was a bucket in
one corner. Another bucket in the opposite corner held drinking
water, but there was no cup. Meals were one cup of boiled rice, and
if we were lucky, a dead cockroach might be in it. Some prisoners, I
discovered later, had learned to leave a few rice crumbs in the corners of their cells to catch crickets and cockroaches and eat them
along with their daily ration of rice. When I was taken into the common room, the jabbering voices ceased abruptly and ebony eyes
considered me warily. A few squatted on their heels, shirts draped
over their knees, tattoos scrambled along their backs and arms.
These men had been in prison more than once, as most Vietnamese
had no use for tattoos; they appeared upon prisoners out of boredom; it was something to while away the time. But the prisoners all
had one thing in common: *the eyes,* cold, penetrating, lifeless, yet
stabbing hard into another's eyes as if they could see to the back of
a man's brain and read his thoughts there. The Saigon jail was the

junction of nonsense and chaos, of madness and dreams, where men were forced to stop deceiving themselves and embrace the vestiges of their birth—the slime and eggshells of their primeval past.

I made endless trips down to the common room and along the corridors whose floors were covered with red-black stains. The air was close in the corridors and smelled stale, like old blood. Occasionally a faint scream would come down one of the corridors, directionless, a hint of the paradox of law enforcement in a city that brought death by night and twisted laws with dark Confucian logic to fit the moment. After a while, time blurred into one Kafkaesque nightmare of arsonists, thieves, tramps, and drunkards, harsh and sullen noises that carried the hysteria of violence. Everywhere I went I was followed by darkness.

Once I passed a prisoner being taken down a corridor to the basement. His eyes were fearful and his lips made sucking sounds over his toothless mouth. He had a slight limp and I looked down and saw that the toes on his right foot had no nails, each toe ending in a pulpy red mass. He saw me looking at his bare feet and began to moan, his voice rising into a high keen, then breaking into a piercing scream. His guards bundled him roughly away, and my guard pushed me hard with his baton in the back, forcing me forward to where Hung waited in an interrogation room.

Perhaps things would have not gone the way they did if I had not seen that prisoner in the corridor at that moment or if Hung had not become so arrogant with his own importance at having an American soldier as a prisoner. He made the mistake of beginning that interrogation by slapping me hard across the face before uttering a single word. I buried my foot in his groin and before the guard in the room could react lifted my knee into Hung's face, taking great pleasure in the sharp *crack!* as his nose broke and blood poured down to puddle on the dirty floor and he curled into a fetal ball, holding himself and moaning.

The guard swung his baton at my head. I ducked and caught the baton on its backswing under my arm, coming up with my elbow under his chin. His teeth clicked together and his eyes rolled back into his head under the pith helmet he wore. He slumped to the ground. The second guard was a little wiser than the other and came at me holding his baton in two hands like a saber. He swung and I slipped inside the swing and sliced with the edge of my hand at his neck below the ear. But he felt it coming and hunched his shoulder, taking most of the blow on the thick muscle there. He grunted and slipped back, spreading his feet wide, standing flat-footed, his weight anchored, his eyes close-set and glaring. He came forward again, spinning the baton in short slices left and right. His reflexes were sharp and fast, his thighs and buttocks coiled like springs. His eyes had a steady heat in them and I knew he would accept any pain I gave him to get in the one sharp blow that would snap my ribs like kindling. He sliced a short stroke at my temple, thinking I would react away from it, but I stepped forward, bringing the heel of my hand up hard against his nose. His face went gray and his eyes rolled back, eyelids fluttering like bruised flower petals. He wove drunkenly for a second, then crashed forward onto the floor.

I stood in the middle of the interrogation room, looking down at the two. For a moment I was tempted to run, but I knew that I would probably never make it out of the place alive. Sighing, I bent and removed a pack of cigarettes and a silver lighter with a curious design on its casing from Hung's pocket. I pocketed them and went back to the chair and sat, waiting patiently for someone to come down to check on us.

At last, a guard opened the door, took one look, then yelled. Immediately other guards swarmed into the room, looking from me to the two on the floor and back again. I sat calmly, watching, until finally someone arrived to take charge. I thought I would be in for a beating, but curiously enough, I was led respectfully back to a cell—a different one this time, and cleaner. A thin cotton pallet lay over the steel springs of the cot.

My trial began the next morning and was over by noon. It was a sham even by lax Vietnamese standards, a Beckettian play dark and onerous, a vile statement about man and society. I was sentenced to the prison island of Poulo Condore off the southwest corner of Vietnam. An American officer attended the trial but said nothing, and as I was being led away, I knew that nothing good had come out of Galilee.

10 In Poulo Condore, the guards had freedom to shoot and kill or play any games that they wanted with any prisoner who made his way into their whimsical thoughts. The floor of the bay was littered with the white bones of prisoners, and you could see them as the bay bed rose up from the drop on a coral incline to the dock.

We were taken ashore in shackles, our wrists in manacles, and shuffled along the wooden dock bleached near white by the burning sun. Off to the left was a small hut where a prisoner lay in the shade, bluebottles flying around his dung-encrusted legs where he had shat himself after a beating. Two guards lounged near him, smoking and chattering as they ignored the low moans coming from the prisoner's throat.

We made our way past several iron boxes, which we soon came to know were scattered around the island. Those boxes quickly became cauldrons of pain when one was forced into the interior, where one could neither stand nor sit and was finally forced to lean his back against the walls that became searingly hot as the day burnt itself away. Bamboo doors allowed a little light to come into the interior, but the noonday heat from the sun beating down upon the box made steam form inside as sweat dripped off the prisoner's body and landed on the iron plates. Every prisoner eventually made a trip into one of the boxes for an infraction of the rules that nobody seemed to fully comprehend and were changed daily at any guard's whimsy. Finally, a prisoner learned that there really were no rules and to exist was to make oneself as invisible as possible by keeping one's eyes always on the ground and learning to watch warily from the corners instead of facing anyone.

We were taken to a long, low building with thick white walls. Inside, my head throbbed painfully as my eyes tried to adjust too rapidly from the bright sunlight to the cool, dim interior. American fans whirred rapidly back and forth from the tops of filing cabinets. One by one, we were taken in to see the commandant, a Colonel Trang, whose face was like a pie plate, hairless, eyes anthracite, and so fat that his breath wheezed inside his chest. He smelled of fish heads and cooked rice and sour beer that he drank from a large ceramic mug with a Black Forest design on it of boars and hunters. The boars had huge tusks.

"Ah," he said with relish when I was brought to him. "This is the American who kills helpless girls."

I remained silent and the guard behind me rapped me smartly on the head with his baton. Caught unprepared, I staggered forward a step, and the guard struck me hard across the backs of my thighs, nearly driving me to the floor. I caught myself in time and stood at attention, staring impassively at Trang.

"Answer Colonel Trang!" the guard yelled.

"He didn't ask a question," I said in Vietnamese.

Trang's lips spread in a slow smile. His teeth were yellow and crooked, his eyes pinpoints, and I became aware of the sweetish smell of an opium smoker lingering in the room.

"I do not ask questions," he said. "But you will answer when I speak."

"All right."

"You are the American who kills helpless girls."

"No."

He frowned and tapped his fingernails impatiently on the desk in front of him. "That is the wrong answer."

"It is the right answer."

"Sir."

"Sir."

"It is the wrong answer."

"No. Sir," I added.

But I had hesitated just long enough for him to feel insulted. He glanced at the guard behind me and gave a tiny nod. Pain leaped through my back just above my kidneys as the baton was laid hard across it. I gasped and arched my back away from the pain, then straightened the best that I could.

"You are the American who kills helpless girls," Trang said again, his tone becoming monotonous, anticipating my refusal to agree.

"No. If he strikes again, I will take that baton away from him," I said quietly, keeping my voice low so Trang would not hear the anger behind my words.

Trang's eyes widened; then his lips moved down into a frown. His eyes glinted dangerously.

"Enough! You are arrogant when you should be humble. Perhaps a couple of days in the box will change you."

"*Con dê hoang,*" I answered.

I felt the blow, and darkness fluttered in front of my eyes; then I fell forward, watching the edge of the desk approach and strike me hard on the forehead. Then, the darkness washed over me like a black tidal wave.

I felt myself melting before I awoke. My body oozed away like a cartoon rabbit; then dull orange light crept through my eyelids and I smelled old rusted iron. My tongue filled my mouth like a ball of cotton. I tried to straighten my legs and the soles of my feet touched red-hot iron and I jerked awake, banging my head against the ceiling of the iron box. I looked for some water, but there was none. Light filtered in through the bamboo gate chained shut in front of me. The bamboo was blackened from where madmen had clutched it with sweating hands, trying to pull the gate apart from its wire webbing.

I knew the purpose of Poulo Condore and the theory behind which it ran. This was where the Vietnamese tried to loose the souls from the bodies of the prisoners by making them feel daily the grief and terror and see it every day, everywhere they looked. This was where men were unstuck from their mortal fastenings. Even when they tried to avoid the island and its grim reality by gazing out at the sea, they sensed that the sky had been sawed loose from the earth's rim. The light shimmered inside the iron box like a protean light dancing in the heat waves, washing over me like a nauseating faintness, and I knew that I was close to heat stroke or heat exhaustion, salt being pulled from my body like iron filings to a magnet. How much longer would I be able to last in this box? How long had I been in it? I didn't know and that was why I had to cling to reason of a sort, *any* reason that would keep my wiring from shorting out. I concentrated on what lay outside the box, ignoring death as death would come to some inside the iron boxes when rodents squeezed in through the gaps between the bamboo staves to gnaw their way inch by inch through a man's entrails, working ever deeper into his liver and stomach, separating tendons carefully until he was alone with them in the dark and they sat across from him in the hut and leaned forward to plant a wet kiss on his lips like an old waterfront whore. I closed my eyes and forced an image forward behind my eyelids of palm trees purple against a flickering sky, the sea rolling gently, as if the water was streaked with quicksilver.

Then the image began to crinkle at the corners and fold in upon itself and I tried desperately to bring it forward again, but it gave way to a dead city like a Bavarian village painted by Adolf Hitler beneath a black ink-washed sky, in which the buildings radiated fear and the empty streets had pools of light from sodium lamps that allowed creatures to hide behind them in the shadows, and I knew that their wise and caring Apollo was not the caretaker of the sun but simply a grim driver of the chariot of Helios with his face averted from this island.

I had to go with the hallucinations beginning to creep out of the mental cell in which I had locked them and knew that I had to learn how to work with them, listening to the screams in my mind spiral higher and higher toward an anonymous pitch, but biting back the sound so no one would know how weak I had become. Silence would become my weapon; I had learned that very quickly in Trang's office.

They came for me the next morning just after false dawn, that deception by Morpheus. My legs wouldn't work and they dragged me to Trang's office, the sand and old shells peeling the flesh off the top of my feet. I tried to stand but fell in a heap in front of Trang's desk.

"Get up," he said monotonously.

There are always lots of possibilities to consider when you encounter the psychological mutants posing as police officers in a police state or country torn by war. The Saigon police were no different, and Trang's men were the worst of the lot, isolated on Poulo Condore Island as much prisoners as the men they were guarding. Ten minutes with one of them in a room and you were willing to swap your Saint Michael medal for a lifetime membership in the National Rifle Association. These were the type of people who believed habeas corpus is the scientific name for a social disease. Perhaps it is.

I tried to rise and fell back again, rolling onto my back. I felt the moist touch of the policeman's hand sliding over my stomach, the tip of his knife not quite breaking the skin but pushed just hard enough against it for me to know that the slightest increase in pressure would send the knife slicing neatly through my flesh and deep into my entrails. His eyes were black, without the slightest trace of moral light slipping from them, the eyes of a man just slipping into an opium dream where he knows he can do no wrong. My chest felt as if a piece of barbed wire had been wrapped tightly around it.

Trang's chair creaked as he stood and walked slowly around his desk to stand before me. He wore jodhpurs with well-polished knee-high Wellingtons. I watched silently, stoically. He nudged me in my ribs, hard enough to let me know he could have broken them if he wanted.

"So," he said softly, his eyes amused. "You are learning already. Perhaps that is too bad. A quick death, painful as it may be, is the choice of many who come here. Many do not last two days in the iron box."

Had it been two days? I hoped he was trying to play mind games, because if it had been two days, then I was already losing the one connection with reality that I needed. Despite what man thinks he needs, he must always have a connection somewhere with something to keep the chaos of the universe at bay. He must have *some* sense of order within his life or he becomes nothing more than flotsam upon the seam of time.

I remained silent.

He frowned and nudged me again, sharper this time, and I hissed with pain but kept my lips pressed tightly together. His brows came together in a furrow of disappointment; then he smiled and moved away.

"Silence can be an answer, Mr. Wingfoot. A useful and successful answer. But not if it is used too often. Then it becomes a weapon." He stopped and swung back to face me. "Am I making myself clear? Lessons come expensive here. You had one. There will be others. Always others," he said softly. "Until you are numb with trying to remember what you need to remember to survive in order to stay out of the iron boxes. Do not make the mistake of thinking you are here to be in prison; you are here to die."

He nodded at the guard, who unceremoniously dragged me from Trang's office, my feet leaving bright smears of blood on the salt-weathered gray boards. The guard dumped me unceremoniously in the sun of what could have been a parade ground and left me.

I rolled painfully to my stomach and pushed up on my elbows to stare around me. Other prisoners looked back impassively and I knew they were waiting for me to either live or die. The choice was mine and mine alone. To interfere with my choice would be to obligate themselves for something that they did not need; their own lives were enough pain and worry for any one man to bear without taking on an extra.

I tried to stand again, but my legs were still frozen in cramps and I hunched my shoulders, pulling myself painfully over the crushed shell and sand to the shadow of a thatched hut, and levered myself up until I could rest my back against the seagrass wall in the shade. I looked down at my feet and grimaced; they were raw chunks of meat, one toenail barely hanging on to a thin strip of flesh. I sighed and looked out toward the sea. A roll of lightning-forked clouds moved angrily south, spreading from horizon to horizon like hard ebony planks upon which hammers pounded relentlessly. Dimly I heard the murmur of voices like a mainline injection of schizophrenia, and then a figure in dirty white shirt and pants squatted beside me. His knobbly toes were in rope sandals. His thin white fingers gently lifted my feet, and I heard a rag being rinsed in water and wrung out. Gently he bathed my feet.

He had a shock of white hair that lay thickly over his forehead. A conical rice hat hung on a leather strap down his back. His white skin was burnt mahogany now, but his blue eyes were soft with pity above a salt-and-pepper beard.

"I am certain that you won't make that mistake again, will you?" he asked in a French-accented voice. For a moment, I was confused; he spoke in English and I had let English slip away from me over the past few weeks—or had they been months? "No, it's best to remain silent here except for the few you meet that you can tolerate. You won't make any friends here, but there will be some that you will be able to tolerate more than others, and they will have to do as friends for you."

"Who—who are you?" I croaked.

He smiled and handed me a bamboo cup of water. I sipped at it, feeling the pain as it laced through the dryness in my throat. He nodded appreciatively.

"At least you know enough not to gulp. You've been in situations like this before. At first, I thought you were a Vietnamese—a bit large, perhaps, but a Vietnamese all right. Then I heard you whispering in English and knew you were not."

"Indian," I whispered. "American Indian. And you?"

"Father André Devereaux," he said. "I had a leper colony up north and made the mistake of treating a few Vietcong soldiers who had been wounded." He shrugged. "Apparently all of God's creatures are not seen as all of God's creatures by others. I was found guilty of giving help to the enemy and sentenced to stay here for the rest of my mortal life. Well, I suppose it is God's work all the same. We just don't know where He will find a need for us."

"How long?"

"Twenty years," he said. "I shall try and get ointment for your feet, but it will be very difficult. We must trade for things we want or need here."

I nodded toward the sea. "The salt water will help," I said.

"Be careful out there," he warned. "If the guards think that you are trying to escape they will shoot. And be careful of where you put your feet. This is the largest area for giant clams. If they clamp down upon your feet, no one will come to help you. That is what passes for amusement here. Prisoners and soldiers both like to bet on how long you will last until the tide drowns you." He nodded toward the center of the island. "There is a large mangrove forest in there that is sometimes harvested, and sea turtles come up to lay their eggs from time to time in the sand. We watch for them because that is how we get some of our food. If you find a marker by one of the beds, do not move it. You will be killed, because that is someone's find."

"Honor among thieves?" I cracked.

He nodded soberly. He squatted on his heels and stared intently into my eyes. "There is that. We must have something on this island that is ours. Break any of the 'laws' of the prisoners and you will die." He swept his arm out to indicate the bay. "You will be dumped out there and will go missing only when and if Trang decides to check on you." He gave a bitter smile. "That doesn't happen very often. We are a long way from the mainland, and the riptide and the current through the channel is very fast."

"No one has ever escaped?"

He shrugged. "Who is to say? We do not know of anyone who has escaped. But even some managed to escape from the French prison on Devil's Island. You know of that?"

"A little. A penal colony in French Guiana, right?"

"The worst of the worst," Devereaux replied. "This place was French as well and modeled after Devil's Island. It was bad, very bad. And this place is becoming worse, as some of the Vietnamese have an infinite appreciation for torture that puts the worst of the French to shame. But you will find out about that and it is best that you do not dwell on such things for long, as that is the way into madness. I shall see if I can get you something to eat. There are still a few who have not lost their souls here."

"Acolytes at Mass?" I said, trying for a lightness to relieve the situation.

He stared soberly at me. "No, there is no God here. Here, I am not Father André Devereaux. Only André. Make no mistake about that. This is hell and you are in it. Let me see what I can find."

He rose and slipped away in a shambling walk. I watched him go as I sipped the cold water from the bamboo cup. It had a slight alkaline taste that reminded me of the Rosebud Reservation just before it slipped away into the Badlands of South Dakota. I thought again of how I hated that place, which right now seemed a far better place to be than where I was at the moment.

I took a deep breath, smelling the sour mud flats, the slit trenches the prisoners used for defecating, the sour stench of bodies that hadn't been washed in a long time because to wash meant that you anticipated going somewhere and no one was going anywhere here. Poulo Condore was an island of hopelessness where one would at times even dream back to the time when he was first placed in jail in Saigon.

I closed my eyes and listened to the sounds of the jail once again: steel doors clanging, trustees dragging wooden buckets of shit and urine down the stone-floored halls, criminals yelling at one another and promising to whack the balls off the officers who had arrested them. I took off my shirt, rolled it, and used it as a pillow as I stretched out on the cold stone floor that smelled like old urine.

There had been another white man in the cell, a man with the glint of true madness in his eyes, a washed-out blue, blond hair like melted gold coins, his flesh like tallow. He smelled like vinegar.

"Hey," he said softly. His voice sounded like a saw rasping through teak. "You the one in for murder?"

I stared at him, waiting for whatever he had in mind when he opened the conversation.

"And you?" I asked. "What are you in for?"

He rubbed his meaty hand across his heavy chin, bristles rasping like a file against rough steel. His shoulders were massive, powerful, his thighs bulging the white pants that ended high above his ankles. His feet gripped the concrete floor like Anteus sinking his toes into rich, black earth.

"Contraband," he said, and laughed. "The whole fucking city is filled with contraband—you know Bring Cash Alley? Shit, the police could raid down there and have a few thousand people in jail for contraband without working up a sweat. So, what do they do? They arrest me and confiscate my boat."

"You are French?"

He shrugged. "Another strike. You have to be careful of committing yourself down here. But, in my case, I'm pretty well known."

"What were you bringing in?"

He laughed. "That's the beauty of it. French brandy. Can you believe that? They could get the same thing from the Americans, but a man has to make a living somehow."

"Uh-huh," I said. "And that was all?"

His eyes narrowed watchfully. "What are you suggesting?"

I shook my head. "That wouldn't have been enough to get you in here. What else did you have?"

He remained silent for a long while, then laughed again. "What difference does it make, now? I brought dreams and took away nightmares. Opium."

I felt the approach of the good Father before he dropped down on his haunches beside me. He held a small ball of rice with some pieces of fish tucked in it wrapped in a palm leaf.

"It isn't much," he said, "but it is all I can do for now. Tomorrow, I will be able to start earlier and then we shall see. You can't afford to remain idle long." He looked critically at my feet. "I can get you some rope sandals. They are easy to find, for we take them from the dead men before they are taken out into the bay and there are always dead men here. We try to hide them, as then we can still claim their rations. Tomorrow morning, I will collect the rations for myself and four others who are too sick to do so themselves. Another prisoner is dead; I shall bring you his." He turned his attention back to my feet. "But you will not be able to wear the sandals on your feet until they are healed properly. And that will take time. The sun will come hard upon them and you must bathe them in the salt water as much as you can to keep the infection down. You will find maggots will form in them, but do not remove the maggots, for they will only eat the dead flesh and help draw the poison from your feet."

"Why are you doing this for me?" I asked.

He looked startled for a moment, then smiled. "I may not be a priest here, but that is still my nature—to help others. God may have forsaken us here, but man has not forsaken himself. That is all that we have before we become animals." He frowned and raised his head, nodding toward the inner island. "There are some in there who have forgotten they are men. Watch carefully for them. Even the guards do not like to go far into the interior. There is much danger there."

"I'll remember," I said.

"Good," he answered. "Now, would you like to try and make it into my hut? There is an extra pallet there and no one will bother you. If you sleep out here—" He shrugged. "The night is dangerous. Can you walk?"

I shrugged and pushed myself to my feet, gasping from the pain of tortured skin suddenly stretched tight. He shoved an arm under my shoulder and lifted gently, taking some of the pain off my feet. Together we hobbled into a hut fifty yards down from where André had found me. It was one that was close enough to the water to give us the fresh salt air yet far enough that water wouldn't be a problem at high tide.

He took me into the hut and placed me gently upon the pallet. It was still damp and I knew that he had washed it clean in the sea before making it up for me. There were two others in the hut, Vietnamese, thin and wasted, with a yellow cast to their skin that told me they would not be long for the world. I could smell death in the room. Death is not an abstract. It is the smell that rises like a green and putrescent fog from a body bag suddenly unzipped; luminescent pustules gathered over the skin of a soldier suddenly unearthed from a bog or marsh during an Arc Light raid; faintly purple mushrooms that grown from the hidden graves of soldiers who tried to run through the rubber trees to safety before an M60 stitched rose petals across their uniforms and shirts.

He brought another bamboo cup of water and placed it beside my bed. "You will have a fever soon. Drink the water and when it is gone, awaken me and I will get you another. You must have water in you all the time. Meanwhile, go to sleep."

He pressed something into my hand; it was a crude rosary made out of roughly carved wooden beads, the cross at one end a simple affair. At the other end, a small wooden medallion with a tiny figure cut into the surface and the single word "Raphael" chipped into the wood. Then he slipped away, a shadowy figure in the dusk. He slipped onto a pallet not far from mine, turned once or twice, then lay still.

I watched his figure for a long time until his breathing rose and fell steadily and I knew he was asleep. I lay on my back for a long time, studying the thatched roof overhead, listening to the rustlings of the mice through the thatch and the other nocturnal sounds, the type that made primal man nervous without his fire. Then, I fell asleep and dreamed the dreams of my youth:

—gathering chokecherries along the banks of Bad River in South Dakota
—making small wickiups out of green willow branches
—trying to learn how to chip arrowheads out of flint from the old men
—hunting rabbits in the patches of green in the Badlands where the ranchers would not accuse us of trying to run off their stock
—being taken into the men's sweat lodge for the first time
—the ritual of my vision quest alone on top of Harney Peak in the Black Hills

Then a stained white radiance slowly descended over my dreams and I awoke to my heart beating wildly, out of control, my mouth dry from fear, and my heart plummeted through the depths of despair to the bottom of the abyss where primeval creatures crawled in primal ooze.

Heat lightning flared outside the hut—*my* hut, now, I thought—and I thought of a frosted mug of beer backed by a double Johnnie Walker and wished hard for that shuddering rush of heat from that special amber light that would flash through my insides and roast the writhing snakes and centipedes inside me and that the rest of the night would be free from the disembodied snores that rose softly around me, building into metamorphic shapes whose shadows grew larger with each flash of lightning.

Trang's words floated back to me. *You are here to die.* My freedom would be my death, and I had little doubt that he meant what he said. The only reason I hadn't been executed in Saigon was because there were too many witnesses and an American being executed for killing a South Vietnamese woman would have been golden publicity for the North. But here, on Poulo Condore Island, one death would be pretty much like any other death and my bones would join the bones of nameless others out in the bay. Ben Wingfoot? There is no one here by that name.

I came wide awake, staring into the dark, my thoughts finally folding their wings and settling into a logical order. Of course I would die here. But not from old age. Someone knew that I was here and still alive and to that someone I was still a threat, if only because I still drew a breath in the same world as he. I swore softly. I had been so consumed with self-pity that I had failed to think about the forces that lay outside my immediate presence. I was innocent; I knew I was innocent; I did not belong here. That had been the sum total of my thinking since my arrest. You are here for a reason and that reason is that *someone* had to be here for the death of Lisa Lee. If not you, then someone else, someone who had so much more to lose than Wingfoot that he could order Wingfoot into this hell to take his rightful place. Someone more powerful than the rank and file of faceless clerks and filers.

But who was responsible for this epiphany?

11 Dawn came up over the sea in brilliant reds and greens and I knew that a storm was building just below the horizon—red sky in morning, sailor take warning—and the green was the snot green that became the poet's color. I rose and hobbled to the small shaving mirror hanging above a chipped enameled washbowl. Someone's razor was there, an old razor, the ivory split, with dirty gray soap still clinging within the crack. I looked into the mirror, seeing myself for the first time as others saw me. I remembered ideas and sensations for the first time since coming to the island.

Pain soared up from my feet through the calves of my legs. I felt feverish but still saw things with a crystal clarity that brought the pain to a bearable point, but I focused upon the pain, concentrating on it, willing it to come to the forefront of my mind, using the pain to fuel the hatred that was beginning to work like an ugly cancer within my stomach. I stared across the waters, imagining myself walking the streets of Saigon, smelling food cooking in open braziers, feeling the heat upon my shoulders except when I walked through the cool shadows of the tamarind and chestnut trees. I saw the hot concrete of Tan Son Nhut, the cubicles of Lincoln Library, forcing myself to remember the conversations that I had with Black and with Fell.

"Are you feeling better this morning?"

I turned to the speaker, recognizing the priest. I shook my head. "No, not really."

"It's not simply the pain of your feet or the iron box, is it? No, I didn't think so," he said, without waiting for my answer. "You are trying to remember what brought you here." He shook his head sadly. "It would be better if you would just learn to accept what has happened for now. A man cannot live with the pain that you are imagining, that you are feeling. That type of pain is a hatred that can destroy you here faster than it would be able to destroy you on the mainland or even back in the United States. Or France." He rubbed the palm of his hand across his face ruefully. "I know. I lived with that pain for a long time before I began to accept it. Once I did that, I began to heal. I saw others around me who had greater pain than I had or could even imagine."

"You became a priest again," I said.

He shook his head sadly. "No, I have *always* been a priest. But for a while, I forgot about being a priest, and that has been a good thing for me. To be a priest openly here is to commit euthanasia, and although I do not mind dying for my God, to die with no purpose is a sin. Do you understand that?"

"Like a soldier," I said. "A soldier of Christ."

He shrugged. "A jesuitical approach, I suppose, but there has to be something more than that. A soldier must also serve a purpose, and that purpose is not simply to kill or be killed. There must always be a purpose behind a death. Always. Sit down."

I frowned.

"Your feet," he said gently. "You must take care of your feet."

I nodded and sat down as he collected a few things from a shelf above his cot. I looked out at the sea, looking out again at the waves, always at the waves, and the sea, the sea. Xenophon's sea.

I felt Devereaux's gentle hands upon my feet, gentle hands upon the sores, spreading gently a cooling cream. I looked down. He smiled up at me.

"I make it from coconut," he said.

"Playing the role of the Magdalen?" I joked.

He shrugged. "For three days we shall use this ointment upon your sores, but on the fourth day, you must begin to bathe them in the sea. The salt water will be good for them and help to toughen them after we have moistened them for the healing to begin. That is the secret here where we do not have the proper medicines. We must allow the body to heal itself and then we can manipulate the body to what we want it to be. First, we must soften the skin so that it will grow back together. Then, you may begin rebuilding."

I looked out again at the sea. "Did you ever think of trying to escape?"

He sat back on his haunches and stared out at the sea. "There is not a man here who does not dream about escaping. But there is no escape. Many have tried. All have failed."

"Or," I added softly, "do you *think* that all have failed? Perhaps they didn't. Would they let you know that they had managed to escape?"

"No," he said. "They would not. Even if knowing such a thing would give hope to those still here."

"So, then we must build our own hopes?" I said, laughing.

"Only if you are Jude," he said solemnly.

"Then, I shall become Jude," I answered. "Tell me: are there any fishermen on the island?"

He sighed and shrugged. "On the far side where some prisoners have lived so long here that they know of no other life. But even they are well guarded, and when they take their boats out they cannot go beyond sight of land, or a patrol boat will be summoned. They guard their boats well themselves, for to lose them would be to lose their way of making a life for themselves and their families, because then they would have to go back to the convict life."

He glanced down at my feet and wrapped them gently in strips of white cloth that had been sea-washed and used many times as bandages.

"This will not keep you from working, but we should try to keep you out of the water in the paddies and out of the honey pits where some ladle the excrement used as fertilizer. There is a guard." He hesitated. "He sometimes will help. Sometimes he will not. But I shall see if I can't get you in the threshing hut. It is hard work there and hot work, as you use a flail to separate the chaff, but at least you will be given time to heal."

"What do you have to give this guard to help me?" I asked.

He smiled tiredly. "He is a man who does not like women."

"No," I said, shaking my head. "No, I cannot allow that."

"You have no choice," he said, rising, his knees cracking and popping with the movement. "Nor do I. It is a part of my penance." He looked down sadly at me. "At least, this way I feel that I am accomplishing something. We all serve—in different ways, but we all serve according to our abilities. This is my death in life."

I watched him shuffle out of the hut, his back bowed with the weight of his world heavy upon it, his white cotton shirt and trousers as clean as he could make them from frequent scrubbing with sea salt. A salt-and-pepper beard made his thin face seem more hollow than it should be, like a painting by El Greco. There was an absence of something to him, like looking into the dark. I sensed the pain and agony that he bore and had not earned by himself but had voluntarily become a victim because it was the only way that he had left to serve a god who had abandoned him although he had yet to abandon that god's creation.

And so time began to pass as my feet slowly healed in the threshing hut where I wore a bandanna around my face like an Old West bandit to keep from inhaling the chaff we beat away from the rice. At night, I would walk down to the beach and wash the chaff from beneath my clothes and out of my sweat. And always I would look out across the sea, feeling the tug of the mainland pulling at my breast, trying to draw me to it. I knew that if I was going to make the escape across that wide expanse of water, I would have to do it soon. The diet we were kept on was slowly sapping my strength, drawing me down into the earth of the island. Escape was not an option; it was a necessity that had to happen soon or I would be unable to leave and would become one of the skeletal, hollow-eyed men walking around as stilted figures that once had life. I could see them everywhere I looked: men as gaunt as aged crones shunning the daylight as much as they could, as the sun left its leathery mark upon their skin by the days. No tears fell from their eyes, as the sun had baked the tear ducts dry, and their shuffling steps raised the powdery earth in tiny clouds to cover their feet and shins like brown flour.

At night, I dreamed of three coaches coming from the gate of hell and felt my life to be a wheel on the axle of one of the coaches, turning and turning with no way of escape under the sorrowful moon. The blossoms from the last spring are only a figment of my imagination, for the apparitions appear in demonic form, faces awful with golden eyes and bloodred horns.

I awoke, sweating profusely upon my couch, realizing how close I had come to letting Poulo Condore take my mind as it was taking my body.

Never, I told myself fiercely. Never. You are still free in your mind as long as you do not let them get into it. They can chain you in those damn iron huts where day is only a red glow, but you do not have to accept their tyranny.

I rose and took a drink of cool water from the bamboo cup tied to the rope handle of the bucket. My tissues soaked up the water so rapidly that I felt light-headed for a moment, but in the center of my brain a tiny heat began to glow, widen, and expand. In the darkness, I had found a dwelling place where the heat of the noonday sun that drove dogs and Englishmen mad could not touch me. There were no crevices between which it could creep. Here, in the dark, I could think and listen to the voices of my ancestors coming to me on the wind. For a moment, I thought I saw the spirits of my ancestors as well, floating across the sea to me like a marsh meteor light, and the legends sung by the sun dancers warmed me, reminding me that even in this far-off land I was still a Sioux and within my veins flowed the blood of great warriors who disdained surrender and remembered their honor when taken far from their homelands by soldiers and imprisoned.

At that moment, my spirit lifted from me and soared high on eagle's wings, circling ever higher in a widening gyre until, in the distance, a snowcapped mountain range appeared and my spirit flew toward it, through the polar day, heading always toward the snowclad offspring of the sun. Yet there was a combat soul within me as well, a hunter of the hills, a follower of the deer and the wolf, and I knew that this spirit would have to be freed and allowed to return to the alleys and byways of Saigon to search out the truth, for no soul can ever be free without the truth being known.

Poulo Condore is a living grave, isolated from the rest of the world by the massy waters that pour up onto its low beaches at high tide, when the spray from the incoming sea blows like a fine mist over the huts clustered along the back end of the beaches. Yet I knew what I needed to live, to slip away in the mist and gain a few hours before being missed.

I began to trap rats in the cane fields in the interior of the island and around the rice paddies, using running nooses made out of fine wire that I stole, because the rats' sharp teeth would chew through the vines that I would have to use to make bamboo cages. I caught the rats and I cooked them and ate them to keep up my strength.

Sometimes I would cut thin slices of flesh from the carcasses and soak them in sea salt and dry them in the sun against the time when food would become scarce. I cut back my daily portion of rice by an eighth and hid it safely in an old biscuit tin I found washed up on the beach one morning after a heavy storm during the night.

I lived. Lived, while others died and were scooped into shallow graves or taken out into the bay and buried without ceremony for the crabs and fishes. I could tell when those were ready to go, when their soul stooped, ready to take wing, and during the night I would listen to their labored breathing, ready to pounce upon whatever meager belongings they had. I would take those across the island to the fishing villages and there make gifts to those fishermen willing to talk about their trade, the coming of the tides, the currents, the course one might have to steer.

Slowly, I built a map within my head of the course I would have to follow to cross the sea, and realized that it would be best for me to try for another island in the west and find a way of sailing from there to Saigon. I might be able to pilot a small boat to Vietnam's shores, but not before the patrol boats with their powerful diesel engines could catch me. But they would be looking for someone trying for the shores of Vietnam and I might gain a day or two trying for another island in the west or south.

The monsoon rains came and with them a tempest that threw the sea up higher than before on the beach. The next day, I discovered a small boat aground in an inlet and managed to pull it into a stand of bamboo where I covered it with elephant grass to hide it. As far as I could tell, it was still seaworthy, and although I had no idea how to sail it, I knew that the time had come for me to try. Impatiently I waited for the passing of the moon, readying my supplies, knowing that I had little chance of succeeding, yet ready for the gamble I was going to take. Odysseus had managed to sail farther than I was going to, but he had the gods on his side. Mine had forsaken me.

"When are you going to try to escape?"

Startled, I looked up at Father Devereaux standing over me. His face was wrinkled with concern, his blue eyes worried.

"How did you know?" I asked.

He gave a small shake of his head and said, "You have been storing rice and dried meat for days. There is only one reason for that; you think that you have found a way off the island. And you have had that absent look about you that I have seen in others before they made their mistake and tried. One man lashed together a raft from bamboo, but the patrol boat caught him before he cleared the bay, and shot him with the big guns. Others have tried to slip aboard and hide on the supply boat. Two of them died in the iron huts. The other two went quite mad before they were let out of the huts. A man can last only so long in those iron huts. You know that. You have been in them."

"I found a boat washed up in the last storm," I answered.

He sighed. "Is it worth the risk? Knowing what has happened to others who have tried to escape, is it really worth the risk? At least here, you are alive. Out there"—he gestured toward the sea—"you will probably die."

I shrugged. "A man is lucky if he can choose his own death. Here it has already been chosen for me. Out there I have a chance to live. A small chance, I know, but there is still a chance. To do otherwise, to stay here when there is still a chance, is to commit euthanasia. What does your god say about suicide?"

He bit his lip and looked away. His face seemed contorted with pain as he tried to resolve the hurt his priesthood had created for him. I sensed the conflicting emotions working within him from having been too long on the island and too long away from the altar. When *had* been the last time he had said Mass? Had sought the transformation of Christ into wafer and wine? Had heard confession and granted absolution? Had sought confession? Had felt God's hand upon his shoulder?

He drew a deep, ragged breath and said so softly I had to strain to hear his words, "Will you take me with you?"

I lay back on my cot, studying him. I could use him—I had little doubt that he knew more about sailing than I did about his god— but I had some misgivings about him.

"Well, let me ask you the same question you asked me: is it worth giving up all this on a chance that you might get killed out there?"

He nibbled on his lower lip and cocked his head as if he was listening to the rats running through the thatched roof of our hut. A lone tear trickled down one leathery cheek.

"It is time that I return. I have neglected my duties long enough here."

He looked down at me and this time I could see the pain in his eyes.

"I should have left long ago. Or tried to. But"—he gestured with one hand as if trying to push a burden away—"here I am safe. I do not have to answer to God here. Only to those who keep us here." He looked embarrassed for a moment, then said quietly, "There comes a time, though, when one cannot ignore what has been laid out for him anymore. It is time that I go back."

"All right," I said. "The company will be good. And maybe your god will guide the boat."

"When are you—we leaving?"

"When the moon dies," I said. "And hope for a starless night as well."

"Then that will give some order to my prayers," he said. He turned to go, then said, "Thank you. Is there anything that I can do?"

"If you can find a sail, that would be good. And a set of oars," I said jokingly.

"I shall see. Maybe God will provide."

"Maybe," I said. "So far, He has remained steadfastly silent. I am always wary of those who sit silently and wait. They remind me of predators."

"Perhaps He is waiting for you to ask Him."

"For forgiveness?" I shook my head. "He needs to ask me for that. That is, if He isn't too arrogant to seek forgiveness for His own wrongdoings. I am not Job and I have little use for a god who indulges in bets with Lucifer, using His own creation as a poker chip or pawn in a diabolical game of faith. I don't care much for someone who rigs a game."

He smiled gently and said, "Perhaps there is a reason for that. We are not given to know—"

"The ways of God, Father? Then why were we given the ability to decide for ourselves only to be punished for making the wrong choice? We are not children anymore. Nor do I have any intention of being one again. I have served my apprenticeship."

"It is dangerous to challenge the gods," he murmured.

"It is slavery not to," I answered. "The first moonless night, unless the stars are too bright. If there is a storm, so much the better. Radar won't work in stormy seas very well. Especially with a little boat like we have. So gather your supplies, Father, for I'm putting out at the first opportunity. And that won't necessarily be predictable."

He nodded and left silently. I watched him make his way down along the beach, hands clasped behind his back, his head bowed deep in thought. A nagging worry suddenly cut through my thoughts, and I wondered about his lack of earthly hope, placing his faith in that which forbade a selfish death.

Four days. Then the moon went under and a fierce storm blew up, taking light and bringing darkness. The vortex hit around midnight, taking with it the air. Devereaux and I crept from our hut, carrying our supplies in an old tarp that we had found behind the paint shed. I had no feeling, no thought, other than a quick run for the boat and a struggle against the rising waves to clear the headland before being discovered.

The good Father had worked well in the short time allotted him: he had found a pair of oars, one weathered and cracked but still serviceable, and a many-patched sail. We had made a mast and spar by cutting mangrove branches and trimming them with an adze. The mangroves grew in the salt flats on the other side of the island, so the wood was well seasoned with salt and would serve us well on our trip.

We made our way across the stones. I was barely conscious of slipping through the blank and bleak and black night, fixing my mind on what needed to be done, the vacancy of immediate thought occupying space, aware that there were no stars, no earth, and no time once we put out onto the raging seas. We would be guided by instinct, busy enough for the moment, while trying to clear the headland with the oars, to not be aware of life or death.

We found the boat and had to bail some water from it before anchoring the mast in its box. We kept the sail down, storing our supplies where the seas crashing over the bow would not wash them away. Then, with great difficulty, our muscles straining until the tendons threatened to snap like overstretched rubber bands, we pulled our way with the oars through the heavy surf, riding high upon the waves and coming down the other side with dizzying rapidity that made our stomachs float to the backs of our throats. Blisters appeared quickly on our palms and popped and the salt water stung them as we pulled stubbornly on the oars against the seas, refusing Poseidon his victory.

And then we were clear of the headland but still fighting the surging seas that wanted to throw us upon the reef. Yet we had an easier time now, for the seas were running away from the land, a rapid current that carried us swiftly south and west—or as near as I could figure south and west in that blackness.

Day came rolling up grayly with the gray seas, but we were alone now on the swollen sea and able to raise the mast, clumsily, as neither of us was a sailor. Yet I knew there were more invisible than visible forces around us. The mast bent with the force of the wind and the bow dipped and bobbed its way through the rolling seas, and we exalted in the sense that we were free for the moment, even if that freedom could end in death at any moment.

The next day, the sun rose on the right and I knew that we had made a mistake in the darkness, heading north instead of south. A south wind blew behind us, but not a single bird followed. Occasionally a fish would roll to the surface to examine us and our hearts would lodge in our throats, for each one was big enough to sink us with a casual flip of his tail.

I thought for a long moment about turning back to the south and west, but I had no idea how long we had been blown north and everything was guesswork to begin with. I decided to trust to fate and keep a steady course north. A fair breeze blew and white foam peeled back away from our bow. We kept a sharp watch for a ship, but we were alone upon that silent sea, and the sea miles dropped rapidly behind us as we slipped in and out of pockets of fog and mist.

Then one morning came when the wind died and we stood alone on a glassy sea, the red sun rising hot and bloody. We stayed motionless upon the ocean, a painted ship upon an ocean painted on glass. We began to ration what little water we had left, but the sun seemed to leech the water out of us as soon as we swallowed it.

The second morning, the sea snakes came, migrating south, gray-green worms rolling joyfully through the waves. That night, Saint Elmo's fire danced along the mast and spar like death's fire, burnt green centered with glowing yellow, tipped with white flames.

Our food went the third day, and the third also saw the last of our water dripped down our parched throats. But on the fourth a green line appeared on the horizon and wearily Devereaux and I bent our backs to the oars, rowing as strongly as we could for the line and shore. We landed near evening, riding the last few hundred yards on a rolling surf, lying weakly in the bottom of the boat, our oars beside us.

Somehow, we slipped through a gap in the barrier reef whose sharp coral should have ripped the bottom out of our boat and flayed the skin from our bodies. But we did and slid smoothly through the fine sand of the sloping beach on the rising tide.

We had no idea where we were but slid weakly over the gunnels and crawled up through the sand to the cool gathering of palms. We found coconuts and with herculean effort smashed them open and drank the milk carefully, letting it trickle slowly into our parched throats. Wherever we were, I knew that we were not on Poulo Condore Island. But it would take us three days of eating coconuts and gathering our strength before we could move off the beach and search the land.

We found a fishing village where lines of fishing stakes ran out from the shore into the water like a mysterious system of half-submerged bamboo fences that formed a maze with the right angle of a bay. At first, there was no sign of life anywhere in the village. Huts sagged, and stone walls that had been erected as a barrier against the storms seemed to have fallen in upon themselves. Back away from the village nearly obscured by palms was a megalith of some ancient god, its face nearly overrun with liana vines crisscrossing its features. No sounds came from the village or even from the woods behind the village. No canoes showed, no bird swung on motionless wings in the sky, and the sun striking off the water like brilliant bubbles burnt my eyes and made me rub them.

Then, in the distance, we heard faint chanting, and canoes came slowly around the point. They appeared to be laden with fishing nets and flowers, and I wondered if this was a combination of funeral and business.

The fishermen were happy to take us to a neighboring island where we could catch a berth on a Swedish freighter working the coast up toward Vietnam. The captain was a good man who had once been forced to spend days in a lifeboat after his ship struck a reef in a storm and sank. After he realized Devereaux was a priest who had escaped from Poulo Condore Island along with an American friend, he gave us a cabin to ourselves, clothes, and promised to set us ashore in Singapore. It was only after a long and heated argument that we talked him into taking us as berth passengers to Saigon.

He shook his head sadly. "You are leaping into the fire when I can give you safety," he said. "This makes no sense to one such as myself. Why would you want to go back to where you were a victim?"

But I had no words for him that would make him understand, and remained silent. Heated anger still smoldered deep inside me at being made a victim when I was a hunter, and I ached to become a hunter once again. This time, however, there would be a difference, and the expected thrill of a hunt began to work its way along my limbs, making them tingle with anticipation.

12 I stood alone at the boat's rail and watched the three hills that marked Vung Tau come closer and closer and the mouth of the Bay of Gan Raie begin to appear from the faint mist that the sun had not burnt completely off the water yet. Behind me, I heard the faint shift of boxes as they moved against their roped bindings that lashed them to the deck of the ship. In the boxes was the contraband being smuggled into the country. The boats seemed to move magically across the bay and entered the river that wound up in a twisting path to Saigon. Thatched huts clung to the edges of the river, and where tree branches hung over the water naked golden bodies showed graciously as they glided through the leaf-dappled water. Boats like Venetian gondolas, high-prowed and high-sterned where a boatman managed a large sweep, moved slowly up and down the river. They passed a boat village where boats were anchored close together and planks laid across their rails to make an artificial passage. Ducks swam at the end of their tethers tied to the boat railings.

I felt, rather than heard, Devereaux move to the rail next to me. He stared out at the approaching hills as well.

"What will you do?" he asked softly.

"Try and find my men," I said. "But I don't expect much luck in that. I'm certain that the team has been broken up and the men sent to other duty stations. But I may find one or two. If not"—I shrugged—"then I shall simply have to make do."

"Saigon can be a very unfriendly place," Devereaux said softly. "Some of the old members of the Binh Xuyen are still around. They aren't a faction anymore, but they do keep their hand in the black market. You can find some of the old ones in Bring Cash Alley. Look for a man called Leclerc. Mention my name. He will help you if he can."

"Thank you," I said. "I'll remember. Leclerc. Bring Cash Alley."

He sighed.

"What will come of you?"

"I'll go back to the cathedral and claim sanctuary first," he said.

"Then, I'll make my way back up to the leper colony. They need me there."

"That's the first place the police will look. They'll find you there," I said.

He smiled. "Yes, probably."

"And this time they will kill you."

"Yes, probably. But a man's death is his own, and frankly, I have lived enough and done enough for others that I think I can choose my own ending or, at least, a part of my own ending. God may have His ideas about that, but I have no intention of allowing Him to be dictatorial in that respect." He laughed. "You know, I never gave a thought to that cliché that dying is easy, living is hard. But there is a great truth to that."

I turned to face him, feeling the sea spray on my face.

"What I don't understand is why you elected to stay where you were all these years? I know what you told me, but *why*?"

A soft laugh came from him. He swayed naturally, easily, to the movement of the ship upon the waves.

"I felt that only the convict knew the isolation that Adam felt, the isolation that man needs to understand the horror of the world, an isolation that could not be learned in a monastery, the isolation that man must experience with others experiencing the same isolation in order to understand the horror that waits around him in his world since he was cast out of Eden."

He turned and faced me and sighed, deeply, as if dragging the pain of the world from deep within his own soul. "My illusions were destroyed one by one until they became a grim humor. Why do some men experience such dangers as only curiosities, consumed with only wondering if they will come out alive or dead?"

"And what did you learn?"

He laughed quietly.

"Men are taught to believe that they cannot live without this thing or another. I discovered that if death becomes meaningless, it is simple to follow that life itself becomes meaningless. And if life becomes meaningless, then God becomes meaningless. And if God is meaningless, what then has meaning?"

We stood silently together at the rail, watching as the captain brought the ship around and dropped anchor to wait for the pilot to come aboard. I climbed to the wheelhouse for a better view of what the French had called Cap St-Jacques, a resort that they had built out of an old fishing village to escape the summer heat of Saigon. In those years the French had tried to a create another Riviera to remind them of the world they had left behind, an arrogance that assured them their civilization was better than the one that had been old when theirs was still being weaned by minor warlords.

The captain grinned at me, his gold tooth reflecting the sun's rays.

"It won't be long. But," he continued soberly, the smile slipping from his face, "there is still time for you to reconsider. Why go back into hell once you have escaped? That suggests only arrogance."

"Questions must be answered," I said quietly.

He nodded and stared out at the sea for a long moment before speaking.

"Revenge? If that is the reason, then it is better to forget and remember that such individuals eventually create their own downfall."

I nodded and remained silent. He started to speak again, then sighed, and together we watched the play of the sunlight upon the waves rolling lazily toward the shore.

We stayed at anchor in the bay until the pilot came aboard to take the ship up the river. The ship slipped into the mouth of the river and began to carefully make its way through the flotsam and garbage drifting down the river and piling up on the lazy bends, but the pilot always found the ever-changing channel. Even here, the forest pressed against the banks of the river, dark green and hostile. The river moved sluggishly here and the pilot nudged me and grinned, his teeth stained red from chewing betel nut.

"Soon," he said, "they will have to dredge the river again or the American boats will not be able to go up and down the river. But they do not like to do that very often, because then they discover the bodies that have been put into the river since the last time they dredged the river. Then the police have to come down and take the bodies away and burn them. Unless the bodies are Americans. Then they have to call the Americans to come and get them and take them and send them home."

He shrugged. "But it doesn't matter who they are. If they have been in the river long, the fish and eels have eaten on them and when the bodies are brought up they stink of death and the stink goes all over the river. That's the best time for us, though, because we do not have to concern ourselves with patrol boats because they are too busy patrolling the dead."

He laughed at his little joke, but he kept his eye on the water ahead, pointing out where ripples gathering in the middle of the river would indicate a snag, where the water swung in a lazy near oxbow and silted the bottom.

The boat landed at the Quai de L'Ysère by the huge old customs shed. But only one customs official was on duty, the others lying up somewhere out of the midday sun. The pier was deserted. The official watched the boat dock, idly swishing away sluggish flies with an ivory-handled flyswatter.

I bowed my shoulders beneath the peasant's clothes I wore, keeping my face averted from the official, hoping that I conveyed the impression that the weight of the world had been draped over my frame. Out of the corner of my eye, I saw his gaze sweep lazily over me, dismissing me contemptuously. I was a faceless nobody in a crowd of faceless individuals whose death would mean only the inconvenience of removing the corpse to an anonymous pit and covering it with lime to help keep the rat population down.

I moved slowly, keeping pace with the others around me. We moved down the quay, groups slowly splintering off as we came to side streets running away from the river. My mouth watered as we walked by stalls of frying foods, melons, fish, and hot and cold drinks. I had no money, though, and swallowed the gushing saliva as I hurried through the market, moving through the city in search of Fell. I desperately needed money and a weapon and his discreet inquiries within Colonel Black's office. But I could not find Fell, although I searched in his old haunts. I dared not go to his office, but I did quietly check his apartment, above a tobacconist on Tu-Do Street after Fell had moved from the Majestic. He wasn't at home.

Then I remembered Nguyen Diem and walked toward the university, where I hoped to find him in his office. First, though, I thought grimly, I had to get there without being recognized by anyone. But other than my height and the slant of my eyes, I blended fairly well into crowds moving slowly along the streets in the noonday sun. I knew, however, that as I came closer to the university I ran a greater risk as clothes climbed the status rank. Then I would stand out from the others—unless there were groundskeepers working. I could slip among them, carrying a hoe or shovel or simply an armful of clippings. The real trouble would come when I tried to enter the buildings, and I had no idea as to which building held Nguyen Diem's office. Or, if I was lucky enough to find it, if he would be willing to help me. The university was a place for the children of old families that had money. Fortunately, old families are like ancient civilizations—they wither and die despite their clinging to crests and the nobility of their ancestors.

I remembered our conversation many weeks ago and hoped that he would be willing to believe me in regard to Lisa Lee's death, although he had no reason to at all. He could even have been the one who had betrayed me. But I had no place else to go unless I left Saigon and tried to find work in the rice paddies where there was not enough work to support a single family, let alone a stranger.

Surprisingly, I moved through the streets without mishap. Few gave me a look, and I realized that there was safety in assuming anonymity. If one did not make eye contact, then one maintained a sort of neutrality and remained invisible to others. Fear has that effect upon people.

Halfway to the university, I could see that I was beginning to draw stares, and abandoned my plan to find Nguyen Diem in his office. Instead, I began the long walk to Old Plantation Road and moved through the heat of the day, feeling my thirst grow, my stomach rumble. I began to grow faint and paused in the shade beneath a banana tree, squatting on my heels like a peasant. I hung my head and panted, watching the world swim before the sweat dripping into my eyes. I felt like driftwood in a pool washed back to shore by bitter waves.

A breath of cool wind came from the south and I raised my head and turned my face into it, enjoying it almost as much as I would a drink of cool water. The leaves rustled above my head. I looked down at my shadow on the dirt, watching it weave slightly from side to side with my movement. I felt drawn down to it and tried to remain motionless. A beetle wiggled up from the dust and moved in small circles before gathering its direction and moving off. I heard a growl and looked up to see a yellow mongrel staring at me, its lips drawn back from its teeth. I held its eyes and slowly it stalked stiff-legged across the road, giving me a wide berth. I heard a loud screech and looked up to see a kite gliding gracefully on the breeze, wings outstretched and trembling.

Heat came down like an anvil, shimmering waves rising from the dust of the road. I began to fantasize, remembering the Lake of the Hidden Sword where Vietnamese royalty often took their walks beneath the leaf-dappled paths toward the Garden of the Moon. A watchman beat the hours on a drum to warn the commoners when the hour had turned and it was time for them to make themselves scarce so the royalty would have the leisure of solitude among themselves.

Suddenly a sorrow heaped itself upon my heart. My shadow looked as gaunt as an aged crane and I felt the marks the past days, weeks, and months had left upon my body like the beating of waves upon a graveled beach. Tears gathered and began to drip from my eyes to fall like scattered dewdrops from a shaken flower into the dust and onto my peasant dress.

Then, a darkening came over the day, and I saw a horse ridden by an aged man coming across the dry-brown prairie grasses dotted here and there with buffalo wallows. A white colt passed by, leaping and kicking its heels in the joy of freedom.

"Wake! Wake!" the old man cried. He waved a coup stick at me.

Then, behind him, riding upon a red horse, I saw a beautiful woman with raven black hair, dressed in white doeskin. She guided the horse with her knees. Behind her rolled heavy black thunderclouds with streaks of lightning leaking from them. She pulled the restless horse to a stand and looked down at me. I knew her; She-Who-Comes-In-Dreams, and knew that at that precise moment Vietnam had ceased to exist and I had been swept back for the moment by the cold winds to the Rosebud Reservation.

"You have been searching for me since you left home," she said. "I am White Buffalo Woman."

"I searched for you before I left home," I said.

"Yes. But you were not ready for me then."

"And now?"

Her face remained sober. "Your anger covers you like darkness. You are a demon dwelling deep within your own thoughts. You must cleanse yourself of this, for otherwise you shall never find the spring that feeds my heart. The drums will speak always for you, but you shall never know peace until you have passed over the Wheel of Fire that sears sinful flesh and shatters bones to dust. See the future you yet may change!"

She waved her hand and the blackness rolled up and over us. Lightning and thunder came over us. I saw the old man's horse leap into the lake and die while the old man's body smashed like dry driftwood upon the spray-splashed rocks. His angry ghost rose from the waves with a nerve-shattering howl, and in one hand he gripped a redstone peace pipe and in the other a bloody war ax, and with the ax he slashed the waves crashing against the rocks until they turned red with blood.

Then, out of the waters rose a black tower, ominous beneath a bright moonlit sky, and around it stretched an impenetrable forest. At the far end of the forest, a magnificent snowcapped mountain rose majestically toward the sky.

A hand jerked my shoulder back and forth rhythmically.

"Wingo?"

I blinked and looked up into the dwarf's face peering closely, anxiously, into mine.

"Wingo?"

"Yes," I croaked. I felt laughter bubbling up inside me and opened my mouth to let the laughter out but only released a bullfrog's croak.

"You've been out in the sun too long," he said.

"Add the Indian to mad dogs and Englishmen," I said, or tried to say, but the words caught at the back of my dry throat.

He pulled at my arm, trying to help me rise. I stumbled to my feet and stood swaying despite his balancing hold. We staggered toward his car parked on the shoulder of the road beneath a banana tree.

"Come on," he grunted with effort. "I can't carry you all the way."

I placed one wooden step in front of the other, concentrating on each as if a stiff, wooden-kneed puppet at the mercy of a puppet master. My joints ached, and fever seemed to settle upon my brow, and I knew that the grueling diet on Poulo Condore Island had begun to take its toll. Yet I knew I was lucky, and I wondered how the priest was making it after staying longer on the island than I. And then I remembered his plan to seek momentary sanctuary at the cathedral, where he would be able to rebuild his strength.

Yet where was my sanctuary?

Nguyen Diem opened the passenger side of his car and turned me so I sat down abruptly on the seat, cracking my head against the top of the doorjamb. Stars and spirals looped in front of my eyes.

"Sorry," he mumbled, struggling to swing my legs inside the car. "Come on; help me."

Woodenly I lifted my legs, and Nguyen pushed hard against them, forcing them inside the car. I leaned my head against the back of the seat as he rushed around and climbed behind the wheel. We moved away in a cloud of dust and a squeal of gears as he shifted his way through the transmission.

"What were you doing alongside the road?" he asked.

"Waiting for you," I said. My legs began to tremble. I gripped my knees hard to try to stop them, but the trembling moved up through my hands, my forearms, my biceps, then my shoulders, and soon I was shaking like Saint Vitus' dance.

"Waiting for me?"

"I had nowhere else to go," I mumbled.

He glanced nervously into the rearview mirror. "This is bad, Wingo. Word has already gone out that you and the priest have escaped from Poulo Condore. There's a reward out."

"A large reward?"

He shook his head. "Doesn't matter. People will sell their mothers for a few piasters right now. There's nowhere safe for you in Saigon."

"Maybe," I said.

My eyes began to droop and I struggled to keep them open.

He made a rude sound, then sighed. "Did you kill her?"

"No."

"How can I be certain?"

"You can't. But why would I be here if I didn't think you'd believe me?"

"And you're not a foolish man."

"That's debatable," I answered. "Wouldn't a foolish man be in this situation?"

"Yes, but so would an honorable one," he said. "The question is, which are you?"

"Just a man," I said. "Nothing more."

I yawned.

"I can hide you for a few days," he said. "I don't get many callers out on Old Plantation Road and my neighbors are far enough away not to notice, either."

"I need clothes. Some money. A weapon."

He sighed. "We'll talk about this later. After you're rested."

I think I fell asleep at that point, for I vaguely being aware of stumbling from the automobile to the spare bedroom of his bungalow before collapsing upon the bed. Dimly I recall a mosquito netting being tucked in around the edge of the mattress, then falling into a deep well, smelling dank decay as I was falling, falling down into the supreme folly.

I awoke to the smell of fried bananas and coffee. A small carafe of water had been placed on a table next to my bed during the night. I reached under the mosquito netting and took it, draining it in one long drink. A great thirst had come upon me in the night, and I felt light-headed despite the sleep that I had. I rose and found that Nguyen Diem had replaced my clothes with white linen pants and a long-sleeved shirt and espadrilles. The shirt was loose and the pants too short, but the espadrilles fit comfortably. I dressed and went out into the living room of the bungalow and found my host busy in the kitchen, walking along a small ramp that had been built to allow him a decent access to the counters and stove and zinc sink. He moved nimbly along the walkway, briskly cutting melon, readying toast and muffins, a platter of cheeses.

"Good morning," I said. "And thanks for the new clothes."

He waved my thanks away impatiently. "No matter. It is safer if you dress like one of the decadent French in a casual parody of Somerset Maugham." He laughed. "And it will be safer in case one of my neighbors who has never cared what happens here before suddenly becomes curious about who is staying with Nguyen the Dwarf." He bowed mockingly. "The reason my neighbors tend to avoid my presence is the result of a mysterious merging of the duality of man, the physical and spiritual. The physical is composed of matter; the spiritual of the mind, the aesthetics, if you will. Oddly enough, size in one connotes to certain people the status of the other. Yet they do not see anything odd in the Neanderthal giant who cannot tie his own shoelaces. Odd, don't you think? What man decides to award his prejudices to?"

I shook my head. "The sign of the devil, the harbinger of evil, short people have been the bane of man for centuries. Quilp in Dickens's *The Old Curiosity Shop*, for instance."

"Yes, I am quite aware of Dickens's Quilp," he said drily. "In some ways Dickens set progress back two hundred years. Still, he was a great writer for some of his work. Would you help set the table, please? I would imagine that you are a bit hungry, by now."

Obediently I carried the plates into the living room, where a small mahogany table spread with a gleaming white linen table-cloth stood. Within minutes, we had the table readied, and I was enjoying my cantaloupe when he asked again, "Did you kill her?"

I shook my head. "No, I didn't. In fact, I had decided that I wasn't going to follow up on the assignment. Then, she simply disappeared. That was Saturday, the day that I had planned on going into headquarters and telling them that I wasn't going to follow up on the assignment. But instead, I was congratulated, sort of backhandedly, if you understand"—he nodded—"on having completed my assignment. That was the first time that I saw the photographs that had been taken of the crime scene.

"I was sent back to my unit with a new assignment. But the assignment was a setup; we were meant to fail. In fact, if something could have gone wrong and didn't, I don't know what it could possibly be."

"They found one of your dog tags near the body, I understand," he said, his eyes steady on my face.

"Yes. But I didn't lose it there, because I wasn't there. The third day I was in Saigon, I noticed that my boots had been cleaned and polished. The laces had been replaced with new ones, and that is when I saw that the dog tag I normally have tied in the laces of one boot was missing. I carry another in a pocket. I never wear them around my neck. Superstition, I guess. Although," I added, "in this instance, a costly one for me. I still have the one I carry in my pocket. Or had. When I was arrested, that was taken from me."

"So, who had taken your dog tag? The valet or bootblack who cared for your boots? Did you ask them?"

I shook my head. "I made a casual inquiry at the desk and then forgot about it."

"So what are you going to do?"

"Find who killed her. If I can," I said grimly.

"Even then, you might not succeed in clearing your name," he said. "Have you thought about that?"

"I've thought about it," I said quietly. "I thought about it every day I was on that damned island. It's not something that you easily forget."

He nodded and toyed with his food for a moment, and suddenly I was aware that he had deliberately fixed the large breakfast for me. I was grateful. And still hungry.

"Will you help me?" I asked, helping myself to the cheese plate.

He looked startled for a moment, then smiled, his lips turning up into deep scimitars in his cheeks. He sat back in his chair, his eyes shining like black diamonds.

"By help, I presume you mean not to escape, but to find the one responsible for killing Lisa Lee? By the way, that wasn't her name, you know."

"Her name doesn't matter. It was a death that shouldn't have happened. Not in that way."

He sobered for a moment, drumming his fingers on the tabletop. His brow furrowed in a deep frown.

"You do know that she was an agent for the North?"

I shrugged. "That still doesn't matter. She didn't deserve to die in that matter."

"One could argue that there have been atrocities committed on both sides."

"One could argue that war is an atrocity by itself and lends itself to such things. That still doesn't make that death right."

"Which is why you were going to refuse the assignment," he mused, resuming the tapping of his fingers. "It wasn't the death that mattered; it was the manner in which the death was to be committed. An ethical question rather than a revenge."

"That, too," I said.

"A soldier with ethics. An *American* soldier with ethics who has seen unethical approaches to war and still holds to principles. That is unusual." He shook his head. "I might be compromised on *both* sides if I help you. One side is bad enough for a man in my position."

"What is your position?"

He pressed his lips together, thinking, then rose and went to the drinks table.

"I think we might consider this a bit over a glass of wine. I know it is early, but I have no lectures today and my office hours can be canceled." He shrugged. "And it is an interesting diversion to consider. Theoretically, of course."

"Of course," I said as he selected a bottle and brought it back to the table.

"What about your friend Fell?" he asked.

I paused, considering. What about Fell? He had his strengths as a friend, but he also had been through more than most soldiers, most humans, for that matter, go through in the course of a war. I had seen his hands shake when he talked about the possibility of going back into covert actions, the look of quiet desperation in his eyes when he talked about the new project that the Lincoln Library boys were beginning to put in place and had tabbed him for an active part in even though his wounds were still healing. His *physical* wounds. Those boys didn't care much for the mental wounds such physical wounds caused. Being shot was not highly traumatic for some, but for others it was a major shock, a trauma that they tried to hide as best they could. I wasn't certain that Fell had managed to learn that yet or even if he would ever be able to learn that. Some are destined to keep their horrors alive for one reason or another or are afraid to tuck them away for fear that they will spring upon them when they are unaware and destroy the happiness of the moment that they are enjoying.

So, what to do with Fell? He could be valuable, but he could just as easily become a liability when I—perhaps we, if Nguyen Diem accepted the responsibility of helping me—could least afford such a liability. I liked Fell and trusted him to a point. But where I was going now was tenuous at best, and would I be able to watch Fell and my back and still move in the various directions I would have to move all at the same time?

"He may be useful," I said cautiously.

Nguyen Diem pursed his lips, then said, *"Ban cung sinh dao tac. Sometimes,* we must take a chance on people. They may surprise us when we least expect it."

"True. But I think chances on people must be taken with a great caution."

"You are taking one with me," he said.

"Co chi lam quan, co gan lam giau," I answered.

"Ah, you seem to have more than a simple command of our language; you know our proverbs as well. Yes, fortune does favor the brave, but sometimes the brave can be foolish."

"You don't think involving Fell is a good idea, then?"

"I didn't say that; he is your friend and you know him much better than I. I think the question is whether you feel the situation, the moment, is serious enough to trust old friendships that may have withered like the late-blooming jackfruit in autumn; it appears to be sweet and edible as it is in the spring, but one bite will tell you it is bitter."

"But still edible to a starving man."

He nodded. "Yes, but in this instance, you must remember the consequences of what will happen to you if you are caught by the Vietnamese: you will be shot. And, if your trial is any indication, if you are caught by the Americans, you will probably be turned over to the Vietnamese." He shook his head as I started to speak, and held up his hand to stop me. "We are in political times, now, my friend. A country's loyalty is not to the individual at the moment. The war is not going well, despite what your superiors tell the newsmen and correspondents. What was once a simple war is now a tightrope, and politicians have stepped into where the military should have complete control. That comes from not having a decisive victory. Right now, the war is in a delicate balance. Neither side has a clear advantage. Do you follow chess? No? I have followed it for years, the great matches between the grand masters. The majority of those games end in stalemate because no one can gain a distinct advantage over the other, and they replay the game over and over by themselves to see where they could have made a different move that would have changed the outcome. Sometimes, they find it; sometimes, they don't, because there isn't any precise moment that could have changed the outcome of the game. The United

States had the opportunity to end this war early, but it elected not to bring its queen into play by pursuing the war as a war instead of electing to fight it in the way North Vietnam had decided to fight it. The United States tried a modified Sicilian defense instead of attacking at certain strategic moments when North Vietnam was extremely vulnerable. Your country has an incredible war machine, but where does your commander keep the strength? In Saigon, so he can show visiting politicians how strong the American forces are, instead of committing them to the field. The queen is never brought into play, my friend, and because of that, South Vietnam and the United States will eventually lose the war. The cautious player who has strength on his side and elects not to commit it against one who has little strength is one who will lose the match."

"So the war is lost, then?"

He nodded sadly. "Yes, I think it is. Although that will not be determined for many years yet."

"So we should not use Fell?"

"Fell is your queen. If you use him and lose him, then you could lose everything."

"But if he proves to not be vulnerable?"

He spread his hands. "Who knows? It depends upon how much strength he has. I do not know this. But you do. A good chess player is one who guards his queen at all times, but not to the extent of losing the game."

I nodded. "He may have to be sacrificed."

"Yes. But the queen must always be guarded, and yet you have to be willing to let her go if the proper moment arrives."

"Then we shall use Fell, but cautiously. He will be able to get us some information that we can't get ourselves."

"By 'we,' I presume you have already decided that I will help you in this endeavor?"

"Won't you?"

He nodded solemnly; then his face split into a wide grin. "Yes, I will. Because I also do not believe the death of Lisa Lee was a good death. You have read Camus?"

I nodded.

"Then you understand. Although there are no good deaths, some are better than others. It is the way one dies that is important. As important as the way one lives. Besides"—he paused to laugh—"no one has ever had such a use for me before. It is good to be seen as something other than a misfit to society."

I stretched my hand across the table and he took it, his small and pudgy, not much larger than the hand of a half-grown child, but the hand of a man nevertheless. He gripped my hand firmly.

13 I found him at the Club Eve, working on a martini on the rocks with a stick of olives in it, alone at an isolated table for two. The room was cool and dark, with black and white tiles on the floor and potted palms scattered here and there, as I remembered them, to give a sense of privacy to its "clients." There were no serious casual drinkers here; a few soldiers who proved to be too rambunctious for the clientele were being politely but forcibly removed. A low and familiar susurration slipped satisfactorily back into the room once the soldiers had been removed and people once again relaxed and turned to their own private moments.

Fell sat, staring deep into his glass as if it was a scrying mirror, his brow furrowed as if trying to discern the future. I waited for a moment, considering him: a muscle twitched in his left cheek, his fingers drummed the table, and I noticed that the ashtray on the table was nearly overflowing from his chain-smoking. I was surprised; Fell had never smoked when I knew him or, if so, rarely, and only when he *wanted* a cigarette and did not *need* it. He had been a man who carefully guarded his weaknesses, held a rigid hold upon himself with everything. But since I had brought him back from the camp where he had been taken—or would *prison* be a better word?—he had slowly slipped away from the person he had been. I became aware that I was watching a man who had fallen away from the road he had taken and was now lost in the briars and brambles leading up the mountain to the mouth of the cave that led down deep into Dante's hell.

He glanced up and saw me standing by the bar. His mouth dropped open in surprise and he squinted, trying to bring me into sharp focus. His features were slack, and I knew that the martini in front of him had not been the first of the evening. I crossed to his table and stood beside it.

"Hello, Fell," I said. "Surprised to see me?"

"Wingo!" he exclaimed loudly, then glanced around, fearful that someone might have overheard him. "Wingo. How—what are you doing here?"

"Visiting you," I said casually.

"I mean—"

"May I join you?" I asked, interrupting him before he began the surprised exclamations that might draw attention to us.

"Join me?" His brow furrowed, then cleared. He made an attempt to rise, but he was "too much with drink taken," as he liked to say in the old days, and slumped back into his bamboo-slatted chair.

"Of course. Of course. I'm sorry. I should have—"

"Forget it," I said, pulling out the other chair and sitting.

A waiter slipped silently up to our table and I ordered a glass of cognac that I didn't really want, but beer was considered gauche in the Club Eve, where the French elite who had elected to stay after Dien Bien Phu still maintained their evening cocktail hour. I glanced at his glass. He caught my look and smiled lopsidedly.

"Evening time," he said, molding the words carefully, as one does who has drunk more than he intended. "Debating on where to go to eat. But food hasn't any appeal to me right now." He managed a smile. "I've got my orders. Bien Hoa. I'm going back in."

"Sorry."

He shrugged. "Well, that's the name of the game, isn't it? Once in, never out." He laughed, but there was a falseness to the laugh nearing hysteria. He took a deep drink of the martini and held the glass up at the bartender, who nodded. Fell finished the drink and began to chew the olives off the stick one by one.

"Isn't that sort of like escaping from Devil's Island?"

"I don't know," I said. "I've never escaped from Devil's Island."

"But you have Poulo Condore."

"Yes."

"You know they'll be looking for you, don't you?"

I gave him a small smile. "Even here? Do you think they'd believe I am dumb enough to come back here?"

He gave a short bark of laughter. "But you *are* dumb enough to come back here. You're sitting in front of me right now."

"Yes, but *they* don't know that, do they?"

"You do have a big pair, you know?" he said quietly as the waiter appeared with our drinks. He sat back and waited while the waiter silently placed our drinks in front of us, then left.

Fell leaned forward, hands cupping the glass, his eyes intent upon mine.

"So how did you get out of there?"

"I found a boat. At the turning of the moon, left."

"But you don't know how to sail."

"Sometimes all a man needs is a bit of luck. Like now."

His eyebrows rose. He puffed out his cheeks and blew softly through pursed lips. "So. Now, you come to me? What luck do I have anymore?"

"You're alive," I said simply.

"I'm not certain that is an endorsement," he muttered. He took a swallow, a smaller one this time. "What is it you want from me?"

"First, money. But not yours. That's too easily traced. Get it from the office. You know, paid informer and all that rot."

"I'll have to have something to show for it," he warned.

"I'll get you something to show for it," I said. "Then, when you go to Supply to pick up your gear, get a double issue. Try to get your hands on a grease gun. People know I like the Thompson, but you've always favored a grease gun. They won't think it too odd that you want more than one. You can spin some sort of story, if you like. They won't check it out."

He shook his head. "Supply is tightening up since the sergeant major got caught with his hands in the till."

I thought a minute. "Then take a clerk with you and have him outfitted. Someone my size you can trust."

"Why not just pick it up off Bring Cash Alley?"

"I've got some other things that I need from there. I want to spread what I need around so it won't all point to one person."

"How much money you going to need?"

"A grand ought to do it," I said. "I need more, I'll come back. By the way, do you have any right now? I just remembered that I need a pistol."

He reached into his pocket and pulled out five twenty-dollar American bills. They would be worth three times that on the black market. "Will this help?"

"Thanks," I said, pocketing the money.

"Where you going? Bring Cash Alley?"

"The best place to get something off-line."

"You have a contact?"

"I have a place. That's enough. Now, what about the grand?"

He shook his head. "We're on the edge, now. My orders are in, and it won't be long before the office starts shutting my files down. We've got a day, maybe two. No more."

I nodded. "I figured as much. That's why you're going to have to pull some late hours, wrapping up the final files. You know, the dedicated soldier who doesn't want to leave a problem for his successor."

He laughed. "There's nothing there that can't be dumped in the wastebasket without a loss."

"Again, they don't know that. Meanwhile, I want the Lisa Lee file."

He stared at me, the glass frozen halfway to his mouth. "Now I *know* you are mad. Do you have any idea where those files are?"

"No."

"COMSACINTEL, T-3 section. I know because I saw the label on the envelope before it went into the courier's briefcase. How the hell am I going to get into there?"

I sat back in my chair, musing. The T-3 section was highest security in-country. Only a few individuals even got in through the door, let alone into the back rooms where the legendary black file cabinets were kept for covert operations. Rumor had it that only three people could go into that room outside the commander. I tasted my cognac—watered down like almost everything else in the country. I replaced my glass.

"Now, why do you suppose that file would be sent there? It's only a murder file. What is there about it that would warrant sending it there? What is in that file? Did you get a name or number concerning who was to sign for it?"

He shook his head, looking miserable. "Hell, I could have been shot just for recognizing the designation label. We can fuck around with a lot of things, Wingo, but there are some things that you just keep yourself away from. T-3 is one of those. You know that; you've been around as long as I have."

"Mm-hm," I said, absently making wet concentric circles upon the top of the table with my glass. Condensation gathered on the sides. "So, why would the file on the murder of one whore in a city of whores draw such attention?"

He wiped a shaky hand over his closely shaven head. "Obvious. There's something in the file that no one wants seen."

"Then why keep it where there's a danger that it could be?"

He laughed. "And who's going to get into T-3 to see what is in the file?"

"That may be, but the only safe way is to destroy everything. Something isn't right here."

I drummed my fingers on the tabletop, trying to think. Why? It didn't make any sense at all. In a country where every other cleaning man and woman worked for the North, why take a chance? Some things need to be destroyed as soon as possible.

"Who's in charge of T-3?" I asked.

He shrugged. "You mean the office itself or under whose umbrella it can be found?"

"Both. I may need to get to both."

"Jesus," he moaned. "You don't do things halfway, do you? Colonel Black handles T-3 along with Major Frank Norris. But both of them work directly under General John Parker Davis. Chances of getting to any of them is nil. Give it up."

I smiled at him. "There's always a weak link when more than one man is involved. Always. The trick is to find it."

"The trick is to not get yourself killed *before* you find it," he said morosely, then added, "and, come to think of it, *after* as well. What are you going to do if you do find something?"

"I'll know more about that when I find it," I said quietly.

"And if you find the one who did kill the girl?" Fell asked.

"I'll kill him," I said.

Fell had a hundred dollars that he let me have before we left the Club Eve, he to weave his way home and start working on digging out what information and money he could get away with before Black's office closed him down on pending orders while I made my way to Bring Cash Alley a few blocks from Tan Son Nhut. I wore black trousers and a white shirt to blend in with the Vietnamese, trusting my Indian features to allow me to slip past the bored MPs who would be looking for trouble with American soldiers and not a Vietnamese who seemed to be going about his business.

Nguyen had promised to spend the day canvasing his friends to see what they might have heard about Lisa Lee's murder. When I offered to go with him, he smiled and said that there were places that it would be better I avoided. Although I might fool the American soldiers, the Vietnamese would know that I was not one of them. The tribal instinct is strong and although many soldiers were convinced that all the "slopes" looked alike, they weren't.

Bring Cash Alley was a narrow street that wound its way through several connecting alleys down to the quay where the boat people had made their own village after being forced down the Saigon River from the north, living in tight boat colonies where the river looked wide and yellow with silt and oil slicks floated down in rainbow patterns with dead fish floating belly up in the current. The alley pulsed with all walks of life and could be a dangerous place for soldiers who were not careful to watch their backs. Street gangs walked the walk, boldly eyeing those who might prove weak. It wasn't that unusual to see someone forced down a side alley where he would be murdered and stripped of what he had, which would appear within minutes at one of the crowded stalls. The smell of fried foods hung in the narrow walkway, the jabber of voices arguing prices bouncing off the smoke gray walls of the buildings that had been old before World War I. My mouth watered as I smelled boiling shrimp and rice and meat being slowly turned over glowing braziers. Cartons of American cigarettes were boldly displayed, filched from PX warehouses. Penicillin could be bought at a dear price. Clothes hung on ropes stretched between the supporting timbers of the stalls. Battlefield souvenirs: dog tags, Zippo cigarette lighters, wallets, keys, Saint Christopher and Saint Michael medals, ponchos, boxes of canned heat, tubes of ointment for jungle rot, other tubes for hemorrhoids—the infantryman's curse—boxes of C rations, boots, socks, jungle blouses, anything could be found that might bring a few piasters.

Behind the stalls were the narrow doorways of shops that specialized in other items, however, and that is where I headed. I stepped into a small doorway and met a man squatting on his heels, chopsticks clacking busily against a bowl of rice mixed with pieces of boiled fish. He stared at me impassively, studying me shrewdly.

"I understand that this is a place where one might buy something unusual," I said.

"Oh?" he replied. He tweezered a piece of fish and carried it to his mouth, chewing with his mouth open. "And where might you have heard that?"

I made an offhand gesture. "Here and there. You know how talk is on the streets."

"You speak Vietnamese pretty good for an American," he said.

"Thank you," I answered.

"How do I know you are not one sent by the police? You look enough like us to pass for the Americans, but the Americans are very stupid. They think we do not know the difference between a snake and an eel."

I shrugged. "There are Americans and there are other Americans."

"And which are you?"

"One who does not need the other Americans to know where he is."

He smiled. His teeth were black from betel nut and opium pipes.

"And how do I know this?"

"You don't."

He nodded and went back to eating his rice. I squatted on my heels, flat-footed as the Vietnamese did, and waited. When he had finished, he wiped his mouth with his sleeve and placed his bowl and chopsticks to the side.

"What is it you want?"

"I understand that it is possible to buy a weapon here."

One eyebrow twitched and he looked behind me at the door. He shouted an order, and a young boy appeared from a beaded curtain behind him. He told the boy to go out and look and see if Americans were in the street or the Vietnamese police. He nodded and left. The man smiled again.

"Of course, that means nothing, you understand. Just a precaution."

"It is a wise man who takes precautions," I said politely.

"You do not take offense?"

"There is no reason to take offense."

The boy reappeared and shook his head and disappeared again behind the beaded curtain. The man pursed his lips, then nodded.

"All right. What is it you wish?"

"I want an American pistol. A .45. I am told that you might have such a thing."

"Such a thing could be very expensive," he said.

I knew then that we were about to enter into negotiations and waited politely for him to name a price. He did: a hundred thousand piasters. I shook my head.

"If I buy one that is a good one, I will pay in American dollars."

This time his eyebrow rose higher and he looked uncomfortable for a moment, but I could see the interest in his eyes. American dollars could be doubled on the black market exchange if someone had the right connections. I had no doubt that he had those connections.

"It is illegal to trade in American dollars," he said.

I shrugged. "It is illegal to sell weapons."

He nodded and studied me carefully, then made up his mind.

"A hundred dollars."

I shook my head. "That is very expensive. Fifty."

He laughed and rubbed his hands together. "I cannot sell at that price. You are not being very reasonable. Ninety."

"Seventy," I said.

"Eighty." He spread his hands in front of him. "That is a fair price."

I pretended to ponder his last offer. It was a fair price and I knew it. But I also knew that if I snapped at his offer, then he would know that I needed the pistol and needed it now. That might affect any future deals we might have. I didn't know if I would ever have need of him again, but this was not the time to burn bridges.

"All right," I said at last. "But this is much money to pay for something that I have never seen. And I would want three clips as well for that price."

A faint smile touched his lips and I knew that my response had been correct. I had given more than I really wanted but wanted more in return. Not that much more, just a gesture on his part, and ammunition clips were among the easiest items to obtain. He would lose nothing on the exchange but might gain a future customer who would want more.

He called and again the boy appeared behind the beaded curtain. The man gave the boy orders, and he disappeared.

"This will take some time," the man said. "I do not keep this merchandise here. Would you care for some tea while we wait?"

He gestured toward a copper kettle setting on top of a brazier. Coals glowed softly beneath soft ash beneath the kettle. A porcelain tea service sat on a small black-lacquered table next to it. Delicate stems of bamboo had been painted on the cups and saucers.

"Tea would be nice," I said. "Please."

He nodded and reached over to remove the kettle. He took a handful of dried leaves from a tin, crushed them gently between his palms, and placed them in a small pot on the table. He poured hot water from the kettle into the pot and replaced the lid.

"It may not be to your liking," he said apologetically. "It is oolong. Not many Americans care for it."

"Oolong is a good tea. If the leaves are lightly fermented."

His face broke into a broader smile. "I see that you are not the American we have come to expect in Vietnam. Have you been here long?"

"Yes," I said, remaining vague. "But I plan on remaining longer. It is a good place. Or could be if it were not for the war."

"Yes," he said sadly. "The war. That doesn't not make this a good place. Still, there are some places where the war has not touched. And those are the places where Americans do not go, for they are the places where they are not welcome. They are also those places where the American soldier cannot find what he wants."

He looked knowingly at me, and I nodded back sagely. I knew the places he referred to were those places where the American's narcissistic vanity would be frowned upon. If an American visited them, he would have to be an apologist for not only his country but also himself, and American soldiers were not given to undergoing an apotheosis, for they did not want to see themselves as others saw them. They preferred the neon places with long mahogany bars and brass foot rails and wood-bladed fans hanging from the ceilings and the air thick with the smell of draft beer and whiskey and cigarette smoke, and young girls, many of them still in their early teens, wore *ao dai*s that the soldiers called Suzie Wong dresses, slit up to the hip to show the entire gleaming leg, and no undergarments. These were the places where the soldiers could go and forget that their souls had been branded by sudden machine-gun fire spitting out from tall

elephant grass while they raced for the cover of banyan trees, holding their helmets tightly upon their heads against the thump of mor-
tars raining down upon them, and hoping that they would not step
into a hole where punji sticks covered with human dung waited for
them.

"Yes, I would imagine there are those places," I said. "There is a
need for those places where people can go and remember what
they are."

He remained silent for a long moment, considering me, then
said, "I think you would be welcome in those places."

The boy reappeared and silently handed the man a package
wrapped in plain brown paper and slipped away. The man took a
small knife, cut the twine holding the package together, then un-
wrapped the paper, carefully folding it to save it for its next use.

A Colt .45, lightly oiled, lay in his lap. He picked it up, slid the
slide half-open to check the chamber, then handed it to me, butt first.

I took it and quickly disassembled it, checking the parts. It had
been used sparingly, the grooves in the barrel showing no wear, the
trigger assembly still nearly blue, the hammer face shiny, with no
pits. I had been lucky; it had been a good buy. I reassembled the
pistol and laid it in my lap. I reached into my pocket and removed
four twenty-dollar bills and handed them across to him. He glanced
at them, held them up to the light, sniffed them, then nodded with
satisfaction and folded them, slipping them inside the black shirt he
wore. He handed me three clips; I was surprised to see that they
were fully loaded, the fat cartridges gleaming softly with oil.

He noted my surprise. "Clips are not much use if they are empty.
It is my gift to you. I think that you are one who has need of help.
There is much talk in the market of two men who escaped from
Poulo Condore. An American and a French priest. The priest has his
church to help him, but the American is alone and must stay alone.
Yet there may come a time when such a man might need a place to
go where others cannot find him. There is a place in the mountains.
A small inn that is owned by a woman whose husband was Cao Dai
and killed by the police, who thought he was working with the people from the North. Her name is Simone. It is a place where war has
not touched it. Near the Cao Bai Pass. You will find it west of Lang
Vei. Go to the first tavern and ask for it. A man will take you to it."

"Thank you. You have been most kind to one you do not know you can trust."

"A man in my position learns quickly who he may trust," he said. "You may use my name when you get to the tavern. The man who works there has a bad eye. You will know him by that. Tell him that Quang has said he is to take you to the Place of Whispers."

I thanked him again and rose. I slipped a clip into the Colt and concealed it beneath my shirt. I put the other clips into my left-hand pocket, bowed, and left.

Outside, the alley looked dark and surreal with the smoke rising from the cooking braziers but spreading out down the alley instead of dissipating into the air. I glanced up at the sky; the sun was gone and thick gray thunderclouds were rolling in. Lightning flashed within their depths and I knew that a heavy shower was about to settle over the city. It didn't seem to make any difference to those who moved up and down the alley intent upon business, though. From somewhere came the sharp twang of a musical instrument accompanying someone who sang in a high-pitched nasal voice that reminded me of the screech of a windmill needing oiling. I felt like electric sparks were jumping off my terminals and stepped into the shadows next to the doorway to scan the street, searching for whatever it was that made my nerves hum like high-voltage wires. I saw nothing that I wouldn't have expected to see in that alley, and that bothered me greatly. Bring Cash Alley always had something unusual happening in it. The unusual was when everything seemed normal, as it did now.

Cautiously I stepped down into the street and slipped in among the crowd, working my way through the mass of people with my elbows and shoulders, keeping my hands close to my waist. Garlic and onions seemed to rise from the people around me, clogging my nose, and I breathed gently through my open mouth to keep from gagging. I glanced around, feeling myself in a concrete jungle, my senses reacting as they would in the high mountains or walking across an exposed rice paddy, trying to sense what could happen before it did. Many soldiers were wandering among the stalls in the five o'clock afternoon, looking for bargains, finding a few.

The .45 felt heavy in my belt and I made a mental note to try to visit a leather worker and have a shoulder holster made that would fit beneath a loose shirt or jacket.

I stepped under an awning and pretended to study the wares of a betel nut–chewing woman who did her best to sell a cigarette lighter made out of a .50-caliber cartridge. I pretended interest while watching out of the corner of my eye for someone who also stopped at a stall.

And saw him.

An American. Black hair and eyes, dressed in casual slacks and a Hawaiian shirt boldly decorated with parrots, which hung outside his pants. The shirt was unbuttoned halfway down his chest and I had little doubt as to why. I probably wouldn't have noticed him—there were other Americans in the alley wearing strange clothes—but Americans don't stop in front of a booth selling eel blood for sexual potency and pretend interest in buying an eel, watching its throat slit with a small filleting knife and the blood caught in a glass to be drunk immediately.

I smiled thinly, then shook my head at the arguing harridan and turned abruptly away, walking rapidly down toward the quay, smelling the cool, dank smell of old brick in the alleyways. I took a sharp turn into a narrow, twisting alley, then ran along it. Behind me, I could hear his feet slapping the bricks like wet mops. I ran easily, looking for a deep doorway from which I might surprise him as he passed.

I heard his footsteps quickening as he came down the alley and discovered that I had disappeared. I pulled back deeper into the dark recess of the doorway, waiting.

He came abreast of the doorway and passed. I stepped out, slipping the pistol from my waistband, cocking it. He froze, keeping his hands away from his body.

"You have a piece," I said conversationally. "Let it drop. Two fingers. I see more, I'll put a .45 in your back."

He began to argue in Vietnamese.

"I know you're an American," I said quietly. "Besides, your accent is terrible. The Presidio should really focus more on teaching dialects. Now, who sent you?"

He remained silent. I sighed. There were always some who believed that they still had control of a situation when they were caught. But they were never trained for what the other person might be willing to do. There was still some Galahadic concept of war floating around among certain departments and with certain soldiers. I knew him: valiant dreams, romantic returns after the brave wound in the shoulder, a chest filled with medals, and sweet Suzy Sue throwing her pale white arms around his neck and pressing soft breasts hard against his chest with a promise of what would be delivered later that night.

"Turn around."

Slowly he turned around, his face set hard, but with a certain smugness about his eyes that suggested he knew that he was safe from being shot.

I smiled at him and suddenly slashed him across the face, dragging the front sight of the Colt along his cheek, slicing it open. He staggered and automatically dropped his hands in a defensive mode. I took a rocker step backward, then forward, the toe of my shoe connecting solidly with his groin. He fell to the ground, his hands cupped around the hurt deep within him. I stepped forward, reversed the pistol, gripping it by the barrel, and hammered the butt into his mouth. Teeth snapped and broke and blood gushed out of his mouth. He moaned, and I pressed the barrel tightly against his temple.

"If I shoot now, your head will explode like a pumpkin and muffle the sound of the shot. So it doesn't matter to me. Not one way or the other. Might matter to you, though."

"Shoot," he said through gritted teeth.

I shrugged, then slipped the pistol down to his knee, pressed the barrel hard against the top of his knee, and pulled the trigger. The explosion was loud in the alley, but I knew we were deep enough into the labyrinth for the sound to muffle itself before it reached the street. Those who lived in the small rooms that fronted on the alley kept away from the windows. There was danger in knowing too much in the district.

He screamed, then, and his eyes bulged as if they were about to burst from his head. He screamed again as he saw the raw wound where his knee had once been, one limb held to the other by tendons, the kneecap nothing but fragmented bone.

"Oh, Christ. Oh, Christ. Oh, Christ." He moaned again.

I leaned forward and whispered into his ear, "Christ is not here. Only hell. Last chance. Who sent you?"

He started to shake his head, then flinched away as I jammed the barrel of the .45 hard against his temple.

"Black," he said thickly, trying to force the words around the blood welling up inside his mouth and through the pain stretching his nerves taut. "His office."

I rose and walked to where he had dropped his pistol. I bent and picked it up: a Baby Browning .25-caliber. Just what I would have chosen for a hide-out. I slipped it inside my pocket.

"Help me," he gasped.

"No," I said.

I turned and left him lying in the filth of the alley, moaning and helpless, with one shattered leg. He might make it out of the alley before they found him—both the rats and the street gangs that patrolled the alleys in the district, hoping to find the helpless. But I doubted it. And I didn't care.

Black.

Somehow, I knew it would be Black. Or his office. But Black was the office and the office was Black. This was not a Hydra where one had to work his way through the various heads until he found the immortal one. Black was the key. Without him, the office would flounder for a few days until the new station chief could figure out where the order had once existed and what was left of a shattered command.

What I didn't know was why.

But I sure as hell was going to find out. A snake will break up a henhouse quicker than anything, because the hens cannot believe that they are in danger. But they are. It's the disruption of the secure feeling that throws a person into panic, and once a person is panicked, then he is easy to manipulate. It wouldn't be Black, though. He had eyes like two candles guttering down into the sockets of iron candlesticks. He could be broken; anyone can be broken; there is no such thing as a complete tolerance of pain, even among those who emerge liking it. But there were others around him who had wasted away with worry until they were as thin as broomsticks and the flesh of their faces had shrunk so far back that the bones appeared as white lines just under the skin. Those were the ones I would work upon. If I could. One at a time, beginning at the bottom and working my way up the ladder so that each person would know when it would be his turn. Eventually, I would find one who would be ready with the information I needed and give it willingly to keep from becoming the next victim.

But that wouldn't be his salvation. Here there were none who were not victims. Even those who did not know that they were victims yet. That would come later, in the dark of the night when they lose their grip upon their mind for just a moment and the nightmare hornets swarm out of their hidden hive and sting them screaming awake, leaving them caught in that pulsating rift between asleep and awake for one brief moment that seems an eternity. You can tell when that has happened to a man because the next morning, when he looks at you for the first time, his eyes are blank and his face looks like it had been hacked with a blunt ax out of pig iron. And at that moment, he is vulnerable.

The sky was the color of sulphur matches by the time I made it to the cathedral. I waited outside until a group of Vietnamese started inside, then took my place with them, working my way slowly to the center of the group. Inside, the cathedral was cool but muggy and my shirt became damp quickly and clung to my back like paste. There was a woman in the middle of the pews, sitting and fanning herself with a handkerchief. I thought she was French from the look of her dress and the white hat with the wide brim that cocks down over the eyes that are still so popular with the French, who stubbornly cling to the old styles as if frozen in time since France officially pulled out of the country. Once, I asked a plantation owner why he didn't go home. He gave me a surprised look and said, "But this *is* my home. My family has been here since 1909. We are buried here. We'll never give this land back despite what the Vietnamese want. My family bought and paid for this land not only in gold but in blood as well. The arrogance of governments is not our concern. Only the land. Our rubber trees, our sugarcane fields, are our only concern."

She sensed that I was staring at her and turned her head quickly. She looked familiar and I tried to remember where I had seen her before. She had golden-brown hair and brown eyes, fawn eyes, wide and innocent-looking, although one was blood-flecked from drinking. There were tiny wrinkles around the corners of her eyes and a tiny softness beneath her chin. Her mouth was wide and generous, and I did not think there was that much innocence in the world that could mask the sensuous cheekbones and that mouth. Her dress was white, like the hat, and the top button undone against the heat. I could see the dampness along the tops of her breasts and up the column of her throat. She raised an eyebrow at my stare, a tiny quirk followed by a small frown that wrinkled her fine forehead. Her skin looked like ivory, and I knew that she came from one of the wealthy plantations upriver where the women did not have to go out in the noonday sun to help their men with the running of the plantation.

I dropped my eyes and continued down toward the front. When I passed her, she put out a gloved hand to stop me. Her fingers trembled and I could smell the old odor of cognac on her breath. I kept my face down, looking at her open-toed white shoes with high heels. Her fine calves were covered by silk stockings.

Up front, a priest was muttering a kerygmatic recital on the truth of revelation. His words came back to us strung together in a soft whispered echo that was distorted by the cathedral itself.

"Pardon me, but I believe I know you. Have we met?"

Her voice was low and vibrated with warmth, sensual. Up this close I could see her age and knew she was older than I had thought when I first saw her.

"I'm sorry, but I don't think so," I said.

She pulled her hand back, and her lips curved slightly in a smile. "Oh, but I'm certain that we have met somewhere before."

I shrugged.

She glanced around. We were alone. She placed her hand on my forearm again and spoke so softly that I had to bend to hear.

"We met once at the Racquet Club. Don't you remember? Christmas. We shared a bottle of wine," she said.

I frowned and shrugged my shoulders helplessly, pretending I didn't understand.

She pressed my forearm harder. "Do not be that way. I know who you are. All of Saigon knows. I have heard what you are said to have done. But the bottle of wine that we shared told me that what I heard was not the truth."

I studied her silently for a long moment. Her face was wan, tired, sober now, but resigned to the series of drinking spells that would carry her over the harsh days. But there was a pleading innocence to her as if by accepting her offer I would give her the last chance to do something worthwhile with what was rapidly becoming a wasted life. I decided to take a chance that she would be useful, and if she wasn't, then little harm would be done. I hoped.

"It wasn't," I said softly. "But this is not the time or the place to go into that."

Our words barely carried from one to the other, so softly did we speak in that acoustical nightmare of a cathedral. I slipped my hand into the pocket where I had placed the Baby Browning. I kept turning my head as if I was embarrassed about being stopped by her. I kept my features frozen in sullenness, suggesting to anyone watching that I was being scolded by her for some affront.

"I may be able to help," she said. "I am staying at the Continental."

"No, I am known there," I answered. "It might be better that you did not get involved in this."

She frowned again. "As you said: you have few friends in this town. I think you can use another."

"Why are you doing this?" I asked. "It's not because of a bottle of wine."

"There was a man," she began, then fell silent. "He was being— forceful. You stopped him."

I remembered. A fat Frenchman who had come to town without his family and gotten drunk somewhere before he came to the Racquet Club. He had tried to force her to go with him. I tried to remember her name—Madeleine. Proust's favorite treat—my memory trick.

"Madeleine," I said.

She smiled. "See? You remember. You said you would always remember Proust's favorite sweet. That was very romantic, I thought. But you left early," she added wistfully.

I nodded, then gently removed her hand.

"We are spending too much time together. I must leave."

"Quick! Where can we meet? I do owe you a favor."

I shook my head, then reconsidered. Could I really afford to throw a possible friend away? That is, if she was really a friend.

"The park across from the Majestic. Find a bench and bring a book to read." I shrugged at her frown. "It's the best that I can do."

"That is not what the French would do. A bar?"

My eye lit on the confessional booths across from us. The ones at the far end were unoccupied.

"Watch for me to enter the far confessional booth. Then you take the one next to it. It will appear that you are in need of confession. We shall have some privacy there."

She frowned. "But you do not look like a priest."

"I will," I said. "In about fifteen minutes or so. Can you wait that long?"

She nodded.

I walked away, making my way slowly down to the front of the church where the priest was ending his chant. I caught him as he exited by the side of the tiny altar to Saint Joseph.

"Father," I began.

He waved impatiently. "I do not hear confessions until later," he said abruptly.

"You recently have taken in a priest for sanctuary," I said.

He paused, eyed me narrowly. "If I have, then that is of no business of yours."

"I am the one who came with him on his sea voyage," I said.

His eyes became dark with suspicion. "And how do I know this?"

"Ask him. Tell him Mr. Wingfoot—Wingo—needs to see him immediately. Tell him I remember his razor with the cracked handle. And the favor he did for me when I came out of the iron boxes."

His eyes softened somewhat, but there was still a hint of suspicion to them.

"If I say that I will tell him, then that is an admission that he is here," he said.

"I shall wait twenty minutes. If you do not appear to take me to him, then I shall know that what I have said was in vain and shall leave," I said.

He shrugged. "Your time is your own. Do with it what you will. I might suggest that you spend some time in prayer. I find that it helps me to pass the time if I talk with God."

I smiled wryly. "I'm not certain God is listening to prayers from me anymore. Or," I added, "from most of the soldiers in Vietnam."

He frowned. "God is always there." He pointed to the red lamp burning behind the altar. "That lamp reminds us of His presence. He is always here."

"There are a lot of churches with a lot of lamps in the world," I said. "But I shall wait, as I said I would wait. If the good Father is here, ask him to see me."

He nodded and continued on his way. I walked to the third pew from the front and sat. Then I knelt, pretending prayer, to lend reason for my being there for any who were curious. But no words came to me; I was empty inside, a man made hollow for what had happened to me and for what I was prepared to do.

I closed my eyes, remembering back to the reservation. The early-morning fog at the willows down by the river soaking into my clothes. The prickly feeling of dried prairie grass scratching my feet and legs when I ran naked with other boys across the prairie. The sun burning through my thick black hair and into my scalp, warm upon my back. When we were exhausted, we would throw ourselves down upon the grass and lie upon our backs looking up at the blue sky that turned to red behind our eyelids. The sun's warmth came like a flood over us.

Then, memories began to glide over my closed eyelids: faces, landscapes, Harney Peak, where I went to seek my vision, the murmuring talk of the women, some laughter, not much, for there isn't much to laugh about upon the reservation. The memories floated in smoke, occasionally pierced by a long, thin shaft of light.

My father died when I was eight or nine—I no longer remembered the year, but I remember the women weeping soundlessly through the night, sitting in the hard-backed chairs or squatting on the floor in front of the wood-burning stove where we sometimes burnt dried manure for heat when we could not get wood. I remembered my grandmother's swollen eyes and the crumpled, tear-stained hem of her blouse she used to dry her eyes.

I remembered the smell of rotting leaves in the hot and humid summers when waves of heat would rise from the ground like the spirits of our ancestors. The night cries of hunting birds. Time slipped and the time passed that had been set aside for diving headlong into the river at dusk to swim before the day's heat left the waters cold, and the wonder at discovering the differences between the girls and ourselves.

I heard the quiet swish of his robes before I sensed him entering the pew and sitting beside me. I glanced at him out of the corner of my eye. His face was gaunt but now had taken on an asceticism one found in the paintings of El Greco. His eyes were calm, his silver-gray hair combed straight back from his forehead and allowed to fall in gentle waves to his black-cassocked shoulders. I looked down at his hands, thin, the blue veins showing like map roads.

"May I help you, my son?" he asked softly.

A grin tugged at my lips. "A bit formal, aren't we, Father?"

"We are in a formal place," he said gently. "And you cannot tell who else might be enjoying the formality of that formal place. I would suspect many."

"Have you found your sanctuary?"

He gave a brief nod. "Yes, I am at peace here. But I cannot stay here too long. I put others into danger. I will have to go."

"And where will you go?"

His eyes became melancholy, but I could see that he was once again the priest in charge of keeping watch over the shadows of the dead and remembering their plaintive and painful confessions that would cleanse their souls for the final trip.

"North," he said simply.

"That isn't a direction," I said. "That is euthanasia."

"There are small churches needing a priest. In the villages, there are still some who have not been corrupted by the war."

I remembered what Quang had told me about the Place of Whispers and wondered if there was a church there that Devereaux might take.

"But you did not come here to talk about this, did you?" he asked softly.

"No. I need help from you. You know about the murder of the young woman that I was blamed for."

He nodded. There was no need to go into further explanation. The long nights on the island had given us ample time to explore each other's hurts.

"I am looking for the man who did this crime. *And* the one who ordered it."

He studied me for a moment, then said, "Cannot they both be the same?"

I gave a tiny shake of my head. "No, I don't think so. Her murder was much in the same way that I was to make it for it to be a warning. But that was given to me by another as an order. You see?"

He frowned. "Then perhaps you have already answered your own question. Could it be that this man gave another the same assignment?"

"Probably, but he is not the one who is responsible. He was only the messenger boy."

"I see."

He folded his hands and placed them in his lap, studying them thoughtfully, as if the vein roads would lead him to the answer.

"And you want me to do what?"

"I would like you to ask among the others here if they have heard something."

"They will not violate the confessional," he said.

"That's not what I'm asking. A priest hears other things that are not in the confessional. People feel comfortable talking to him and often say things that should have been reserved for the confessional, thinking that simple conversation is the same."

"Sometimes, it is," he said softly. "Sometimes, it has to be. We learned our lesson well from the past history of our church. Even in the beginning there was a need for silence which was not kept. That is when the doom of man was given."

I raised an eyebrow. "Not the beginning of life? Isn't that one of the tenets of your church?"

He smiled gently. "Yes. But we must also be aware of the fallacy which hides behind the truth. And sometimes, the truth hides behind the fallacy. I will make some discreet inquiries. How shall I find you if I discover anything?"

I nodded toward the confessional. "In there."

A wry smile appeared. "Yes, that would be appropriate, wouldn't it."

"I'll be here next Saturday morning. Will that give you enough time?"

He nodded. "If there is anything to hear, I will have heard it by then."

He started to rise, but I placed my hand upon his knee, holding him. He settled back into the pew and looked at me questioningly.

"There's one more thing," I said. "I need to borrow your cassock for a moment."

He frowned. "Why?"

"There is a woman halfway down the center aisle. She has offered to help. But we need someplace where we can be alone without others thinking evil of her."

"And where you will have some sanctuary," he said.

I shrugged. "That, too."

"But why the cassock?"

I tilted my head slightly toward the confessionals and slowly he nodded.

"Yes, that is where you will find your sanctuary."

"Will you help?"

"Come with me."

He rose and led me slowly into the back where mahogany cabinets lined the walls of a small room. He opened one, took out a cassock, and handed it to me. In another cabinet he found a small black leather satchel, and in another a black suit and shirt with a priest's collar.

"This might help you move around in certain places where you cannot otherwise go," he said as he carefully folded the clothes and placed them in the satchel. From the shelf in the closet he took a rosary, and dropped it into the bag along with a small silver cross on a chain. He handed the satchel to me.

"There is room left for the cassock."

"You won't get into trouble for this?"

He smiled. "Who is to know but you, me, and God?"

"Isn't theft a sin?"

"Yes. But there are enough sins on my soul that another will not matter much. Take them and go before someone comes in."

I shook his hand and slipped the cassock on. Adopting a pious attitude, I slipped back into the cathedral and made my way to the last confessional. I placed the satchel inside and backed in and sat. I closed the door and sat in the dark, waiting. I didn't have long to wait; the door next to my tiny cell opened and closed quickly. I slid the grate back and peeked through the gold-plated screen.

"Bless me, Father, for I have sinned," she said solemnly. "It has been two weeks since my last confession and lately I have been thinking about a man who reads Proust."

A low chuckle came through the screen.

"You have been thinking too much on the man who reads Proust," I replied carefully. "But, if you wish to help, then see what you can discover through your friends at the Racquet Club. Your friends, your husband and his friends—"

"He was killed nine years ago," she replied calmly. "Our plantation is up north of An Loc. He went out to check the fields and didn't come back. We found him hacked to death with machetes at the edge of the grove where we used to hold parties when things were so one could hold parties without worrying about night coming down. We never discovered if it was the workers who did this or if the Vietcong came down and found him there. That is why that fat fool tried to take advantage of me at Christmas."

I knew then that she was a woman born of the war and belonged to it, had been forged by it over the years. She had known war all her life—just as I had, but her war had been much different. Hers had not been one where she had to play sordid games with the "white Indians" of the reservation who had the power to do whatever they wanted and the white high school boys from the small towns around the reservation who liked to come onto the reservation to drink 3.2 beer and to hunt our lands during the upland game season and to try to turn our young women into whores.

Madeleine's war had been one to which she belonged as her birthright. It was one in which there would be no end, for she was French, although she had been born in the colony and had never known another country as her homeland.

Now I knew the parallel between the French and myself; we were both the victims of a war that had gotten beyond our control. Mine was older, however, and my people had learned to live with the result that made them shadows in what had once been their own wild and free land. The French were still trying to stay out of the shadows. But they were fighting a doomed battle, for one day the war would end and there would have to be a reckoning for those who were left behind by the losers. I had no doubt who was going to lose this war; it was lost already; I could see that in the looks of the soldiers who frequented the Saigon bars and the houses of prostitution such as The Flowers, The House of the Bamboo Spirits, and the cribs in Cholon where the naked Chinese prostitutes never left their tiny beds while men lined up outside their curtained doorways, impatiently waiting to spill their seed into the now mechanical woman who often would eat while a man made love to her, occasionally pausing to push a necklace made of wooden beads up his anus and pop them free, one at a time, when he started to climax, bringing him through a rapid series of climaxes that left him spent and nearly dead, and vowing to return again and again.

But it was the stare in the eyes of the young soldiers—I felt much older than they were, although we shared nearly the same age—who saw nothing in their futures, not even the hope of being able to one day leave Vietnam when their tours were done and fly back home, because by now home was only a distant dream that had never happened, a wistful wish as true as the wooden Pinocchio suddenly becoming flesh and blood with the touch of a fairy wand in reward for good deeds that were, by now, only a figment of someone's imagination.

"You didn't do it," she said softly.

Startled, I tried to stare through the grille into her face, but the shadows of the confessional distorted it.

"Pardon me?"

"I said, 'You didn't do it.' "

"This is true. But how can you be so certain?"

She remained silent for a long moment and I wondered if she had slipped a drink from a purse flask before coming into the confessional and was now having second thoughts. I knew the dark depression that was working on her, had been working on her for the years when she had spent under one war or the other, trying to hold a family and home together in a time when nothing worked right, when nightmares became unbearable and she sought solace in opium pipes and French cognac and wine, when her world tightened like a hard iron band around her forehead and tried to squeeze belonging out of her until only emptiness remained and everything seemed to become only a few drops of memory to be placed under a microscope that took away the life that she once knew until she could escape only through those deadly "what could have beens." People who once dared not approach her now saw her as prey, and she was helpless because the life she once knew was gone forever. She had become flotsam on a sea where no lifeboat could float.

"I have a gift," she said hesitantly, so softly that I had to strain to hear her words. "There are times when I can *see* things—not all the time, but times when I can see shadows moving around behind a gray veil and I know they have a meaning, but I cannot tell the meaning. My grandfather once said that I had a gift for seeing things that had happened to others. But I did not know the others. I cannot tell you why or how, but I know that what happened to you did not happen *because* of something you did. Yet it is related to you and what happened to you because you avoided what had been set in motion for you."

I tried to make light of the moment, as I sensed she was remembering things that she had heard from somewhere when she had been drinking or had seen in an opium dream and seeing me at that moment in the cathedral had attached those—what? sensations?—to me because of the small favor that I had done for her that was not a small favor to her but an *obligation* that once had come naturally to her in the old days.

"And what is it you have seen?" I asked tactfully.

"I don't know," she said softly. I heard the despair in her voice as if she was truly regretful that she could tell me no more. Then my flesh pebbled when she added, "But I feel that you must be very careful to whom you give your confidence." She paused, then added, "You must always remain alone in what lies ahead of you. You must remain alone."

"Do you know—"

"Do not press me further," she said softly. "I cannot tell you any more than what the shadows suggest." I sensed the shrug. "The gift is not absolute. We are not given to know everything. We must discover some things for ourselves. No man is to know everything."

"Perhaps I should be wary of you. Two hundred years ago you would have been burnt for what you said."

"Two hundred years ago I wouldn't have said it," she answered. "I can tell you this: evil is always where you least expect it."

"Thank you. I'll be careful."

"And I'll see what I can find among the Racquet Club crowd and some of the places that a proper lady is not supposed to know about. Shall we meet here at the same time next week?"

"All right," I answered.

"And if I need to get in touch with you immediately?"

I hesitated, then gave her Fell's name and address. "You will be able to find him at the Club Eve about five every afternoon. It is where he begins his day. His circadian cycle is out of sync. He only comes alive at night. During the day, he slips through the hours as unobtrusive as possible."

She made a clicking sound with her tongue. "The poor man. Was he a victim?"

"Is there anyone who isn't?" I replied.

"No, not in this land," she said sadly.

I listened as the door opened and she exited the confessional. I peeked out and watched her enter a pew and kneel to suggest serving the penance that had been handed out for her sins. I had forgotten that point to make to her, but she had remembered the small formality herself. You need to be more careful, I warned myself. It is the little things you forget that can bring you down.

I slipped from the confessional as a Vietnamese merchant headed impatiently for the door adjoining my booth. His eyes flashed angrily when he saw me emerge from the booth. I smiled and shook my head gently, pointing at the confessionals at the other end where a long line of penitents wove back to the door.

I reached inside the booth and took the small satchel and made my way down the aisle toward the door, remembering to bless myself and genuflect before stepping out into the bright sunlight. I walked around to the side of the cathedral, glanced around, then stepped between some bushes and slipped out of the cassock, folding it carefully and placing it in the satchel.

I turned and walked Tu-Do Street, trying to keep pace with the groups of Vietnamese around me. I emerged around Lam Son Square. Suddenly a policeman stepped in front of me. I smiled nervously and tried to step around him, but he slipped again in front. He held out his hand.

"Your papers," he demanded.

I frowned, pretending not to understand. He shook his head impatiently.

"Your papers."

He made the "give-me" motion with his hand. I nodded enthusiastically and stuck my hand in my back pocket, pretending to pull them out while I stepped close to him. I reached out, grabbed his arm, and pulled him close to me, jamming my knee into his groin at the same time. He gagged, his face turning chalky white, then green, and I stepped back hastily as his breakfast of rice splattered onto the concrete. I reached down, snapped his pistol free, and ran hastily from the square, weaving my way through the warren of narrow alleys covered with slippery bricks, dank and evil-smelling, working my way toward the river.

All alleys seemed to eventually lead their way toward the brown and muddy river moving sluggishly toward the sea, a highway of freedom for those who could find their way down its twists and turns to emerge near Vung Tau. I found a wall, plaster peeling to reveal old red bricks beneath. I leaped up, gripping the edge of the wall with the edge of my fingers while I brushed my fingers gently over the top of the wall, feeling for embedded glass. Finding none, I pulled myself up and dropped gently down into a garden filled with rubber plants and bougainvillea and ivy vines twisting wildly untamed. Flowers grew in ragged patterns, some volunteer here and there where wind had blown seeds. It was a garden in disrepair, left to its own devices, a sort of metaphysical scramble of vegetation rambling helter-skelter as if a breath of nature or raindrop of pathos had found its way into the middle of some fantastic imagery that barely clung to the depths of rich, dark earth.

Yet there was something far more sinister about it as well. I found a stone path overgrown with dried weeds leading up to a mansion that had begun to crumble into the same pattern of old civilizations and old families once wealthy and important until a newer and more important life came along and the ways of the fashionable became unfashionable and, bit by bit, belongings were sold off in an attempt to maintain a lifestyle that had become sorely dated.

I followed the path up to the house. As I neared the front door, I could hear the faint notes of a violin being played, sad and melancholy, as if the playing of the violin was the sole purpose to the day in a movement from substance to shadow, ready to move from this world to the next.

I paused beside a concrete pond a carriage width from the front door and watched the koi move in graceful gold and speckled patterns through mossy water. The fountain no longer spouted water to the sunlight, and yet the koi were sleek and well fed and apparently content in their soft-green world. Despite the seedy appearance of the house, someone apparently cared enough for the fish to keep them well fed, although a gardener had become a luxury that could no longer be afforded. Tiny weeds grew flatly among the gravel of the drive and the brass around the bell-turn mounted in the center of the door had not been polished in months and a long dirty crack ran a ragged pattern down through one of the long lead-glass panes in the door. I was looking upon and standing within a tragedy of time.

I slipped silently away from the door and made my way down to the bottom of the garden where I could see the timbers of a gazebo still standing, now pearl gray in the sunlight instead of the dazzling white they would have been years before when young men and women dressed in white would sit languidly, beginning conversations with, "I had too much to drink last night." Feeble attempts at giving meaning to a life that had no meaning other than pleasure.

Now there were only ghosts there in the ragged cushions on splintered rattan furniture. But I did not need the ghosts of the past; I needed shelter for a few hours, time to reflect and gather my thoughts, time for pursuit to fall away from the area.

14 After dinner, Nguyen and I sat in his little gazebo at the back of his garden, listening to the quiet lapping of the river as it rolled by. At the front gate to his bungalow, an old woman dressed in black trousers squatted alongside the road, chewing betel nut. The night might have been too cool for her old bones, but she always squatted there as if she had posted herself a lookout for any intruder. Nguyen always took her a bowl of rice heaped with meat at the evening meal. When I questioned him about it, he simply said that we owed a life to someone and for him it might as well be the old woman. Yet I had a feeling that she meant more to him than what he was willing to admit. Once the police had tried to arrest her, but Nguyen went down and opened the gate and let her squat on her heels just inside the gate, which gave her legitimacy in the eyes of the police, and grudgingly they released her.

I thought of several jests that I could have made at that—the old woman and the dwarf—but I had seen too many old women rousted by the reservation police while I was a child to feel anything but contempt for the police and pity for the old woman. And I had no desire to hurt him or her or, for that matter, myself. The pain I felt at the memories of the old people on the reservation was long enough that I didn't need to take on any more. I could hear her singing in her old, cracked voice that carried faintly over the crickets' chirruping and the whirr of night insect wings. Bats swooped through the garden, bright tongues of fire stabbing the unwary insects.

The mosquitoes were thick, but Nguyen had lit a fragrant smudge pot that kept them from bothering us. Through the smoke and the thin light pouring from the French doors that Nguyen had left open I could see the dark shadows of puppets hanging from their places on the walls. They looked macabre in the light, twisted forms dancing on air like the feet of newly hanged men jerking uncontrollably as life strangled out of them.

Nguyen smoked a long-stemmed opium pipe, the ivory bowl

stained a dark brown from the many pellets that had been kneaded into it and fired with a tiny lamp. The stem was two feet of straight bamboo and the bowl two-thirds of the way down so he could easily tilt the pipe into the lamp fire. He drew the smoke into his lungs in steady puffs, not the long single draw of a practiced smoker. He did not want the deep dream of the practiced smoker but rather the fresh and relaxed mind of a tired professor and writer.

Nguyen sighed and laid the pipe carefully on a small bamboo table beside him and stretched. He smiled gently as if he was about to give me a blessing. I half-expected him to sign through the air, but he contented himself with stretching his short arms behind his head and clasping his hands.

"How was your day?" he asked pleasantly.

I made a face. "A policeman tried to arrest me on Lam Son Square."

His black eyes studied mine thoughtfully for a moment. "Did he come straight to you or did he stop others first?"

I thought a minute. "He came straight to me."

"So he was looking for you. And knew where to find you."

I sat back against the damp cushions of the chair and stared up at the ceiling of the gazebo. Had the policeman been looking for me? And did he know where to find me? I found that hard to accept in a city of a million or more people. Yet there was the suggestion of the coincidence and I couldn't afford to believe in coincidences. Not anymore.

"It appears so."

"Logically so," he amended.

"Yes. Did you find out anything?"

He sighed and sat still for a moment, gathering his thoughts. "I have some friends who were with the Cao Dais and Hoa Haos—you know them?"

I knew them. Or, I amended, *about* them. The Cao Dais came about through the backwash of French culture sometime in the midtwenties when the small farmers, merchants, and civil servants, who had been touched by the grand finger of French culture, thought they had discovered the root of French superiority. But they were not culturally focused upon what was reality and what was fiction. Semiliterate, they thought they had discovered through a spiritualist or a medium or a vision—I was a bit vague on that—that a spirit who revealed himself as the Cao Dai, or supreme god of the universe, was to give to them the "third amnesty of God." Apparently, the first amnesty had been Christ and Moses, the second Buddha and Lao-tzu, and the third a hodgepodge of modern happenings.

The French were heavy into the Masonic order and so the Cao Dais adopted the Masonic eye of God and lumped all the world's religious leaders into one boiling pot, including such figures as Joan of Arc, Victor Hugo, and some minor deities who had surfaced along the way. The Cao Dais modeled their church along the lines of the Catholic Church and immediately began to gain followers who flocked to the new order that was promised to them by the first grand master or priest or whatever titular title he used.

The Hoa Haos, however, came out of the new Vietnam. Their self-styled prophet, Huynh Phu So, the "mad bonze," came from the northwest corner of the Delta near the Bassac River, where the Vietnamese had settled in an uneasy alliance with the Cambodians and together they had colonized the uninhabited wastelands that nobody wanted. The area quickly became a breeding ground of magicians and prophets who through strange incantations managed to reveal the future to those who had no future and who so desperately wanted a future.

So a sickly young man suddenly found himself "miraculously" cured and began to preach a type of enlightenment, proclaiming the coming of a supreme sage who would rule Vietnam in the three religions—Catholicism, Cao Dai, and Hoa Hao—with a little Buddhism tossed in here and there.

The Cao Dais and Hoa Haos eventually became strong enough to have their own armies, and the Hoa Hao prophet eventually made the mistake of attacking a Vietminh stronghold and was assassinated. But the will of heaven did not come down for them, and the religions began to slip away into the past as all religions eventually do before disintegrating altogether when a new and stronger god is eventually discovered by another prophet. White Buffalo Woman had begun to slip away into the mists of time when the black-robed friars came into my people's lands, and I had little doubt that the modern gods would find their way into that same other world where the ancient gods wait patiently for their moment again in time. All civilizations have their own concept of the Eternal Return. It is man's one frantic grip upon the immortality of his mortality.

"Yes, I have an idea of the two sects," I said.

He nodded and continued. "Although they are not really active—at least not the Hoa Haos—they still keep close to each other. There is a sense of belonging to each other. Since it has been many years since they practiced, what they were is often forgotten by those who are willing to hire them as workers—gardeners, laborers, that sort of thing." He laughed. "And the Americans, well, they have a tendency of thinking that the Vietnamese who work for them are as silent as the walls. But their servants hear things and they keep that to themselves because today such knowledge can be either very dangerous or very valuable."

"And these people are willing to share this information with you?"

He opened his arms wide and laughed again. "What is there to fear from a dwarf? There is little that we can do. A flyswatter would take care of us."

His face darkened for a moment and I knew that he was revisiting the moments when he was young and the source of countless tortures the young inflict upon one another. Unfortunately, the youths often keep their cruelties when they become adults and then the cruelties become much worse as they realize more power.

"And you learned?" I prompted gently.

He sighed and rubbed his hands hard across his face as if he was trying to scrub fire ants away.

"You knew she was pregnant?" he said quietly.

I nodded, a flash of the ugliness I had seen in the pictures laid out across Black's desk flashing across my memory—the child removed from her womb and laid neatly beside her, hardly recognizable yet as a human being, the mother's intestines removed and draped ritually over her shoulder. It was a scene of ugliness not that far removed from what I had seen many times in many places in Vietnam, but this particular moment had been far more brutal and bloodthirsty because of the innocence of the moment when it had happened. War does not violate the sanctity of the person; only man can do that. A demented individual for whom life has fully ceased to have any meaning.

"That is why she was killed," he said.

I raised my eyebrows in surprise.

"I thought she was an agent for the North."

"She was. But that is only an incidental in Saigon anymore. Everyone is an agent for someone. There is no innocence anymore. Innocence is a luxury that is no longer affordable. Even the shoeshine boys are not to be trusted."

I knew that. I had seen one black soldier place his jump boot on the shoe box to get a shine and the next thing he knew he was lying in the gutter, trying to stop blood from leaping from a severed femoral artery. The boy had palmed a razor from his box and run it up lengthwise along the vein to make a tourniquet useless. The soldier bled to death in a matter of seconds.

"Everybody will also tell you what they think you want to know," Nguyen added. "So." He spread his hands. "It becomes a matter of trying to decide what is true and what is not true, what someone has to gain from giving you certain information and what he hopes to gain in return. Yet, sometimes, there is a grain of truth in one lie, another grain in another, and when you put the two grains together, you come up with a projection of what might be true."

I nodded. "And what have you managed to come up with?"

He studied me for a long moment, then sighed and said, "I do not know *who* killed her, but I do know why."

He looked away, watching the bats unfold against the dark of the night. A mosquito landed on my arm. I slapped it and watched the blood splatter against the dark skin. Had I just slain a new prophet? A new god? And how many had I killed who might have brought a semblance of order to the disorder around us at the moment over the past year alone?

"You know about 'Big' Minh?"

My stomach muscles tightened at the name. General Duong Van Minh had been one of the star pupils at the École de Chartres and slipped back and forth from one side to the next during the wars that rolled across Vietnam like a dirty flood from the Red River. He was taller than most Vietnamese—nearly my height—and had an uncanny grasp of which side to choose at the right time, constantly emerging with more and more power and riches and strength. At various times, he managed to make the Buddhists, students, and intellectuals—many of them, at any rate—recognize him as a "king-maker" in establishing new order when the old began to fold at the seams like an overused picnic blanket. When the Americans came into the war, he quickly ingratiated himself among the generals by hosting elaborate parties at a plantation he had bought by convincing the Frenchman trying desperately to hold on to his family estate during the transition from French colonial rule to Vietnamese that it would be in his best interest to sell cheaply and leave for his "native land," where the Frenchman was, for all practical purposes, a foreigner, having been born in Vietnam. The rumor was that Minh had a follower hold a pistol to the head of the Frenchman's wife until he agreed to sell out for the equivalent of a hundred thousand dollars in an overinflated Vietnamese currency and four tickets to France—one for the Frenchman and one each for his wife and two daughters.

The soirees that Minh held on a regular basis, however, were designed for jaded tastes that appealed to all who attended, and those who objected to the happenings at the plantation on Old Plantation Road were discreetly omitted from future invitations and rotated back home by those American officers who enjoyed the distractions Minh provided from the war.

"I can see that you know," Nguyen said softly. "He is a very powerful man. Very powerful. And no one wants to talk about what happens out at his plantation for fear of disappearing somewhere. Like Poulo Condore. Or somewhere worse.

"Boys, women, even animals, I am told. You understand that this is all something that no one talks about. *No one,*" he emphasized. "To do so is to risk going there. It is said that he even makes movies with captured North Vietnamese women and young boys who are . . ." He hesitated. "Well, does it make a difference as to the manner of execution? A bullet in the head is as much a degradation as any other, isn't it?"

"Only to the one who is killed," I said. "To all others, it may be a blessing or opportunity. So, we have the place but do not know who. A party, but which of the party would it be?"

"She was pregnant," he reminded me gently. "Who has the most to lose if such knowledge would be brought to light?"

It wouldn't be Minh. He had the power to ride through anything that might affect him personally. His army was a private army—that was the problem with Vietnam; too many of the province chiefs and area generals had carte blanche in operations that gave them unlimited power. And, I knew, Minh was quite capable of leading his men down on an attack against Saigon and unseating the central government. He had been involved in that once before.

No, it wouldn't be Minh. He might react like a butcher to protect his name, but he wouldn't have anything to lose if Lisa Lee's death became common knowledge and tied directly to him. Not even the police would have the power to arrest him.

So, it had to be someone else.

Someone who was a frequent visitor to Minh's parties.

But who? From what I understood, the guest list was vast and some had special privileges to come and go as they wished. I felt like I was on a carousel, spinning faster and faster, my wooden horse riding up and down on its pole with more furious intent, and the watchers in the shadows observing the riders become more and more faceless blurs.

I met Madeleine at the old Vieux Moulin after Father Devereaux delivered the message to me at our next meeting. The Vieux Moulin stood beside the bridge to Dakow. Stalls of the new dirty magazines had once again reappeared despite the attempts of Madam Nhu to outlaw them. But the Nhus were no longer a faction in Saigon and now French magazines like *Tabu* and *Ilusion*—the old copies once outlawed—were again displayed, the edges of their pages brown from having been stored, along with others of a newer and more frank approach.

Armed police stood by the bridge on both sides, but I had no idea what they were protecting or from whom as people streamed across in an endless river of brown faces and white *ao dais*.

The restaurant had an iron grille covered with a fine mesh of wire to keep out grenades or Molotov cocktails, which some of the more ambitious youths had taken to, finding wine bottles and filling them with gasoline and cotton wicks. Some had learned to put liquid laundry detergent in the bottles for homemade napalm.

During the day it was fairly safe to cross the bridge, but at night

Dakow was an open area filled with after-hour bars and girls who would do anything for a few piasters. Anyone who went across the bridge after dark took his life in his own hands both coming and going. The police were quite willing to let anyone go over the bridge from the Saigon side, but getting back was something else. Usually you could pay a bribe. The police on the Dakow side didn't care that much; they were already deep into someone's pad but sometimes would demand a fine for the inconvenience of guarding the one crossing over.

In the early morning, when the tide rolled the river away, leaving the mud banks exposed on either side, the police would roll up their trousers and remove their shoes and slog through the mud to the exposed bodies from the night before, quickly collecting anything of value before the coroner's boys got there and robbed the bodies. Sometimes, however, not even the police would go down onto the mud flats, and that was when the bodies showed that they had floated down from upstream and the crabs and the fish had been at them. One had to work quickly in this climate and city. The toss-up was who would get the tip, the stench of the dead bodies, the city police or the coroners.

After the bodies were taken back to the mortuary, not much changed since the day of the French with its smell of urine and injustice, the American and Vietnamese security officers would make their appearances to see if one of their men had "been turned" and, if so, who had to be warned immediately, because no one could resist torture forever and salvage operations had to begin immediately. Or else rebuilding a network, which would be time-consuming and expensive, and even then the question would be who to trust.

The Vietnamese controlled the main roads until 7:00 P.M. or until it became dark enough that shadows could melt within other shadows in a war of shadows. After that, the Vietnamese preferred to remain in watchtowers, which were silly, because the watchtowers were death traps for rocket launchers or even demolition squads that the Vietcong would send in under the watchtowers' pylons. They wrapped stolen C-4 compound or Symtex around the pylons and brought them down in one concussive blast. Being not quite as experienced as the North Vietnam Regular Army, their enthusiasm would often lead them to overload the pylons and nearly send the watchtowers into orbit or smash them into kindling wood or strange twisted sculptures that had become fashionable among artists of no talent.

Madeleine had a table in the far corner of the room beneath a potted palm that allowed for a sense of privacy without becoming obvious. I moved around the side away from her, burying myself deeper into the palm's shadow. I eased my pistol around in front to the left and leaned back against the rattan chair, keeping the room in view. She smiled at my precautions.

"My husband used to do that when the war was going very badly," she said. "I think all soldiers who have been in a war for a few years become like that. Of course"—she shrugged—"it wasn't this that killed him."

A waiter approached and I ordered a vermouth cassis while Madeleine asked for a glass of Chablis with pomegranate dripped into it. The waiter nodded and moved away on his felt slippers across the tiles.

"Have you found anything?" she asked.

I told her about what Nguyen had uncovered during his wanderings among the backstreets and cafés of Saigon. Her eyebrows rose slightly when I mentioned Big Minh's parties, and a tiny smile touched the corners of her full lips. Then I asked her what she had discovered among her friends at the Racquet Club.

She shook her head. "Not much. It would appear Minh is using his house as a retreat for the Americans and not the French—although he does like to go to the old Grande Moulin over in Cholon on occasion. Do you know it?"

I did. Once it had been elegant and the service good and the food and wine excellent. But over the years it had fallen into a seediness that mimicked the French taste instead of maintaining the reality of the old. Some members of the old Binh Xuyen still visited there to talk about the old days and sometimes the new as well, for although the Binh Xuyen had been driven out of Saigon officially in the fifties, many of them had simply moved their operations underground. The Binh Xuyen was still active, although its leaders now lived in Paris. Most of the prostitution in Saigon was still controlled by them and practically all of the gambling and much of the drug market.

"He finds many willing participants there. Some he hires from the old men—you know them?" I nodded. "Of course. You would know them and how they earned their power and how it was ended but not ended." She laughed, but there was a hardness to her laugh that did not belong with her. "Many do not believe that."

"Then they are fools," I said. "Simply saying that there is no crime does not make it so. Those are only words."

She nodded and picked up her glass, sipping. "I feel you will find what you are looking for at the Grande Moulin. Or, at least, you will find something there that will take you elsewhere."

"Yes," I replied. I reached out and pressed her hand. "Thank you."

She nodded. "It isn't much. But you may need some help again. You will find my plantation up near An Loc. We can help you there more than we can help you here when the time comes that you may need that help." She paused. "They will hunt you, you know."

"Yes."

"And you will have to have someplace to go. You will not be able to spend a long time there, for the tongues of servants are given to wagging and there will be some in An Loc who will know you are there before three days pass. But from there we can make arrangements for you that we cannot make down here."

I nodded. "Who's 'we'?"

A tight smile crossed her face, bringing her features into a saturnine look. I sensed then the steel that was behind her, forged in the years of war that she had experienced.

"Some of us did not beat our swords into ploughshares," she answered. "This is our land as much as it belongs to anyone. We will be buried here."

I had nothing to say to that, for I recognized the truth behind her words. Regardless of which side won—the North or the South—her time was limited by the desires of those who would emerge in power. It was the nature of the beast.

André waited for me in the confessional of the Saigon cathedral. I slipped into the booth next to him, and when he slid the small door open to reveal the grating that suggested anonymity to the confessor I said, "Forgive me, Father, for I have never confessed."

For a moment, silence came from the other side, then a quiet chuckle.

"And why is that, my son?"

"I'm not Catholic."

"Would you like to be?"

We laughed together quietly, content again in the closeness of ourselves, one to the other, that bond that sometimes joins men closer than blood ties. I felt his spirit move through the grate to gently embrace me and then return. A warmness that I had never felt before from him and I knew—suddenly I knew—that he had at least found peace within his tortured spirit and the world that had once appeared to him only through a nocturnal mist now came forth in softness and warmth.

"Have you been all right?" he asked softly.

"Yes. But they do search for me. And you," I added.

He laughed quietly. "I am not hard to find. I am always here."

"Yes," I said, "but the Church is here as well. It would not be in the best interests of the government to take you from here. The Church is still powerful enough to influence the United States and French governments. The Australians as well and others that signed the SEATO treaty. And the United Nations must be considered as well. The Vietnamese are not fools; they know that whichever side wins the war, eventually they will have to gain the recognition of the United Nations."

"I think you assign too much influence to a poor priest," he said. "I do not believe politics should have a place in any religion. Not mine . . ." He hesitated. "Not yours."

"Yet some bring politics into religion."

"Yes. Sadly, yes. And some make the Church a brothel."

I was taken aback by his choice of words and leaned in closer to the window, whispering, whispering, whispering the world down to words.

"You have heard something, then?"

"Yes. Many are torn by what they have done or are about to do or have had done to them. They seek forgiveness. And there are some who want forgiveness but are not penitent persons."

"Saint Augustine, wasn't it, who prayed to God to make him a better man but not yet?"

"You are repeating yourself; you said that before."

"Perhaps I have, but that doesn't make it any the less true. *And* applicable today more than during Augustine's day. Your own bishops showed that in the past."

"I have begun to say Mass again," he said. "And to hear confessions. But I find it hard to grant absolution to a man who is not truly penitent. There has to be a limit to hypocrisy. And so, I do not believe that such people are worthy of the silence of the confessional even if the Church feels that must be between the confessor and his God.

"It is not only the rich who come in here to confess," André said, "but the poor as well and those who must continue to make their way upon the streets because there is nothing for them. But there are those who prey upon those who walk the streets, for they know the poor do not have the choices of the wealthy and must take a few grains of rice wherever they can find it. I detest those who make victims out of those who are already victims. But I detest even more those who want to make God their co-conspirator.

"One of Big Minh's men came in to confess about his part in one of Minh's parties at the plantation. He said that when a young girl refused to do something an American general insisted upon, she was beaten until she agreed to his demands."

"Who was the general?"

"I do not know. But the man who confessed was the man who beat her with a whip made from elephant hide, and I could tell that he took great satisfaction in his work. His was not a confession but a brag that he thought could be hidden by the confessional. Perhaps it should have been, but there must be a time when God must hold such a man accountable."

"Did you give him absolution?"

"No," André answered. "And he was furious when I told him that he needed to make a severe act of contrition before I could forgive him for his sins. You see, I *knew* that they were not sins to him but moments of triumph."

"His name?"

"Yes, I know his name. I know it well, for I had seen him swagger in many times to other confessionals before I took one. He uses the name 'Belloc,' which he claims he is entitled to, but he isn't. His mother was only a worker in the Belloc house and spent her days tapping rubber trees."

"She could have spent her night with Belloc," I murmured.

"No, not with Belloc," André said. "You see, Belloc was an old man and childless. When he was young, he suffered a riding accident that left him impotent. No, this one who claims his name is not a Belloc. He is Vietnamese. One of those who tries to be more than he is or ever will be. It shouldn't be too hard to discover his real name."

"Perhaps," I said. "Is there anything else?"

He gave another of his soft laughs. "No, that is all. Except that the man for whom you search is an American general."

"There are a lot of generals in Vietnam," I said.

"Not that many who attend Minh's parties," he said, and slid the door shut, leaving me in the gloom and darkness of the confessional, where I could feel the sweat begin to run off my skin like snakes.

Fell was not in his usual haunts, and it took some looking before I found him hunched over a large glass of scotch to which little, if any, soda or water had been added. The bar was little more than a hole in the wall with a dirt floor and frayed red beads separating a room at the back where tired women with faces pasted white to hide pox scars took their customers. I smelled the sickly-sweet odor of opium and noticed the brown spots on the wall where water had leaked through the whitewash. I pulled a chair out from his table and sat. I touched the tabletop, covered with flies feasting on some sticky substance, and grimaced. He looked up, frowning, blearily trying to bring my face into focus. His face was bloated from drink and his eyes red pools. A stubble covered his chin and spread up onto his cheeks. His shirt bore the stains of last night's meal.

"I've been looking for you," I said.

The frown relaxed and he gave a lopsided grin. "Wingo. Was won-wondering when you would show up."

"You had your doubts?" I asked casually.

He waved his hand, nearly upsetting his drink. "No, no. Just wondering when."

A tingle began to run down my spine like when you step into a clearing for the first time in the jungle and just *feel* the sights upon your chest. I tried to study his eyes, but they kept shifting from mine to the left and back again as if they had Saint Vitus' dance. His hand trembled when he lifted his glass to his lips and drank thirstily.

"What's wrong?" I asked quietly.

"What makes you think something's wrong?" he replied half-angrily. "Just because I have a few drinks—"

"You've obviously had more than a few," I said. The pistol suddenly felt heavy beneath my shirt. "You don't do that alone. You know that. We were *told* that we were to never do this alone."

He studied the contents of his dirty glass for a moment; then tears started rolling down his face. He snuffled and wiped his nose with the back of his hand. I wondered how many opium pipes he had had over the past few hours. He was like a stray misanthrope who had been brought in off the streets.

"I'm going out in two days," he said dully. "Wingo, I'm going out in two days. I don't think I can take that anymore."

"You can take it," I said quietly. "You know that the majority of what you are going to do is office work."

"But I *will* have to go back out into the field. You know that. I'm a field op, for Chrissakes. Why the hell do you think they would have assigned me there if I wasn't a field op? Shit. Motherfuckers are always after you."

He held out his right hand. It trembled so violently that you wouldn't have been able to balance a penny on the back of it.

"Does that look like I'll be able to work the field? Meet the contacts? Bring back what these assholes want? I'm done, Wingo! I'm just a walking shadow, a corpse that has a few last breaths in him, and they want even that." He shuddered and took another long drink. "All I want to do is go home. That's all, just go home. I'm finished. Take me out of Saigon and I'm finished. The razor's edge is gone."

He laughed, but the sound was sharp and edgy, like a man clinging as hard and fast as he could to the last vestiges of self-control. I leaned back, studying him hard. He was like a photograph of a derelict caught on the waterfront in one of the old films. For a moment I thought my eyes could see through the black-and-white grain of that photograph and pull myself inside it with him, the two of us thumbing a ride down the highway toward the Rosebud Indian Reservation, where he could lose himself from the world that was pressing so hard down upon his shoulders.

But I knew that I was making a complexity out of histrionics.

"All right," I said soothingly. "Are you still at the office?"

For a moment I didn't think he understood the question; then he nodded and burped.

"Last day."

"Then let's get you out of here and cleaned up. I need you to do a last favor for me."

"You mean outside of getting your gear? I got that. It's in my pad. In the hall closet."

"Good, good," I said. "But now, there is one more thing that you have to do. Lisa Lee. Remember?"

He shuddered and gulped the dregs of his glass. He placed his elbows on the table and leaned into his hands. He shook his head slowly back and forth as if trying to rock memory away. Then, he took a deep sigh and sat back, staring with haunted eyes at me.

"I'll never forget that," he whispered.

I frowned. "What do you mean?"

"I owed you, Wingo. I owed you!" he blurted.

Tears began to streak down his face and a coldness entered the pit of my stomach.

"It was you, wasn't it, Fell?"

He nodded. "You weren't going to kill her and that would have finished you. They couldn't let you live after all they had told you. You can see that, can't you? That's why they sent you on that mission. You were meant to fail. You were meant to. I didn't know that then, but I knew that if you didn't do it, they would have had you killed somehow. That's why they brought someone in from upcountry for the job. Can't you see that? When they sent you back, you would have been killed in a firefight or something. Or set up as you were. But I didn't know that. Didn't think about that. I just thought if she was dead, then you would be all right."

The coldness began to creep up from my stomach. I stared across at him, feeling anger beginning to work in me.

"And you let me go to that fucking prison?"

He shook his head miserably. "No. After you were sent back up north, I was given courier duty to Australia. You know. Bring the money back from the Nugan Hand Bank for the warlords up north. I was out of the country when you were arrested and then you were gone and there was nothing I could do then. Nothing. I'm sorry, Wingo. I'm sorry."

I sat back, thinking. Fell had been the one, but he was only the arm. There was someone else who put the events into motion, and that was the one who was really guilty. Fell had been trying to repay me for pulling him out of that camp and had unknowingly slipped into their plan, finishing what I would not have finished. And now he would have to live with that for the rest of his life.

"You know about Big Minh and his parties out along Old Plantation Road." I knew Fell was aware of them, but I wanted to remind him of that, to focus his mind away from the moment.

He nodded. "Sumbitch."

"Yes, that's right. That's what he is. Now, I have information that Minh threw a special party out there and that Lisa Lee was hooked up with a general who has peculiar tastes. I need his name."

Fell rubbed his hands hard across his face as if trying to push the bloat away. He shook his head.

"Man, there's a lot of brass in Vietnam. Could have been anyone."

"No," I said, spacing my words carefully so they could penetrate the alcoholic fog in his brain. "No, there won't be that many. *And* there's a record of the movements of all generals so they can be reached on a moment's notice. You know that. It's been standard operating procedure since we've been in Vietnam. You need to find the log for those two months before Lisa Lee was murdered and get them to me."

He stared unbelievingly at me for a long moment. "Are you out of your fucking mind? Do you know where those logs are kept?"

"Lincoln Library," I said simply. "All you have to do is to get into Lincoln Library and 'check' the books out."

"You know you're taking on the Good Old Boy network, don't you?" he said. "Those fuckers don't forget anything. Never. And they have the longest arms—bunch of goddamn orang-orangutans. He's protected by the Long Gray Line stretching back to the banks of the Hudson."

"And that doesn't include the Langley crowd."

"Bunch of goddamned Baptists," he growled. "But they're a big problem."

"All right. But you can do it. I need to go through those records to find out which one has been a regular at Minh's parties. Minh's *special* parties."

"Jesus, you think a *general* offed her?"

I shook my head. "Generals don't get their hands dirty. But they pass the word down unofficially to get things done."

"Maybe Black knows."

"He does," I answered. "But he'll lie. I'll still see him, but I know he'll lie. He's in the lying game right now, and that is a game that he has to play to the hilt."

Fell heaved a great sigh and reached again for his glass, but I gently moved it away from his reach. He stared down at the table again as if reading ancient writings in the sticky swirls and whorls upon the surface.

"All right," he said dully. "I still owe you. Let's do it. Fuck, if I'm going to get killed one way, might as well be another."

I helped him up out of his chair, quickly moving him around to my left so I could support him and keep my hand free for the pistol in my waistband.

We walked outside the bar into the light, and the heat struck hard, like a match flame against our skin.

It was early morning but still dark by the time I managed to get Fell cleaned up and reasonably sober. His face looked like a death's-head, but I knew we had to work quickly, before his nerve left him.

We made our way to the gate. Fell took a deep breath and crossed over to the guard and showed him his credentials. The guard studied Fell for a second, then handed his credentials back to him, and Fell passed on through the gate. I sighed and squatted on my haunches to wait, although I was to meet him in the small park by the Dakow bridge. Dangerous, yes, but I needed to see him safe before the meet.

The minutes dragged by like hours and then I saw Fell coming back to the gate through the darkness. The wind had begun to blow hard from the south, bringing with it tiny grains of dirt and sand. A jeep rolled by and two MPs eyed me suspiciously, but I stayed hunkered down like a weary Vietnamese. The jeep halted beside the guard hut and one of the MPs said something to the guard and pointed back at me. I tensed.

Then an old taxi roared past me, driving straight toward the steel post blocking the entrance to the airfield. He rammed into it and leaned out the window shouting, "To die a glorious death!"

He tried to throw a grenade at the MPs, who were already riddling the taxi with bullets, but the grenade dropped from his hand. I rose and ran quickly for the side alley, sliding around the corner as the grenade exploded. I peeked around the corner as the taxi went up in a ball of flame like a huge Roman candle.

I watched as Fell slipped through the gate behind the MPs and ran for the alley. I stepped behind a stack of cartons and let him go by, waiting to see if he was being followed. But the MPs were intent upon the taxi and a crowd of Vietnamese that was gathering, shouting obscenities at the MPs.

I followed Fell as he ran through the alley, weaving around piles of refuse. He made his way to the quay and paused to draw his breath. Then he walked unsteadily to our meeting place and sat on a small bench just inside the park.

I made my way through the shadows of tamarind trees and slipped out behind him.

"Did you get them?" I asked.

He jumped and then recognized me and smiled weakly. "Yes. I have them."

He handed them to me; then suddenly he was babbling like a child, recounting everything that had happened. I let him talk, hoping that by telling me in detail what he had gone through he would exorcise himself. He trembled and then drew a deep, shuddering breath.

"Thank you," I said.

He shook his head. "Don't. I had to. I owed you."

"You owe me nothing."

"Yes, I still do," he said. "I sent the stuff you wanted to Nguyen." He tried to smile. "I don't think we'll see each other again. I have my orders, you know."

I let him rise and watched as he made his way to the Dakow bridge leading over to Cholon. It was the wrong time of night for him to go across, but I knew the need within him that was making him cross over. Sometimes a man has to put himself in danger only to stop the doubt and demons inside him.

I rose and made my way through backstreets and alleys to the park beside the cathedral and hid inside the bushes to wait until the sun had risen enough for crowds to gather. It was time again to practice patience, although my hands itched to begin reading the binders. I forced my thoughts away, concentrating again on my final day on Harney Peak.

When I had gone to Harney Peak in the Black Hills of South Dakota for my vision quest, the old man who had guided me and prepared me for my individual journey had said that from that point on, each step I would take would be the beginning of a new journey once I had returned from the vision quest. I had starved myself on the mountain for three days and nights, drinking only a little water now and then to keep my mouth from drying out. Then, on the third night, I saw a solitary Indian on a black pony riding slowly toward me from out of the dark clouds beginning to gather around the hills. He was naked, except for a breechclout, and his chest had been painted blue with white hailstones splattered upon it. A red-tailed hawk circled above his head. He carried no weapon save a long staff that he rested upon his hip. His face had been painted half-black, and red tears seemed to be trickling out of his eyes. He said nothing, just rode steadily toward me until I could see the sadness in his eyes. He halted his pony and made a slow circle around his head with the staff, then leaned forward and touched me gently on my chest with it, made the circle again, and was gone.

When I told the old man about the vision, his face grew solemn and sad as we sat together on a hill overlooking the Needles in the Black Hills, and then he softly explained the vision to me: I was to be alone and my journey would be hard and filled with danger and disappointment, but I would eventually find a place to belong, but not on the reservation. That place was someplace in the world off the reservation, which was the world to the Indian.

When I asked him how I would know when I had found that place, he remained silent for a long time, then said that I would know when I saw the red-tailed hawk circling.

I had yet to see that red-tailed hawk.

15

I stood under the shade of a small palm, watching the street and the area around the cathedral, looking for the casual loiterer, one who stayed longer in one place than he should. A few beggars sat on bamboo mats, stretching out mutilated hands to those passing by. Occasionally someone would drop a few piasters or sous in their hands or in the wooden cups beside the knees of the beggars whose legs had been amputated by mines or bullets. There was one who must have been on the fringes of a napalm drop. His flesh had been stretched like fine parchment over his skull, his nose burnt away and now a black hole in the center of his face. The flesh on his arms was shiny pink with dirty gray splotches spattered upon it.

I frowned. Where were the prostitutes? Late afternoon was when the prostitutes would begin to appear to tempt those coming from the cathedral, freshly cleansed and ready to step again into the familiar fire that made Saigon too thick for hymns and temporarily damn their souls again.

But I could see no one who looked like he or she did not belong, and I walked out from under the palm, shuffling my feet, head bowed and hands clasped near the pistol in my belt under my shirt—a proper penitent heading for the confessional.

I stepped into the dark cool of the cathedral and moved to my left to let my eyes adjust to the change from the bright sunlight outside. I smelled the musty scent of old incense, the sweat of the past, and something acrid, like dust shaken from rosary beads dragged out of old pouches for the first time in years.

A few people knelt at altars, praying for deliverance from the wolf that has suddenly come to their door. A small line of confessors stood before one confessional booth, patiently waiting for their turn. Only one booth seemed to be in use, but the one at the far end had the door closed. I took a deep breath and made my way past the line to the far end. I stepped into the penitent's side. The partition was closed and I knocked gently upon the grille.

The panel slid open, but I could not see who was inside. I felt a faint tingle of alarm and slipped the pistol from my belt, gently working the slide back, chambering a round.

"Forgive me, Father, for I have sinned," I whispered.

"Wingo?"

I barely recognized the dry rasp coming from the other side and gripped the pistol harder.

"Is that you, Wingo?"

I nodded, forgetting myself, then said, "Yes. André?"

A heavy sigh came from the other side, then the rasping voice I could not recognize, like a smoker with phlegm caught in his throat.

"Yes. It is I. You must be very careful. Very careful. Do not trust anyone."

He breathed heavily, and I heard his breath rattle in his throat.

"What's wrong?"

He tried a chuckle but was suddenly taken with a harsh cough that seemed to rip his soul from his body.

"I have been found," he said simply.

I slid the door open a crack and took a glance around; we were still alone. I closed the door and leaned close to the grate.

"What has happened?"

"It doesn't matter. Now. It would be best for you to leave Saigon. Go."

"Where?" I asked. "I have no place to go."

"Into the mountains. You are dead, here. There, you may be safe for a while. But they have long arms. Long arms."

"Who?"

"The police. Your people. Those who work for them are everywhere, now, and they look for you. Listen: I don't have . . . much time. Minh's men are on the streets even now looking for you and they will know that you will come here." Alarm suddenly tinged the rasp in his voice. "Were you seen?"

"I don't think so."

Another sigh, this one like bubbles bursting.

"Good. But quickly now. The man you want will be at a party tonight at Minh's house on Old Plantation Road. I do not know who he will be, but he will be there."

"How do you know this?"

"The party will be the type that he likes. Young men and women. Prostitutes. Others. Minh's men have been arresting the street people, but they have all been the young ones. Word has gone out and those who know about Minh's parties and want nothing to do with them have gone into the alleys where they can hide until they are no longer sought. It shouldn't be long. The day passes; soon it will be night, and then—"

Another rattling cough and a sharp breath came from the other side and I heard a *thump!* as if he had suddenly fallen.

I opened the door and stepped out, glancing around again, alert, holding the pistol down by my side where it could not be seen. I saw nothing unusual and opened the priest's door.

André sat slumped against the back of the confessional, his hands gripping his belly, trying to keep his intestines pressed inside, but his grip had weakened and I could see them start to slip away from him. He looked up at me, his eyes filled with pain but still holding that softness that wanted to wash away the sins of the world. Blood had gushed from his mouth and spilled over his cassock.

I started to reach in to help him, but he weakly shook his head.

"Too late. Too late." He tried to smile. His teeth were bloodstained. "Be careful. Go, now. Go with God."

A shudder went through him. A sudden intake of breath, then his hands fell away and his intestines rolled out like thick worms as the light slipped away from his eyes.

I closed the door softly and stepped away. I slipped the pistol beneath my shirt but kept my hand tight upon the butt as I walked away, making my way toward the door of the cathedral, letting everything wash over me, my senses alert for anything that might come suddenly from the shadows and darkness, my stomach a nest of stinging scorpions. My eyes remained dry although I felt the lump in my throat at the loss of one of the few friends I had in Saigon.

I didn't pause at the door but again bowed my head and walked away as fast as I dared, merging myself into the crowd, losing myself in their midst, waiting for the time when it would be safe to go to Nguyen Diem's house.

———

I glanced at the sky; the sun was departing in a last burst of gold and red, and the living things of the night were beginning to stretch and tauten their muscles.

I stepped into the street and hailed a battered Citroën taxi and told him to take me to Nguyen's place. He sped away in a cloud of blue smoke. I craned my head and looked out the dirty back window but saw no one following me.

But I knew they were there like I knew kites were circling above the dead when the jungle was too thick to see the sky.

Thunderheads were rolling in swiftly from the sea when the taxi deposited me at the drive leading to Nguyen's bungalow. Sheet lightning swept across the sky, throwing pale light over the crushed shell drive and the shadows among the trees and bushes, illuminating yet not illuminating and leaving suspicion in its wake. The house at the end of the drive had a single light burning in the room that Nguyen used as his study; the rest of the house was a study in darkness. A tiger seemed to move in the night and I sensed its hunger-seeking through the overgrown garden, stretching across the bare patches of ground, the burning fire of his eyes and black lips slipping back from feral fangs. The night seemed charged with electricity and I slipped from the bath, the familiar comfort of the protective trees and bushes, and made my way warily toward the bungalow, slipping from dark shadow to dark shadow, avoiding the cleared patches of ground wherever I came upon them.

I made no pretense of hiding the pistol but drew it and held it ready as I neared the bungalow. I paused. Lightning cracked and I smelled briefly brimstone and the acrid stench that followed, the smell of a slaughterhouse.

I came up to the bungalow and flattened myself against a wall covered with a bougainvillea vine growing wildly up through the flaking plaster to the pale orange-tiled roof, waiting patiently until I was certain that no one moved within the shadows. I crouched and moved quickly to the French doors leading to Nguyen's study. I turned the handle quietly and slipped inside, finding cover behind the heavily upholstered chair where I had spent nights in conversation and argument with him.

But the room was empty although I smelled the blood, raw and rank upon my nostrils. I moved quickly into the next room where he kept his eclectic collections of Noh theater masks, ornate Javanese shadow puppets, leather and two-dimensional, with black and gold faces, long limbs, and large noses. A metamorphosis of the grotesque into the gods and heroes man needed. Nguyen hung with the puppets, his hands extended in a painful parody of a *wayang* puppet. He hung between the crude Bima and Arjuna, the warrior who had to battle his own weakness before he could be of use to others. Nguyen's bowels had been removed and flung over one shoulder in parody of Lisa Lee. His face was contorted with pain, and as I came closer I could see how he hung upon the wall with large spikes driven through his wrists.

I considered his posture carefully. Obviously he had been posed, and I saw that the left hand had been folded back to form a pointer that indicated the female puppet Srikandi, the princess Arjuna was fated to love, while the right hand had been forced to indicate Arjuna.

Madeleine.

And Arjuna must be Fell.

Someone was playing a cruel joke while working his way through my friends to me. I took a heavy sigh: Fell could take care of himself once I warned him. But Madeleine—I frowned, remembering her words, her promise, and that she would return to her plantation up north. She would be temporarily safe there, but not if I didn't move quickly. *And* I had no way of warning her; telephone lines were haphazard at best, as the Vietcong kept cutting them and tying the lines back to the posts in such a way that each pole had to be climbed to discover the break. There was the radio, of course, but with the lightning storm rolling in from the sea, radio would be tenuous at best. *If* she had a radio. And then again, I didn't know her call sign.

I was going to have to get word to Fell.

I slipped through the rest of the house to the back room where Nguyen had placed a bed for me, close to windows and doors through which I could escape into the thick garden if I needed. Fell had sent my gear in a duffel bag that had been tucked far beneath the bed and somehow escaped whoever had been in the house. I removed it and began laying out the contents upon the bed, aware that the smell of blood was drawing night insects into the room and soon feral dogs would catch the scent and begin prowling around the outside of the bungalow, seeking an entrance, drawing attention from any who might pass by. I dropped the red binders beside the contents of the bag. A jungle blouse and pants, jungle boots, black beret, Special Forces poncho liner to be used as a blanket against the cold nights, canteens, small hip pack, and a Thompson, instead of the grease gun I had asked for, with several clips of ammunition and a knife and machete. Other odds and ends included a compass and a canvas map pouch. Enough.

I dressed quickly and packed as quickly as I could. The blood smell grew thicker. I took the red binders and slipped through back doors, melting into the shadows of the garden, following them down to one wall. A snake slithered away into the underbrush. I came to a wall, scaled it, and dropped down into the other side, crouching, holding the Thompson ready, but I did not feel the tiger here and moved away, into the overgrown garden that had not seen a gardener's hand in a long time.

The house was in equal disrepair, windows broken by the poor looking for something to sell, vandals, soldiers looking for souvenirs, and riffraff looking for a place to shelter temporarily. I slipped in through a sagging French door and quickly made a tour of the house. I was alone. I made my way into what must have been the sitting room and took refuge in a corner where I could use a small penlight to work my way through the red binders.

Seven names came up with enough regularity to indicate they would be at Minh's house for dinner. Three of the names appeared each time together in the first two binders, but in the final binder, only one. I stared at it, amazed, but knowing I had the answer. *If* he was at Minh's house tonight.

But where was Fell? What had happened to him? I had not heard from him since he placed the two red binders in my hands and staggered away in the general direction of the Dakow bridge. Was it an opium den he sought, peace found and lost in the gray smoke from an oily pellet deftly rolled by an old woman? I had recognized the haunted and hunted look on his face in the skin stretched tightly over his skull and the way his shoulders hunched, stuck up like the wings of a vulture resting in the high branches of a dead tree. He carried the sour smell of fear with him always, now, like old whisky leaking out from his pores with his sweat.

I had seen men like that before, on the edge, ready to go one way or the other. Sometimes, fear became so great that the only relief was to go mad and do crazy things in the bush; sometimes, simply putting the muzzle of a pistol or rifle in the mouth and pulling the trigger; sometimes, simply going raving mad and being sent home to spend the rest of their lives in electric shock treatments that would leave them turnips instead of carrots. The choice was a living death or simply blessed darkness forever.

But right now, I had other things to consider.

Rain began to paddle harder, and that would help.

I gathered the binders and carried them outside under the eaves of the bungalow and burnt them, watching the covers blacken and curl, the pages spring into bright flame. When the last flame flickered out, I gathered the ashes and carried them out into the garden, scattering them.

I came back to the room. I heard rats scurrying in the other room and took one last look at Nguyen the Dwarf hung between the puppet dwarfs.

There was nothing I could do for him now. I couldn't call the police because I needed the time, and for now, I had to let the dead bury the dead.

While I made more.

I gathered my gear and left.

The rain had stopped by the time I made my way along the edges of Old Plantation Road to Minh's house. The gate was heavily guarded and I slipped back along the edges of the road and found where a thick vine crawled up and over the wall. I tugged at the strands. They held firm. I wondered why Minh had not had the vine cut back; it was a security risk. But when men become too powerful, they also become careless, secure in their own dominion, mini-gods in their mini-heavens invulnerable in their own minds.

I scaled the wall and dropped down inside the walled garden, falling flat and lying motionless for a long moment on a pile of dead leaves that smelled like old smoke. I crawled forward and made my way slowly through the garden, slipping from tree to tree, looking for the guard I knew had to be there. I found him leaning against the thick bole of a barian kingwood tree, carelessly smoking a cigarette without cupping the coal in his hand. I slipped the Fairbairn from its sheath. I rose from behind a bush and was on him while he had the cigarette in his mouth, his eyes intent on the burning coal. I slammed the cigarette back into his mouth and held my hand across it to keep him from yelling a warning while I slipped the Fairbairn under his ribs, ripping up into his heart. His eyes bulged and he tried to pull my hands away. I pushed harder, twisting the blade to open the wound, and he slumped. His legs jerked involuntarily a couple of times, and I felt the life rush out of him like a floodwater.

I lowered him gently to the ground and stood still, searching for another guard that should have been there. I saw no one and turned my attention to the house.

The general's house had a manicured lawn that sloped back and down toward the river. Azaleas bloomed and night-blooming jasmine filled the air with a heavy perfume. I listened to the quiet of a man-made waterfall as it puddled into a pond. Along the pond edges, brightly colored koi fish nibbled at the thick moss, their mouths making tiny plunking sounds where the water met the stone, mistaking the drip of rain from palm fronds for insects. A cool breeze drifted through the bougainvillea, and the date palms rustled as rain-swollen clouds slipped over the garden.

I heard music coming from the house and laughter and occasionally a woman's excited yip. Light poured from the windows and from the French doors that led out onto the terrace. The doors were wide open to take advantage of the rain-cooled breeze, and a man and a woman stood half-naked on the terrace, intent on each other.

I slipped the bolt on the Thompson back slowly and chambered a round. Cautiously I made my way around the house, staying out of the light, working my way to the back of the house. The kitchen doors were open and I could see three solemn-faced Vietnamese preparing trays of food. I waited until two of them picked up the trays and carried them through swinging doors into the house. I went in rapidly. The Vietnamese man saw me, eyes widening in surprise. He grabbed a meat cleaver, but too late, as I swung the butt of the Thompson hard against his head. He fell hard to the floor. I picked up the cleaver and sank it into his head.

I glanced around and saw a small stairway leading up to the second floor. I took it, climbing rapidly up on my toes, keeping close to the wall where the planks met the joists, hoping the wood had soaked up enough humidity to keep from creaking.

I opened the door a crack and looked out onto a carpeted hallway. The carpet had an Oriental design woven into it: reds and greens and cream strands woven into intricate flowers. At the far end of the hallway, a curving mahogany staircase led to the floor below. Laughter rolled up the staircase. Six bedroom doors stood on each side of the hallway. I slipped out and began to work my way down the hall, opening the doors a crack and peeking in at couples on beds. They were too intent upon themselves to notice me.

Halfway down, a couple appeared at the top of the staircase. A young woman and the man I sought. They were laughing together and he had his arm tightly around her, his huge hand cupping her tiny breast as she squirmed against him. A blue Masonic ring gleamed from his ring finger. I knew him well from the articles that had appeared about him in *Time* and *Life* magazines and *Stars and Stripes*.

Brigadier General Thomas Jefferson Jackson Worland. West Point Class of '50. Old Virginia family that could trace its roots back to John Smith. He had been as good an officer as any who was being groomed by the Old Boys' Club for a command position at the Pentagon. He had been a general who choppered in T-bone steaks and beer to whatever unit made favorable headlines after an operation. He had a special liking for the First Cavalry Air Mobile people instead of the Airborne soldiers because paratroopers had their own sense of elitism that defeated the need of the journalists who always went with the Air Cav on their operations and Worland often rode with them, knowing his own invulnerability, always wearing a yellow cavalry scarf in remembrance of the Seventh Cavalry commanded by George Armstrong Custer, and often referred to the Battle of the Little Bighorn as a classic attack strategy that had gone wrong. He failed to mention that it went wrong because my people had won and Indians were not supposed to win battles against the mighty U.S. Army.

The couple saw me and stiffened. I raised a finger to my lips to silence them and lifted the Thompson.

"What—," Worland began, then fell silent when I pointed the Thompson at him. The young woman suddenly lost control of her bladder, and urine began to splatter against the floor at their feet.

"Where's your room?" I asked softly.

His eyes shifted to the right and I nodded, moving quickly down the hall and opening the door. I glanced inside. The room was dark and empty. I stepped back and motioned for them to enter. The young girl's eyes rolled with fright as she stepped into the room. Worland hung back, his gray eyes hard on mine from beneath his iron gray hair cut into a stiff brush. His shoulders were big and beefy and strained the seams of his white shirt that he wore outside black slacks. But his stomach still bulged against the front of the shirt, and I remembered the jokes we used to make about him pretending to be a warrior when he had been a desk man most of his life.

"Your choice," I said softly.

He hesitated and I stepped forward quickly, jamming the barrel of the Thompson into his soft belly just above the waistline. He gagged and bent forward. I pushed him into the room and pushed the door shut just as vomit spewed from his mouth. I glanced at the girl; she had dropped down onto the floor in a corner of the room, huddling, pulling her knees tightly to her breast. I could see the dark triangle of her sex beneath the pale green Suzie Wong dress she wore. She hid her face on top of her knees to keep from seeing what she was certain was going to happen.

I grabbed Worland's collar and jerked him upright, pushing him across the room until he sprawled upon the bed. He took deep, ragged gulps of air.

"Sit up," I said quietly.

He rolled over and sat up, holding his belly with his hands, feet barely touching the floor. His face had become ashen beneath its deep tan, and the heavy pouches under his eyes seemed to sag nearly to his chin. Yet his eyes burnt hard with a cold fire into mine when he raised them to me.

"Who the hell are you?" he growled.

"Wingfoot," I said.

His eyes widened and I knew then that this was the man who had given the orders to Black and had somehow arranged for my arrest and imprisonment. I tasted something bitter at the back of my throat, and my finger took up the slack in the Thompson's trigger. I wanted to press it hard and send the whole clip into him, but I forced myself to relax.

"What I want to know is why?" I asked. "I know Lisa Lee was pregnant, but why did you have her killed? What's one young woman with one more baby in a country where hundreds are born each day?"

"She was an agent," he said.

I shook my head. "No, that's not everything, is it? The baby was yours, wasn't it?"

He regarded me silently for a moment, then said, "She and her 'friends' were threatening to use that baby against me in the press. Can you imagine the effect that would have had upon the Pentagon? That would have ruined me."

I noticed he used "ruined me" and not the war effort or bad publicity for the United States at a time when hippies and war protest movements back home were beginning to gather support. That would have happened anyway, but it was his career that had brought him to order her death in such a way that nothing could be traced back to him. Black and his office would have buried or even burnt anything that could have linked Worland to the affair.

"And now?" I asked.

"Now? What?" His lips spread in a scornful smile. "There's nothing that can connect me with the North or with what happened to that woman. Are you thinking that you can change things?" He shrugged. "Your word against mine? You wouldn't even be given a paragraph in any newspaper. No one would listen to you, a convicted murderer who has escaped from a penal colony."

His voice grew stronger, and contempt began to show across his fleshy features. He made to rise, but I lifted the barrel of the Thompson and he settled back down onto the bed.

"Yes, I know. Besides, the Good Old Boy network would protect you, wouldn't it?"

An eyebrow rose at my mention of the West Point organization that protected its field-grade officers earmarked for future promotion.

"I know about that, too. Hell," I said harshly, "everybody in the army knows about that organization. As long as you appear reasonably able to be cleared they'll come to bat for you and make you out to be a paragon of shining virtue. What's on your agenda, Worland? Politics after your tour in the Pentagon? Do you see yourself in the Senate? The White House?"

A strange look came over his face for a second, the flickering of plan and ruthlessness, and the truth of my words suddenly dawned on me, and why he always made an effort at flamboyance: the yellow scarf, the continuous association with Custer and the stories of my ancestors about what happened at Wounded Knee when the remnants of Custer's command took their revenge for what had happened at Little Bighorn, and I knew then that Vietnam was only his battlefield for the politics that Custer craved. The Vietnamese were as much sacrificial lambs as my people had been. This war was only a proving ground for those the Pentagon was grooming to be in public office and its key representatives. The military needed this war as a showplace for increased budgets. It was a place for the making of heroes like Eisenhower had been following World War II. America had been without heroes for too long, and now here was an opportunity to create those heroes, despite the war protestors who objected to the reality of the war. It wasn't the present that the Pentagon was concerned with but the future. Disgust rolled over me as I thought of the many body bags being sent back home, closed coffins, framed photos, sepia-tinged, draped in black on mantels and tabletops.

"That's the real focus, isn't it? Politics. You can't afford even a hint of scandal or you would be crucified at the polls by suggestion. My question is how did you ever get Black to go along with you on this?"

He shrugged. "Black's a career soldier, a professional. He knows what needs to be done."

"You didn't tell him the real reason, did you?"

He actually laughed. "God, but you're naïve! Soldiers like Black don't ask 'why'; they just follow the orders. That's their training."

"Like Nuremburg."

"Armies are armies and soldiers are soldiers," he said. "There's no difference in them. Men are trained to take orders and to carry them out without questioning them."

"And there's no difference?"

"Between the German army in the Second World War and America's army today? No. None. You know that. How many times was your team sent into hard places or ordered to erase a village? Did you question that? No, you didn't. I know you, Wingfoot. I know all about the other teams as well. You and others like you were part of an experiment that the army was conducting to form Phoenix."

A puzzled look must have come over my face, because he laughed and shook his head at my expression.

"You think we would build a special operations plan on a hunch? No, we needed men like you to see if such a plan would be feasible before we recruited men into it."

"And Lisa Lee?"

He shrugged again. "A minor inconvenience that has been taken care of. And now, what do you propose to do?"

I barely heard the door opening behind me, but the stunted gasp of surprise registered and I whirled around to see a drunken major standing with his arm around a young Vietnamese boy. The major must have come to the party straight from duty, because he was dressed in his uniform, with a holstered pistol at his side.

"What the hell?" he shouted.

He tried to draw his pistol. I fired a short burst, killing him and the boy beside him. I whirled back to Worland, but he was already disappearing through the French doors that led to a balcony that ran along the side of the house.

Shouts of alarm rang from below. The girl screamed from her place in the corner. I swore and ran for the French doors. I stepped through just as Worland was nearing the corner of the house. I raised the Thompson to fire a burst at him when bullets thudded into the house beside me. I ducked and ran down the other way, toward the back of the house, bullets buzzing around me like angry bees. I paused to fire a burst over the balcony at the soldiers below. One jerked and fell while others ran beneath the balcony and began shooting up through the flooring. I swore again and ran down the length of the balcony and leaped off it. I hit the ground, rolling re-flexively as I had been taught in Airborne school at Fort Benning. I fired another burst at the soldiers under the balcony and ran into the garden, zigzagging my way among the trees for the wall; then I doubled back and around the house.

Three Vietnamese soldiers stood uncertainly around a jeep, their eyes trained away from me, toward the shooting. I fired a short burst, killing them, then leaped into the jeep, started it, and sped away toward the gate. The windshield suddenly starred with bullet holes. A soldier stepped out to try to stop me, then leaped away as the jeep roared down toward him. I floored the accelerator and hit the gate hard, nearly bouncing from the seat when steel met steel, and then I was through and roaring down Old Plantation Road.

I glanced over my shoulder. They hadn't figured out where I had gone yet. I could hear firing and knew they were shooting wildly at whatever shadows presented themselves. I had some time before they would come after me, but I knew I wouldn't be able to outrun a radio and that would come soon.

A dirt road came up leading away from the river and I took it, driving recklessly away and toward the north, weaving my way along roads and paths that presented themselves, always working my way north because I knew they would think that I would head back to Saigon. At night, a lone soldier would do something like that, seeking safety in an unsafe city simply because there were others there seeking the same safety.

I suddenly came upon a paved road and turned north upon it. A few miles later, I sped through Phu Cuong and knew that Ben Cat would be coming up next after a series of nameless hamlets. I was going into the Iron Triangle and would have to abandon the jeep soon because I was entering the area controlled at night by the Viet-cong. They wouldn't ask questions; they would see the jeep, the uniform, and shoot first.

Like Worland said, armies are armies and trained to follow orders.

I managed to make it nearly to Ben Cat before a short burst fol-lowed the jeep as I rounded a bend in the road. I slowed, then leaped from the jeep, letting it drive on wildly out of control. I hit the ground, rolling, and came up. I fired a long burst from my Thompson and the jeep burst into a ball of flame.

I slipped away into the ditch and crawled across a paddy dike to the forest beyond and plunged in, working my way carefully into its welcoming darkness. The cold dark folded around me and I felt the warm embrace of familiarity come over me and gave myself once more over to the forest and jungle.

16

I had failed. I knew that and the thought was bitter as I moved deeper into the forest, looking for a place to spend the rest of the night where I would have a brief sanctuary from everything and collect my thoughts.

I knew I couldn't go back after Worland; that would be an impossibility right now, but later—later, I might be able to. In the meantime, I had to find a place to hole up and collect my thoughts, find—I didn't know what. At the moment, my life felt purposeless, as if I was simply making movement through life, hunted and wanted and, I was pretty certain, wanted dead, not alive.

The rain had stopped, but the leaves of the trees still dripped heavily, soaking me. I found a jumble of granite boulders heavily entwined with vines. They had fallen together to form a half shelter inside. I pushed aside the vines to enter, and a slim shadow suddenly reared up in front of me, spreading its hood. I knew I had stumbled upon a cobra and froze as it began to weave back and forth in the hypnotizing motion that froze birds and forest mice and rats. I shifted the Thompson to my left hand and slowly eased the machete from its sheath hanging down my back. I waited for that short second when the cobra would stop swaying and strike, balancing myself upon my toes to leap back and away. I tried to calculate the length of its body, but it was hidden in shadows. I knew it would strike only the length of its raised body.

The strike almost caught me unaware and the head slipped past my thigh. I swung the machete hard, cutting the snake in half, and leaped away, knowing that the nerves would still be leaping inside the severed head and there was length enough for it to turn. I crouched a short distance from it, watching the body writhe and twist as pain made its way down the nerve endings. When the body settled into small twitchings, I moved forward cautiously and jammed my boot down on the head itself. I swung the machete again, severing the head as close as I dared to the rest of the half body still connected to it.

I heaved a deep sigh and placed the Thompson at my side as I skinned the snake, slicing it lengthwise and stripping the insides out. I peeled the skin from it, seeing the pink flesh emerge. Carefully I sliced the flesh from the bone, cutting the meat into small chunks. I kept a wary eye upon the half shelter, expecting the snake's mate to follow it out. But nothing stirred in the darkness. Cautiously I gathered the meat from the two sections of the cobra and slipped inside the half shelter.

It was dry inside and I gathered a handful of dry leaves and started a small fire in the back of the half shelter where the flames could not be seen. I cooked the flesh and ate what I wanted, saving the rest for later, making certain that it was cooked thoroughly to keep it from rotting rapidly in the heat of the next day. Then I moved to place my back against the stones, sitting with my Thompson in my lap, and slept.

Morning came up quickly with light laddering through the heavy foliage overhead, and I could feel the heat of the day already building and knew that the forest would quickly become hot and steamy. But that would make it easier and safer to travel. Soldiers are soldiers, whether U.S. or Vietnamese, and the Vietcong were no different. They would not want to move unless they were ordered to, and the chances of running across a lone hunter would be slim in the heat.

I glanced at the remains of the cobra; the ants were already at work, stripping the bones clean. I listened to the sounds of the waking forest and knew that I was alone with the forest. Yet I waited, nibbling on a couple of dried pieces of cold cobra meat, wanting the forest to be fully awake before I began to move. But where?

I pulled a map from the case Fell had left me and opened it, spreading it on the ground in front of me, staring at the contours, looking for a destination. Then, I heard a bird that reminded me of a finch singing and suddenly thought of Madeleine and remembered her words and offer to help. I wondered if she would have returned home near An Loc. I traced a route with my finger, trying to find a way that I could make it through the forest to An Loc without exposing myself to road patrols. It was possible, but there would be a couple of places where I would have to cross where the forest had been cleared for the small hamlets and some farms. Unavoidable, but if I went far enough north along the edges of the forest before crossing, I might miss the patrols. Besides, I wondered if they thought I would go north toward the enemy, then sighed as I realized that they could think little else. My team was somewhere else, by now, scattered, I was certain, among another command, and I had no one else to fall back upon except the Montagnards. I knew I could not go back to them, as that would be a natural place to seek me and there would be someone waiting there for me.

I thought about going back to Saigon and trying to lose myself in the city, but that was too dangerous and Saigon, although heavily populated, still carried the risk of an accidental encounter like that with the soldier who had stopped me on Lam Son Square to ask for my papers. Besides, alone, out here, I could be mistaken by American soldiers for a Vietnamese while the Vietnamese might mistake me for an American. My clothes carried no insignia, so I might have a better chance of passing away from the city.

I looked out at the growing light and felt a great bitterness as I thought about Worland and knew as well that there was nothing I would be able to do there as well. He would be heavily protected now, and even if I did manage to get close enough to kill him, what would I do then? I still had no way of clearing my name. I had been tried and convicted and sentenced and no one would ever believe my story against his reputation and the reputation of the Good Old Boy network and that of the U.S. Army, men created officers by an act of Congress. Oh, I knew there were some reporters who might listen to my story and run a query column or two that would be given little credence by those who had the power to do anything at all.

I was finished; I knew it. I was a man without a country, alone in the world, hunted. I would have to find a place where I wasn't known. But right now, I needed to find a place where I could rest and wait for a decision. I had little choice but to hope that I could get to Madeleine's plantation without being discovered.

I sighed and rose to my feet, stepping out from the half shelter and staring at the thick forest around me. A long time had passed since I felt the warm peace that settled over me now that I had a destination, regardless of how short a time I could spend there. The forest was home now, the only home that I had known in a long time. South Dakota seemed far in the past, Ithaca even farther. I wondered who ranched the old quarter that my great-grandfather had homesteaded. The land had never been out of mortgage since, and my father had died there and been buried beneath its hardscrabble earth. There was no one else. My mother had died when I was born. I had a drunk uncle somewhere still on the reservation, but my last letter to him had come back stamped UNKNOWN in thick, red letters. Since then, I had been alone and now found contentment in being alone. I felt tired, empty, but a certain serenity descended upon me from the jungle, and I recognized the feeling as one the doctors watched and waited for with relish to prove their preconceived thesis that man can only stand so much of the jungle before the jungle descended into him. But at least it was better than Saigon or the prison island.

I stepped out into the forest and began my journey forward, into a new life, a new beginning. I didn't know what lay ahead for me, but it didn't matter. I was seeking what had been given to me to seek. Alone, just as alone as the American soldiers would be when they returned home from the war.

Days passed as I made my winding way north. I found and killed an iguana and paused long enough to roast the meat, cutting it into small, thin slices like jerky. I killed a monkey and ate that, tough and stringy meat that left my mouth tasting like old leather. I found a small deer, debated about killing it, then passed by without killing it, as preparing the meat for my journey would take longer than I could spare in one place for long. I found some wild banana stalks and gathered some of them to take with me.

I moved through the various changes within the jungle: places filled with hard, large, twisting roots like giant worms trying to make their way into the forest floor; up and down slopes strewn with bamboo and saffron-colored flowers; places where the air smelled of rotting leaves. When I rested, the sun beamed red through my eyelids and flooded me with warmth like a high river rushing down its banks. Memories sometimes glided across my eyelids: faces, murmurs I could not make out, laughter, the prairie and the hills. They floated like smoke, shot through with streams of light.

Sometimes, I asked myself when I had last known happiness. *If* I had ever known happiness. Was this, then, freedom? Perhaps. But *freedom* is just another word meaning that you have become a prisoner to something else. Words are slippery eels used by those who mean you to think one thing while they intend another. But in the forest, there were no words, only the aimless cries of birds and screams of monkeys, the guttural growl of a night-hunting tiger. Sometimes I heard the sound of helicopters skimming the tops of the trees, and when that happened I stayed beneath the protective canopy of a tree until the forest sank back again into momentary silence.

It was near the end of my second week of careful traveling when I heard gunfire. I froze, then dropped down behind a large banyan root and waited, listening as the crackle of gunfire grew in intensity. By midday the firing had eased off, and by late afternoon a great blanket of silence lay over the jungle.

I rose and moved forward cautiously, listening hard to the silence that surrounded me, slipping carefully through the trees from one trunk to the other, pausing for a moment before moving on again. I had to be patient; a trait that had been bred into me by my ancestors who had lived as I now lived, alone much of the time in the hills and on the plains where a constantly moving object would be easily picked up by the enemy. Motion was my enemy now, and I had to be constantly aware of it.

I found the small hamlet, the burnt-out huts standing like glowing charcoal skeletons in the nightmare just before twilight. A few scrawny chickens still scratched the thin soil vainly in search of a seed that might have been dropped, but the rains had come too late to this hamlet to help the crops and each seed had been carefully hoarded and carelessness became a sin.

Bodies lay scattered around the hamlet, grotesque and twisted in their death agonies. The ground seemed hot and gave off shafts of steamy vapor. Brass cartridges lay everywhere and I searched among them for some that were still unfired. I found many and filled a small canvas sack I took from a dead body with them and another sack with empty clips that would fit the Thompson. I found a couple of hand grenades and hung them by their handles from my belt. I found a heavy-bladed *coupe-coupe* in its wooden sheath and took that as well.

At the end of the village, I saw where some villagers had fled into the jungle at the first assault. They had made a makeshift altar and were offering sacrifices to show the *ma*, the spirits of the dead who lay back in the village, that they were remembered. I watched as the *songman* directed the placing of tiny cups of tea on the altar. Tiny bowls of rice were placed between burning *joss* sticks. I knew that was needed to keep the Celestial Dog from eating the dead men's stomachs. I slipped away before the villagers could see me. As an outsider they would see me as a *cache-muong*, a change-fated person who might disrupt the movement of the universe and set it on a new path if I intruded upon their ceremony. If they saw me, they would know me as a shadowman who moved beyond the help of the Hearth-Guardian.

I paused when I was again deep into the forest to rearrange my gear and pack everything more tightly. Then I moved again, traveling into the night until constellations burst from the black dome of the sky. I made my way up a hill and paused, staring down into the blackness at the bottom on the other side. A mist seemed to roll up from bottom so thick that I thought quickly that a fire must have broken out, and oily clouds of smoke were rolling toward me. The air smelled dank like freshly turned earth, and the mist rolled slowly halfway up the hill where it wrapped itself around the tree trunks and hung like shrouds. It was a place of death, and I found a thick tree that would partially conceal me, and ate some cold iguana meat before dropping into a light sleep, waiting for the sun to rise and burn away the threat of death before I moved down the hill.

The end of the third week brought me to An Loc. I stayed in the trees, studying the village, the paved road leading into it, and the dirt roads spidering off from it. I squatted on my haunches, studying the dirt roads. Most led to small huts and farms, but one disappeared into a grove of trees, and I could see a red-tiled roof peeking above the tree line. That had to be an old French house, which could be Madeleine's plantation. It could also belong to the province chief, but I had a hunch the province chief would want to live closer to the military camp for protection. Besides, I had little choice. I would start there and perhaps get lucky.

I glanced at the sun; just past midday. I could chance crossing the area and making my way down the dirt road or I could wait until nightfall.

But I knew An Loc and knew that there was a strong guerrilla force operating in the area at night. From a distance, I could be mistaken for a Vietnamese, even by the Vietnamese. Close encounters, however, were what needed to be avoided if possible. The danger would be when I had to cross the paved road.

I decided that in this instance my chances were better if I used daylight instead of night to travel. At night, any friendly forces might mistake me for the enemy and shoot first, while the chances of finding Vietcong out in the open during daylight were slim. I would simply have to be very careful while crossing the road.

I rose and made my way down the hill, watching carefully for punji pits: holes carefully covered, the bottoms of which had sharpened bamboo stakes implanted with human feces spread over them. A bamboo stake through the foot or leg would make the soldier unable to carry on his duty, and the blood poisoning that would come from the feces would keep him further disabled. The Vietcong liked to place punji pits on trails through the forests and jungle and at the edges of fields where soldiers often patrolled instead of staying out in the open. The closer I got to the first field I had to cross, the closer attention I paid to the tops of the trees and the ground.

I found a punji pit, freshly dug, which proved my point about a stronghold of guerrilla activity. I would have to watch carefully, too, while crossing the field. One could often find Bouncing Bettys in the fields, placed there during the night. They were small mines that leaped up into the air when one stepped on them and blew the manhood off and filled one's guts with shrapnel. Strangely enough, most soldiers worried more about getting their manhood blown off than losing their lives and feared the Bouncing Bettys more than they did a firefight.

When I reached the edge of the field, I slung the Thompson over my shoulder and slumped my shoulders like a weary Vietnamese who had been forced to go out in the noonday sun to make a circle patrol. I walked slowly, as if the heat was pressing down hard upon me, and I felt the benign indifference of the universe. It was the way the Vietnamese soldier moved when not around officers, unhappy with his lot but better off than he might have been otherwise. It was not the job, however, but the concept of being forced into doing something he did not want to do at a time when he would rather be laying up away from the noonday sun, playing cards with his friends in the cool shade and drinking rice wine or beer. Yet the slow movement allowed me to concentrate upon the ground.

As I came close to the paved road, I saw a small convoy moving up from the southeast. If I crossed in front of them, it would be close, and such a figure as I was trying to project would halt and wait, watching curiously while the trucks passed. It would be a natural break in the monotony of his walk. So, I waited, my heart hammering wildly in my chest, hand clutching the strap to the Thompson, as the convoy neared in the shimmering heat. I kept my head bowed as much as possible and stood in the ditch to lend an illusion to my height. I offered a salute that helped to obscure my face to the jeep and officer riding in it. He returned my salute indifferently, ignoring the presence of a mere soldier at the side of the road. Then I squatted on my heels to drop my size even lower, waving casually at the men in the passing trucks. Some shouted obscenities at me and made rude gestures; most ignored me.

After the last truck passed, I rose and crossed the road, making my way as fast as I dared down the dirt road to the grove of trees. I noted the twisted oaks and sycamores and eucalyptus trees, large shade trees that had been artfully planted years ago to provide a comfortable and cool place for the plantation master and his family to entertain in the hot days. The grove was overgrown now, the bushes ragged and ill-kept, and I noticed that mines had been carefully hidden in them. Neglect showed in the unpruned branches of the trees and the shoots growing up through once graveled paths that wove gently through the grove. Stone benches stood here and there, some fallen onto their sides. Moss and lichens grew on the benches and were covered with bird droppings. Old families, like civilizations, are doomed to decay and slip away into the past. I was seeing the beginning of an end.

I crossed through the grove to the house; it wasn't a manager's house but the house of the owner. An effort had been made to keep its once splendor, but time weathers plaster and whitewash and in places I could see where brick showed through and the pockmarks of bullets. Several pockmarks. The roof had not been cleaned in a long time, and some tiles had slipped and lay broken next to the house. A shaded fountain still had fish in it, but the water was more of a trickle than a spray, and birdbaths had furry moss growing in the bottom of them. Yet, the windows were clean and the trim around them freshly painted. It was an odd combination: an attempt to maintain the gentility of the old place and yet part of it beginning to fall into ruin.

I made a quiet tour of the house outside, noting that the doors in the back had been replaced by steel doors while the wooden front doors had been kept and been freshly painted with white that stood in stark contrast to the faded walls. I found four heavily armed guards, none Vietnamese, at the corners of the house and slipped back through the grove and made my way to the road leading up to the circular drive that swept along the front of the house.

Taking a deep breath, I made my way up the road, and when I emerged from the bend a shout warned me to stop.

I obeyed and raised my hands to shoulder level, high enough to suggest compliance, close enough that I could sweep the Thompson from my shoulder and press it into action.

One of the guards came down cautiously, his rifle, a nine-millimeter MAT-49 submachine gun once used by the French before the fall of Dien Bien Phu, centered on my chest. I felt my stomach muscles tense, and my weight moved forward onto the balls of my feet, ready to throw myself to one side or the other.

"Ne vous approchez pas. Qu'est-ce que tu fais là?" he asked. I noted that he did not ask in Vietnamese, so either he recognized that I wasn't a Vietnamese or else his arrogance prompted him to use French.

"I wish to see the lady of the house," I said in English.

His eyebrows rose. "American?" he asked.

I nodded.

He thought a minute, then said with difficulty, "What do you want?"

"That is between the two of us," I replied.

He hesitated, then nodded at my weapon. "Give me your weapon."

"No," I said calmly.

His eyes narrowed and his lips spread in a thin line; then a shout from the house caused him to half-turn.

"Raul!" she called. "Allow him to come up."

I looked up at the house. She stood in the doorway, wearing a white dress that dropped to her knees. She held a large pair of binoculars in one hand, shading her eyes with the other. When he hesitated, she motioned impatiently with the binoculars.

He turned to me and gestured with his rifle. "Be careful," he warned. "I will shoot. Believe that."

"Oh, I believe it," I said, dropping my hands. "One must be careful in times like this."

His eyes narrowed, but I smiled at him and moved my hands slightly away from my body as I stepped forward, walking slowly up to the three steps leading onto the small terrace in front of the house. A hammock hung at one end between a pillar and the house, next to a rattan table and two chairs. One had not been used in a long time, its surface dried and splintered from disuse. The other showed a seat polished with frequent use. I turned and looked back down the road and noticed the line of the hills in the west that showed this had once been a pleasant place where one could sit with an afternoon drink and watch the sun set. It must have been beautiful in the days when the French still had a hold on Vietnam. But time had eroded that pleasantry.

"Hello," she said warmly. "I have been expecting you."

"Why?" I asked.

"The radio," she said. "We must have a way of contacting the army when we need them. They speak of you on that."

"What do they say?"

"That you are an assassin who tried to kill General Minh. That wasn't true, was it?"

I shook my head.

"I thought not. It is all right, Raul," she said to the man standing watchfully behind me. "He is one I have been expecting."

I watched as Raul nodded and lowered his weapon and returned to his post at the corner of the house.

"You have some good watchdogs," I said.

"It is, unfortunately, a necessity," she answered.

A smile broke across her face. "Come in. Please. You will be safe here."

"Will I?" I asked as I climbed the steps and stopped in front of her.

The smile slipped a little, but she held it and nodded. "For a while. For now. Please." She gestured at the doorway.

I looked down at myself, grimy from my travel through the forest.

"I'm afraid I'm not very presentable," I said.

She laughed and hooked her arm into mine, leading me into the house. "It can be remedied. I think you may be near the size of my husband. His room has been kept presentable, and his clothes still hang in the wardrobe. Most of them," she added.

She led me into the house. The rooms were high-ceilinged and furnished elegantly, but there was a shabbiness in most of them, the result of time, not use. The oaken floors gleamed with fresh polish, and vases of flowers had been placed on most of the tables. But the air still carried a musty smell like old men, and I imagined that at night ghosts probably filled the house with their silent laughter.

"Would you like a drink?" she asked.

I shook my head. "Yes, but I would rather clean up first, if I may."

"Certainly," she said, and took my hand and led me to the stairs that curved up to the second floor. Her husband's room opened out onto a small balcony at the front, and I could see An Loc in the distance. An elegant spread was on the bed, and mosquito netting had been tied back to the tall bedposts. In one corner of the room stood a comfortable chair beside a table with a marble top that matched the marble top of the dresser. A lamp stood on the table beside an album. The mahogany wardrobe stood in the corner. She crossed to it and opened it, showing her former husband's clothes still neatly hanging, the shoulder seams precisely even. Drawers beneath the wardrobe opened to reveal neatly folded underwear and socks in a variety of colors.

"You may help yourself," she said. Her eyes suddenly became melancholy. She nodded at one door opposite. "That leads to my room. The bathroom is through there." She pointed at another door opposite the bed. "We each have our own, so you do not have to worry."

"Thank you," I said.

She nodded and looked steadily into my eyes. "Did you find what you searched for?"

"Yes."

"And did you . . . ?" She left the question hanging delicately.

"No. I tried, but he got away. Do you want to know who?"

She studied me long and hard, thinking, then said, "Yes. But only because I do not wish to know such a man."

"General Worland," I said.

Her eyes widened. "*Merde!* I had a drink with him once at the club. He was . . . inappropriate with his suggestions. I tired quickly of him and left."

"Lucky," I said.

"Yes. I was." She clapped her hands together once. "Now then, you get cleaned up and I shall arrange for drinks on the terrace and tell the cook to set another plate for dinner."

"Thank you," I said. "You know, you are taking a great chance by letting me stay here."

She shook her head. "No. It is something that I want to do."

She smiled and left. I sighed and sat in the chair to take off my boots. I opened the album. It contained pictures of the house being built. Old pictures, sepia-tinted. The family posed on horses in front of the structure being claimed from the jungle. I thumbed through the album quickly, through generation after generation, seeing happiness, then the faces of all became tighter and the smiles harder, and I knew I was in the war years. I shook my head and placed the album back on the table.

And now the jungle was beginning to reclaim what it once had, the house slowly falling into disrepair, the grove already turning back into the jungle. Soon not even pride would be enough to hold the jungle away.

I sighed and pulled my boots off, grimacing at the odor that rose. I stripped, leaving my clothes in a pile, and headed naked into the bathroom. The tub was deep and lion-footed, the mirror old, blurring my reflection. I could barely recognize the man who looked back. Shaving soap, a straight razor, and lotions stood lined neatly on a shelf beneath the mirror. Pears Soap had been placed in the soap dish.

I turned the bath knobs on and watched the water as it gushed out, hot and clean, into the tub. I stepped into the tub and relaxed against the cool porcelain back, letting the hot water climb slowly up my body, feeling the past few weeks begin to wash away.

Madeleine waited for me on the terrace. She had changed her dress to one a soft yellow that reflected against her skin. A tray holding a variety of liquors, tonic, and a soda siphon had been placed on the rattan table next to her. She smiled as I came to her, wearing one of her husband's white shirts, cotton trousers, and a pair of espadrilles. They were the only shoes that fit. The trousers were too big at the waist and the shirt a bit small in the shoulders, but at least I had clean clothes on and felt better for it. My clothes had been tactfully removed from the room while I bathed. I presumed by a maid, although I had yet to see one.

"Feeling better?" Madeleine asked.

I dropped into the chair beside her, sitting gingerly against the splintered surface.

"Yes. Much better," I said.

"Good." She gestured at the tray. "Would you like a Campari-and-soda? Or perhaps a cognac? Brandy?"

"Campari and soda sounds good," I said.

"It is refreshing," she said, dropping a thin lemon into a glass and mixing the drink. She handed it to me, then made one for herself. She took a sip, then said, "What will you do?"

I shrugged. "I don't know."

"You may stay here as long as you like," she said.

"There will be talk," I answered, glancing at the guards.

She followed my gaze and laughed. "They will be quiet. They are all cousins. Their plantations are gone to the war and so they stay here and keep this place safe."

"You haven't been troubled?"

"Certainly. All French are troubled. But this is our home. I know no other. Like you, I have no other place to go. France is a foreign country to me. So, we endure. If this place is destroyed, then I shall be destroyed with it."

"The Vietcong—"

"Did you know they are the invention of the Americans?" she asked. I looked startled and she smiled and nodded and continued. "Oh, yes. Most certainly. Why do you think that you are here? Because of an old treaty that isn't worth the paper it is written on? America has broken many treaties."

"I am quite aware of that," I said dryly. "My own people are the victims of broken treaties."

"Yes. But it is the same thing here. The United States needs a deepwater port in this part of the world because of China. That is why you are here. The South Vietnamese government gave the United States Cam Ranh Bay on a ninety-nine-year treaty in exchange for your support in their war against Hanoi." She gave a wry smile. "You see?"

I shook my head. "How did the Vietcong get invented by the United Sates?"

Her face turned serious. "It was during World War II. The O.S.S. sent teams into Vietnam with arms and supplies to fight the Japanese. At the request of Ho Chi Minh."

"Ho Chi Minh?" I frowned. I thought I knew the history of Vietnam; I had known about the Deer Teams. My own team was formed on that same principle. But that Ho Chi Minh had requested U.S. assistance was news to me. I knew about Cam Ranh Bay and the lease, although that was not really made public in this manner. It was supposedly a lease paid for by appropriations to the South Vietnamese government. That the lease might have included a demand for military support was new to me. But, as I thought about it for a minute, it made sense. The U.S. now had interests to protect in Southeast Asia. The deepwater port was essential in case the situation with Communist China became worse and war broke out. It gave the U.S. a strategic port within easy striking distance of the mainland across the China Sea. Now that I thought about it, it all made sense instead of using the old SEATO treaty as an excuse for the military buildup in Southeast Asia. The U.S. was using a bit of political maneuvering to run an end-around play around the public.

"Ho Chi Minh was educated in France," she said, sipping. She placed her glass carefully upon the table. "He and some of his friends began trying to get France to leave Indochina, but the

French government didn't listen to their protests. So, he began to build alliances with other countries. Very subtle. But he is a very patient man."

"You sound as if you know him," I said.

"Oh, all the French still in Vietnam have probably met him at one time or another," she said easily. "All of the old families, that is. Mine are among the oldest. He has been to dinner here. When my father was still alive, that is, and before the revolution. Of course, that was long ago. Now, we live in the shadow of the war. Sometimes, the younger Vietcong decide that we should be driven out and attack us. They are the radicals who want all white people out of Southeast Asia and forget that we are as much Vietnam as they are. They look at us and think that we are French, but we are really Vietnamese."

She waved her arm broadly, indicating the plantation. "They see all of this and want it, but they forget that we did not take the land from them. My family bought the land and it has been ours just as the peasant will scrape together piasters to buy land himself for his rice paddies or farm. We were no different except we look different. And the French government made things as hard upon people like us as it did upon the Vietnamese. We paid a fair price for our workers—more than some others—and paid our taxes to the government just as all other Vietnamese did. No, we sometimes call ourselves French, but we are not French; we are Vietnamese."

She fell silent for a long moment, staring out at the far hills, then said softly, "I will die here. I know that. And I will be buried with the rest of my family, and when this war is over and the South has lost, then some of the peasants will claim the land or one of the new government officials will claim the land and the jungle will claim our graveyard because there will be no one left to take care of it. Or it will be plowed under by a small farmer who buys the plot of land for his little farm. My body will become a part of the soil of Vietnam and I will be forever a part of this country just as the rest of my family is becoming a part of this country. But we shall be forgotten and remembered only in the new history books as the enemy and not a part of the country. This is a great sadness but an inevitability. All things must come to an end, and our end is near. Very near. And I shall see that end and the beginning of the new."

"You think the war is lost, then?" I said.

She sighed and picked up her glass, sipping. "The war was lost when it began. The Americans did not learn from the French mistakes. They try to fight as the Vietcong and the North Vietnamese Army fight. They do not fight as they know how to fight. Some people do not think that an idea can be defeated. That is wrong. It can be. Ours was. The idea of France was. Now, the Americans are following in the footsteps of France and claiming great victories when all they win are small battles that mean nothing. Ho Chi Minh and his armies are fighting a familiar war that they won once before, and as long as this war continues to be fought his way, he is content, because he knows how it will end. He is a very patient man and time means little to him. Besides"—she smiled crookedly—"every nation gets the government it deserves. Even the United States."

"You must worry some about raids here," I said. I drank my Campari and placed the glass on the table. She moved to refill it, but I shook my head.

"Yes, it is almost time for dinner," she said, smiling. "We shall have wine with the dinner. Our wine cellar is still very good, and I have selected some of the older wines for tonight."

She did not answer my question, but it was more rhetorical than a question to be answered. There was no need to worry about the inevitable. The raids would come, and when they came, then would be the time to worry about them. Meanwhile, her people would watch and guard and wait. They had learned the same patience that the Vietnamese had learned, for time meant nothing to them when they already knew the ending. There is a certain serenity that comes over one when one knows how his time will end. A resignation, perhaps, and although they would fight against the end to hold it off as long as they could, Madeleine and her people already knew that the fight was only a fierce resistance to the future that had been forged for them by the past. So time had become only the present.

I wondered about the destiny that had been forged for me. I did not know my own ending, yet, but I knew that it, too, had been forged many years before by my ancestors and those my ancestors had fought. I had stepped out of that future when I left the reservation, but I had not stopped the turning of the earth and the passing of time, and my end had also been made for me. Unlike her, however, I could only speculate upon what that ending would be, as I was solitary in the world, now, and had no land that I could be content with, no land that I could claim as mine. I was only a wanderer over a wasteland.

Dinner was a step back in time to the formality of the past. For the first time, I saw some of the servants, who waited on us at the table, laid with fine china and silverware with Madeleine's family crest upon it. Wineglasses were fine crystal and sparkled in the candlelight that had been lit when the soft night fell upon us. There was a delicacy to the movement around the table where we dined alone although there was room at the table for her cousins. I felt, though, that she had decided that we would dine alone in solitary splendor that formed an intimate ambiance. Soft music came from a record player in another room, music from another time when life moved slowly from day to day with timeless content. She was doing her best to re-create an elegant moment in a world turned chaotic.

The chains of the past surrounded us even while we ate, and I realized that this was a moment in which one could forget the present only for a very short time. I wondered if a return to that present would be more painful than it was because of the fierce attempt to maintain that elegance in a world that no longer cared for cultured taste. Even while we ate, I couldn't help thinking about Charlie squatting in the bushes with a cup of cold rice that made him stronger than the meal Madeleine and I were enjoying together. That which makes us miserable makes us stronger.

Yet one must have his dreams, for the dream by itself is necessary in order to make life durable and dinners like this provided a sense of not only nostalgia but also a wish to return to an ordered life. Here, now, we were actors in an ancient play, aware of the horror, but denying it, bathing ourselves in a poem of the sea reflecting the stars.

We took brandy in front of a small fire in the library, sitting upon a small couch together, close enough to be aware of each other. I watched the firelight play across the fine skin of her face, softening her features into a mellow expression, and when she turned her face to look at me, I leaned forward and kissed her softly upon her lips without a prelude and was kissed back softly in return. A gentle rain began to fall outside, a September rain although it was not September except for us, the autumn of our night together.

She rose and took my hand, leading me up the polished staircase to her room. Candles had been lit by someone and bathed the room in a golden glow. We kissed and slowly undressed each other. I lay in her bed as she moved around it, letting down the mosquito netting, momentarily appearing behind the netting in the soft image of Aphrodite. Her breasts firm with dark nipples a hint only, there in a dreamland that I was about to enter.

I awoke in the middle of the night. The rain had passed and the moon was now up, and in its light I saw her glossy black hair upon my pillow. I rolled on my side and smelled the scent of night-blooming gardenias in the hollow of her neck. She opened her black eyes and caught me staring at her. She smiled gently and draped her arm over my shoulders, pulling me close. I ran my hand down the silky length of her back and she snuggled closer to me, tightening her embrace. We lay in the darkness, and I knew that I had been blessed for the moment and that was enough to carry me through the next day and, if I was lucky, perhaps a week. Or maybe two. But September never lasts; October comes, then the autumn ends, and we enter into the winter of despair that always brings an end to happiness. It was out there, waiting now for the time to be right. Implacable, patient, inevitable, while I fell back into the dream.

We settled into a comfortable routine, mornings spent making the rounds of the plantation on horseback, noons lunching on the terrace or having an occasional picnic in the grove, afternoons reading—sometimes she would curl up at one end of the couch in the library and listen while I read poetry aloud to her—and listening to the radio to hear the news of the outside world, dinners together and alone, and nights lying in each other's arms.

The first week passed and the search for me still continued to be mentioned, but with less frequency, and then a week passed in which I was not mentioned at all. But I knew that the tiger was still out there, searching for its prey. Worland would not be safe until my body was returned to him in a black rubber body bag, and he knew that as long as I remained alive, his plans were like a house built upon sand. And this made him a constant danger, for until I was dead, he would not have his own freedom, a word, I have discovered, that means only that one has nothing left to lose. He was a man at war with himself, and in war there is no substitute for victory. He did not understand that the world is not made on a human scale although he wanted it to be.

I never gave a thought to other lovers that she might have had since her husband's death. They didn't matter to me. The past was the past, and for now I was the present and that was enough for me or should have been for any man.

I recognized this in the American captain Juan Sanchez who came unexpectedly one day to Madeleine's door, a small bouquet of flowers in one hand and a bottle of wine in the other. When Madeleine opened the door, he simply walked in past her as if he had been gone only an hour and was returning to his home.

"Hello, my dear. Miss me?" he said, and bent his head to kiss her, but she gracefully turned a cheek and caught the intended intimacy there instead.

His black eyebrows rose in surprise. He straightened and frowned down at her, his black eyes narrowing suspiciously. His mouth hardened.

"Aren't you glad to see me? It's been a couple of months. I should think that you would have been lonely."

I studied him curiously. He carried himself with that odd self-importance that I had seen in Hispanic officers who had come up through the ranks and through Officer Candidate School before and treated women as if they were personal possessions, demanding this and that from them with a self-assuredness that said they were used to women doing what they told them. He had a mustache that hid a weak upper lip, and his black hair had been cut to hide a receding hairline. His cheeks looked like a chipmunk's pouches, and a soft roll under his chin told me that he did not spend much time in the field. Besides, he still had not seen me standing in the doorway to the library or, if he did, chose to ignore me as one of her staff or workers.

He glanced at her clothes and clucked his tongue disapprovingly. We had been out riding and she was dressed in an old long-sleeved cotton blouse that still showed perspiration stains. Her tan pants had a network of tiny creases in them and her boots were dusty. She had caught her long hair up in a single gather held back from her forehead with a simple sterling clasp.

"Really, you should take more pride in your appearance," he said. "Go and change."

A deep flush appeared along her cheeks and up the column of her throat.

"Hello, Juan," she said. Her voice held a hint of hardness that suggested her anger with his behavior, but it did not register with him as he held out the flowers and wine. She took them reluctantly and placed them on a small table beside the front door.

"Thank you," she said.

His face brightened and he stepped forward to embrace her, but she took a step back and indicated me standing in the doorway. He frowned as he stared at me, hostility gleaming in his eyes.

"How do you do?" I said.

His face darkened as he turned back to her.

"Am I interrupting 'something'?" he demanded.

"I am busy," she said. "You forget that I have a plantation to run."

"And who is he? One of your workers?"

I had enough of his insolence and spoke. "As Madeleine said: we are quite busy."

He drew himself up, looking through hooded eyes at me. "Captain Juan Sanchez. United States Army. And who are you?"

I noticed that he placed himself first instead of asking for an introduction from Madeleine. The muscles along my back and shoulders began to stiffen.

"Thomas Johnson," I said. I made no move to come forward and offer to shake his hand.

"American?" he asked, then: "You are obviously not a soldier. So, who are you?"

I felt a smile begin. My hair was long and had not been cut since I had been sent to the prison island, and covered my ears. I slouched in the doorway.

"Is that really any of your business?" I asked, feeling the smile stretch wider.

His eyes narrowed and a dark flush deepened the brown of his face.

"I want to know."

I shrugged my shoulders. "People in hell want ice water, too."

He took an angry step toward me and Madeleine moved quickly in front of him, placing her hand on his chest, stopping him.

"I think you had better go," she said quietly.

"Go? Me? I drove all the way up here to be with you. I thought we had an understanding between us."

"You presumed too much," she said. Her voice sounded hard. "Now, please go."

"No."

I moved toward him but stopped when she raised her voice, calling, "Raul! Please come here quickly!"

The captain blinked at her, frowning, confused by why she had not been swept off her feet by his charm. He flicked a glance at me and saw me standing close at Madeleine's shoulder. His eyes met mine, then slipped uneasily away and came back. He tried to maintain a stare but saw something in my face, my eyes, that made him uneasy. He shook his head and walked to the small table and picked up the flowers and wine. Raul appeared at the door, his face hard, his rifle held ready.

"Yes, Madeleine?" he said. "What is the matter?"

"Would you escort Captain Sanchez off the property, please?"

"Very well," he said. He stepped through the door and tapped Sanchez on the shoulder. "You heard my cousin. Let's go."

Sanchez pressed his lips together tightly. He turned and left without a word, walking stiffly to a jeep that had been parked in the circular drive. He tossed the flowers behind the seat and placed the wine on the passenger side. He stepped into the jeep and drove away, spinning his wheels angrily as a teenage boy would in his jealous fury.

Madeleine turned to me, her face drained and tight. Our eyes locked and she walked to me and placed her arms around me, resting her face against my chest.

"I am sorry about that," she said. "I had no idea he would come by."

"There's nothing to be sorry for. Unless it is that you would rather have him here than me."

Her arms tightened around me. "No. I don't know what I want anymore. There is no talking with him. He is just interested in one thing. He said he loved me."

"Do you love him?"

"No. I don't think so. I don't know. Until you came, I thought I might. I had had enough lovers and wanted . . . something to last for a change. You understand?"

I did. It was the despair of loneliness and the war that had broken a sense of permanence in her life. Living with doubts and indecision yet being forced to make decisions was hard on anyone who had not been born to it. But she was a woman of the war who had been forced into that situation.

I looked down at the top of her head and saw a few strands of gray in her hair that I had not seen before. A sadness reached deep down into me and I held her close in my arms, feeling her loneliness creep into mine and join it. Her shoulders began to shake and I knew she was crying.

Raul appeared in the doorway, took in the situation at a glance, nodded at me, and disappeared.

We stood there until her sobs stopped. My shirt was wet from her tears.

For the first time, I felt as if I belonged somewhere. Here. At this moment, I belonged here, yet an uneasiness came into me as I wondered if such a thing could last between two people who had not known each other for very long.

The war had brought us together. And now, I felt divorced from the war. I imagined it was like someone becoming divorced from a wife and suddenly finding the one good thing that could have happened to him. Browning, again: somewhere there is the one person that will make your life complete, and you must seize that moment or lose it forever. Still, an emptiness stayed with me as I could feel doubt beginning even though I was happy for the first time in a long time. I knew that was dangerous, as the gods are fickle and those to whom they gave happiness they soon meant to destroy. I knew that, too, had known it my entire life. Happiness was not permanent and would never be permanent for some. I had learned that early in my life by seeing the despair that followed happy moments on the reservation in South Dakota.

I had seen it in college.

And I had seen it in the army.

Yet we spent the days in a sort of happy melancholy. At times, I would look up suddenly and catch her staring at me, sadness deep in her eyes. Our cocktail time grew to two, then three drinks together, and I knew that she was wondering about the happiness that had come to us and if it would last. We were happy, but Sanchez was still there between us, as I knew she was wondering if he would come back. People like Sanchez do not give up easily and keep pressing their wishes upon others even after being warned off.

Then, I began to wonder if she was content with the decision she had made or if she had even made a decision, yet. I couldn't help it; I could feel that certain despair deep inside me that made me question what had happened. She had not told him to never come back or even that she was through with him. She had simply made him go away for the moment. She had not spoken the words, and there are times when words must be spoken, given wings, times when present and past are both present in the future. Eliot's words from "Burnt Norton" began to wander through my mind in the odd moments when a long silence would come between us. Eliot was right, I knew: time is unredeemable, and all thoughts otherwise are merely dreams in a world of speculation.

I still heard the birds in the shrubbery when we went outside and watched tiny dust motes move through the sunlight to settle upon the daily-cut yellow roses in a vase she always kept upon a mahogany table near the French doors of the library, a ritual from time past that she now maintained automatically.

Humankind cannot really bear much reality, and I knew that reality was coming to us like a dark thundercloud rolling in from the sea. We had only these brief moments in which to have happiness, and that reality would bring a dark melancholy upon me. Over and over I kept going over our world together, an unbelievable world. Sunlight seemed golden, for the moment, and yet I knew the dreamworld that we had built together was too much for the two of us to hold, and a great ache would build inside me. I began to wonder if I had the ability to stay happy or if I was to always have unhappiness lurking at the edges of my happy days.

I tried to keep those dark thoughts away and managed to do so when we were together, when we were laughing, enjoying the day together. But at night, I would awake and listen to the night sounds drifting in through the open French doors that led to the balcony outside our room.

One night, I awoke and watched as a moth fluttered in through the open French doors and danced around the flames of the candles we had kept lit on Madeleine's dresser. Then, suddenly, the moth danced too close to a flame and its wings burst into fire and it fell, dead, beside the candle. I slipped quietly away from her and rose, walked to the candles and blew them out, then made my way back to bed. She murmured in her sleep and turned to me, throwing her arm around my shoulder as if protecting me from the night. I rolled my head on the pillow and smelled faintly the jasmine again in the hollow of her throat.

I fell asleep like that but slept badly, dreaming of shadows creeping toward me from the jungle darkness and waking briefly when they came near, then falling again into an uneasy sleep, the shadows again appearing at the edges of my night.

The next day came creeping into our room, gray and gloomy, and I awoke with a bad brassy taste in my mouth and senses that had been buried for the weeks that I had spent with Madeleine suddenly alert again.

I rose uneasily and walked to the French doors and looked out. A low fog hung heavily to the damp ground. I breathed and smelled the damp earth and for no reason suddenly remembered my vision from my youthful trip to Harney Peak in South Dakota. Then I realized I did not hear the birds that always sang to the morning, and went quickly back to the bed, shaking Madeleine awake.

"Something's wrong," I said.

She sat up immediately, her black hair tousled, sleep disappearing from her eyes.

"What is it?" she asked, swinging her legs over the side of the bed and standing.

"I don't know," I said, adding, "I do not hear the birds."

She walked quickly to her wardrobe while I hurried to her husband's room. I dressed quickly in the clothes I had worn the day I came to her house and sat in the chair to pull on my boots, lacing them quickly. I picked up my Thompson and swung the bag of clips over my shoulders. I loaded a round into the Thompson, readying it.

Madeleine appeared in my doorway, buttoning her blouse. Her eyes widened as she saw me.

"My God, help us!" she whispered.

She turned and ran from my room, calling for her cousins as she made the stairs, sounding the alarm.

I stepped through the French doors and onto the balcony that ran along the sides of the house, holding the Thompson ready, the sling wrapped around my arm to help steady it. I looked down as her cousins ran from their posts into the house. I slipped quickly across the balcony to the side facing the grove and saw figures moving quickly through the grove toward the house like tiny black ants swarming toward a rotting corpse.

I knelt, bracing myself against a post, and waited until the first wave came out from the trees, then fired, moving the barrel of the Thompson rapidly back and forth. Figures twisted and fell, some writhing in agony, the others limply, already dead. The bolt clicked open on the Thompson and I quickly changed the clip for a loaded one and fired again as the wave continued rolling toward the house. More fell. I rammed another clip home and heard fire from the floor below as Madeleine's cousins joined in.

The wave hesitated; then a second wave came out of the trees. An explosion came and earth blew up in front of them. Another explosion as the cousins set off the mines, and I heard the familiar sound of ball bearings whistling through the air, and bits of flesh and blood spurted from the Vietcong like tiny red fountains. An arm flew in a lazy arc up, then dropped limply to the earth. Glass shattered behind me, and I realized that the Vietcong had found me on the balcony. I ducked, then rose and moved rapidly across the balcony, firing as I went. More bodies fell as I made it to the other corner of the house.

I glanced around the corner of the house and saw a small group crawling toward the back of the house. I reached for a hand grenade, then realized that I had left them in the room. I swore, stood, and emptied the Thompson into them. I exchanged the clip, then rose and stepped over the railing and dropped down, falling flatly to the ground. I rolled quickly to my right, rising to my knees as two Vietcong rushed me, firing AK-47s as they came. Bullets splattered around me. I pressed the trigger and felt the Thompson bucking and fought the barrel down. The two Vietcong stiffened as if they had run into a wall, then flew backward as the heavy .45 bullets slammed into them.

I leaped to my feet and ran past them, paused to slip two hand grenades from the belt of one, and continued on to the far edge of the grove. I ran through the trees, making my way around and back toward the middle of the grove. I found another small group making ready to rush the house. I slipped behind the heavy bole of a twisted oak and lobbed one of the grenades toward them. It exploded and I slipped around the bole of the tree, firing the Thompson into them. I twisted back behind the tree and squatted, exchanging the clip again.

Quiet descended. I remained where I was, watching, waiting for long minutes until I was certain that the attack was over. Cautiously I climbed to my feet and went slowly through the grove, checking. I found no one and made my way back to the house, pausing behind a tree to yell at the house that I was coming.

Raul's voice answered and I stepped out into the open, making my way through the broken bodies of the Vietcong lying dead upon the ground. One groaned and moved slightly. I put a bullet in his head, checked the others, and, finding them all dead, ran toward the house, my muscles tensing in my back at the expectation of a shot from the trees. But none came, and then I was in the house, standing in the foyer leaning against the heavy door, panting heavily. I lowered the Thompson and tried to swallow past the dryness in my mouth. My throat ached.

Raul appeared in the library doorway. He looked at me and shook his head.

"You are crazy," he said.

"It helps," I muttered, then said, "Is everyone all right?"

"I think so," he said. "We were very lucky."

Madeleine came from the back of the house. She held a small carbine in her hands. A powder smudge marred one cheek. Her black eyes shone. Her breasts moved against the front of her blouse as she took deep breaths to calm herself.

"Are you all right?" she asked, looking at me.

Both Raul and I answered; then Raul whistled and the others came from the living and dining rooms. Together they went out, spreading warily apart as they went toward the grove, checking the bodies again before disappearing into the trees.

Madeleine went into the library and I followed her to the French doors, each of us standing to one side as we watched. Long minutes passed; then Raul appeared at the edge of the grove and waved.

She sighed and her shoulders slumped. She laid the carbine on the desk and went to the drinks table. She poured two glasses of brandy and held one out to me while she drank the other.

"How did you know?" she asked.

I took the glass from her hand and emptied it. She took the decanter from the table and refilled our glasses. This time, I sipped while she drained hers and refilled it again.

"I just knew," I said. There was no way to explain the feeling to one who had not felt it.

"The birds. You said you did not hear the birds," she said.

"That was part of it," I said. I realized I was still holding the Thompson and walked to the couch and leaned the Thompson against it.

She shook her head and came across the room to hug me. Brandy spilled from the glass onto the back of my neck. I felt her body quiver, then begin to shake. Gently I led her around to the couch and forced her to sit. She drank again, emptying the brandy, and took a deep breath.

I brought the decanter from the table and sat beside her. I poured brandy into both of our glasses.

She took hers, leaning against me. Slowly, she relaxed, the tension slipping from her as the brandy seeped through her.

"Thank you," she said.

Raul came into the library and went to the drinks table and collected a glass. He took the decanter from me and filled the glass. He drank while he looked at me.

"Why did you leave the house?" he asked.

Madeleine frowned. Raul explained what I had done. She looked at me. I told them how I had seen the same tactics, the sending of two groups out one after the other to draw the fire while a third group came behind them after a short wait to let the defenders think everything was finished.

"That happened at a Special Forces camp up near Tram," I said.

"That was very reckless," she said.

I shrugged. "It had to be done."

"Yes," Raul said. "It was something that had to be done. But none of us thought to do it. You did."

"History. Mine, not yours," I said.

He raised an eyebrow.

I shook my head, though. Indians are the result of their past, and the stories of their ancestors and how they fought were passed down through generations until they become automatically a part of the Indians themselves. I was as much a part of my cultural inheritance as Sanchez was a part of his cultural heritage, and I knew that there are those who bear as much intense dislike for people like me as I felt for people like Sanchez. I had seen it too many times in the towns off the reservation. What people do not understand they fear and would like to destroy and often do. No one is without prejudices, and suddenly I realized that this was one of the reasons that I had walked through the shadows of the world for so long.

"You have been through much," Madeleine said.

I looked at her and nodded. I had, but it was something that would have to remain inside of me, as I instinctively felt that to talk about what had been done would make the two of them uneasy. They had seen much of war, but only from one side and separated by moments of tranquillity. I had been too deeply involved in it to want to explain the happenings. I knew that we had shared a part of the same horror but not the entire horror. I knew, at this moment, that I had looked too long into the abyss and now the abyss was in me. Nietzsche had been right; I had become a monster, and the thought of that would later come back to me in the quiet of the night and the thought of suicide would become a great comfort, like a calm passage to be made across the night.

How long had I been tired of the war? Wrung out by its intensity, holding it inside of me in a private room of my memory without letting it out as Fell had?

At that moment, I realized that I had held the war out from me in this place that had become, briefly, a sanctuary. And now the war had come again to me. How long, O God? How long must this continue? An answer seemed to be whispered to me: *As long as it must.*

I felt Madeleine's arm come around my waist. Automatically I reached around her shoulders and pressed her close. Raul finished his brandy and excused himself, saying that he needed to make the rounds with the others to make certain that the plantation was now safe and to make arrangements for the removal of the bodies. They would use one of the plantation trucks to carry the bodies down to the ARVN detachment for burial.

Madeleine and I sat, holding each other close, as he left. Slowly, we each seemed to merge into the other and I knew that she now understood me more than I understood myself and I understood her more than she understood herself. The past of each of us had merged into the present with the Vietcong attack and now we waited for time to bury the day. For a long time, neither of us moved, taking refuge in each other, and the silence seemed to gather us into it and we became a part of the silence and descended into the still point of the turning world as we waited for the gray day to be gathered into night.

That night it rained and we lay together, naked, in bed, content with being close to each other and not making love but listening to the rain, still in our own world. We had eaten dinner and drunk a bottle of wine, which was more important to us than the meal of cold chicken and salad. We were gathered into the night and lay with the coverlet over us, snuggled deep into its warmth and letting that warmth draw the day from us. It was a moment of liberation from the war and from the world, but we did not know what to do with it, and so we lay together, waiting for that decision to be made for us. We were not looking for the meaning of our lives but rather for the meaning of that particular moment in which we each had come to realize the depth of the other's life. We had reached a new beginning together and realized that in that beginning was also the end. It was time not to be searching for the meaning in the wisdom of old men but rather to be looking into their folly that always seemed to emerge in war.

We had moved past philosophical meanderings and had arrived at that place where we could look together with isolated detachment at what had happened to each of us both apart and together. We did not have the need for words but only for time to bring us back from that still point of the world into the present that was being forged for us while we waited in the still of the night with only the rain descending quietly upon the roof above us and washing away the happenings of the day.

We fell into a dreamless sleep together, each aware only of the presence of the other. Our September had merged into October.

The next day, Madeleine sent the cook into An Loc to shop and late that afternoon they came for me. We were sitting on the terrace after making the rounds of the plantation, and I could hear the small convoy come up the long dirt road leading to the house. Our eyes met and a deep sadness came into hers as a jeep and a truck came up to the bend leading to the circular drive in front of the house. Sanchez was in the jeep along with a Vietnamese *dai-uy*. A triumphant smile was on Sanchez's face as the jeep came to a halt. He climbed out of the jeep and stood, hands on hips just above a Colt .45 that he wore around his waist. Soldiers spilled from the back of the truck and fanned out behind him as he walked up to the stairs.

"Benjamin Wingfoot," he said, the smile broadening.

I sighed and rose.

"You are not welcome here anymore, Juan," Madeleine said.

He dismissed her with a casual wave of his hand, eyes intent upon me. His eyes glittered as they squinted against the golden sunlight. The smile broadened.

"Benjamin Wingfoot," he repeated. I could see the gloat build in his eyes. I looked at the soldiers watching warily, and shook my head.

"You're making a big mistake," I said.

He yanked a picture out of his back pocket, unfolded it, and shouted, "No! *You* made the mistake, fucker! You should have kept on running!" He glanced at Madeleine, standing white-faced beside me. "Well, my dear. Were you aware of who this man was?"

"No," I said. "She wasn't. I told her my name was Thomas Johnson. She had no way of knowing. Neither did anyone here," I added, indicating her cousins standing by watchfully, guns leveled at the Vietnamese.

"Good enough," he said, folding the picture and sticking it back into his pocket. He placed his hands on his hips again. "I knew it had to be you when I heard the stories about the attack on the big house and the American who killed so many and drove Charlie away." He laughed. "That's the trouble with servants, you know. They can't stop talking among themselves. And there is the matter of the reward for you. Quite enough to make your own mother turn you in. If you knew her," he added.

He had made the mistake of starting to mount the steps as he bragged. When he moved up to the second step, I kicked him in the face, driving him back and off the steps. He fell flat on his back, stunned, blood flowing from his broken nose. I slipped off the steps and dropped down beside him, slipping a choke hold on him, anchoring it with the side of my head as I lifted and spun him to face the Vietnamese rifles.

"*Dừng bắn!*" the *dai-uy* shouted.

The Vietnamese froze, keeping their rifles leveled at me. I heard the clicks of rounds loading into the chambers of the rifles Madeleine's cousins held. There was a heartbeat before the moment when a bloodbath could begin.

"One move and I'll break his neck," I warned the *dai-uy*. I pressed my head hard against the side of Sanchez's neck, forcing it against the crook of my elbow. I could feel the bones in his neck begin to shift. He moaned.

"Listen to him!" he croaked, and gagged as he swallowed a mouthful of blood. He tried to heave, but I held him tightly, and the blood rolled out over his lips and my forearm, staining the front of his carefully starched and pressed jungle blouse that had never seen the jungle.

"For God's sake!" he shouted. "Do what he says!"

"Now," I said softly, "tell them to get back in the truck. I'll go with you, but on my terms. You have that?"

I reached around and slipped the .45 from his holster. I pressed it hard against his ear, digging the barrel into it.

"Tell them!"

The *dai-uy* told them. Sanchez was too busy gagging. Reluctantly the soldiers lowered their weapons and turned sullenly back to the truck, climbing inside. The *dai-uy* stood watching us, however, his eyes narrow and sharp.

"Different, now, isn't it, fucker?" I whispered in Sanchez's ear. "You can't push around a woman, now, with your talk and walk. What do you think will happen when I squeeze the trigger? Think the bullet will go right through or splatter your pathetic brain all over the two of us?"

Suddenly Sanchez's sphincter muscle relaxed and he fouled himself. He moaned.

I felt Madeleine kneeling beside me, tugging at my arm.

"Please, Wingo," she said softly. "Let him go."

I turned and looked into her eyes, dark and fearful, and felt our world spinning us out of our dream and back into reality. The war again. And her plantation. It was all she had remaining of what she once knew. Her cousins would help me, I knew, but I also knew that they would be committing themselves to the forest, the jungle, and the mountains for the rest of their lives. I thought about what they had already lost and knew that I couldn't let them lose this last niche of their old lives that they had clung to so tenaciously over the years, grimly fighting off attack after attack, insisting on their right to be in Vietnam despite the changing seasons within their world.

"All right," I said. "But on my own terms." I turned back to Sanchez. "I'll go with you. But I'm keeping this .45 on the back of your head all the way into the ARVN camp. Then, I'll surrender."

I looked up at the *dai-uy*. "You understand?"

He nodded. His eyes flickered down to Sanchez's spoiled pants and I saw the contempt for him moving in their black depths.

"Yes," the *dai-uy* said. "You will not be harmed. I give you my word."

"Wingo," Raul said, moving up to stand beside me. "We'll hold them off so you can get away."

"No," I said, releasing Sanchez. I rose to my feet, nudging him with my knee. "Get up. No, you will only be making trouble for yourselves. I'll go with them."

A deep blackness descended upon me. I glanced up at the sun. A red haze seemed to cover it. A blood sun. I shrugged.

"Wingo," Madeleine said, placing her hand upon my forearm.

I smiled at her. "It had to happen sometime, Madeleine. It might as well be now."

Her hand dropped, and she turned away, shoulders bowed, walking toward the house. I watched her mount the steps and disappear, without looking back, into the house.

I sighed and turned back to Sanchez. "All right. On your feet. Let's go."

I looked at Raul. He nodded silently and stepped back, still keeping his rifle trained on the truck where the Vietnamese soldiers sat, watching silently the little *Nho* scene being played out in front of them. I wondered if they understood the irony of the situation.

"Up," I said, nudging Sanchez with my foot.

He rose, trying to maintain his dignity and failing because he knew that the Vietnamese had seen him vulnerable and helpless and behaving without dignity or honor. That was worse than any bullet I could have placed in his useless brain, doing the army a favor. I knew that word of this would also trickle down to Nha Trang and the command there.

"I'll kill you," he said thickly as he climbed to his feet. The back of his pants was sodden with his excrement. "You won't live through this, you sonofabitch."

"You had your chance," I said, shoving him with the pistol muzzle. He stumbled forward, and I stepped forward with him, jabbing him constantly to remind him that the pistol was always there, as we walked down to the jeep. He climbed in the passenger seat. I kept the pistol on him as I stepped into the back. The *dai-uy* climbed in beside me.

"You will not need that," he said to me.

"I believe you," I said. "But I do not believe the others who will be behind us."

He nodded. "It will be as you say."

He ordered the driver to return to the ARVN camp. We drove away from the plantation in a cloud of dust. I felt the black hollow I had felt when Worland escaped descend once again inside me and darkness gather once again around me.

I sat quietly in the cool, dark room in the ARVN camp. Once we were inside the concrete wall running around the old plantation quarters they used as their headquarters, I had lowered the hammer on the .45 and handed it to the *dai-uy*. Then childishly, because I had nothing to lose, I yanked Sanchez's head back and hit him hard on the bridge of his nose, breaking it again. He screamed, and the *dai-uy* muttered an imprecation and gestured that I should climb out of the jeep.

He followed me to the old storage room they used as a jail for their prisoners.

"I will make certain that nothing happens to those on the plantation," he said as I stepped into the dark interior. "There will be no trouble there."

"Thank you," I said politely.

"It is nothing," he said. He glanced over his shoulder to where two soldiers were helping Sanchez to the aid station. He spat. "It was good to see that one come down."

It took me a moment to understand what he meant.

"Many Vietnamese women have complained about him," he said. "But he is a favorite with certain of your officers."

"I understand," I said.

"Yes," he said. "But you are not a part of the American problem. You will go back to Poulo Condore." He looked at me, silent for a moment, then shook his head. "Perhaps I should do you a favor and shoot you now for trying to escape. I would be doing you a favor, I think. But"—he shrugged—"there are some things that I cannot do. There are many who would talk about this."

"Very many," I agreed.

"Yes." He fell silent again, regarding me. "Sometimes, the wrong man is put in charge of service to us. Men like this one." He nodded toward Sanchez, who was disappearing through the doorway of the aid station. "That one should be on Poulo Condore. Not men like you."

He shook his head. "I have heard about you, Wingfoot. It is said that you are a man to have in a fight. I regret this. Very much."

"Thank you," I said. "I will remember this."

He sighed and shrugged and motioned to the guard to shut and lock the door. "Yes, but it will not do much good for you or me for you to remember it. You will not come back from Poulo Condore this time. Unfortunately."

The steel door clanged shut on his words.

I turned and leaned against it, feeling the cold steel against my back, the sweat already starting to cool on me. I glanced around the room. There was one other prisoner, a Vietcong beaten badly, lying on a rice mat in the far corner. He watched me with glittering eyes.

I walked to the corner diagonal from him and unrolled a rice mat that had been tied shut and laid against the wall. I spread it out and lay down upon it and gave myself over to the darkness.

"You American."

The words floated to me out of the dark. It took a moment for me to realize that they came from the far corner where the Vietcong still lay on his pallet.

"Yes," I said.

"I will not talk."

A stubborn hatred seemed to blaze from the anger in his words, searing their way from the darkness to me.

"I don't care," I said. "Talk if you wish. Do not talk. The choice is yours."

"They think," he said, and gasped with the pain that the words caused him. I heard his breath hissing through his clenched teeth. "They think putting you in here will make me talk. I do not think you are a prisoner. You are like the viper hiding in the bamboo."

"They think I killed a woman," I said.

He remained silent, breath wheezing from him. I rose and walked over to his pallet and stood above him, staring down at him. His eyes glittered hate at me in the darkness. I shook my head and knelt beside him, gently touching his sides. Something moved beneath my fingers. He gasped and squeezed his eyes shut as pain shot through him.

"I did not kill the woman," I said.

I gently took his shirt from him and, using my teeth and fingers, tore it into long strips. Gently I raised him to a sitting position and wound the strips around him.

"Let your breath come out," I said.

He took a deep, shuddering breath, then pushed it out, and I pulled hard on the strips. He moaned and clutched my hands with hands like talons. I knotted the ends and scuttled back from him.

"That will help," I said. "I think they broke your ribs."

"They did," he gasped, strangling on the ribs.

I moved back to my pallet, leaving him alone with his pain. In a few minutes, his breathing eased.

"Why do you do this?" he asked.

I remained silent. I didn't know how to answer him. Pity for a fellow prisoner? One I knew was going to be shot? Perhaps. And why did it matter to me, now? I had killed many like him before and never gave a thought to their suffering. So why did it matter now?

"I had a prisoner with me on Poulo Condore who did me a favor like this," I said, suddenly remembering André. "He was a good man. I owe him."

"Then why not repay him instead of me?"

"He is dead. They killed him," I said, adding, "after we escaped."

"You escape Poulo Condore?"

"Yes."

"That is not done."

"Sometimes."

"I have never heard of this."

"It does not matter," I said tiredly. "It is a debt I owe. It does not matter to whom I pay it."

A long silence descended into the room, and I thought that he had fallen asleep. But suddenly he spoke.

"I do not know why I believe you. I should not. But I do. Thank you, for your payment of the debt."

"You are welcome," I answered.

"It will not matter, though. Tomorrow, they will shoot me. I know this. First, they question their prisoners. Then, they beat them. The next day they shoot them. It is a pattern."

"It is a pattern," I agreed.

"You have done this before?"

"No. I have only killed. Never done this thing."

Another silence, then:

"I am Durong. I have a wife and three children. In the North. I will not see them again."

"I am Wingfoot," I said. "I have no one to grieve for me."

"No wife?"

"No."

"A man should have a wife."

"A man should."

"But you do not."

"No."

"That is a greater sadness. Who will weep for you when you are gone?"

"No one," I said. Then thought of Madeleine, but remained silent. I wondered if she would cry when she heard about my death. Then I thought about how it would be done. I sighed. I knew the answer. It would be a hard death. They would want to make an example of me for others. A hard death. As hard as those of my ancestors who died at Wounded Knee or starved to death in the cold winter.

"One should have someone to weep for him."

I didn't answer. There was no need to answer, and he knew that as well as I knew it. But there are some in this world who are born alone into the world and destined to die alone within it. Lost souls. As my vision had told me would be my way in this world when I first saw the vision on Harney Peak. I began to understand the old man, now.

For the first time since I could not remember when, I felt a lump come into my throat, then scalding tears as they ran down my cheeks. And I cried for the happiness I had never known except briefly at Madeleine's plantation when for a few brief moments the world stopped spinning on its axis and allowed me to know what others had felt, would feel, during their lifetimes. And I knew that it was the only happiness that I would ever feel. Then, I cried for other soldiers who I knew would never find the happiness they once knew when they returned home, for they would be locked into a dark prison for the rest of their lives as I was locked in this one.

I could sense the tiger grinning in the darkness.

I awoke sometime in the middle of the night, the dark time of despair in men's souls. I lay, confused for a moment in the darkness, listening to the labored breathing of my fellow prisoner, wondering what it was that had awakened me. I felt the jungle moving inside me again, wild and untamable, straining to find the reason for my awakening.

I heard a key rattle in the steel door; then it swung half-open. I spun off my pallet into the middle of the room, squatting on my heels, aware that Durong was awake and listening with me, trying painfully to climb silently to his feet. I could barely hear the whisper as it crept through the door.

"Wingo?"

I recognized Raul's voice. "Yes?" I whispered.

The door was nudged wider and a dark form slipped inside the room.

"Come with us. Did you think that we would let you go as simply as that? My brothers are waiting for us."

A quiet chuckle slipped from his lips.

"I am surprised that the Vietcong have not overrun this camp. The guards are sleeping. Or," he corrected himself, "are now."

Durong moved near me. Raul's voice sharpened.

"Who is in here with you?"

"Another prisoner," I whispered back.

"Viet?" he asked.

"That doesn't matter. He is a prisoner, like me, and will probably be shot in the morning. Let him come with us."

"One of those who attacked us?"

"I don't know," I said. "But it doesn't matter. Not anymore. Does it?"

He fell silent for only a moment, then sighed. "This is not the time to argue about it. Let us go, and quickly. We shall talk about it when we are free of this place."

I groped in the darkness and found Durong's arm. He resisted my pull.

"They will kill me," he said dully.

"Does it matter if they kill you or the others kill you? At least you will not die in here like an animal."

"True," he muttered, and groaned as he allowed me to drag him to his feet.

I hurried him through the door into the shallow light of the quartered moon. Raul looked suspiciously at Durong, then shrugged.

"Who cares? One dead here or later is of no concern to us. Come, now. We have to hurry. They will change the guards soon."

"How do you know?" I asked.

"They change guards in the first hour," Durong gasped. "Yes, listen to your friend. I would rather die somewhere but here."

We waited for a moment until a cloud went over the moon, then hurried across the compound to where the gates stood slightly ajar. We slipped through the gates. Durong began to slump and Raul cursed and grabbed him roughly, hoisting him and helping me as we staggered away from the ARVN camp.

We made our way to where the plantation truck stood in the shadow of a wall. Raul pushed Durong into the truck and motioned for me to follow him. I shook my head.

"What is it?" he whispered.

"There is another that must go with us," I whispered back. "I want Sanchez."

"He is nothing," Raul protested.

"He is to me. And Madeleine. He would return to the plantation, but this time with American soldiers. You know what that might mean."

He sighed heavily.

"You know I'm right," I pressed.

"You are going to kill him?"

"No, I will take him with me."

He stood silently, shifting his weight from foot to foot.

"They will think that the Vietcong have taken him," I said. "Who knows that you are here?"

"No one. All right. Here."

He pressed a pistol in my hand.

"I think that you do not need my help in this."

"Fifteen minutes. If I am not back by then, go without me. And let Durong free when you reach the road leading to the plantation."

"That is crazy," he protested.

"But that is what I want," I insisted.

"All right. Fifteen minutes. But if you are not back in that time, we shall go. I am sorry, but we cannot spend more time. It is too dangerous."

I ran back to the compound and eased inside the gate. I paused in the shadow near the wall, scanning the compound and the walls. No one moved. I crossed the compound in a rush to the aid station. I eased the door open and saw a Vietnamese nurse nodding as he sat in his chair. The cots were empty save one.

I slipped inside and glided on my toes behind the nurse, reversed the pistol, and clubbed him behind his ear. He sprawled silently forward onto the table.

I slipped to the cot and looked down at Sanchez, sleeping, his mouth open to drag in air that his broken nose could not. I jammed the pistol into his mouth, waking him. He gagged. His eyes flew open in fright. Then, he saw who I was and tried to shout, but I cocked the pistol, and he moved the shout to a moan.

"I want to kill you. Now," I said. "But I won't. If you come with me silently. You understand me? I can kill you anytime. I am already dead. It doesn't matter to me. But I think it matters to you. Am I right?"

He tried to nod, but the pistol stopped him.

"All right. One sound, and you are dead." A laugh bubbled up in my throat. His eyes widened. "Let's go."

He rose and groped for his boots, but I pulled him roughly up and shoved him to the door. I grabbed his pants and blouse from the foot of the cot. They had been laundered while he slept. He moved forward, clad only in a pair of tan boxer shorts. His paunch was more pronounced without his pants and hung over the edge of his shorts. But he shuffled forward, wincing as his bare feet encountered tiny pebbles that had escaped the broom.

We made our way outside and across the compound. He hesitated at the gate, but I jammed the pistol hard against his kidneys. His back arched, and he gasped from the pain but moved forward away from it.

I held the pistol against his back as we moved down to where Raul waited with his brothers at the truck.

"You should kill him, now," Raul said. He moved his rifle forward and jabbed Sanchez in his stomach. "This pig has forced us to do many things for him."

"Let's go and worry about this later," I whispered.

I shoved Sanchez. He clambered awkwardly into the truck. I followed him, centering the pistol between his eyes and close enough that he was aware of it.

Raul climbed into the truck and drove quickly away. He kept the lights off as we moved through the shantytown on the outskirts of An Loc and out onto the highway. I wondered about possible patrols, then remembered that there would be none. The night belonged to the Vietcong and no one would be using the road that night.

"Here," one of Raul's brothers said, pushing a bundle onto my lap. "Here are your clothes. Your machine gun is here and everything that you need. A small pack. Food. You know that you cannot come back to the plantation."

"What are you going to do with me?" Sanchez asked fearfully.

I threw his clothes to him.

"Put them on. Watch him," I warned.

"Do not worry about that," the brother said. It was too dark for me to see which one spoke, but it didn't matter. "What do we do with the other one?"

"He will come with me," I said, undressing rapidly in the dark. I slipped into my clothes that I had worn when I first arrived at the plantation. I found my socks and put them on, and my boots. My fingers scuttled over my pack, checking it, and the twin canteens on each side of the pack, then the Thompson. A fresh clip had been inserted. I quickly donned the gear and moved to the front of the truck.

"Will you drive us past the plantation road?"

"For a few kilometers," he answered. "But it is too dangerous to go anymore. We must return quickly to the plantation. There is only one to help Madeleine."

"She will not need help," Durong said in the dark. He laughed. "Those who attacked you were not from here."

"That is what worries me," Raul said. "There are others like them out there somewhere."

"Not at the moment," Durong said. Then, he addressed me. "What will you do with me?"

"You come with me," I said. Impulsively I took the pistol Raul had given me and pressed it into Durong's hand. He jerked in surprise. "You may need this."

Silently he took it, sliding the chamber back to thumb the round and make certain that it was loaded properly. He remained quiet as the truck rolled down the highway. I saw the turnoff to the plantation slip by on our right; then we were around the bend in the road and near the hills when Raul slowed and stopped.

"This is as far as we dare," he said.

I jumped down from the bed of the truck and motioned for Sanchez to follow. Behind him, Durong painfully eased himself to the ground. He bent forward for a second, then straightened. I knew what the effort must have cost him. My ribs had been broken once in a football game when I was in college.

"If he moves," I said, indicating Sanchez, "feel free to shoot him."

"Yes," Durong said, breathing shallowly against the pain.

"What are you going to do?" Sanchez asked.

I ignored him and ran around to the driver's side. Raul leaned out, handing a small leather bag to me. Surprised, I took it, and felt a tiny jingle within.

"Gold," he said. "Not much, but enough that might help you if you can get to a place where it might be used. I am sorry," he said regretfully, "but there is nothing more that we can do for you."

"It's enough," I answered. I slipped the bag into one of the thigh pockets of my pants. "Tell Madeleine that I shall write."

He grasped my hand and held it for a long moment, pressing it hard.

"I do not think that would be wise," he said.

I remained silent.

"They will be watching us for a long time," he said, explaining. "All mail will be examined. I think it best if you"—he paused— "forget her. And us."

I felt an ache begin in my throat. "I don't know—"

"If you care for her, you will do this," Raul said.

"Does she agree?"

"I do not know," he answered. "But it is what must be done. Surely you can see this?"

Reluctantly I had to agree, although the lump in my throat grew larger and I no longer trusted my voice. I nodded.

"I will tell her what you wished to do," Raul said. "But now, you must go. We have been here far too long and must return. And you must get into the forest."

"Thank you," I managed past the lump in my throat.

He shrugged. "It is a favor owed," he said. I turned to go. "There is one more thing."

I turned back to him.

"In the bag you will find her father's ring," he said. "She wished you to have it."

The lump threatened to choke me and I reached up to grasp his hand. He placed both of his on mine, then pushed me away.

"Go. Now. Quickly."

I nodded and returned to the rear of the truck. Durong held the pistol steadily upon Sanchez. Even in the pale moonlight, I could see his legs shaking.

"Let us go," I said.

"Where?" Durong asked.

"North. Where else?"

He studied me for a moment, then nodded and looked up at Sanchez. I placed my hand on Durong's shoulder and squeezed gently.

"No," I said. "He comes with us."

I felt Durong shrug; then he stepped down into the ditch and made his way up to the other side where the trees came down like a hard dark line to the edge of the ditch. Raul swung the truck in a tight turn and drove quickly away. I looked at Sanchez, a coldness settling in my stomach.

"What are you going to do?" he asked.

"Take you into the jungle," I answered. "I think you need to discover what the rest of us have discovered."

"What—," he began, but I raised the Thompson. He hesitated briefly. "I don't have my boots."

"Neither does Durong," I answered.

I gestured.

He turned slowly, shoulders rounded with the weight of a world he did not know, and he slid carefully down the side of the ditch and pulled himself to the top of the other side. Within moments, we were within the safety of the dark wood. Durong was waiting for us.

"Can you lead us north?" I asked.

"Yes," he answered. I knew he was looking at Sanchez. "It would be better if we killed this one now. He will be a problem later."

"Perhaps," I said. "But that is my problem."

Durong turned silently and moved into the darkness, slipping through the trees. I nudged Sanchez with the barrel of the Thompson.

"If you lose sight of him, I'll kill you," I promised.

Sanchez didn't pause to answer but moved off rapidly after Durong, yelping softly when his feet met thorns and rocks, but he did not stop. I followed as we made our way through the darkness and the trees and bushes, and a feral familiarity descended upon me as I felt the spirt of the woods come within me and make me one with it.

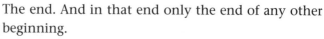

17

The end. And in that end only the end of any other beginning.

I came awake with a start and stared at the blue sky through the thick branches and leaves overhead. Somewhere a pig grunted, and my stomach rumbled as I remembered my hunger. I rolled over and pushed up to my feet. Automatically I ran my fingers around my belt, checking my canteens, the Colt .45 pistol, the old Fairbairn commando dagger at my side. I glanced down at the Thompson and checked the action. All my weapons are old friends and comfortable, but no more comfortable than the Baby Browning I carry in a small belly holster beneath my jungle blouse. For some reason, I take a greater comfort in that small automatic than I do in the other weapons. It is the prenatal hope of the warrior, the joker in the deck that the soldier always carries with him, how he will play the last hand being dealt to him at the last moment. A possibility of birth instead of death.

Not all soldiers have a joker. But they haven't felt the sudden *whump!* of a mortar round that knocks the oxygen out of the air around you and leaves you gasping for breath; the hard thump of a bullet slamming unexpectedly into you the way you used to sneak up on your buddies on the playground and whap the shit out of them while yelling, "Tag! You're it!" and taking relish in slamming your fist as hard as you could against them so that they really *felt* that they were "it" for the moment, then running like hell before they could return blow for blow; how suddenly you remember a gunshot snapping past your ear later when the sound finally arrives when you least expect it; maybe the strange look of a white pebble covered with tiny black dots lying in a dry creek bed in front of you while you wait for Charlie to come humping unexpectedly down the Ho Chi Minh Trail into oblivion.

Some soldiers haven't learned the *necessity* of having a joker in their deck.

They are the fools who insist on playing with the house cards. There's a joke so old that moss grows on both sides of it: A soldier is in a crap game and his friend pulls him aside and tells him that the game is as crooked as a general's dick and the soldier says he knows it, but it's the only crap game in town.

You *had* to have a joker. Otherwise, it was like knowing Mickey Mantle was coming to the plate and the only thing you had to throw at him was a fastball straight down the middle of the strike zone. Sooner or later Big Mick was going to lash one over deep center and you'd be left standing alone on the mound, naked, alone, and dead.

I wondered if I should have just taken the assignment and killed Lisa Lee myself. It would only have been another death, and the whole country was nothing but death: death in the cities, in the towns, in the villages, in the hamlets, in the rice paddies, along trails in the highlands, in the swamp in the Mekong Delta, everywhere, so much of it that one death merged into another and was quickly forgotten because there was nothing unusual enough about death to warrant anything more than a moment's grief for those who knew the dead. Even then, however, there were some who never knew the dead they mourned: professional mourners who hired themselves out to send a dead person away with a little dignity by pretending to wail and pull hair and pound the ground while the dead were being carried to their burial. More often, however, the dead were carried out of the city of the living and into the city of the dead, where they would be placed upon a burning pyre. The ground could hold only so many dead, and the Vietnam ground was already well glutted with dead bodies. Even the tombs were full, so that burning the bodies and scattering the ashes seemed natural.

I sighed and rose, slithering through the trees, trying to slide in shadows around the shafts of sunlight slipping through the branches. It is dangerous to be caught in those shafts and it is dangerous to think too much on the sunlight, although I would like to feel the healing sun warm upon my shoulders. Here sunlight is an occupational hazard. When you are the hunted you do not want illumination but raw animal instinct, keeping the edge of primal fear always on the conscious and not buried in the subconscious of civilized man. Reaction is more important than thought.

A bird calls, the note sharp and high and clear.

Musty rot reaches strongly from the jungle floor.

Bluebottles dance in still air, weaving a gauze of sound.

a pool must be near a water source for Charlie

I pant.

Cobwebs seem to clutter my lungs.

I glanced around, seeing spiders scuttle quickly from leaf to leaf.

Softly I work around the trees and discover a small stream seeping through the old leaves, pliable, oil-skinned, a transfer of liquid shadow.

My throat sickens and cold sweat prickles along heated skin.

I look with deliberate care, thrilling to the expectation of discovery, and find him hunkered down at the base of the tree shadow, black hair plastered down over brown forehead, black clothes merging with shadow-black, training his sights on me.

But I refuse to panic, and step sideways, bringing the Thompson down quickly, my thumb slipping the safety, my forefinger pressing the trigger hard back toward the guard, and in a slipstream of slowed seconds see the bullets speed toward him, strike him, drive him back, blood spurting in red streams from him like burst pipes.

I squat behind a tree, pressing my back against its rough bark, automatically dropping the spent clip out of the Thompson and slamming a new full one home, pressing the button to slide the bolt forward, chambering the cartridge.

Then, the familiar terror comes like a sharp-clawed rat and I feel a sudden urge to urinate. I shrug my shoulders up around my ears, waiting for return fire.

But there is only silence and I know then that he was alone as I am alone, with only the jungle between us and common fear.

I edge around the tree and stare into the silence of the warm, waiting.

Seconds speed. Minutes crawl.

Then a raven lands on a branch high in the banyan tree above the sprawled man, dead and alone, known only to the world now as Charlie.

I draw a shaky sigh of relief.

At least it isn't me.

floppity-floppity-floppity-floppity

Helicopters.

They are still searching for me and I know they will always be searching for me like dust motes in a light stream of sunlight.

The ground was thick with pine needles. I came upon a tea-colored stream rushing rapidly over polished rocks and stones. The ground by the stream seemed spongy, with dark ferns rotting against the humus. I knelt and refilled my canteen, then sat back on my heels, staring around me. I had the illusion that I was in a cathedral and everything I touched coming to this place bore the mark of failure. My heart seemed shriveled, poisoned, the very earth stricken with disease. A sudden wind kicked a screen of pine needles across my eyes like bits of dried parchment, and I knew that grief and loss would never become acceptable with the passing of time.

I lay on a limestone outcropping above a deep gorge that cut through the mountains. I didn't know which one; the borders were indifferent this high, and I could have been in one of three different countries. The trail far below seemed to play hide-and-seek among the huge rocks that lay as if carelessly tossed by a giant's hand. I stretched out my hand and let it dangle in space, idly passing time, until movement caught my eye. There had been no movement for a long time, not even an animal, for the sun was high and hot in the hard blue sky and the animals had long hidden up in what cool shade they could find. I stretched carefully, like a leopard loosening his muscles, taking care not to send a pebble crashing down the side of the mountain. I squinted across at the jagged line of mountains that looked like a broken-toothed comb on the other side of the gorge. The mountains, I had discovered, had magic in them. I knew this although I had never seen the magic work as magic should work, but I *felt* the magic and knew that the mountains knew I was there and was a part of them, and that was enough for me to make them feared and revered. I remembered the one night beneath a pine tree when Tawna Littlebird, who had an anxiousness that made her willing to make boys into men, made my body vibrate with such exquisite agony in the Needles of the Black Hills of South Dakota following my vision quest. We had bathed naked in the cold waters of Sylvan Lake and, shivering, made our way into the sleeping bag that the old man had brought for me.

Thinking of that now made me ache with a pleasing desire, but I ached for Madeleine and not Tawna. I closed my eyes and entered once again that small darkness that had wrapped itself around us in the deep shadows of the pine tree, but this time Tawna became Madeleine. I leaned into the memory, remembering Madeleine, aching for her, wondering if she ached for me as I ached for her. I remembered once when she had ridden into the forest to a quiet glade where a small pool lay in the middle of the clearing and orchids burst in bloom from each tree trunk surrounding the glade, a natural Eden not touched by man but allowed to exist, she said, without man's interference. We made love in that small glade and I noticed for the first time what perfect moons surrounded her nipples and the slight bulge above the waistband of her trousers that introduced the matron from the maiden yet made her all the more exciting for that, and the clean line down to her navel, and the descent into Adam's desire.

I watched as the movement metamorphosed in a man, carefully making his way along the trail I had followed to where I lay. I wished I had a pair of binoculars, but I didn't. I could tell from the way he moved, though, that he was a soldier and either a South Vietnamese soldier or an American soldier; the jungle fatigues marked him. Of course, he might have stolen them, but I doubted if that was the case. He carried a scope-mounted rifle and I had a hunch that he was one of the Special Ops boys who had been assigned to me. Some of them liked to work alone. I remembered one who took out a warlord in the Golden Triangle after the C.I.A. had purchased his opium crop with the understanding that he use his men in guerrilla warfare along the Ho Chi Minh Trail snaking down from the North over into Laos and Cambodia before looping back at several points into South Vietnam. We had taken him to a ridge that was about a thousand meters from the warlord's house. When the warlord appeared, stretching and smiling in the morning sun, the shooter shot him, the bullet slamming into the warlord with such force that he was driven backward halfway through the doorway that he had just left.

This man moved just like that shooter had moved, careful, watching everywhere automatically as he followed the trail. I wondered if he had found Sanchez where I had left him, alive but screaming, then choking into silence as he looked wildly at the forest surrounding him.

"You can't leave me here alone, Wingfoot!" he yelled. "I don't know which way to go! I don't have a weapon!"

I pointed at the Combat Infantryman Badge he wore on his blouse. "You should be all right. After all, you're a combat man, right?"

His nose widened and his eyes bulged wildly as I turned to go.

"Wait!"

I turned back. He was sitting on the ground, his feet, torn and bloody from the thorns, stretched out in front of him. He pointed at them, tears beginning to run down his face.

"I don't even have boots," he complained.

"I know," I said. "But a man like you should be able to improvise something." I glanced around the forest elaborately. "And, if I were you, I wouldn't stay here. This is a pretty hot area. A lot of Vietcong activity. Right, Durong?"

Durong grinned and nodded. His skin was stretched tight over his skull, and his eyes burnt like black coals in his face. We had moved steadily north for two days, forcing Sanchez forward until finally we both grew tired of his constant whining. Durong wanted to kill him, but I refused, although I knew that Durong was right; Sanchez was a liability. But by the time he made it back to An Loc— *if* he made it back—his credibility would be destroyed. I knew Raul and his brothers and the *dai-uy* would have had time to file their reports with Nha Trang when they notified headquarters about Sanchez's disappearance.

I remember his yells and the fright in his voice as Durong and I left him by the stream. A few kilometers later, Durong went away from me, heading back to his village and family. At first, he took a long look back down the trail we had followed, frowning, and I thought he might go back and kill Sanchez. But he shook his head and said, "I think that you better be careful."

"What do you see?" I said, straining to see what he had seen. But there was nothing behind us, only the forest.

"Nothing. I *feel* something, though."

I knew what he meant; everyone developed a certain sense of survival, and with some who had lived for a long time in the jungle that sense was honed to a fine edge. He had demonstrated this ability earlier.

We had been following a small game trail through the jungle when suddenly he froze, then lowered himself behind a thick banyan root.

"What is it?" I whispered, straining to see what he had seen.

"Up ahead."

"I do not see anything."

He shook his head. "But they are there. I know it."

"What do you want to do?"

He shook his head. "They will welcome me. And you because I will say that you are with me. But I do not know about him." He jerked his head toward Sanchez, who lay flat on the ground, as close as his buttons would let him.

I looked up into the tiny grove of thitka trees and shook my head. "I don't know. You never can tell what'll fly out of a tree until you throw a rock into it."

I rolled onto my back and stared up at the sky, at the plum-colored thunderclouds rolling in from the coast. Then, I shook my head. "But this is one time I don't really care what the hell is in that tree. Let's go around them."

A shaft of sunlight fell through the tree branches upon Durong's face, and for one strange moment his face became a mahogany mask pieced together from the broken parts of other masks. He gestured toward Sanchez.

"He is too slow." He looked without pity at Sanchez, scorn filling his face. "We should kill him. What difference is it to you? You know what will happen if you are captured. The same as for me."

"It is not time, yet," I said. "We are still too close to An Loc."

"And the woman," Durong said. "Your woman?"

A great sadness came upon me. "No. Perhaps she might have become my woman. But he"—I motioned toward Sanchez—"took that from me, as he wanted the woman."

"Did she want him?"

"No."

"Then we should kill him for that."

But I refused and reluctantly Durong led us on a wide detour around the suspected ambush. We constantly had to change direction to avoid the Vietcong who had camps sprinkled like frost throughout the forest. There were tunnels, too, that honeycombed the area. We found one by accident when Sanchez blundered into it, falling to his armpits and yelling that he had fallen into a punji pit and by the grace of God and Holy Mother Mary would we please pull him out?

I was tempted to leave him there. I could tell by the look in Durong's eyes that he felt the same way, but despite all my hatred for the man, he was still a soldier and, God help me, I still thought of myself as a soldier as well. I suppose it was a nostalgic clinging to what I had thought had finally brought a sense of order to my chaotic life, although I knew that it had simply changed the direction of my flight through chaos.

At last, we came to where Durong regretfully told me that he needed to leave. We had gone far enough north into Cambodia where the Mekong River laced through on its rush to the sea. An old moss-covered boat swung in the shallows, and I could smell death upon it. Durong grinned.

"It is always here. We call it 'The Death Boat,' but we use it as a marker. There are weapons stored in it as well, but it takes a brave man to go into the boat to get them. There are some American rations there, and you are welcome to them if you wish."

"Won't you go and get them?"

He shook his head. "I am not superstitious, but those who go aboard die within the next three days. I think it is only a coincidence. But"—he shrugged—"if one tempts the gods they will answer him in a manner which he does not want."

Heat lightning suddenly trembled above the trees, and clouds painted like horsetails began to scuttle across the sky. Thunder rolled down, echoing from the valleys and gorges and ravines in the mountains.

I glanced at the boat. The hairs on my arms stood up.

"Well," I said uncertainly, "we each need rations. If there is food there, then one of us needs to go get it."

"I mention only that there are arms there as well as to suggest which one of us will go," he answered solemnly. But there was a glint of laughter in his black eyes and I wondered if he was teasing me about the "curse" that had come downriver with this derelict.

"All right," I said. "I'll go. You watch him." I motioned toward Sanchez, who had stumbled to the bank and was puddling his bloody and swollen feet in the shallows of the river. I didn't bother to tell him that it wasn't a good idea, as the river had wound through many hamlets by this time and those people still used the river to carry away their garbage and fecal matter.

I stepped aboard and cautiously made my way to the back of the boat, my head filled with a strange wet sulphurous smell. The horse-tail clouds had dropped down to the river like a shot glass of bourbon down a drunk's throat, and gathering mist now rolled in gray clouds down the river like gathering puffs of smoke. I found the boxes of C rations stacked neatly at the back of the boat under a tattered bamboo and palm frond roof, a gray furze covering the cardboard. I pulled two cartons out and the cardboard folded softly into mush in my hands and the boxes tumbled out onto the deck. Some of the boxes split open and the olive-drab green cans rolled across the deck—ham and lima beans, sausage and eggs, beef stew, other "dinners" prepared in mass and sealed in globby forms in tin meant to last forever and a day—I believe it; I glanced at the package date on one can: 1944, only twenty-four years in the keeping. Tasty.

I gathered the cans and brought them back to the riverbank. Durong grinned as I dumped them into his arms.

"American ingenuity," he said. Actually, he never said "ingenuity," but the intent was the same—a slang reference to American efficiency.

"Hey!" Sanchez whined. "Don't give him all that! I'm hungry."

I glanced at Durong. His eyebrows rose. Together we said, "Ham and lima beans."

I fumbled through the cans and found two marked "Ham and Lima Beans" and tossed them to Sanchez along with a P-38 can opener.

Awkwardly he fumbled the can opener around the edges of the can, then ate eagerly, smacking his lips. I knew then that he had never spent a full day in the field, dependent upon C rations for a meal. Every soldier knew enough to hate the thought of ham and lima beans in the field, as, although there were pluses to it like

pound cake dessert and a small five-cigarette packet of Pall Mall cigarettes and a candy bar, the beans would give you the runs four
hours later and you would be hanging your ass over whatever log
you could find, splattering the ferns. Fortunately, some wise individual also had included a small package of toilet paper in the meal
kit as well.

I didn't give Sanchez the toilet paper.

"Hey, all right!" he said. He belched. "This is great." Then, his
face sobered as he noticed us staring at him. His eyebrows folded together and hooded his eyes. He looked warily from one of us to the
other.

"What . . . what . . . what are you . . . well—"

"We're going to leave you here," I said. I smiled.

He stared in disbelief at me, then laughed. "A joke! A grand joke!
Leave me here!" He laughed wildly and looked around him. Durong
and I slipped away into the forest while Sanchez was babbling and
turning around to look fearfully at the forest. And we heard his first
forlorn and frightened cry when he discovered that we were missing
and had left him alone.

His despairing cries followed us, faintly disappearing as we disappeared faintly through the jungle, emerging at last to the point of
our separation.

"You will travel alone from here," Durong said. "And you must
make your own way. Be careful. There are tribes warring against
each other the farther you travel. Have you decided where you will
travel?"

I shook my head. "West. I'll go west and perhaps I shall find a
place where I might remain. A home."

A sad smile came over Durong's face. "There is no home for one
such as yourself. Only temporary lodging here and there. You have
made an enemy of a very powerful man who knows that his power
is in danger as long as you live."

We clasped hands and Durong turned, loping down the hill and
disappearing into forest. I sighed and turned, making my way up the
Mekong River. I wandered aimlessly, directionless except for maintaining a general westward movement. I kept a wary watch on my
back trail but saw nothing. Yet I *felt* that there was someone following
me, and I knew that it was someone who had been sent to kill me.

I moved away from the river, climbing up the hills, unsure of borders but having no need for them as well. I was not bound by borders and simply made my way through the jungle, moving as whim presented itself. I found the Shans, whose women are the most beautiful in the world, and stayed with them for a while. But the feeling that someone was coming became stronger each day and finally I slipped away early one morning while the cooking fires were being lit. I traveled lightly, making my way through the hills, going deeper and deeper into the jungle, seeking isolation, trying to merge myself in the wilderness far from any form of civilization.

Each night, I would clean the Thompson and my pistols and lay them within easy reach while I slept, contented, knowing that I was fairly safe. I stayed away from pools of water at night, as that was the time when the night hunters would come down to drink. I always filled my canteen with fresh water and existed upon what animals I could kill with the least noise and trouble. Usually, I existed on rice, beans, barley, and millet that I brought with me when I left the Shans.

Once I crossed through a deserted village and found small bags of beans and barley neatly tied and stored on a shelf high above the ground to keep the animals from eating them. I took them with me, scavenging, saving the money that Madeleine had sent to me. I found the ring in the sack with the gold coins and slipped it on, but the ring reminded me too much of Madeleine too soon, and I placed it back into the bag and carefully stored it at the bottom of my pack. For days I moved ever westward, wondering where I would end and what I would find when I arrived there.

For a while, I thought I had lost the man hunting me, but then I caught sight of him from the limestone edge. A deep melancholy came over me as I watched him make his way laboriously up the trail at the bottom of the gorge. I sighed. The war had again found me. I slipped the action on the Thompson and checked the dull brass cartridge; the clip was full, as were the other clips in the bag I carried.

It was time to end the search for me.

I moved back from the edge of the gorge and stood, carefully studying the options. The land top of the gorge ran back on a northwest jaunt. At the far end of the plateau the forest began again. But there was an oddness to it, almost as if it had been planted by man a long time ago and been allowed over the years to fall into ruin.

I glanced down at the figure. He suddenly stopped and leaned back, shading his eyes with his hand, staring up at me. We remained motionless for a long while; then he began to climb the trail, moving faster than before.

I turned and jogged quickly toward the forest. In the open, I had no chance against him. His rifle had far more range than my Thompson. But in the forest the rifle might become a liability. I had to get across the open before he made it to the top of the ridge.

Something warned me and I took a sharp turn right and heard the snap of a bullet going past me. I glanced back and saw him kneeling, the rifle leveled. I swung the Thompson from my shoulder and fired a short burst, holding high, watching the bullets splatter in front of him, raised it more, and fired another burst. The bullets came near enough to cause him to roll away from them. I turned and plunged into the tree line, zigzagging my way deeper into the cool depths.

I found an abandoned temple covered with creeper vines. Monkeys screeched and ran madly from me when I appeared from the forest. They scrambled up the side of the temple and sat, screeching angrily at me. I studied the temple carefully before making my way up the steps and inside. Several large blocks had tumbled from the walls and lay in a jumble around a reclining Buddha.

It was as good a place as any to make a stand. I took a position in the shadows just inside the doorway to the temple and squatted, my back against the wall, watching and waiting.

I knew when he was coming, as birds rose from the trees at his passing. Then, he stopped, a shadow among the trees at the edge of the clearing. He raised the rifle and swung it slowly back and forth, using the telescope to try to locate me. I remained still in the shadows and watched as the rifle swung slowly past the doorway. Then, he lowered the rifle and stood, staring at the temple. He knew I was there, and didn't like it. If he came up to the temple, he would be losing the advantage of his long rifle. But as long as I stayed hidden, he had no target.

He moved back deeper into the forest, but still close enough that he could observe the temple. I watched as he squatted and began to wait.

The shadows lengthened around him, making him harder to see, but I knew where he was and I knew that although he was patient, he also would try to use the night to come to me. But I intended on using the night as well, and this time I would be a hunter.

The monkeys had begun to accept me by the time twilight came to the forest. I wondered if they would continue to accept me once I started moving again or would screech and scamper away from me and give him a warning.

But he moved first and the monkeys saw him moving and began their screeching. I rose and quickly slid outside the temple, clinging to the wall and the shadows as I slipped down to where a huge block of stone lay. I dropped behind the stone and watched, waiting for him to come up the steps. I shrugged out of my harness and placed it quietly in front of me. I laid the Thompson across the pack and slipped the Fairbairn from its sheath. I took the .45 from its holster and soundlessly slipped the slide back, chambering a round.

He came in a rush, crouched, weaving slightly as he moved with the shadows and ran up the stairs. The monkeys screeched louder at the new intruder. He flattened himself against the wall next to the doorway, then slipped around and inside.

I rose and ran quietly down to the door and dropped to my knees, looking cautiously around into the darkness. The holes in the roof caused by the fallen stones allowed light to trickle in. Not much, but enough that I could see movement.

I moved around the corner and slipped behind one of the larger blocks of stone.

"Who are you?" I asked.

My voice echoed in the room, and I heard him gasp and fall flat on the floor. Minutes passed. I waited, unmoving. I strained to hear the slightest scrape, a tiny pebble rolling, the soft brush of cloth over the floor of the temple. I glanced at the corners of the room: each was hidden in darkness. Cautiously I moved out from behind the block and, crouching, slipped to the back wall, moving on the balls of my feet. I slid down the wall, careful not to touch it, then found a corner and dropped down into the darkness, waiting.

I emptied my mind of the thought of time, concentrating only on the room. Then, I heard it, a soft leather scrape against stone, and knew he had imitated my movement. But he was not content to wait in dark corners. He was too used to being the hunter, not the hunted. The coyote does not wait long, but the rabbit will wait until the last moment before trying to flee.

I caught the faint outline of him as he passed close to a spot on the floor of the temple where light from the moon streamed in from a hole in the roof. I waited until he was nearly upon me, then struck upward with the Fairbairn, driving it into his belly just above his groin. He gasped with pain and tried to bring the rifle around, but I was in too close, now, and I rose, ripping upward with the Fairbairn, gutting him.

The rifle clattered to the floor as he slumped to his knees, both hands holding tightly to his belly. I reached down and slipped the knife and pistol from his belt and squatted beside him, keeping the .45 trained on his head.

"Who are you?" I asked.

He shook his head and grimaced. The slightest movement sending pain shooting through him.

"You . . . know . . . ," he gasped.

"Worland? Langley?"

"Yes. . . ."

"Are others following you?"

"In . . . nine . . . days . . . if . . . I . . . don't . . . report. . . ."   His gasps were coming shallower and shallower. "I . . . didn't . . . want . . . this. . . ."

The word ended on a hiss. He took in one last shuddering breath, then fell slowly on his side, twitched once, and lay still.

I waited with him through the night until false light began to show. I could see him now, face painted in camouflage blacks and dark greens. He looked too young to be doing what he was doing, but I knew that was deception only. The young are far easier to bend to the will than the more experienced soldiers. A great weariness came over me at what I had become. I sighed and quickly searched him, finding nothing other than a Swiss Army pocketknife, a small waterproof tube of matches, and a map, folded and snugged into one thigh pocket of his jungle pants. No dog tags. I didn't expect any. People doing what he did refused to carry them. They were seldom captured, and dog tags became a nuisance and had an odd habit of tinkling at the wrong moment, even if you taped them together. He would have left his gear out under the trees.

I rose and left the temple, collecting my gear, then went down to the edge of the clearing to search for his. It took only ten minutes. He had placed it under a thick bush draped by a huge frond. I opened it: C rations, extra ammunition, more maps, a small radio, canteens of water, and a poncho liner. He had learned to travel light, but he did have a British Sten gun with him and clips of ammunition in pouches that hung on a garrison belt. I wondered why he brought the rifle with him into the temple. Old habits are hard to break. The Sten had been for use in the jungle, but up here the Sten was more useless than my Thompson.

I squatted, thinking, then rose and went back to the temple, this time with my Thompson and clips in their bag. He lay where he had fallen. I picked up his rifle: a 30.06, the barrel floated, large Starlite scope attached that could be slipped for another for day use. I placed the Thompson beside him along with a couple of other items that could be identified as mine. I backed up to the doorway and, taking careful aim, blew his head apart, shattering his teeth. I left the rest the way it was; the animals would be at him soon, and that would take care of all possible identification otherwise. I hoped. At any rate, it would buy me some time to get farther west from pursuit. Maybe far enough that I could lose myself in the outback.

But there was Madeleine. I would be just as safe back there with that soldier dead and carrying my identification. Maybe more so, as once I was at Madeleine's plantation there would be no new trail to follow if I could stay close to the one we made coming up here.

I felt tired but knew that I had to place as much distance between us as possible. I took his pack, keeping the food, leaving the rest, and dropped my pack by him. Then, I left the temple, collected his gear as mine, now, and set off at a steady pace through the trees, working my way back through the jungle, heading south.

I moved through the weeks across jungles and open plains, keeping as far away from people as I could, coming in close to villages only at night when I needed food and could steal a few chickens, bowls of rice, and other grains, whatever I could find. Occasionally I came upon another traveler who looked warily at me. One, an outcast or outlaw—I didn't know the region at the time—tried to rob me.

I had to make a detour once when I found a large NVA body moving south and entered a valley filled with red colocassias so thickly that I felt that I was walking through a haunted labyrinth. I traveled in circles, coming back and back again to the same place where a bramble bush grew between two heavy boulders. The valley was chilly and gray and I felt the spirits of others who had been lost in the valley around me, watching, waiting. The sides of the path I was following when I met the man were choked with violet flowers and silver leaves of creeper vines. I took the machete and warily hacked my way through them, watching for the green snakes that could suddenly lash out and bite. By late afternoon, the north wind began to howl through the valley and I thought I heard the strains of a bamboo flute.

I traveled another hundred meters and found myself in a stand of giant colocassias whose trunks twisted into a single gnarled root the size of a palm tree. The shadows became dark and clammy. And suddenly the man was in front of me, wearing a tattered uniform. His face mirrored my own surprise. He raised his rifle. I was forced to kill him, and that haunted me as well as I moved south.

I stumbled across the body of another soldier, an American, his skeleton lying in tattered clothes, and I knew that I wasn't the only one who had suddenly taken to the forest to escape. I wondered how many I had passed by without seeing, soldiers looking for a peace that they needed badly enough to take their chances alone in the forest, walking their way to the Western world because they sensed that that would be the only way they would possibly reach home. They knew the odds were against them, but still, the one chance that they had was better than the no chance that they felt with the many patrols and search-and-destroy missions that they went out on where return would only be by chance.

I knew I was in danger here—had been for a long, long time—what with patrols by NVA soldiers, but I continued working my way up through the deep mountains, avoiding the small villages as much as necessary.

Near the Cao Bai Pass, I remembered the words of the man in

Bring Cash Alley who had sold me the .45. I made my way west of Lang Vei and found the first tavern that he had mentioned. I entered and found the man with a bad eye and asked for the Place of Whispers. He gave me a strange look and motioned to the back of the tavern. He disappeared and returned with a young boy who had to be his son.

The boy gestured and I followed him out the back and across a small clearing and into the jungle. We made our way carefully up through the hills and then came upon the small inn. Our approach had apparently been watched, as a middle-aged woman with gray streaking her coal black hair stood shading her eyes in the doorway.

"Quang sent me," I said, my mouth dry and sticky from our walk.

She studied me quietly for a long moment, then said, "You are the one the soldiers hunt for."

"Yes," I answered.

She nodded, considering. Then she motioned me inside and I stepped into the cool interior of the inn. "How long you stay?"

I shrugged. "I don't know."

She glanced at my tattered clothes, the weapons hanging from me. "You have traveled a long way."

"Yes. Far to the north, then back here again."

A faint smile touched her lips. "That was good. The soldiers will not think that you would come back here."

She looked closely at me. "You are an American?"

"An Indian," I said.

"Ah. You could almost be one of us. With the exception of your nose. And your eyes. They have seen much. Too much, I think."

"All war is too much. It is born of politics by people who do not have political beliefs but have something they want. But it is the soldier who must fight to give the politicians what they want."

"Yes. My husband was killed by such as those," she said. She considered me thoughtfully for a long moment. "You may stay here. It is quiet and no one speaks of such things that they should not. But it would be better if you stopped being a soldier and became one of us. Keep your weapons. But you need clothes."

"I have money," I said. "Gold."

Her eyes lit at that and she smiled wider. "Then we shall make you Vietnamese before you leave here. When it is safe, I will get you to where you wish to go. There are many who owe me favors."

I stayed a week at the Place of Whispers while the woman took my clothes and burnt them. Clothes were brought to me: white shirts and black pants and shoes that would make me something other than a field worker and would help to explain the difference between me and those who tilled the fields. She brought a wizened old man into my room one day to take my picture with my hair combed to the right, leaving a large shock draped over my forehead to help hide my features. A week later, he came back with papers that said I was Luy Tien and worked as an accountant in a small firm in Saigon. That gave me a little to play with as I made my way back to An Loc.

That night, the woman came to my room. She stood in the doorway, studying me. Then she shrugged and sighed.

"I think it is time that you leave," she said. She swept her arm around. "The Place of Whispers also has ears, and there is a large reward for you. Where will you go?"

"To Saigon," I lied.

She nodded, knowing the lie when she heard it. "We will take you to the village, where you may take a bus. It will take a long time, but I will make you food to eat along the way."

"Thank you," I said.

She gave a half smile and stepped forward, placing her hand along my face. I could feel the rough callus on the palm of her hand. "I do not take sides in this war. All men need a refuge. If you have need of it again, return. But use that time wisely. You will only be able to return once. Then, it would become too dangerous."

She patted my cheek and left.

The next morning, the boy from the tavern appeared and we made our way back down the trail to the village. I left the Thompson there but kept the Colt and the Baby Browning, tucked in the waistband of my trousers, leaving my shirt to hang over them. I glanced in a window and was surprised at what I saw: the American Indian had almost disappeared. I saw the face of a Vietnamese until I looked into my eyes and saw the war there.

The bus came and took nearly fourteen hours to reach An Loc. I slipped off the bus, telling the driver that I needed to get food and would find a place to stay until the next bus came along. He said that would be a week, but his uncle's sister had a small place in an alley off the market that she would let me use for a few hundred piasters. The price was good and I promised to find her. He smiled and nodded and I knew that I had effectively disappeared. If I left a few hundred piasters with his uncle's sister, that would be enough to keep them from going to the police, as the police would treat them as co-conspirators.

I rented a room and waited until late afternoon before I took my small bundle and made my way north from town, following the dusty road to the cutoff that led up to Madeleine's plantation.

They saw me coming and came down to meet me, suspicious at first; then Raul's eyes smiled and he gripped my hand.

"I did not expect to see you again," he said.

"I know," I answered.

"It is still dangerous," he warned.

"No, they think I'm dead," I said, and explained what had happened in the hills to the north and what I had done with the man who had been sent after me.

Raul tugged at his ear for a moment, considering my words, then said, "That may stop them eventually. But there will always be the threat, the suspicion."

"Yes, and that may be enough," I answered. Worland would always be suspicious until he was able to see my body bag. He would not know what I might have left with a reporter or correspondent or if I had told others about what had happened. He would have to live with that suspicion for the rest of his life, and it would haunt him at night and haunt him while he tried to work his way through the political arena, not certain if the next question from a reporter would be one about the death of a prostitute in Saigon. They say generals do not have consciences, but they are only men and a man's mind is his own worst enemy, for he always has his fears closest to him.

"How is Madeleine?" I asked.

Raul smiled and gripped my hand. "She waits for you," he said. "I do not know how she knew, but she knew you would be coming."

I wondered when the vision had come to her or the sense that I was returning. But that didn't matter. All that mattered was that

I was here and for now the war was far behind and, with luck, would remain far behind for a while longer. Perhaps long enough that I might learn happiness.

He turned and I followed him up the road to the main house. She stepped out of the doorway to see who was coming. As we neared, I saw her hand go to her throat; then she was running down the road to meet us.

I looked up above the white house and saw a red-tailed hawk circling high overhead.